I0760772

Hill City Press



Edited by Sara Lawson.

Cover and jacket design by MiblArt.

Hardback cover art by Damian V.

Interior art by Janelle Hovde.

SECRETS OF THE FAE

# The Shadow Heir

C. F. E. BLACK

To the ones who feel broken.

Sign up for reader VIP treatment including bonus content and sneak peeks at all new books by heading to
vip.cfeblack.com/join

# 1

## Zara

I had only seconds to reach the ground before the night guard returned, but my ruffled skirt snagged as I swung my legs over the balcony's stone railing. Timing my descent with quiet breaths, I held my weight in my arms and lowered myself down.

One.

A small ripping sound rent the quiet night, stealing another second as my attention stalled.

Two. No time to waste. I felt with my toes for the trellis anchored to the whitewashed walls.

Three. Ignoring the way the leaves tickled my ankles, I released one hand from the railing.

Four. I released the other hand.

Five.

Only twelve seconds before the guard reappeared. With a racing heart and careful movements, I slipped down to the grass below my bedroom window.

In my haste, I'd knocked a pair of passionflower blooms to the ground. I snatched up the fragrant blossoms and took off toward the wall of boxwoods marking the inner garden on the west side of my family's estate.

On a good day, running flat out across the grass from the house to the privacy of the inner garden on my short legs took nine seconds. But tonight, I also wore flamenco shoes and a tight dress.

Holding up my dress, I pumped my legs so hard that a quiet scream tore from my lips as my muscles burned.

I darted through the opening between the boxwoods and heaved in gasps of air as quietly as I could, tiptoeing around the burbling fountain in the safety of the shadows while holding back the laughter that threatened to spew from my lips. The moon was out as well as a host of stars, but the darkness seemed thicker tonight, as if it welcomed me.

A flicker of fear sent gooseflesh down my arms as I scanned the deep shadows of the garden. Memories of stories recounting the many beasts that prowled the worlds at night flashed through my mind. I'd always considered the tales nothing more than entertainment, until one month ago, when I'd seen the Wild Hunt with my own eyes outside of Puerta de los Reyes as I sped there on horseback beside my best friend, Talia. That night had changed everything for me. That night, the Wild Hunt had stolen a woman, and Talia had disappeared into the fae lands, and I'd been forced to admit that my father's warnings about a bargain he'd made many years ago with what he simply called *la sombra*—the shadow—might *not* actually be lies meant to scare me into good behavior.

Stolen. Disappeared. Bargain. The words rang in my ears as I picked my way around the happy, oblivious fountain. My heart was bursting from my sprint, and a wave of lightheadedness swept over me. I bent to brace my hands on the fountain's edge, breathing heavily.

Dull bronze coins glinted in the water, coins I'd tossed in every year—on my birthday, on every holiday, on my father's birthday, and during the harvest festivals, where otherworldly creatures were said to be present among us in greater numbers. I'd hoped my father's words about his bargain with the shadows was a ruse, but deep down, I'd feared it was true. These coins were proof. But with each coin tossed in, each hopeless prayer offered to whatever deity listened to humans, not once had anything happened. Not once had my father come to me and told me the bargain was broken, that his foolish mistake was remedied, that I wouldn't have to leave my home on my twentieth birthday because of a magical deal he'd made long ago.

In a matter of hours, I would complete my twentieth year. Tonight was my last chance—one more night to break the curse he didn't seem able to break. It was a half hour to midnight, which meant I had less than one hour until I learned whether my father's bargain was, in fact, real.

I stood straight and inhaled deeply. I had enough time. I was so close to breaking the terms of my father's bargain, to no longer being *maldita*—cursed.

The man I loved would break the curse. He would end this tonight.

Because in all the fae stories, all the fantastical tales of *los malditos*, true love always broke the curse. And I'd found it.

I just needed to tell him. To know my love was returned.

With renewed excitement, I hurried toward the back of the garden to a pale brick wall that marked the edge of my father's property.

The flowers I'd grabbed now wilted in the sweat at my neckline, where I'd stuffed the blooms. Ignacio, the stone-faced guard who paraded the west side of the estate at night, had a way of *knowing* when I wasn't in my room, no matter how flawless my escape. He might have counted the flowers before his patrol this evening, but I couldn't be certain. He never seemed to miss anything, and my father had been quite clear about what would happen if I got caught without a chaperone one more time. I'd have to marry one of the rich boys he approved of, and at my birthday celebration, no less. The party could easily double as my wedding celebration.

But I wouldn't be marrying one of the stuffy gentlemen's heirs. I'd be marrying Jorge, and my father wouldn't be able to say no when he learned that love broke the curse *he* created.

As I neared the edge of my father's property, a man emerged from the shadowy forest and hopped over the wall, arms extended.

With a quiet gasp, I sailed into his open arms, wrapping myself in Jorge's warm embrace. We tipped backward against the wall, and for a moment we laughed as we tried to untangle ourselves.

When we regained our balance, his fingers pushed a stray curl from my face. "Señorita," he said, voice low.

His dark eyes carried a seriousness in them tonight, a hunger that made my belly flip over inside me. He brought his lips down to mine, and for a moment, I thought the world was for no one but him and me.

A moment later, I traced my thumb over his mustache. "This is new."

He pulled my wrist to his lips and kissed it. "Do you like it?"

I pulled my arm down and smiled. "No."

His eyes widened, but he pulled me into another kiss. "Now do you like it?"

I placed my hands against his chest, and I could feel his heart beating madly. My own heart rate soared. "You'll always be handsome to me," I replied, ready to move to the road and head into town. His affection had grown rather insatiable in the few weeks we'd known each other, and my mind prickled with uncertainty, recalling past mistakes, but my heart urged me onward. Love was meant to be ravenous, unstoppable—who was I to question it when I'd finally found it?

My heart hammered in my chest as I waited for him to take my outstretched hand. Jorge was different than all the other boys. In him, I'd found a love that would surmount all obstacles. A love that would break the curse that bound my life to the darkness.

Twenty years ago, my father had made a rash decision. That decision had shaped every day of my life from the moment I was born. My father and mother had wanted a child, desperately. To stop my mother's grief, my father had sought out the supernatural—a man he only ever called Oscuro, a creature with incredible power who appeared to be comprised of night itself, like his name implied. *La oscuridad*, the darkness. He'd promised my father a child, but my father hadn't been sensible enough to ask what the cost would be. He'd accepted Oscuro's terms without question, so pleased to finally be able to tell his wife the news that they would conceive.

Only after my father had agreed did Oscuro explain the terms: they would have a child, but after twenty years, the child would have to return to Oscuro's court. The Court of Shadows.

Jorge's fingers entwined with mine, and I snapped out of my fearful reverie. I let out a long, quiet breath as I calmed my racing heart, trusting that my curse would be broken when Jorge declared his love. Even my father believed love was the answer, as he'd threatened repeatedly to force me to marry on my twentieth birthday if I didn't find love on my own before then.

Jorge and I walked hand in hand toward a waiting carriage. The best parties in Leor didn't start until midnight, after the restaurants finally closed their doors and most of the late-night dinner goers finally went home. We'd be right on time if we left now. Jorge had promised to bring his sister and her husband, both who were eager to meet me. Before we climbed inside the carriage and lost our moment of privacy together, I pulled on his arm and he swung around toward me, looping his other arm behind my back.

I tugged his head down so I could whisper in his ear. "Tomorrow is my birthday. I'd like you to meet my father."

Jorge pulled back a little, his arms still around my waist. "You think so?"

A little surprised by his response, I nodded. "I love you."

His lips broke into a smile as they pressed against mine. "You love me?" His hands began to roam, his touch becoming stronger, harsher.

"Yes, but—"

He angled his face down and went for my neck, but I shoved my hand against his forehead, pressing him back.

"What now, *mi corazón*?" he cooed, trying again. My palm barricaded him as I recalled other men who'd attempted to win my inheritance with false affection. One other, in particular, who'd left me with memories I'd tried to blot out. But Jorge wasn't like the others. He pulled my hand aside, and for a moment, I was nearly lost to the feeling of being so desired.

"Do you love me?" I asked, smiling as I waited for his reply.

He stood straight and locked eyes with me. "I want to be with you."

A note of happiness burst from my mouth, but it was cut short. "You didn't answer my question." Everything hinged on his response.

He backed away, a pinch forming between his dark brows. "Zara, you know how I feel about you."

"How, exactly, do you feel?" I propped my hands on my hips.

Jorge shook his head. He looked handsome in his suit, even though it wasn't half as nice as those worn by the noblemen at my father's parties. I'd never cared that his clothes weren't as fine or his carriage as grand.

"I…I want," he stammered, running a hand over his short hair. Then he swallowed, as if rallying himself. "Of course I love you. I'd be a fool not to admit it. Come on, Zara." He grabbed my waist and tugged me toward him.

Heat flared up in my palms and a sinking chill gnawed at my stomach. His confession fell flat, perhaps because of the way he cracked every knuckle in his fidgeting left hand as he stared down at me with hooded eyes. A flash of fear surged in my gut at his look. Two years ago, I'd learned the hard way that some men wanted something other than money, and it had nothing to do with love. I'd been young and uncertain and I'd believed his every word, and it had only left me aching and empty and alone when he'd vanished the next day.

But not Jorge. He was different. He was...

When he tried to kiss me again, I turned aside. Sweat bloomed up my torso as memories jarred my mind. His hands trapped my hips in a strong grip.

"Please stop," I said as evenly as I could, but my heart was beating between my ears, and I couldn't think straight. I glanced at the carriage. There were people inside. His own *sister* that I'd never met. We weren't alone. Yet the carriage was awfully quiet.

"I'd like to meet your sister," I said, ignoring the panic rising inside me. Jorge was probably only edgy after his admission, right? Love wasn't a word one tossed around lightly. He was likely as nervous as I was.

An almost imperceptible chuckle left his lips, and I froze. "My sister," he said, his forehead tilting down to rest on my exposed shoulder. "You can meet her in town."

"You said you'd bring her with you." I ducked out from under him as playfully as I could with all my nerves in knots. I couldn't be wrong about him. I couldn't be *that* wrong.

"Afraid of a little alone time? If you love me, show me."

My mouth fell open in a silent scoff, my body's alarm bells ringing at full capacity now. "Jorge, I...Please...I don't..." I couldn't form a complete sentence. I had been wrong. *So* wrong.

Deep in my chest, a sharp ache prickled like I'd been stabbed. I backed away from him.

"Zara," he said, coming closer. I could no longer deny the look in his eyes. I'd seen it plenty of times before, but out here, we were entirely alone. The carriage driver was likely expressly told not to interfere with anything happening inside the carriage. I had to run.

"Don't look so scared," he teased. "I heard you were fun."

"*What*?" I shouted, voice cracking.

"You have a reputation, you know. All the other men you've left behind said it was worth it."

My jaw couldn't open any wider, and my rage couldn't boil any hotter. "They *what*?" I couldn't believe this, couldn't wrap my head around the lies, around what my *reputation* must be to him. Then it hit me. All of this—all of the persona he'd portrayed—was simply a ploy to get me alone, because he believed a pack of lies crafted by men with wounded egos. I pressed both palms to my forehead, smearing away the sweat beading there and feeling a growing urge to vomit. I backed away quickly.

"There you go," he said, rolling his eyes. "You enjoy tossing out men like the food left on your plate, don't you?"

My stomach dropped to the ground, and I hunched forward, dumbstruck.

"They warned me you'd run. I only assumed it would be after." He half-turned aside, his hands again going to his hair.

At those repulsive words, I bent down and yanked the dagger from its sheath at my calf. I'd taken to wearing it everywhere after witnessing the Wild Hunt mere weeks ago.

The blade glinted in the moonlight as I held it at arm's length, pointed toward Jorge, my heart in little dusty pieces at my feet.

"Leave me alone," I warned.

Love was supposed to be powerful. It was supposed to break class barriers and expectations and curses. But all it had done for me was ensnare me. I swallowed and stood straighter, harnessing my emotions before they spiraled away with the breeze.

Jorge chuckled dryly. "I thought you wanted me to meet your father. I thought you loved me, Zara."

An angry huff escaped my lips. "That's what you call love?" I said, eyeing the carriage with a shiver of unease. To think that's why he'd courted me. I lifted the knife a little higher, trying to steady my shaking arm. Grateful my father had insisted on putting me through weapons training, I wouldn't let all those years of training fail me now, despite feeling like I was cracking at the edges.

Jorge lifted his hands, palms out. "*Cálmate.* I'm leaving."

That command—*calm down*—smashed any remaining bit of tenderness I felt toward Jorge into the dirt at my feet. My stepmother, since she'd arrived five years ago, had used that command more times than I could count, whenever my emotions rose to a level that made her uncomfortable. The words always had the opposite effect, though, and my breaths came faster through my clenched teeth as I glared at the man I'd hoped to marry, the man I'd dreamed would set me free from my father's bargain.

And with that, he spun toward the carriage. Before the door closed, he spat one word over his shoulder, "*Maldita.*"

My chest cracked from the inside. He couldn't possibly know. My father had been diligent in his efforts to contain the fact that I was a gift from some magical being. No one would have done business with my father—bought his wine or invested in his vineyards or his ships—if they'd known that. Magic was for stories, not for noblemen.

But what if the truth had leaked out somehow? Was *that* why each of the men had left me?

As the carriage rolled away, I stood still, heaving quick breaths, a tear tickling down each of my cheeks.

"Stars," I hissed between clenched teeth as I slipped the knife back in its sheath at my calf. I grabbed a rock from the ground and threw it across the road into the trees, where it made no sound at all as it was swallowed by the night. I tilted my head up and stared at the starry sky. "What now? Aren't you supposed to have some sort of power?" My father had never taught me to pray to anyone, although he cursed the stars often enough that I assumed they held some sway. But if they did, the stars didn't like me very much. They sent me too many failed loves. Too much heartbreak. And a life that was over before it really had time to start.

I had mere minutes until my birthday, hours if this Oscuro creature waited until the hour of my birth passed. But that wasn't enough time to find true love, no matter what my father orchestrated. Marrying a gentleman's son wouldn't fix anything. As my twenty years drew to a close, I'd be gone. Whisked away to the Shadow Court, wherever that was.

No stars, no bargains, no miracles were going to help me now.

An owl launched into the air nearby, startling me. Peering up at the dark forest, an old, familiar verse from a children's song echoed in my head: *The shadows come to steal and to kill, and they dance away with your heart. If you think them kind or a good place to hide, you'll die alone in the dark.* The song was meant to keep children from wandering away after dark, but it hadn't done much good for me.

As I hurried home, Jorge's words plaguing my mind, I knew that if Ignacio caught me and my father and stepmother found out I'd sneaked away again, I'd *feel* cursed. But their greatest threat, I realized with a huff, was now my last resort. I'd have to marry whichever bachelor my father could rope into a marriage by sundown.

I wasn't in the mood to return to my room. Not yet. I'd only weep into my pillow, which didn't sound fun or productive, so I picked my way north across the garden, avoiding the areas visible to Ignacio on his nightly vigil between my bedroom and the external doors nearest my wing of the house. To take my mind off of the emptiness growing inside me, I visualized the row of wooden targets lined up at the edge of the shooting field adjacent to our forested acres. Loosing arrows into the center of a target sounded like the perfect way to pass this dreadful night. Besides, if my aim was true, I might even be able to slay this Oscuro whenever he came to claim me.

# 2

## Casimiro

"Curse the stars," I grumbled as I stared at the door of a grand mausoleum in the center of a human cemetery. This wasn't where I'd hoped to find the next mortal on my father's list. With a flick of my wrist, the heavy stone door responded to my magic and swung open with a grinding sound, releasing a wave of cold air and the stench of embalming fluid. I cringed. The way mortals preserved their dead remains prickled my skin.

Even through a sealed box, my nose could detect the awful smell.

The coffin I sought sat on a shelf above another cobwebbed box. This one was studded with gems. I propped my hands on my hips and shook my head. Stealing dead people was never as fun. They didn't fight or scream.

I took out my knife and popped off six of the rubies lining the edge of the smooth wooden coffin. Humans were so wasteful—especially the rich ones—thinking jewels would do any bit of good against the nightmares facing them after they left the mortal world. I tucked the small stones into my pocket as my mind flashed with images of crooked little waist-high *duendes*, with their pseudo-magic and their annoying way of always smelling like rotting garbage, who would likely tunnel into this mausoleum later this very night in search of gems. These lesser fae, often serving in the homes of the high fae, hoarded jewels like dragons, even though the long-nosed creatures couldn't access the magic inside the stones like a high fae. A *duende* could use a ruby or an emerald as a nice little bargaining chip, though, anytime they happened upon a desperate fae or the occasional unsuspecting human. Better that I use the valuable stones.

I shrugged and extracted one of the tiny rubies. Humans knew very little about the magic in their world, and more times than not, their attempts to ward off the shadows only succeeded in bringing us closer. This man had bargained with the Shadow King—a fool's plea—and assumed a handful of rubies would keep my father from taking his dead body. Well, not my father. Me.

While Father was away visiting other courts, his errand of collecting mortals fell to his heir. As of one year ago, I was his oldest heir.

The last time my father had been away, it had been my older brother, Augustín, who'd collected the mortals bound to the Shadow King. A stab of anger pierced my chest as I rolled the faceted stone between my fingertips. The ruby thrummed with a pinprick of welcoming heat—just enough magic to fuel a spell for five minutes, six depending on the spell. A waste in most cases. But when dropped into an elixir, a ruby or amethyst or sapphire of this size would increase the potency threefold, a far more useful application of the stone's magic.

Even though Father would be angry that this mortal was dead, I was grateful for the gemstones as I slipped them in my pocket. As if hearing Augustín's voice, the words *don't waste what we've given you* echoed in my mind.

With a huff, I shoved the painful memories aside and placed my hand on the coffin and envisioned the place in the woods where I'd agreed to meet Felipe, who'd agreed to help me on my second night of collecting mortals. When I opened my eyes again, I stood in a dark forest beneath thick pines. The coffin rested beside me on the ground.

Crashing footsteps—a mortal's by the sound of them—preceded Felipe as he strolled into view between the tall trees, pushing a middle-aged man whose hands were bound.

"Getting cold, princess?" he called over the man's loud footsteps.

I rolled my eyes at his epithet. "Did you enjoy harassing the mortal with your brute strength?" I asked.

Felipe shoved the man to the ground. He grunted and didn't attempt to get up. After spitting on the forest floor beside the mortal—also unnecessary—Felipe propped one foot on the man's back.

I pursed my lips. "My father wants them whole, not broken."

After a small kick, Felipe removed his foot. "There. Happy?"

"Not usually. But that's not your fault." I turned and stared at the coffin. "Father doesn't appreciate the dead ones. He'll blame me for this when he returns." I flexed my fingers as the ghost of pain lanced up my arm from my father's last display of anger.

"Do you think one of ours killed him?" Felipe muttered, his eyes flicking to my hands and back to my face.

My mouth turned down as I studied the coffin. Mortals died if they broke a bargain with a fae, but a fae only suffered a temporary loss of magic, unless the deal had been specifically crafted to end in death. High fae from every court, including ours, frequently killed mortals bound to my father in an attempt to weaken the Shadow King, a man whose reign had stood unbroken for three thousand years, ever since he'd forged a fifth court when there were only ever meant to be four. But in three millennia, no one had succeeded in dethroning my father.

I shrugged. "I've no doubt there will be another coup attempt, as usual, while Father is away, but I doubt this"—I indicated the coffin—"was one of ours. Wouldn't give anyone in our court much advantage to weaken him while he's on the other side of Rivenmark."

Felipe half-smiled as he kicked a pinecone toward the mortal who was awkwardly trying to get up with his hands bound. "No, indeed."

As my father's current heir, my errand was to bring to the Shadow Court all the mortals my father had bargained for, and that meant collecting bodies—living or dead.

That's why we were out here in the mortal world, fishing for humans he'd bargained with, while he proved to the Star Queen—*again*—that his court was a powerful ally, and they couldn't afford to turn on us, should another court attempt to attack our own.

Felipe chuckled and pulled a tiny bottle from the inside of his waistcoat. "We could always try this."

"It's a coffin. Not a sickbed," I said, flicking my wrist at the box.

Felipe frowned, clearly disappointed that I wasn't in the mood to joke with him. Since I was placed in the role of acting sovereign in my father's absence, nothing really seemed funny anymore.

Felipe, however, persisted. "If this could imbue that corpse with enough strength to walk into your father's throne room, it might be worth it. Just to see the look on his face."

"Even if we put a dozen rubies in that vial and made the corpse dance for a fortnight, Father would not be impressed. And besides, he's not returning for an entire year. By then, this corpse will smell too foul to dance for us."

Felipe offered a dry chuckle and tapped his chin. "So we bring back one living captive?"

"One?" I arched my brows at Felipe. "Oh, there's more than one. What, did you think my father was *modest* in making these bargains?" I cracked my knuckles. "That's why I brought you with me, to save time."

Felipe snorted. "Efficiency. Who needs that when you're immortal?"

His joke fell flat as I stared back at him with a look of mild horror.

He coughed. "Sorry."

The ghost of Augustín might as well have been standing in the moonlit forest with us, so vibrant were the memories of him playing in my head. Of the last time I'd spoken to him, taking from his hand a worn journal. Of the way his arms had turned a solid black as pain racked his body. Not all of us were immortal.

The bound mortal stared between us, his rasping breaths loud as a saw in my ear, grating on my nerves.

Felipe's smile returned and he filled the silence. "Let me guess, rich, stupid noble makes bargain for a child? Doesn't think to add any specification clauses?"

I nodded crisply, thankful for the reminder of why we were here. "Yes. Should be easy enough."

With a simple spell, Felipe lengthened the bound man's chains to wrap around the coffin. It wasn't very nice of us, considering how much humans feared death, but we couldn't have him running off like a rabbit while we collected the last mortal from this region.

The forest was a lovely place at night, dark as any place under the moon could be, save the underground halls of Nightsong, where my court made its home. The shadows danced for us as we walked between the trees, down a little road with wagon ruts, toward a large manor house on the outskirts of a city called Leor. Little faces peered at us from the darkness, and I heard the hushed exclamations of both fear and wonder. The night-dwelling creatures in these lands worshiped the Shadows, ignorant of the existence of our oldest enemy, the Night Sovereign, whose court had never fully recovered its strength after the war that granted my father his throne.

One such creature padded out onto the road on soft paws—a *dip*, his furry back as high as my waist, his pointed ears flattened, and his tail tucked in submission. I'd never even met this particular animal, but he knew his place. The hound likely smelled Diego on my clothes and knew he could trust me. I knelt to rub its belly as it rolled over on its back, tongue lolling out, gleaming red eyes glowing. This one smelled atrocious and its fur was matted.

"Don't tell me you want to keep it," Felipe drawled, rolling his eyes.

I cleared my throat. "Not at all." I stared down at the dog—or hellhound, as the humans often called them—and scratched at a tick lodged behind one of his ears. With a quick spell, I dislodged the blood-bloated bug. The dog hopped up and flopped his ears back and forth.

Felipe cringed away. "It'll fling fleas onto us."

I stood and brushed away the black fur clinging to my white shirt. "You do realize these animals work for us? You could treat them with a little less disdain."

Felipe sniffed.

The massive dogs didn't have much magic, but they could be excellent spies. Few fae possessed the magic to speak directly to an animal's mind, so the dogs were most often employed as trackers or fearmongers, but the dogs *could* reveal much, if they were trained.

"Come on, if you pet every hellhound, we're never going to get there before sunrise."

I shot my companion a pointed glare. "I'm coming. And there's no need to rush. This is a nobleman's daughter we're talking about. She's likely never lifted more than a paintbrush in her life, and I bet you these rubies in my pocket that we'll have her walking out after us willingly, like a good little puppy."

Felipe grinned. "Deal."

The words had no sooner left my mouth than an arrow whooshed out of the night and stuck straight into my shoulder.

"Ah," I groaned as the arrow shook my frame. I frowned and shot Felipe a pointed glare that dared him to say a word. But instead of teasing me, Felipe tensed, shifting his stare from me to the forest.

I rubbed the muscle around the puncture wound, more concerned with finding my attacker than dealing with the wound.

My eyes spotted a figure, deep in shadow but not invisible to me. The shot had been impressive, considering the range, the dim lighting, and the tree branches hanging across the road. The person must have noticed me staring, because it nocked another arrow and let it loose. I tipped sideways and let it fly straight past me.

Then, with a small yank, I ripped the arrow from my shoulder and tossed it aside. The skin instantly began to knit back together, leaving me with little more than an ugly bloodstain on my loose white shirt.

At that, the human—for I detected no glamour or traces of magic—darted out from its hiding place and bolted for the distant manor house.

I stormed toward the attacker.

Her. I stormed toward *her*. As she ran, I saw an enormous swath of dark hair swish out behind her and the distinct outline of a ruffled dress. I'd been shot by a mortal woman. She moved with the speed of youth.

Rage seethed in my blood as I stalked my attacker. Despite the fact that most Avencians stayed up to midnight—a result of my court's influence on their lands—it was an odd hour for a mortal woman to be out shooting arrows, alone. I had time enough to handle this mortal and still collect on my father's bargain. Lucky for me, this attacker lived in the same house as the last mortal on our list.

The last *female* mortal. Who, as of today, was twenty years old.

But a nobleman's daughter wouldn't be out at the edge of her estate at night. Would she?

Nostrils flaring, I decided to end this chase. In the blink of an eye, I slipped into the darkness itself, becoming one with the night in my Shadow form, and placed myself directly in the woman's path.

As was customary, she screamed bloody murder when I appeared in front of her. However, contrary to all my other encounters with human females, this one didn't melt with fear or swoon at my glamour.

She shoved an iron dagger into my stomach.

# 3

## Zara

I stared at the face of my pursuer. His dark hair hung across his brow and touched his cheek, hiding his eyes. A smile played on his lips, which just made me shove the blade in harder, until the hilt was the only thing sticking out.

The flesh of his abdomen was hard as a brick wall against my knuckles, now slippery with blood. He'd disappeared and reappeared without moving at all. A trickster, a fae, just like the one I'd met in Puerta only weeks ago, the one who'd married my best friend and taken her away. But if he was fae, the iron should be working already. Instead, he watched me, as if waiting to see what I would do next. He appeared in no great discomfort, other than the blood pouring out of him and the slight flex in his jaw muscle. If I hadn't been so panicked and trying to balance the bow on my shoulder, I would have aimed better and hit him where it mattered.

My breaths came so angry and fast that my cheeks puffed out like the gills of the decorative koi my father kept in the garden pond. I'd been collecting an arrow that had sailed over the targets along the forest's edge when I'd seen his white shirt—a trespasser on my father's land—and taken a shot. That hadn't hurt him, either. Silver-white moonlight barely touched him, as if the darkness clung to him.

The iron worked slower than I'd expected.

The man bent over, head dropping so much that his longish black hair touched my extended arm. For a moment, I wasn't sure if I should yank the blade out and call for Ignacio, or if I should leave the blade in so the iron would keep his magic at bay.

The legends were all such a jumble, considering the stories shifted every year as the storytellers attempted to earn more money. Mortals seldom paid well to hear stories of the fae unless they were ridiculous accounts: how a single mortal hero brought down the entire Wild Hunt or slew a fae king. I could hardly trust such tales to give me accurate information on how to defeat the fae.

So, I stood there, my hand growing wetter with hot blood by the second, unsure what my next move was. Father had omitted this particular conundrum from my years of training.

I elected to leave the knife in, taking my chances on running while the intruder was magicless. He'd pulled my arrow out easily enough, so I supposed he could have the dagger out in a matter of seconds as well, and as soon as that iron left his body, he would likely be strong again.

Using every ounce of my adrenaline and training, I charged toward the garden entrance at the back of my house, which was still far enough away that I couldn't see Ignacio. He'd see me soon enough, though, which was a strange comfort, considering how many nights I'd spent trying to avoid him.

As I raced through the garden, heart beating between my ears rather than in my chest, I tried to smear the blood off my hand with each pump of my arms. My mind flashed to everything I knew about the fae—which wasn't much.

They were real, all right. And they took humans.

I leaped over a stone statue of a frog and decided to abandon the winding path for the more direct route to the door. So far, I couldn't hear anyone pursuing me. But my footsteps and breaths were so loud, I doubted I would hear a horse if it galloped up behind me.

Which was why I was caught completely unaware when a white-shirted torso appeared two steps in front of me. I didn't even have time to slow down. My body crashed into his, and instead of knocking him down, I cracked like I'd run straight into a wall.

I was on the ground, groaning, before I knew what had happened.

He stood there, bloodstained and smug, as if nothing had happened.

Anger spewed out. "But that was iron!"

The man, glamoured again to be so stupidly attractive it was unfair, held the dagger up to the moonlight, examining the blood-soaked blade. "You mean this one?"

His eyes flicked to something over my shoulder, and I scrambled to my feet, chest heaving. Only then did I see the second man, standing behind me as if he'd been there all along. He was sheathed in shadows and as silent as the night. His features were dark—and he tilted his head down, away from the moonlight—that I couldn't see his eyes or mouth. He had wavy hair and wore dark colors, an exquisite suit by the looks of the cut and the sheen of the fabric.

He must be the one who didn't do the chasing. This riffraff, with his crinkled white shirt, must be the errand boy.

I couldn't outrun them. So instead, I grabbed an arrow from my quiver and, with a quick spin, aimed it at the second man. It flashed in the pale light as I held the tip at his temple.

But the man moved like smoke and was gone before I'd even seen him take a step.

Then a sticky blade was at my throat, and I knew I'd lost.

All those years of training, and I'd *lost* in a matter of seconds. Father hadn't told me what creatures would come for me. Hadn't told me anything at all about the bargain, other than that my time here, in this home, in this life, would expire after twenty years. He'd never said *fae* were the ones he'd bargained with, though I'd pondered endlessly the places I might be taken if I were ever captured by a supernatural being. Secretly, I'd always hoped Oscuro was some sort of apothecary, someone who used herbal remedies few others knew about and had gained a reputation for miraculous powers. I'd hoped he wasn't *truly* magical.

"My friend Felipe is an excellent warrior. I wouldn't threaten him," whispered the man I'd wounded twice as he held me with unyielding strength. I stared at the only part of him I could see, his forearm, ridged with veins up to his elbow, where his white shirt made a stark contrast with his dusty olive skin. "Are you going to stop fighting now?" he asked, his voice like hot wax poured over my shoulder as he held the blade close to my throat without touching it. Each word stung, marking my defeat.

Fae had magic. Fae stole humans. Fae ruined my life less when they took Talia.

Each panicked thought pounded through my head to the beat of my pulse.

"You're not going to steal me. Ignacio will be here any minute."

"You mean the guard I put to sleep over there?"

I followed his gaze and ground my teeth as I spotted a dark shape on the garden's path. Desperate, I tried again. "I'm the daughter of a wealthy man. He can pay you whatever you like."

Behind me, the man's chest shook twice as he chuckled. "Oh, but he's already paid."

My blood ran cold.

"You see," he said, dropping the blade so I could spin out of his grip and look him in the eye, "he paid twenty years ago, when he bargained with the Shadow King for a child."

My throat closed up, and my ragged breaths sawed through my lungs as I tried to breathe.

"You had your twenty years, now it's time to come with us." The man flicked the iron dagger aside the way someone might toss a piece of fruit when they discover a spot of hairy mold, then shoved his shirt sleeves up once more and hooked his thumbs on the top of his pants. He tilted his head so the moonlight rested against his upraised cheekbone and the bridge of his nose. Stupidly, I imagined him under a spotlight on a dance floor. He had the perfect thin yet strong build of a dancer. A panicked shiver raced down my spine at the thought of dancing with him.

He smiled. "You're going to be fun."

# 4

## Zara

Hatred seethed out of my pores as I marched between the two men, away from my home and away from my family—dysfunctional as it was. This could not be happening.

But as I walked back into the woods, helpless to defeat these magical beings, I couldn't tell if I hated them or my father more.

I'd known about his bargain since I was six years old, when Papá sat me down and told me about it against my mother's wishes. It hadn't made sense to me then, and over the years—other than my weapons training and my father's unusual spurts of affection around my birthday—the bargain was never again mentioned except once. I was fifteen. My father had just betrothed himself to Nina after seven years as a widower. He had allowed me to be present while he told Nina of the curse on my life. She, of course, was appalled, but my father's wealth beckoned louder than her fears. I would never forget the way she looked at me that night, as her expression of horrified shock transformed into one of quiet delight. In those eyes, her intentions were plain: she hoped to give birth to the heir who would inherit Papá's fortune, and I would be left to the whims of fate.

I stopped walking, too rattled by the reality that was starting to sink in.

The well-dressed fae I hadn't stabbed, Felipe, paused before he crashed into me, but I could feel his breath over my shoulder.

I whirled on him, elbow first, and rejoiced as his eyes closed in the tiniest flash of discomfort. It might not have hurt his immortal, perfect body much, but at least I'd surprised him. His friend, marked by two bloodstains I'd given him, smirked.

"I can't go with you," I blurted out.

Felipe's brown lips curled like drying apple peel. "You don't have a choice. Your life belongs to the Shadow Court."

I looked him up and down. Between his ostentatious black suit and baked-in look of disdain, he definitely seemed like he belonged in the shadows. "You said my father made the bargain twenty years ago. But twenty years ago, I wasn't born yet."

The man's onyx eyes sparked as he shot a look at the other fae. "How old are you?" he asked me, eyes attempting to puncture me with their intensity.

My stomach knotted. "Nineteen." It was true. At least for a handful of hours.

The other fae moved so quietly I spooked like a horse as his shirt brushed against my upper arm. "You can't be nineteen. You are Zara Valencia Calderon, and you were born this day twenty years ago."

These creeps knew my name.

"The time for your life in the mortal realm has come to an end," he continued. "My father requires you at his court."

"*Your* father?" I glanced between him and the suited fae.

His thick brows lifted. "We really don't have time for questions. We can compel you to follow us, but we'd hoped you'd come willingly."

I shook my head, desperation mounting.

The fae sighed. He was so tall that my head only reached to his collarbone, even though he slouched with his neck tipped sideways and his hips at a lazy tilt.

"The problem is, if you don't come with us on the twentieth anniversary of your birth, your father will have failed to uphold his end of the bargain. You know what happens to people who do that?" He leaned forward so his eyes were nearly level with mine. "They die."

A shudder rocked my entire body. Rage and fear and hate, like too much chili pepper poured into a dish, mixed and turned my blood to fire.

The man in the white shirt started walking again, as if he'd solved my dilemma and there would be no more arguing. When I didn't follow, he turned around with a huff of anger and stormed back to me.

"Do you want your father to die?"

After a moment of stunned silence, I fumbled out, "I was—I was born one hour before midnight. That's...it's...technically, as of this hour, twenty years ago, I wasn't born yet."

The prince—for that's what I assumed he was—frowned. "But it *is* the day of your birth." He almost sounded pleased I was arguing with them.

Felipe cleared his throat. "It'll be dawn in a few hours, sweetheart, and we are to have you and the others back at court before the night is done."

"You can't take me until my twenty years are complete. I have until one hour before midnight," I nearly shouted. My voice came out sturdier than I felt, but I lifted my chin and inhaled loudly to drive home the point.

The two men exchanged a glance. Then, the prince whose father was apparently the ruler of the Shadow Court, pinched his lower lip between his perfectly white teeth, deliberating.

Desperation churned inside me. "If I don't show up to my birthday celebration tonight, people will ask questions."

"People will ask questions, eh?" The prince's smirk fanned the flames in my blood. "I'm ever so worried about mortals' *questions*." He sighed and ran a hand through his floppy hair. "But she's right," he said, startling the sneer off my face.

The suited man snorted and turned aside.

"At one hour to midnight, your time here will end," the prince continued. He winked at me, sending a shiver of disgust over every bit of my exposed skin. "You have your request, but when the time is up, you *will* come with us. You can't run from the shadows, señorita Valencia. So don't even try."

As I stumbled into my bedroom not five minutes later, I was out of breath. My hands shook so violently, I couldn't light the candle by my bedside. I pulled away the mosquito netting that surrounded my bed, shoved aside the pile of cushions meant to mimic my body under the covers, and crawled onto my tall bed. My mind rang with the words of the shadow fae. *At one hour to midnight, your time here will end.*

I punched one of the pillows lined up under the covers then flopped on top of them, crying silently.

"Spare me, please," came a deep voice from the corner of my room.

I screamed like a little girl running from a spider.

Without thinking, I hurled a pillow at the voice, but it only knocked into the netting and bounced back onto the bed. Through the faint silvery sheen of the net, I couldn't see anyone in the dark.

One of my daggers was outside the net, resting on my bedside table. The gossamer fabric felt like a cage around me, keeping me from my weapon. My eyes darted to the blade, but before I lunged for it, I sensed movement in the shadows.

Swatting away the curtain, I growled low through my teeth as a hand, dark as the inky night sky, slipped over the hilt of the blade.

"You won't be stabbing me again, I'm afraid."

The voice of the prince sounded from the darkness, but no one was there. My room was painted in shades of gray and black, lit only by the moonlight falling in from the tall windows on two sides.

I saw no one.

"Where are you?" I couldn't keep the tremor of fear from my voice as I slid my hand onto my bedside table. My fingers closed over the cool handle of my brush. In a pinch, it could serve as a weapon.

"Everywhere."

"That's poetic."

A satisfied *hmm* emerged from the darkness. He was moving, but I still couldn't see him.

"Let go of my knife."

"I don't like getting stabbed by iron."

My pulse raged in my ears like the jangling belts of the belly dancers in the market square. "You didn't seem too bothered by it earlier." If this fae wasn't affected by iron, then I'd wasted my money having an iron dagger forged.

The darkness chuckled, and I shivered despite the sweat on my back. Each long second that he remained silent, the muscles in my chest tightened.

After a minute, my fear burst out. "Are you going to stay hidden, or will you show your face?"

"You are afraid," came the prince's deep voice.

My father had tried to teach me to conceal my emotions, but I'd mostly been terrible at it—at least, according to his continual lack of approval. Never good enough. Never stoic enough. Never unfeeling enough. I'd assumed it was because he wanted me to fit into proper society, where women were expected to remain quiet and demure at all times, but perhaps it was because he didn't want the fae to be able to read me so easily.

A frenzied knock at my bedroom door triggered another small yelp—I couldn't remember the last time I'd been so jumpy. A soft chuckle from the shadows made my upper lip curl as I hurried into bed, spending five agonizing seconds tangling once again in the frustrating net.

The door opened, and I went still as a statue, despite my heart trying to explode from my chest. Candlelight flooded the room, and my eyes did a quick survey of every corner. No one was there.

The upstairs housemaid poked her head in. "Everything all right, señorita?"

If her definition of all right included being stalked by shadows as they awaited the moment they could steal me from the mortal world, just as my father *agreed* so many years ago, sure, I was fine.

For a split second, I thought about screaming again, telling her to wake the guards and muster the troops—we didn't actually have any troops—and ring every alarm bell in Leor until this sticky shadow fae was lying in pieces in the woods somewhere and I could go back to normal life.

But then my father would die.

And, though my thoughts toward him at this moment were muddy and painful, I couldn't breathe at the thought of him dying. So I nodded, forced a smile, and dismissed the maid.

"Good girl," the man said as soon as the door closed.

I sat up in bed, scanning the room until my eyes fixed on the silver flash of moonlight on a twirling blade. My blade.

He sat—no, lounged—in the chair before my dressing table, which was half-turned toward the enormous windows overlooking the western side of the estate, one leg hooked over the armrest while his head was tilted back against the ornate wing of the chair.

"I hate you," I blurted, lacking anything more intelligent to say to him.

"I'd be disappointed if you didn't. It'll make everything much more fun."

My throat tried to close up. I wanted to ask him what he meant by *everything*, but I couldn't bring myself to do it. I didn't really want to know what these fae had in store for me. Not yet. After all, I'd marry in a few hours, and maybe that would be enough to break the curse.

I flung the covers off and hopped out of bed. I would *not* be sleeping in the presence of this pointy-eared creature.

"Where do you think you're going?" he drawled, not moving from his relaxed position.

Sweat blanketed my back, and I was nowhere near sleepy. "If I only have one day left before you—before *I* go, then I'm not going to waste time sleeping."

"You don't have to sleep, but then I wouldn't touch any doors or windows, if I were you. They've been enchanted to put you into a *very* deep sleep."

I glared at the door to my bedroom, as if I could see the magic infused in the wood. He might be lying. But fae weren't supposed to be able to lie. I sighed heavily.

"I really hate you."

His shadowy features broke into a smile, then he stood. "I'm thrilled by your level of affection toward me, but I really must be going."

I blinked. "You're leaving?" Hope filled my chest.

"I only needed to escort you back here and place my enchantments. Now that you're trapped in here, I'm free to go." He moved toward the window. "I don't have time to sit around with you all night. The enchantment will shift to include the entire house when the sun comes up so you can move about your day. I'm generous like that. But you won't be able to run." With hands braced against the window casing, he looked back at me. “I will return tonight. Look for me. My name is Casimiro. Oh, and happy birthday, Zara Valencia.”

Before I could so much as clench my jaw, he was gone, dissipating into the night like smoke and taking my dagger with him.

# 5

## Casimiro

In the cover of night, my shadow form wasn't visible to her, so I turned, my wings silently holding me aloft, and watched the mortal as she hurried to her bed and collapsed facedown. For a moment she lay so still, I wondered if she'd fallen asleep. So much for her claims of not wanting to sleep on her final day in the mortal world.

Then she slammed a fist into the blankets, and a muffled scream reached my ears.

A flicker of dread filled my chest. She might be angry now, but she too would break. She too would die. Mortals loved to talk of their heart, their driving beliefs, and their passions, but in the face of death, they all cracked.

My father made sure they did. No, not him anymore. While he was away, breaking mortals was my responsibility.

As I flew away from her house, my eyes traced the forest, penetrating the darkness better than a cat's, but I couldn't focus on the hunched duendes, the tall dryads, or the tiny pixies scurrying about. My mind filled with the image of the curly-haired woman's eyes as she'd pressed an iron blade into my stomach.

Her little stunt had proved that the many years of building up a resistance to the magic-stifling metal had paid off. And now she knew it. Anger flared in my chest as I angled toward the place where Felipe waited. She could not discover anything else about me that might give her an edge in what was about to take place. Father had been clear: no mortal can prevail in the games.

They all must die.

And given what I'd seen of her so far, I fully believed this mortal, when given the chance to choose her fate, would elect to enter the games. The proud ones always chose the games.

But I couldn't let myself be concerned with her for the next several hours.

Felipe yawned dramatically as I landed silently on the forest floor, shifting back into my physical form. "Ready, princess?" he asked.

I rolled my eyes and tossed my hand out toward the empty space between two large pines. A crack appeared in the very air as my magic split the worlds and opened up a fissure in the shape of a rectangular door, blacker than the night, a door to Nightsong.

"I needed to make sure she wouldn't run. She seemed the type to try it," I replied, flexing and curling my fingers as a dull ache throbbed in my bones.

Felipe nodded and stood up from his seat on the coffin. "That she did. If she chooses to entertain, she'll be a favorite, I'm certain."

My mouth curled into a sneer. "She'll burn out like all the rest. I give her two trials and she'll crack."

The mortal still chained to the coffin looked between us, confused.

"Let's go," Felipe said, tugging the man to his feet.

"Did you give him the choice?"

Felipe nodded and jostled the man. "We've got us an entertainer."

Only then did I notice the man was crying quietly, and I whirled away from the sight of his foul tears. I couldn't stand the sight of tears streaking a human's face, as if they had no ability to control themselves, no capacity to staunch their emotions and get on with their short lives.

And now he'd chosen a path that would end his life much sooner. Likely before the sun ever rose.

A brief notion pricked at me—this man likely had a family he was leaving behind. We'd taken him from a gambling hall, so I hadn't seen his dwelling or any family who might be waiting for his return.

*These people will live and die before a fae child ever casts his first spell,* Father had frequently reminded me when I was young enough to still question him, young enough that most of his ire was directed toward Velazques, the brother I'd barely known, older even than Augustín. After Velazques died, all my questions had stopped.

I shook away the memories and stormed forward, grabbing one end of the coffin by its embedded handle. Felipe bent to collect the second handle. The chained mortal moved with us, his reddened eyes fixed on me, as if he could plead with nothing but his repulsive tears.

Even if he was leaving a family behind, he was the one who'd made the deal with my father. Anyone desperate enough for that had to pay the price. Leaving him here, the bargain unfulfilled, would be a death sentence as much as bringing him with us.

We walked awkwardly toward the doorway I'd opened, the coffin and the bound man between us. Felipe angled so he could back through the door first and tossed a smirk at the human.

"Ready to enter the Shadow Court?"

The man shook his head.

"No one ever is," Felipe replied with a broad smile.

We passed through the cleft between worlds, and darkness swallowed us.

The surge in my magic as we returned home felt like a plunge into a cool, refreshing lake. I breathed deeply as my feet touched the smooth rock surface of the hall buried deep underground. Two stairwells branched off from the wide hall, leading up on each side, and a dark passage ahead led toward the human servants' quarters. The hall was empty, save for the fae guard waiting here to collect the mortals I was supposed to bring with me.

Without a word, the guard, Farrin, raced forward to collect the chained man. The briefest of frowns crossed Farrin's face as he eyed the coffin, but he said nothing. I strode toward the stairwell leading up to the right.

"See you at sundown," Felipe called up to me.

With a nod, I jogged up one flight of steps, then another, and exited the palace into the starlit night, relishing the snap of cold air against my face. Descending into Avencia's summer, even at night, was like taking a swim in a molten lake. I relished the cold.

I strolled up a flat path cut into the mountainside and climbed one more flight of steps that deposited me onto a small balcony that overlooked the deep valley below. The lake below reflected the pale light of the moon, which was already almost hidden behind the opposing mountain peak. Wind howled through the crevices and crags, singing to me the music of the shadows. Lights glowed along the paths crisscrossing the mountainside, making the darkness glisten like a wood full of fireflies.

The sconce behind me flickered to life, its white flames burning without a sound, as I removed the bloodstained shirt and tossed it at the wall behind me. The frigid air danced over my skin for a moment before a clean shirt materialized in my hand. As I pulled the fabric down over my head, the muted sound of hurried footsteps brought a smile to my face.

"Fae move without sound," I teased as I whirled around, just in time to accept a smash in the stomach meant to resemble a hug.

"You brought home a dead guy!" my sister said as she peeled herself off me, shaking out long dark hair that paled as it fell over her small shoulders until it was the color of spun honey. Tonight, Alba had one long chunk of hair tied up in what looked like a donut at the top of her head.

I eyed the strange pale circle of hair resting atop her head only to discover it had twigs and feathers sticking out of it as well. I frowned to keep from laughing. "Did you build a bird's nest in your hair?"

Alba planted her hands on her hips. "A dragon nest, actually. My mother is from the Star Court, which means I should have at least a *little* spring magic in me. And dragons are kind of like birds."

I snorted, reaching out to muss her hair. She ducked away, hands up.

"Kind of like birds? Except huge and with a particular aversion to our magic?"

She straightened and crossed her arms. "There are many breeds of dragons. Some of them are quite small."

"And they live in the jungle. Not here. And they'd hate us just as much as the big ones."

She huffed. "Well, perhaps they only hate us because we *steal* their young."

The smile tugging at my lips fell away. Stealing was what my court did best. We stole dragon eggs. We stole humans. We stole power from the other courts. It had made us many enemies.

She glared up at me. "A dragon will find me. It will see that I'm no enemy."

Alba hadn't yet seen what we did to the dragons that outgrew our cages and our magic. The creatures hated us for more reasons than a few stolen eggs. "One girl won't change the hatred seared into their natures, Alba."

Her crossed arms fell away, but her lips pursed in annoyance.

"Besides," I said, "do you really want dragon dung in your hair?"

The frown on her face loosened and she made a disgusted face. It was all I could do not to wrap her in a hug and procure a dragon-shaped shadow to sit in her hair all night. But a creature made from darkness wasn't what she wanted, and it would only make her sad. So, instead, I tried to ignore the nest on her head—and the things the other fae were likely saying about it—and thought of what she'd first said.

"There was nothing I could do about the dead man. He'd been dead for two days. If Father felt the effects of the broken bargain, he felt them two days ago."

Her eyes went wide as realization dawned on her pretty face. She had the pallor of the Star Court. The freckles dusting her skin from head to toe resembled the court's beloved stars. Her clothing, like her hair, always attempted to wed the customs of the two courts that flowed in her veins—the result of one of Father's trips to the Star Court. Tonight she wore a black dress with pale blue sequins huddled at the waist. A mix of darkness and starlight.

"I thought you had three mortals to collect tonight?" she said, tilting her head so that the nest would have dumped out any eggs, had there been any.

"I did. But the hour of birth hadn't passed yet for the third, and she knew enough to understand that she technically had until that hour."

Alba clapped. "Oh, a mortal who knows about us?"

My look cut off her little celebration. "I doubt she knows much. And, Alba, no meddling with these new arrivals. You know they'll die soon enough as it is. Their lives are a vapor."

Her face fell. "That may be, but birds don't live long either, and we still love their songs."

"Planning to make the mortals sing for you?"

She smirked. "Perhaps. If blades can sing."

"You can't gut them, Alba. You know the rules."

My sister planted her hands on her slender hips. "I'm not going to kill anyone, Cas. Unlike *you*." Her words stung, but I brushed off the feeling. As acting sovereign, I didn't have the luxury of remorse. "Father instructed me to keep practicing with my blades, and you're too busy now," she continued. "I need a dueling partner, and how fun would it be to pick a *mortal*? They'd be so terrified."

"You just compared them to songbirds."

Alba lifted her hands in frustration. "My point," she seethed, "was simply that their short lifespans aren't the reason we despise them."

I rolled my eyes. "So, find one to duel with, if you wish. But do not interfere with the games."

"I won't."

I turned away, rubbing my chin. "The mortal I met tonight could handle a blade," I said, rubbing a hand over the place where the iron had pierced my flesh. If Alba knew that woman had stabbed me, she'd never let me live it down.

"Excellent. I want to practice with someone who knows how to fight."

"A mortal against a fae is not a fight."

She snorted. "That's why it'll be so much fun!"

"Don't get too excited. She has to survive her first trial."

Alba clapped, and I wasn't sure if it was because of the upcoming trial or the fact that there might be a mortal she could duel with.

When my sister's footsteps moved away, I spun back around.

At only eighty-one, Alba was still a novice at magic, born of a union created during one of our father's travels to the Star Court in an attempt to forge peace between us. She'd been here only two decades, not long enough to have known Velazques or Augustín. Not long enough to know the pain I knew. Not long enough to hate our father the way I did.

As she scampered up the stairwell that led up to her quarters, I muttered, "Never stop dreaming, Alba."

I half considered flying a little more tonight, feeling the need to let the wind carry me, but there were more pressing matters. So, with a last glance at the night, I turned and entered my bedroom through a heavy wooden door set into the mountainside.

Bypassing the bed I rarely used, I marched straight to my study, where books and vials all called to my attention.

I had time, I reminded myself. A quick, deep inhale helped me settle my thoughts, and I moved to the rows of vials. My fingers traced the edge of a shelf stocked with everything from remedies to stomach ailments to balms for burned skin. I found a dusty vial labeled *Brittlebloom Extract* and tipped it forward. The shelf loosened from the wall, and I pulled, not far enough to open the room behind the shelf, built centuries ago by a brother I'd never known, but enough to access the hidden panel that looked only like the back of the shelf. I pried open the tiny slot that housed a single book.

When the compartment was again hidden away behind my shelf, I sat and thumbed to the last page I'd read.

*Entry 612: I should add to my last note that lithewart leaves are the important part, not the buds, as I expected. When crushed and added, they offer a bolstering effect to the goosenettle, which I believe is an essential ingredient for the way it dulls the pain.*

I glanced at my shelves, finding the tin of dried lithewart and the oil of goosenettle, both plants that had been discovered in the neighboring realm, Verindal, a thousand years ago.

The handwriting on the page, browned with age, was elegant and slanted in the old style, the letters shaped with precision and grace, even in the language no one else could read but those who owned this journal. I traced the lines with a finger, absently wondering who or what had interrupted Enzo when he penned this entry some seven hundred years ago.

A flicker at the corner of my mind told me someone had passed the boundary spell outside my room.

I stood and quickly hid the journal back in its slot behind the shelf and took a seat at my desk, grabbing the book nearest me and feigning interest.

A knock sounded.

"Court business, Your Highness." It was one of the fae in charge of setting up the mortal games. I'd brought home one man and he would have to perform for the fae court at dawn.

"Coming," I called, abandoning my books. With a sigh, I grabbed my suit jacket from the back of my chair and jammed my arms in the sleeves. Then I quickly snatched the black stone crown from my desk, tossed my hair back, and settled the crown on top of my head. It might as well have been a chain, binding me to the will of the Shadow Court.

# 6

## Zara

With the frenzy of activity in the house and grounds as final preparations for tonight's ball were made, I had few options for where to pass my time—the library or the shooting range or the stables. The fae prince had warned me that magic bound me to the estate.

After sneaking a few small blades and holsters from the family armory, I settled on the library, hoping to find a book that contained information I hadn't yet read about the fae—some jewel of information that could save my life. I'd read every fictional tale we owned, but maybe one of the historical tomes mentioned these otherworldly creatures. They *had* to. Talia and I couldn't be the only humans to meet any fae.

As I searched the library, I assessed what I already knew of them. I now knew that iron didn't kill them, as many of the stories claimed. And if my arrows and knives couldn't kill these creatures, then I would arm myself with knowledge.

The library had been polished to a high shine, and the midmorning light pouring in from the tall windows reflected off the reading tables and brass book holders. Talia had always loved this place. I admired my friend, who'd gone with that mysterious fae so willingly, just to help her family, but now that I was faced with the same possibility, I would do anything *not* to. Perhaps the two strange men I'd met earlier would know what had happened to her.

By the time Raquel, my personal maid, collected me from the library in the early afternoon to begin prepping me for the party, my eyes were numb from scanning old texts, none of which included any useful information. A dusty tome called *Mysteries of Avencia: Unsolved History* described enough accounts of disappearing humans—both men and women—to indicate that I would simply become another statistic on a time-yellowed page. Of the sixteen accounts listed in the book, two included quotes from family members that mentioned the fae were responsible for stealing their loved ones. Both were considered accounts from confused or aggrieved subjects. All my hours of study had simply shown me that this had happened before.

"I need to speak with Papá," I told Raquel, suddenly panicked that my time to do so was running thin. He'd been in Leor by the time I came down the stairs from my room this morning, apparently called to town early to finalize the wedding negotiations with my bridegroom.

My maid informed me that he was still meeting with the delegation from Cavaria, but that she would relay the message.

With a reluctant huff, I followed Raquel up to my bathing chamber, determined to have a word with Papá before the ball—which would double as my wedding.

Two hours later, I stood before a tall mirror as my stepmother and three servants bustled about, fussing over my hair and clothes and cosmetics. I could barely hear their chatter over the buzz of blood in my ears.

Night had fallen again. My final day had come and gone like a held breath, rushing out faster than I could hold on to it. The hours had slipped by, and I'd arrived here at my birthday celebration, unable to recall what I'd done of note since that shadowy man had left my room.

But now that I waited in my bedroom above the noisy ballroom, preparing to perform for my guests—a request my father had reluctantly granted, perhaps because he knew he owed me—I had run out of time to talk to him. It felt like he was avoiding me on what might be the last day I would ever speak to him.

If today turned out to be my final day in the mortal world, I'd regret having spent so much of it on my hair, but my curls were unruly, according to my stepmother, and had to be tugged and smeared back into a tight knot, as was only proper for young ladies.

Despite all the fears creeping in, I had one last hope: this marriage. At this point, I didn't care who my father had chosen. Love wasn't what I'd believed, and if being married was enough to break the curse on my life, then I'd take it. I'd find a way to survive a loveless marriage more easily than I would a trip to the Shadow Court. A place that, to my knowledge, no one had ever returned from. There were no stories about the shadow fae. Not one. As if they didn't even exist.

The chatter of a hundred voices filtered up from the ballroom's open windows and into my bedroom, through the same window the Shadow prince had departed. I could picture the light of the chandeliers reflected on the smooth wood floor downstairs and the massive stacks of sugar-dusted *mantecados* displayed at the back of the large room. My mouth watered just thinking of them, but per tradition, the birthday dessert wasn't to be eaten until the hour of birth—the same hour I was apparently going to be whisked away by two handsome mythical creatures. If that sly prince thought he could keep me from my pastries, he'd get another dagger in his gut.

"Breathe out," my stepmother barked, poking me in the ribs as Raquel tightened the knots at the back of my dress.

Instead, I pulled in a deep breath, expanding my ribcage.

A frustrated sigh issued from Nina's painted lips. "Be reasonable," my stepmother spat under her breath so no one standing outside on the terrace could hear. "Don't you want to perform tonight?"

Raquel pursed her lips and squeezed the dress into place over my ample bosom until it hurt. Nina nodded her approval.

Three weeks ago, when I'd won the dance competition held during the midsummer *Festival de los Cuentos*, my stepmother had realized that my dancing held a possible benefit for her. She saw the way men looked at me, and she'd salivated at the notion that I'd finally find a husband and free her from having to bother with me, leaving her to be the woman of the estate once and for all. I was to perform tonight, finally, in my own home, and woo the man my father had chosen as my spouse—Baron Montrose, a gentleman from the distant country of Cavaria, where they spoke no Avencian and wore fur coats in the winter. I wasn't sure which would be worse, the Shadow Court or deeply cold winters.

I lifted my chin—still dramatically lower than Nina's—and fixed her with a hard stare. She assumed I desired the gaze of men. Everyone assumed things about me. Jorge had assumed I wanted…well, something I only wanted when I was married and in love. My father assumed I wanted to be married, if it would free me of this curse. Nina assumed I wanted to marry Montrose simply because he was wealthy.

"There, now, remember what's at stake." My stepmother tapped the side of my face waiting for my answer.

She knew of the curse, but the look in her eyes said she wasn't worried about where I went after tonight, be it a fae court or an estate far to the north, as long as it was away from here. She almost ruined this for me. Almost. But I wouldn't let her spoil what might be my final dance ever.

"I must speak with Papá."

Nina pinched her lips and a look of true disappointment crossed her brow. "He wishes to speak with you as well, but it must be after you dance. There is no time!"

Raquel finished securing my dress and stepped back.

"No time for what?" My father's deep voice came from the antechamber outside my bedroom.

My heart leapt, and I rushed to him.

"Papá!" I sailed into his open arms.

We didn't usually embrace like this, but we both felt the weight of what was at stake tonight. Nina cleared her throat behind us.

"I apologize, *Zarita*, for being absent much of today. I heard that you wished to speak with me." He held me at arm's length, his eyes already filling with tears. In my entire life, I'd seen the man cry twice. The first time when he told me of my curse, and the second when my mother died. "Your wedding arrangements have been made. Montrose is ready to marry you tonight."

I didn't want to ask what Papá had done to enable a wedding to take place so quickly. It didn't matter. With a deep inhale that made my tight dress creak, I lifted my chin and nodded.

"Do you really think it will work?" I asked.

Nina dismissed the maids, leaving us to speak of this disaster alone. My father's hands tightened on my shoulders, but he said nothing. For a man of many words, seeing him speechless sent a wave of tingling panic down my arms and legs. My breaths shortened, and my body heated as my stomach twisted inside me.

"It will work," Nina said, walking up to us with a fixed, poised expression. This conundrum was of little consequence to her. "Now, we have guests waiting."

"They came earlier," I whispered as Nina walked toward the door. "I met them. They are fae. *Shadow* fae."

Papá's face dropped to be level with mine. "You met Oscuro?"

I shook my head. "He said his name was Casimiro, the son of the Shadow King."

Papá straightened. The breath leaving his lungs smelled of his prized wine. "Oh, Zara. This marriage will be our salvation. You were right to tell me that marriage breaks these kinds of things." He never used the word curse...or *maldita*.

*Love breaks curses*, I'd told him. Not weddings. But maybe to a fae bargain, they were one and the same? We could only hope.

Nina scoffed. "Be glad that you are marrying at all, under the circumstances. At least your beauty will please Montrose."

I glanced down at my cleavage. "By beauty, you mean this, right?"

She pursed her lips.

Whenever she spoke of my body like a painting that was for sale, I winced. I grabbed the fringed shawl she held out toward me and wrapped it around my shoulders, crossing it over my chest.

Flamenco dresses were not worn by the high nobility in Avencia, save for once a year. During the *Festival de los Cuentos*, when any costume was allowable, many women opted to wear flamenco-style dresses, embracing for one week the form-fitting dresses stacked with ruffles. That festival had ended weeks ago, and I'd be the only one wearing this style tonight.

All the more reason, according to my stepmother, for my soon-to-be husband to be fawning over me.

An unwanted chill raked down my spine as I recalled the disheveled princeling who'd stolen my dagger. I didn't want to think of him. By the time he returned to collect me, the bargain would be broken. It had to be.

Grinding my teeth, I focused instead on the dance I was about to perform, moving through the opening steps in my head as I exited the room on my father's arm, Nina walking behind us.

"You are a dancer," Nina hissed over our shoulders. "Great men think nothing more of women on a stage than they do of a fancy chair or a nice wine goblet. Entertainers are like ornaments at a party. Something to be admired but nothing more. I'm shocked Montrose agreed to let his bride dance tonight."

A weight sank in my stomach as all the blood rushed from my head. Usually, the moments before a dance amplified my spirit and gave life to my bones. But in one statement, my stepmother had stripped everything joyful about this moment. Nina was pale and generally unassuming and she even had freckles, something rare among the Avencian people. Some of the storytellers considered freckles a curse by the sun on those who were tasteless. I knew better than that, as most of the stories told at Festival were solely for entertainment, but at times like this, I was tempted to believe that one held a little truth.

Without another word to her, we descended the stairs, pausing only as we approached the ballroom.

My father turned and kissed both of my cheeks. "We will see the end of this tonight," he said reassuringly. "Don't you worry. Now, go and have fun." He smiled, but the expression was strained. He took Nina's arm, and the two disappeared into the ballroom as the announcer called their arrival.

Raquel reappeared from the side hall and handed me my castanets. Within the ballroom, I heard my father announcing the upcoming wedding, a fact greeted by loud applause. Then the room quieted, and my father announced my performance. It was time.

I cleared my throat, made sure my castanets were secured in my fingers, then slipped quietly through the doorway onto the dance floor. A hush fell over the crowd as the tinkling glasses and laughter died down. A few snickers trickled through the seated guests, and immediately the sweat of doubt prickled through my skin.

I lifted my hands into the air, twisting my fingers around artfully. My heart pounded in my ears. Before the music began, I curled my arms in a snakelike fashion over my head, face lifted to the light above.

The music began. My foot stomped to the beat and my hips moved, the ruffles in my dress flipping as I cocked my heeled shoe sideways and spun.

The crowd watched in perfect silence.

The chandelier above was so bright it was hard to see faces in the room, which made it easier for me to concentrate on the dance. Soon I lost myself in the movements. The tension from a moment ago melted into my hot blood. The thrill of the sound, the rhythm, and the reverberations running through my legs every time I clicked my heels into the floor, erased all the anxiety and brought about a welcome oblivion.

The music was drawing to a crescendo. It was so quiet I wondered if every person in the room was holding their breath. This part of the dance required that I edge closer to the people sitting in the chairs. This was the part that had brought the crowd to their feet three weeks ago, winning me first place.

Clacking my castanets and heels in faster and faster succession, I stomped up to the nearest table to finish this performance, selecting, as usual, one man to approach for my final pose. I noticed a dark suit, though I was spinning too fast to take note of his face. He angled his body toward me, leaning one elbow against the table, the other splayed against the back of his chair, as if he was pleased with my choice, like he was some peacock worthy of being singled out in a roomful of nobility.

He eased back in a comfortable position, knees splayed out, lounging backward as I danced faster and faster, nearer and nearer. I was right in front of him, clacking and stomping as the music reached its final crescendo.

When I stomped the last step of the dance, I threw my arms up and turned my chin dramatically to the side. I had to hold the pose for five seconds, at least, for full effect. Out of the corner of my eye, I noticed that the man had scooted his feet out so that they were on either side of mine, just under the ruffles of my dress. Heat blazed up my shins at his boldness, but I didn't break my pose to see who the man was.

As the first applause began, I straightened and finally looked at the man sitting right in front of me. It was Casimiro, and his was the only face not smiling.

# 7

## Zara

Icy fear prickled my skin, though my blood was still pumping quickly from the dance.

The lone sound of a chair scooting backward across the wooden floor rose over the polite applause. Casimiro stood, so close that I edged away from him. He lifted his hands and began to clap, his applause continuing long after everyone else's had stopped.

Every eye in the room stared at him. His sweeping dark hair was slicked back, revealing his pointed ears for all to see. On his head was a crown that appeared to be made of onyx.

When his applause ended, heavy silence filled the room. No one moved.

Except Casimiro, who bent at the waist, his eyes still on me, and said, "A most moving performance. Do me the honor of dancing with me tonight." He straightened.

The wedding ceremony was to begin directly after my performance. We didn't have time to dance beforehand. My heart fluttered nervously as I glanced to Papá to give a reply, but when I spotted my father, his face was frozen in open-mouthed shock, a visible sheen of sweat twinkling on his brow as he stared at the fae prince. My knees almost buckled beneath me.

I cleared my throat. "There is no time, I'm afraid," I replied, hoping my voice sounded calm and confident despite my rushing pulse.

The fae prince sneered. "There is time if I say there is. We shall dance," he announced, lifting a hand to the musicians. "Though I believe your first dance is already taken by that gentleman over there."

Casimiro turned toward Lord Montrose, whose pale features stood out in the room full of dark-haired Avencians.

"Indeed," Montrose said, rising from his seat. He bobbed a polite bow to Casimiro, who did not return the gesture. A few people gasped at the impropriety. Others whispered the word *fae* loud enough that the prince's lips curled into a smile.

Lord Montrose walked toward me with a stiff frown, his eyes cutting toward Casimiro twice, but still no one else in the room budged from their seats. My cheeks heated as I took Montrose's hand and stepped back onto the dance floor, away from the fae.

This wasn't how the evening was supposed to go. We were supposed to join hands and exchange vows after my dance. But Lord Montrose didn't know *why* the timing mattered. Avencian parties never started until all the hues of sunset were gone, which in the summer was not until after ten o'clock. We had less than one hour to be wed before my time was up.

Casimiro sat down, but the tension in the room only amplified, as everyone launched into furious whispers, forgetting, perhaps, that the stories all claimed fae had excellent hearing. My pulse remained high while the music started again. As Montrose swept me into the first steps of the dance, I caught sight of the fae prince sipping my father's prized wine, a bored expression on his face.

Lord Montrose asked me something, but my brain hadn't stopped thinking about Casimiro's request for my next dance. I responded with a half-dazed *hmm*.

"I look forward to getting to know you better, tonight," he said in his heavy accent, offering me the slightest ghost of a smile. This was the man I was to marry, and I should look at him as my savior, my ticket away from the Shadow Court. Instead, my eyes raked the room for Casimiro. Was he about to snatch me right this minute? Did I even have time to hug my father one last time?

My shoulders tensed a little when I realized Papá wasn't sitting where I'd last seen him. The fae had indicated that my father would die if the bargain was broken...I nearly lost the contents of my stomach on Lord Montrose's shined shoes.

No, Papá was fine. Likely speaking to someone on the terrace, that was all.

"Thank you," I said to Montrose, unsure if this was the right thing to say in the moment. My mind was spinning faster than my shoes. The wedding was about to take place, as planned. We still had time.

My future husband spun me around and gripped me with a featherlight touch. His light skin and freckles certainly stood out against my darker tone, but he was pleasant to look at and not yet thirty-five. I should be pleased with my father's choice. Love was meant to surmount all obstacles, after all. Perhaps, in time, I'd find love with Montrose.

The dance ended, and I stared blankly at the table of *mantecados*, hoping to have time and appetite enough to enjoy them later. It was time for the wedding ceremony. Montrose bowed and I curtsied, my heart in a frantic tangle of emotions. For a brief moment, my eyes glazed over and I pictured Talia the last time she'd been in this ballroom. How I longed to see her again.

But when I blinked, I saw another face before me.

Casimiro.

He snapped his fingers at the musicians, and their strings slid seamlessly into a fast tune. The prince didn't wait for me to take his hand. Instead, he swept me into a dance as the music began.

His hand was tighter on my waist than Lord Montrose's had been, forcing me closer and moving me faster. Instantly, my body responded, heating as I realized I danced with someone who matched my skill and passion. My blood flushed with anger and fear and the twisted desire to outdance this fae, to prove that I was not some toy for him to toss around.

I pushed against his hands, testing the strength of his lead in the dance. He matched my aggression and soon my arms burned as they pressed back into his hold. His lips held the faintest curl at the edges as he charged across the dance floor with the precision of a marching soldier. Confined in his grip for the duration of the dance, I allowed myself to really look at him. His features were as precisely shaped as the stone of his crown, chiseled and smooth as if age did not touch him. He stared at me with deep-set eyes the color of fresh coffee. My stomach flipped over inside me. If it weren't for the fact that he'd only come to steal me away to the Shadow Court, I might have wanted to dance with him again. The dance raced toward the first dip, and my body moved on its own, lost to the rhythm.

He held one strong arm under my back and leaned forward, pressing me down toward the floor with such grace and gentleness I let out a small gasp. As he bent forward, his entire face fell into shadow, lit from above. This close, the spark in his eyes was undeniable, though I couldn't tell if it was simply because he'd beaten Montrose by proving his superior skill or if he truly enjoyed dancing with me. As he pulled me back up, a shiver interrupted my next move, and his grip tightened, as if to remind me who was really in charge here. Angry at my slip, I stormed toward him, commanding the dance as my own once again.

"You think getting married will break the bargain?" he asked, his voice low and threatening.

At that moment, he released me into a spin. When I slammed into his grip once more, my heart drummed against my ribs. "Yes," I spat back. "The stories all say love breaks curses."

Without missing a step, he tilted his head back and laughed. Doubt clamped around my lungs, pushing out all my air.

"Getting married will not save you from your fate. It will only leave that man a widower. For I will take you, married or not. Better to let him avoid that, don't you think?"

The word *widower* sat heavy on my chest, making it difficult to breathe. My feet missed a step of the dance, and Casimiro's chest bumped against mine.

"Will your father kill me?" I managed to ask.

Casimiro's eyes darkened. "No. That is not his job."

As my fear rose, the prince's hold on me tightened, not allowing me to miss another step. And it seemed that no one in the room—my betrothed included—felt bold enough to cut in on my dance with the fae prince. "But you said—then whose job is it?" I blurted out.

"Mine."

My gasp was covered by the final crescendo of the dance. Shock caused me to go limp, and I felt my body falling to the floor.

No, I was being lowered, carefully, in a set of strong arms, into a deep final pose.

Casimiro stared down at me with blazing eyes, his crown somehow not falling off his perfect brow. When he lifted me, he maintained eye contact, drilling in the last word he'd spoken.

It was *his* job to kill me.

While our faces were still close, he whispered, "If you do not want to die, then choose wisely."

"Choose? What do you mean?"

But Casimiro's hands let go, and he stepped back.

My gaze shifted to Lord Montrose. He seethed with envy or anger or both, his jaw flexing and his lips pinched.

"It is time," the prince muttered.

“Wait!” I stepped toward the fae prince, and the entire room sucked in a scandalized gasp. I ignored them. “It's not eleven o'clock yet!"

"We have to be in the Shadow Court by the hour of your birth, or your father dies."

His words hit me like a volley of arrows. This was it. We really were out of time.

"I will say goodbye to my father.”

Without waiting for permission, I stormed away from him. Sweat poured freely down my chest as I marched through the crowd toward the head table, decorated with a heap of white and purple flowers. Papá was standing, gripping the back of his chair, his eyes on me. *Every* eye in the room was on me.

As I edged around an older couple, the pair’s clasped hands briefly stole my attention. I blinked down at them, overcome with a pang of jealousy. They were entering the last season of their lives and were well wrinkled with age, but still, they clung to each other.

I’d never have that chance.

I readied myself for my stepmother’s attack regarding my dancing with the fae, but my shoulders eased as Papá swept me into a tight embrace.

“Don’t be afraid,” he said against my hair.

A half-laugh, half-cry sounded in my throat. “I’m terrified.”

He groaned. “I know, *mi cariña*.”

After a moment, I stepped back, swallowed the emotions clogging my throat, and finally mustered the courage to ask the one question I’d always longed to ask him. “Why?”

His eyes slowly closed and opened. “Your mother and I desperately wanted a child.”

I shook my head, willing the tears budding in my eyes not to fall. “No. You’ve told me that before. Why did you do it?”

My father's shoulders sank, and he glanced at Nina before turning his attention back to me once more. "I loved your mother, and I would have given her the moon if she'd asked. But she didn't ask for the moon. She asked for a child."

I swiped at one pesky tear that got loose.

"And when the doctors told us it was impossible, I thought I was going to lose her to the grief. I'd heard the stories of a wish granter who walked the woods at night, so I sought him and I simply...made the deal. It sounded so simple at the time." Tears poured freely down my father's cheeks now, tracing the lines of the intimidating scowl that had given him a reputation as a heartless man. People were staring. "Oh, Zara, I am so sorry," he mumbled, taking my hand with both of his.

A deep voice cleared his throat behind me. I stiffened.

"We must go," the fae prince said in his rough voice.

Had the room grown darker when he approached?

My father did not spare a glance for Casimiro—his eyes never left my face. Nina glared at me, as if totally oblivious to the prince. She wasn't one to be impolite to well-dressed men, so I wondered if the fae was employing some trickery that made him invisible. I grabbed a full goblet of wine from the table and took a large gulp.

A dark figure now stood before me, composed entirely of thick, writhing shadows, as if made of smoke. He still wore his fancy suit, still had all the same chiseled features, but everything, his face and clothes alike, were monochrome black and my eyes had trouble fixing on him.

"What are you?" I murmured.

He smirked. "The prince of shadows."

That didn't explain his current form. I tried to move away, but I bumped into the table, rattling the glasses and cutlery. Nina gasped.

Casimiro leaned forward, grasping my wrist with a strong hand. "You belong to the shadows now, señorita Valencia. You can come willingly, or I can force you."

I jerked my arm free, trying to calm the terror rising in my blood. "What will you do with me?" Stories said the fae stole mortals as brides or servants. One tale even claimed the fae turned humans into all manner of unusual creatures. But this prince had said he was going to *kill* me—and yet, somehow, I had a choice in the matter.

He lifted his elbow as if he might escort me. I scoffed at him.

"You will do what all mortals do in the Shadow Court," he said. "You will either serve us or entertain us."

My face twisted in disgust. "I won't serve you."

"Then you will entertain? How fitting." His lips twitched.

"I will do no such thing."

An annoyed sigh escaped his mouth. "You will serve forever, or you will entertain us for one year. My father's bargains offer all mortals this choice."

My spine straightened. "One year?" I blinked at his strange, shadowy form. "That's it?"

"Oh, I assure you, it is the worse of the two options. Remember what I said. If you do not want to die, choose wisely."

I didn't care what he thought. "If the options are forever or one year, the choice is easy. I'll entertain for one year."

"That is your choice then? For it is, as always, the mortal's choice. I cannot force your decision."

"Who would choose forever?"

His shadowy face inched forward. "Those who want to live. I hear you mortals are afraid of death."

I tried not to flinch. My father was still standing behind his chair, only a step away, but he was entirely still, his head hung low. Nina was scanning the room, as if searching for someone.

A shiver of unease raked down my spine. No one in the room seemed concerned with the figure comprised of twisting shadows. "Trying to scare me into a life of servitude?" I snarled at him. "Well, it won't work. I choose one year of entertainment." This was *so* much better than being taken away for the rest of my life—my father must not have known about this aspect of the bargain. I was a good dancer, and Papá had ensured I was good with a blade. I could survive a year of entertaining the fae. A year. A single year. Relief filled my lungs, though the prince's smoke-like eyes unsettled me.

A slow nod was his only response. He again lifted his elbow toward me. For a moment, I hesitated, then I took it, trying to reassure myself that all I had to do was endure one year in his court.

His dark fingers clamped my arm to his, and he murmured in my ear, "You have made a bold choice, mortal, and my father has entrusted me with the mortal trials. If you make it past the first trial I prepare for you, I will personally invite you to dine at my table."

The room melted away before I could so much as scream.

My hand on the fae prince's arm tightened as the walls and the crowds dissolved, leaving us standing in a moonlit forest next to the second fae I'd seen last night.

As soon as my feet felt the solid earth and the cool night air, I leaped away from the prince, who was almost entirely invisible in the dark. The other man, Felipe, flashed me a bright smile that did nothing to ease the pounding of my heart.

"All set?" Felipe asked, tucking his hands behind his back.

My entire body began to shake, and I looked around for something to steady me, but I only saw the two fae, and I wouldn't cling to them for support. This was what my father had chosen for me.

For love.

His words in the ballroom had carved a hollow in my chest and filled it with sorrow. He rarely spoke of my mother, and I longed to hear of his love for her. It was *that* kind of love I'd always hoped for. But their love had driven them to make desperate choices, and in the end, it hadn't lasted. Death had parted them too soon.

My skin prickled, and my heart thumped loudly. These fae really were stealing me away. I could delay no longer. All my efforts to break the bargain had failed.

Deranged visions of Jorge plagued my mind as I imagined him sweeping in with a sword to battle these monsters. But he wasn't the man I'd thought he was. No one was coming to save me. All I had was the tiny knife strapped to my thigh, high enough that it didn't show during the spins in my dance.

"I'll need your blade," Felipe said.

My shoulders sank, and I crossed my arms.

"She's a feisty one. She won't want to give it up," spat the prince.

His illusory form moved beside me, and I felt the hem of my dress being pushed aside.

I yelped and kicked, and the toe of my shoe connected with his temple. The shadow groaned.

"Don't you dare touch me," I yelled, bending to gather my ruffled hem and yank out my knife.

Felipe cackled. "Don't tell me. She chose to entertain?" He sighed. "Cas, you're supposed to explain it to them."

Casimiro stood and swept dark, smoke-like strands of hair from his face. "I did." His dark eyes glowed a faint blue-white, hot as a smith's fire. I blinked at the alarming sight.

The other man shook his head and tsked. "I'm sorry if our prince forced you into a choice you'll regret. He was told to explain things better, but he's not one to listen to anyone." The broad-shouldered immortal stepped up in front of me. "I'm Felipe."

He reached out a hand and traced the edge of my face with a cool knuckle.

I slapped his hand away.

Felipe snorted and walked past me. "Shame. She would have made a fun servant."

At those words, the prince's glowing eyes flared brighter, illuminating a hard scowl on his face as he tracked his friend's movements. Then the light in his eyes dimmed.

"Come on," the prince said. "It's almost midnight, and if your birthday expires before you reach my court, you will die. I can chain you if I must, but the ones who choose entertainment are always so proud of coming *willingly*."

I tried to swallow, but my throat had gone dry. I stepped forward.

Casimiro chuckled and nodded his approval. "See, she's compliant."

I wanted to hit him, but it wouldn't do any good, considering an arrow and a dagger hadn't even fazed him.

"She's also proud," Felipe added. "Which will make the games shorter for her." He spoke over me, like I was a child. "The proud ones never make it." Now he focused on me as a smile played on his lips. "Remember this: it's the ones who break quickly, accepting our help, who end up surviving." He pinned me with a sharp gaze. "Because mortals are made to break, and the sooner you learn that, the better it will be for you."

Before I had time to reply to his awful words, a strange hissing sound filled the night as a strange black line sawed its way through the very air, as if the world was tearing at the seams. A second later, an open doorway stood in the forest beside us, darker than the night, as if no light at all could penetrate it.

I choked on my next breath as Casimiro strolled through the archway and vanished into the dark. My hands shook at my sides, and my lungs quaked. One year. That was all. I could survive for one year. I *would*. And then I would return to my father. He'd lost his first love, and I couldn't let him lose me forever too.

As if reading my thoughts, Felipe announced, "Your turn."

My muscles clenched as I stepped toward the doorway that would take me from this world. Then, with a deep breath, I walked into the darkness.

# 8

## Zara

I looked first left, then right, and then down. Initially, I saw nothing but blackness. Then cool air bit my cheeks, and a light pulsed to life in a wide, dark hallway. Ahead, the heir strode down the hall away from me. His features had solidified and no longer appeared like writhing smoke. Shiny black walls, unbroken by a single window, surrounded me and a stairwell opened to my left and right, both reaching up.

Dizziness washed over me, and I stumbled sideways until my hand braced against the cold stone wall. Under my fingertips, small veins of a lighter colored stone streaked through the otherwise black walls.

Felipe strode around me and nodded at me. "Wasn't so bad, was it?"

I scowled at him and wrapped my arms around my shoulders to fight off the chill sinking into my skin. I took a step forward, but Felipe held up a hand.

"Wait here. Someone will be around to fetch you." He sounded annoyed, as his eyes scanned the hall and quickly flicked to the stairwells on either side, as if this *someone* was late.

Without another word, the tall fae marched away, toward the prince's retreating form. The two men exchanged a quiet word, and the prince tossed a single glance back at me.

For a long moment, he stared at me with a cold, shuttered expression. I stiffened under his gaze. Then, with a small huff, he said, loud enough for me to hear, "Let her try."

To my horror, a shadowy figure separated from the prince's frame, the same dark form I'd seen in my father's ballroom. This *second* prince sprouted wings from his back and vanished down the wide hallway, leaving me pinned to the wall with two hands clapped over my open mouth.

Casimiro, whatever part of him was still standing in the hall beside Felipe, chuckled at my reaction. Pushing aside his suit jacket, he shoved his hands in his pockets and strolled away down the long, dark hall. Felipe nodded once to me and spun to follow the prince.

My eyes cut to the stairwells, then behind me. A solid wall stood in place of the dark passage that had brought me from the mortal world. On the wall was a door-shaped etching, intricately carved with a pattern of trees that mirrored the pines I'd just walked through. The stone was cold when my fingers touched it, tracing the lines of the forest.

I backed away, and without a second thought, I charged up the stairwell to my right. If they thought I would wait patiently in this cold, creepy hall, they were wrong.

The arched ceiling above the stairs echoed my footsteps back to me. A light, pale and almost entirely white, glowed to life atop a wall sconce as I climbed. At the top of the steps, I glanced right and left down another long, pitch-black hall. Across from me, illuminated by the light from the stairwell, was another carving in the stone wall.

This one depicted a massive dragon, talons out like an eagle about to snatch a fish. But instead of a fish, this dragon was about to grab a lone figure with an upraised sword.

A shiver shook my body. If the Wild Hunt was real, then dragons might as well be real too. I only hoped I never had to encounter one.

Fast footsteps behind me startled me so forcefully that I jumped, nearly toppling down the steps. A man wearing white hurried up the stairs toward me. He had a shaved head, putting his rounded mortal ears in full view. A dark shadow of a beard hugged his chin, and he wore a long tunic that fell to his knees with white pants beneath it. The neckline of the tunic was sewn with a dark purple thread. A metal cuff on his wrist partly shone under his long sleeve.

When he reached the top of the steps, he took a breath before he said, "Don't run off like that. You'll only anger them."

I glanced back at the bottom of the steps. "The fae? They already told me they plan to kill me. I'm not sure how angering them makes any difference."

The man ran a hand down his face and blew out a frustrated breath. "I'm Malik. And believe me, angering the fae will make things so much worse. And not just for you, but for us as well."

My brows lifted. "Us?"

The man's lips pinched before he spat, "The servants. Those who chose not to entertain."

"Are there many mortals here?" Somehow, knowing there were others like me here, others *not* destined to die, brought a wave of comfort, despite the fact that he'd called them servants.

Malik's frown deepened. "Yes. Now, come. I'm to prepare you for your first trial."

"Now?"

He nodded. "Those who choose to entertain complete their first trial the night they arrive. And the fae care deeply about their entertainment."

The way he said the last word sent a chill down my arms.

I swallowed. "What kind of trial?"

The man's honey-colored eyes narrowed as he looked me up and down. "I'm not certain. But I do know that the mortal games, as the fae call them, are designed to kill you." At my gaping mouth, he added, "Welcome to the Shadow Court."

All the air in my lungs whooshed out. Casimiro had warned me of my imminent death. But he'd also told me I only had to survive for one year. How hard could it be?

I lifted my chin. "I'm not dying tonight. Now, tell me where we are. We're not in Avencia anymore, though I was just there a moment ago."

"This is Nightsong, the palace of the Shadow King. Tell me your name."

"Zara Valencia Calderon."

"Nice to have met you, then."

The servant turned and walked crisply down the windowless hall, but I planted my hands on my hips and called after him. "Malik. You are mortal. You serve this court, I presume?"

He turned and fixed a stony gaze on me.

"Shouldn't you be telling me what I can do to survive here?" I asked. "Do you not care that they're going to try to kill me?"

Malik's eyes widened but the scowl on his face lessened a bit. After a brief pause, he said, "The other human servants here do not like the entertainers." His gaze averted briefly. "The entertainers are treated...like kings compared to us."

"But you just said the trials are designed to kill us. Not exactly kingly treatment."

A slight pinching of his eyes hinted at an unspoken apology. "Indeed. I believe the animosity arises from jealousy on both sides. The entertainers envy us our guaranteed safety. And we envy the way they treat you. I'm sure it delights the fae to no end that the mortals in their palace don't get along. They want to watch us suffer, make no mistake. When they give you the fancy clothes and the good food and the lavish rooms, don't let it get to you. They hate us."

I nodded slowly. "I won't forget."

"Come, we have no time to stand here and chat. I am sorry, Miss Valencia," he added.

"Where are you from?" I asked as I stepped after him. I wasn't used to being called *miss*, though I'd heard foreigners in Leor use the term.

A more genuine smile ghosted over his mouth. "You are Avencian?" At my nod, he added, "I am from Votna. Though it has been many years since I left."

My eyes widened. "I've never met anyone from that far east. Your Avencian is perfect."

He waved away my enthusiasm. "It's the language we all speak here. The fae are the ones who brought this language to your lands, did you know that?"

I shook my head. I was quickly realizing there was much I didn't know.

Malik continued, "You'll meet many people here. The Shadow lords and ladies travel far and wide to wreak havoc on mankind."

At those happy words, he led me farther into the palace, which with its lack of windows and cold stone walls felt eerily like it was underground. As we moved through the darkness, white flames leaped to life in sconces along the wall. We traveled up another flight of wide stone steps, to an atrium of sorts that ended in a pair of massive wooden doors braced with ironwork. The ceiling soared over my head, and the white light cast dancing shadows on the stones that appeared to move entirely more than candleflames called for. As I squinted up at the writhing shapes, I sensed that it was not merely a dance of light and shadow but actual forms. Casimiro had turned as black as night and sprouted wings. Perhaps other shadowy beings cavorted in the darkness.

Malik caught me gaping and whispered, "It's best not to stare. You don't want to give the fae any reason to dislike you more than they already do." He sighed. "You asked what you can do to survive? Do not question anything you see here. Do not stand out. Do not anger them. Keep your head down—and fight."

I tried to respond, but my throat had closed up at his words, and I simply nodded.

Images had been expertly embossed on the walls of the atrium and threads of gilded paint outlined the shapes. Great, sweeping scenes unfolded on the walls as we walked toward the doors—battle scenes, throne room scenes, and one that looked like a winged man blocking out the sun from a panicked crowd below.

Some of the artwork depicted things I didn't want to see, so I averted my eyes, shocked at what these fae considered art. By the time we reached the tall double doors at the end of the hall, my cheeks flamed with heat. Dread filled my stomach as I contemplated what I'd agreed to in choosing to entertain these creatures.

"The fae are waiting," Malik said, nodding at the doors crisscrossed with ornate iron bracing.

"Waiting for what?" I asked, throat dry.

"You. It's midnight. Time for you to perform."

# 9

## Zara

I swallowed, lifting my chin. Talia had been brave when she faced the fae. So I would be too.

"May the stars watch over you," Malik said, urging me forward. The ironwork clicked, and the massive doors swung inward.

A cavern larger than any ballroom yawned before us. The floor slanted gently toward a massive underground lake that stretched out so far into the darkness that I couldn't see the other side. Round tables of smooth, black stone dotted the sloping cavern floor and stopped at the edge of the lake. Above each table hung enormous, wrought iron chandeliers dotted with glowing lights that looked nothing like any lights I'd ever seen. But as I stared at the nearest chandelier, I noticed something moving within the orb-shaped iron bars. They weren't just chandeliers. They were *cages*.

All manner of creatures huddled or paced within their metal confines, many I didn't recognize. In one cage a sphinx was sleeping, one dark paw dangling through the bars. In another, large antlers kept the animal inside from being able to move at all. In yet another cage, a flurry of bats darted around, never squeezing through the bars. I jumped as a wolverine snapped its jaws.

I pulled my eyes from the chandeliers and looked instead at the seated fae. The tables had been hewn out of the rock floor itself, and space had been carved around each one to make a bench. Fae lounged at each table, some engaged in heated arguments, others in passionate embraces. A few of the immortals lay flat on their backs, reaching across with lazy arms to grab a piece of fruit from the heaps of food stacked on their plates.

At a glance, the wealth in this room mocked the richest in Leor. Jewels hung over foreheads and dripped from the men's ears as well as the women's. These fae were adorned with dresses and tunics and suits of the highest quality, all made from a fine, drapey material rather than the stiff fabrics of our upper class. But the most surprising detail of all was the strangeness of their features.

A fae at the nearest table had antlers that glittered in the light diffusing from glowing cages above. Another male—by the look of his suit—had the same blue skin of the lizards back home. At one table, a massive jackrabbit sat eating a wad of lettuce between a pair of women in fine silks. A great dog the size of a bear lay on the floor between two tables, its red eyes tracking my movements. I jerked with fright at the sight.

A few chuckles greeted my burning ears, and fury rose up from my toes. These immortals thought I was a toy. I straightened my shoulders and attempted to walk with all the grace my father had always expected of me.

"As is customary, you will perform alone tonight," Malik explained as he led me down the sloping floor. His voice had lost its sympathetic tone and was now curt and businesslike. "Every new arrival is evaluated and given a task suited to your abilities."

"Evaluated? Right here?"

"Oh, no. You were evaluated earlier. The master of the mortal games has already created your first trial." He inclined his head down the walkway. "You must walk the rest of the way alone."

Casimiro had said he was in charge of the *games,* as he called them. Death games—what a morbid paradox.

I glanced at the lake, then back at Malik. For a breath, I didn't move.

Then Malik made a subtle shooing motion, and I stumbled down the sloping path, my shoes slapping the stones and finally drawing the eyes of those seated at the lavish tables. My eyes raked over the crowd, desperate for someone to stand up and tell me this was all a dream, a joke, an immaculate play—anything but reality.

Strange animal noises filled the vaulted space, and I glanced around, nervous that my first trial would involve dragons or some other mythical creature. Though, I supposed, mythical wasn't the right word anymore. My eyes snagged on a single figure dressed in white, standing on a table in the center of the cavern, near the edge of the lake. He was staring directly at me.

The heir's dark hair and rich skin tone stood out against his loose white shirt, unbuttoned at the neck. He wore a gray suit jacket, also unbuttoned, and his shiny black crown sat on his head. He was the kind of man who could wear soil-stained farmer's attire and still be impossibly handsome, which just made me loathe him more.

He lifted both arms at his sides and the room fell silent. I ground my teeth and fisted my hands.

"Shadow Court, meet your newest entertainer," he announced, his deep voice filling the cavern. "I'm especially looking forward to watching her performance." He lowered one hand, leaving the other still angled toward the lake.

The water's reflection was utterly smooth and perfectly black. A square platform sat atop the water like a dock, though there were no ships. My heart hammered angrily in my chest. I was no great swimmer.

My stomach dropped as my eyes flicked back to the wooden platform. A single glowing orb hovered directly over it. That was no dock—it was a dance floor.

I swallowed as I spotted a pair of castanets resting at the base of a small staircase leading to the platform.

As I walked slowly toward the platform, Casimiro's voice echoed around the cave. "Entertain us, señorita Valencia. Show us that passion you showed me."

My head whipped back around in time to see him wink. I snatched the castanets as a chorus of laughter rose from the crowd. Casimiro had dropped to sit on the edge of his table, feet swinging as he picked up a cluster of grapes from the centerpiece.

The cave was cold, but sweat broke out across my chest and back as I climbed the few steps to the platform. My stomach rumbled, and I ignored it, relieved that all I had to do was dance. I'd brought the heir to his feet with a dance once. I could do it again.

*Get a grip, and get this done*, I told myself as I stepped onto the platform, convincing myself this was no different than any other performance.

While I walked to the center of the dance floor, I was careful to keep my weight on the soles of my feet, saving the clack of my heels for when the dance began. I slipped the castanets onto my fingers and envisioned the dances I knew best. I couldn't repeat the dance I'd performed just an hour ago at my party, since the heir had already seen that one. I needed something new, something riskier. I'd picked my most tasteful routine for my party, given that I'd thought my betrothed would be offended by the kind of flamenco I liked best. The corner of my mouth flicked into a grin as I settled on the dance I would perform for these creatures. If it was passion they wanted, I'd give them that.

"Dance well," a quiet, accented voice spoke from nearby.

A man in a white tunic identical to Malik's wove between the tables, a guitar slung over his shoulder.

"Any tips?" I hissed, taking my stance for the start of the dance.

The man shrugged, strumming a single chord. To my horror, the stairs to the platform evaporated, trapping me on the dance floor. A few notes of laughter floated across the cavern.

*Don't panic.*

This was only another performance.

The servant strummed once more, a fast chord, snapping my mind into sharp focus. I clapped my castanets together and fixed my arms in their starting position a heartbeat before the music launched me into the dance.

I threw myself into the beginning steps of a familiar dance as every fae turned their face toward me. They had blank, almost bored eyes. *Don't look at them.* I glanced instead at the glowing orbs above their heads. And soon, the music and the sound of my feet drew me deeper into the dance. I stomped harder, the echoes rising as the sounds drifted across the water and bounced against the cavern's walls and ceiling, growing until a deafening, thunderous clamor blocked every fear from my mind.

As I moved outward from the center of the dance floor, the platform beneath me tilted under my weight. I tipped sideways and lost my balance entirely, crashing onto my hip. The floor tilted higher, and I began to slide toward the edge, where large ripples peeled away from the spiny back of a massive creature lurking just beneath the inky surface.

Laughter erupted from the crowd. I scrambled onto my knees as the floor again teetered beneath me. Panicked, I clawed my way toward the center, digging my fingernails into the varnished wood like a cat. The dance floor tilted in the other direction, causing me to crash onto my chest and push the dance floor into an even greater angle. This dance floor was going to toss me into the lake.

*No.* I would not fall.

The laughter of the fae nearly drowned out the lone guitar still strumming through the song. I couldn't let them beat me that easily.

My face slid toward the water even as my hands pressed against the wood, desperate for purchase. I wished desperately for a blade to jam into the wood and hold me steady. I'd be in the water in seconds if I couldn't think of something. I spun onto my back and rolled. The floor slowed and tipped the other way. In the brief moment it rocked from left to right, I pressed backward on my hands and knees, then threw myself onto my rear until the dance floor tilted back the other way.

As the heavy floor wobbled on its fulcrum, I leaned forward. When it tipped forward again, I leaned back, edging a little to the right so I was directly in the center. When the floor stopped wobbling, my heart was pounding so hard I barely registered that the song was still playing. A few cheers rang out, as well as a few boos.

"Keep dancing!" a woman shouted from somewhere in the crowd.

Carefully, I moved my feet underneath me and shifted onto my ankles. The fae were shouting at me now, calling for me to fall, to die. Others were screaming at me with lifted fists to *dance, mortal!*

Blood seething, I stood slowly, arms out for balance. The dance floor wobbled, but it didn't tilt. Many in the crowd launched into hysterical laughter, but the sound only fueled my rage. These creatures wanted to see me die. That crafty brat of a prince had put me up here to watch me dance to death. But I wouldn't give him the satisfaction. Slowly, I lifted my hands above my head once more, clacking my fingers to the rhythm of the music.

The laughter died down.

It was quickly replaced by boos and the sound of fists hitting tables. I lifted one foot quickly and stomped my heel down. The loud echo reverberated around the cavern. Again, I stomped. This time I was ready for the small way the dance floor trembled. This trial was not over yet.

I placed all of my weight on one leg, adjusting my stance so that the floor barely moved. Then I kicked my leg out and spun, my ruffled dress following behind in an arc.

When I stomped again, the entire place rose to their feet. Some shouted obscenities, while others cheered drunkenly for me. I kept the dance at the center of the dance floor, restricting my movements to stay alive.

The dance was nearing its conclusion. I could feel the ending of the song approaching. *Just get through it.*

Stomp. Catch my balance. Click my castas. Spin, stomp, click, wobble. This was it. This was when I would normally advance toward the nearest person in the crowd. Several of the creatures had their arms crossed and were staring at me with gloomy, disappointed expressions. They had wanted to watch me fall.

Well, I'd give them something unexpected.

The thought of falling into the water terrified me, but judging by the increasing severity of the jeers hurled at me, these creatures were not pleased. Staying safe in the center wasn't what they wanted. With a deep breath and a quick halfway-reassuring calculation, I prepared for the final steps of the dance, stepping outward again, and then again. The dance floor immediately tilted. I only had a few more steps before I would fall.

Then I charged directly toward the edge, which clunked down into the dark waters, sending out a wave that splashed against the retaining wall only a step away. With a scream of determination, I jumped from the sloped surface toward the wall. But I hadn't accounted for how my body would be sinking toward the lake when I pushed off. My chest slammed into the wall, and I clung with aching arms, my feet dangling in the cold water for a second before I hefted myself to the top of the wall. The guitar player strummed his final chord, and I dove forward onto my knees, arcing my head back until it touched the ground, my hair lost in the wet ruffles of my dress.

I was breathing hard, and my knees screamed in pain, but I swept my arm above my head, fingers curled as I clacked the final note of the dance. For a count of five, I held the final position, as I'd been trained. Then I pulled my body upright and rose to my feet. The entire cavern full of fae stared at me, many with open mouths.

Someone began a slow applause, and soon half the cavern was cheering for me. The other half stared in bemused silence. My eyes raked over the crowd and snagged on a single face. The prince stood a short distance away, his dark brow knitted together in a fierce scowl.

# 10

## Zara

My lips curled as I returned the princeling's stare. I lifted my chin, chest still heaving from the dance, and dipped into a mock curtsy. A few of the nearby fae laughed and pointed at me, amused by my boldness. Well, wasn't that the point? To *entertain* them? I wasn't sure if angering the heir was a smart move, but right now, I didn't care.

I'd survived the little death trap that he'd crafted specially for me.

Someone tugged at my arm.

"The table for the entertainment is this way," drawled a woman in a servant's white tunic. It appeared she'd rather be anywhere but standing here talking to me. She was tall and thin, her skin paler than I'd ever seen in Avencia. Her long red hair was tied back behind her head but still hung halfway down her back. I stared at her a little too long, and her brows lifted.

"Sorry," I mumbled. I hadn't met many redheads in my life.

"Come on, if you linger here, someone is likely to give you a glass of wine. I don't want to be around for that." She walked ahead of me, indicating I should follow.

As I trailed her through the large cavern, I peered at the wine goblets. My mouth was dry, and my curiosity called for the dark red liquid. As the daughter of a man known as much for his wine cellar as for his business dealings, I craved a taste of their wine, to see if it was any better than Father's. Our vineyards were famous throughout Avencia, and if there was one thing my father and I had in common, it was our fascination with the nuances of flavors in a single glass of wine. But I couldn't risk an ounce of distraction here, and I didn't know how strong the fae liked their wine. Better to leave it alone.

*Survive*, I told myself, tearing my attention from the glittering wine to the rest of the tables' contents. There were mounds of grapes, elaborate towers of apples, and small statues of everything from dancing maidens to dragons in flight. I squinted at a pale-yellow statue of a goblin bent in a deep bow. *Cheese.* The statues were made of cheese.

"What's your name?" I asked.

"I'm Ariana. I'm to be your...I'm to show you...I'll take you where you need to go, when you need to go there, and that's it. You look like you came from money, but I'm not your servant."

I stopped abruptly. She noted my pause but didn't stop walking. As I glanced around the room, I realized she wore white, as did all those who were filling goblets or replacing food on the tables. Not one person in white was seated—save the heir.

Malik had explained why the servants and the entertainers didn't get along. But we were all mortals, trapped here against our will. The animosity seemed pointless.

I hurried after Ariana, trying to think of the right words to disarm her. "Is there anything I should know about these fae, to help me survive?" Maybe if she thought I trusted her, that would help.

Instead she whirled on me, her pale brows furrowed. "You entertainers think you deserve *everything* since you're facing death."

My mouth hung open, and I couldn't think of a single thing to say before she marched onward. Desperate to find at least one friend here, I hurried after her. "I don't think I deserve anything, but I *do* want to live. I only barely survived that"—I gestured back toward the dance floor—"and I have no idea how I'll survive the next terrible thing they make me do. But I'm going to try."

Ariana's frown didn't relax as she eyed me up and down. My dress was wet up to my knees and sliding pitifully across the stone floor, and my hair had long since wiggled free of its hold and tumbled in unruly curls over my shoulders. I must have looked a total mess. The woman, not much older than me, sighed loudly through her nose. "They're not your friends," she said, flicking her gaze at the fae. "No matter what you think. They will try to woo you with their riches and their looks and their endless temptations, but they're just trying to weaken you. They know mortals can hardly resist the flash of wealth." Her expression remained hard as she stared at me. The fae sitting near us paid us no mind.

"Ariana, my life was just snatched away from me. I'm here until the fae kill me or a year elapses. I couldn't care less about the wealth these creatures offer." I glanced up at the prince's table, but his back was to me as he spoke to the woman beside him. "I hate them as much as you do."

The tension between her brows lessened, but only marginally. Still, I considered it a victory. "They can only kill you in the trials," she said, her voice low, "and never outside of those events. Be that as it may, these fae have one year to prove their superiority over your mortality, and believe me, they always succeed."

I pinched my lips before responding. "Always?"

Ariana turned and kept walking. "I've only been here for three years. In that time, not one entertainer has survived their year of trials."

The heaviness of those words made it hard to keep walking, but I put one foot in front of the other, forcing myself to follow.

Ariana slowed her pace, allowing me to walk beside her. "Their fruit is often enchanted as well. St. John's wort or cayenne pepper can help ward off enchantments, but it's best to avoid the fruit."

I nodded firmly. "Thank you."

She straightened. "They always assign me to wealthy women like you. And in my experience, people who've come from privilege and comfort die the fastest." She let those words sink in a moment before she added, "That scowl on the prince's face a minute ago when you survived his task...whatever trial he creates next, he'll try to pay you back for beating him tonight. I know you want a friend, but I can't—they've all—I just can't." She wrung her hands at her waist as she spoke, her gaze pinned to the floor. She'd watched entertainers die over and over again. I couldn't imagine what that did to someone.

It was doing a fair amount to my roiling insides at the moment.

We continued weaving through the tables toward the edge of the cavern, far from the lake. The rock floor was as smooth as glass, and streaks of gemstones in the walls sparkled in the light of the glowing orbs. Fear pricked inside me, but I continued to follow the woman, glancing up at the cages every few steps. Ariana led me to a tight corner of the cavern, where the slanted ceiling was lower, and a trickle of water dampened the nearest wall.

"This is your table." She waved a stiff hand at the people already seated, then she nodded and marched away with hurried steps.

The five faces watching me were not smiling. Their eyes traveled up and down my frame, some lingering, others flicking away in disinterest. Not a single gaze appeared welcoming. Among the people seated were two women and three men, all of whom appeared older than me. One woman and one man had gray hair. I couldn't imagine them performing trials like the one I'd just completed.

I'd intended to smile at these people, to disarm them, but my eyes were drawn to movement in the cage above their table. My jaw fell open in shock. A small dragon shuffled uncomfortably in the cramped space, its wings rising partway, then clamping back down against its back. Its long neck was curled upward, pressed against the iron bars.

My mouth hung loose as I watched the creature squirm. I'd never known they were so...beautiful. The black scales glinted like oil-slicked water. The orange eye facing me rolled here and there and its nostrils flared in annoyance. The claws that gripped the cage were as long as the dinner knives on the table.

"The cages are iron." The man who spoke had a beard and, of the seated humans, was the only one not frowning or staring off into space. "And the cages are enchanted so nothing...falls on us while we eat."

I couldn't contain a disgusted twist of my lips. Dragon dung wasn't something I wanted to experience ever, but especially not as an addition to the chocolate fountain that bubbled on their table like some poisoned brook.

Then one young woman, whose face was mostly covered by a curtain of her mousy brown hair, scooted over so that a space opened up beside her on the bench-like seat.

"Here, you can sit by me," she said, her voice quiet but friendly. Her eyes looked like they hadn't seen a full night's rest in a while.

I smiled down at her as I stepped toward the vacant space. "Thank you."

As I hitched up the hem of my damp dress to step down onto the bench, every person facing me at the table straightened and paled, their eyes fixed on something behind me.

"I'm offended," said a deep, familiar voice. "And here I was assuming a human wouldn't possibly deign to ignore my dinner invitation."

# 11

## Casimiro

She whirled toward me with a wide-eyed scowl, but her ruffled dress, still wet from her encounter with the lake, stuck to the floor, temporarily tangling around her legs. Her brown eyes flashed up to my crown then down to my open shirt collar.

"My face is up here, Valencia."

She let out an angry huff of air, and I couldn't keep the smirk from twisting one side of my mouth.

"Shall we, then?" I asked, offering her my elbow. She did not move to accept it.

This woman had discovered how to finish her performance in the center of the tilting floor, where it was safe, moving with all the passion she'd shown me in the dance in Leor. I'd been impressed then.

But she hadn't stayed in the center.

She'd run for the edge, forced the dance floor to tilt once more. Most mortals feared death, though I'd encountered a few over the years who had a reckless death wish. But as she'd pulled herself from the waters, dripping and heaving, only to drop to her knees at the final note of the song, I'd known then she was not like the others.

"I do so desperately hate to wait," I drawled, elbow still lifted toward her.

This woman perplexed me. She seemed eager to survive and yet eager to anger me. If I was to craft a trial that would kill her, I needed to know who she was, what she was likely to do or not do.

"I do so desperately hate to be taken captive and forced to act against my will," she spat back. Two people at the table gasped. At least one tried to hide a snicker.

I stepped toward her, pausing when I was close enough that she had to tilt her chin up to meet my eyes. She *hmphed*, a sound I found most amusing. The gazes of the other entertainers fixed on me, but I didn't spare them a glance.

"You chose to entertain, did you not? I did not force that on you."

A loud breath hissed from her nose as she held my gaze. "And were you entertained?"

A full two seconds passed as I stared down at her, waiting for her to flinch, to see if she would look at me differently now that she'd survived a task intended to kill her, a task I'd designed in a matter of minutes upon her arrival. Over half the mortals collected by my father died the night they arrived. Those who did survive their first trial all perished within the year, most within the first six months. I'd brought home only two mortals since my father had left.

And she was the first to survive.

"Yes," I replied.

She held my gaze with piercing intensity, perhaps waiting for me to look away first. I did not. Finally, she lifted her hand and placed it in the crook of my elbow, her fingers brushing my skin where my sleeve was rolled up. The featherlight touch contrasted so vividly with the fierce pressure of her hands when we'd danced only an hour ago. Oddly, I wanted to feel that same purposeful grip in her tiny hands again rather than this polite, delicate touch.

"You will sit with me tonight," I said, remembering why I'd walked to her table. She didn't want to die, but she didn't want to play it safe either—and I needed to discover what motivation she had to survive. All mortals had their reasons—a lover, a family member, a dream, sometimes a religion—but those never seemed strong enough to push them through the hardest nights. This woman would be dead in a matter of months at most.

Every pair of eyes at the mortals' table bored into my back as I walked away leading the woman on my arm. I strolled slowly, casually, through the tables, nodding and smiling at those who greeted me. Their gazes flashed suspiciously to the mortal on my arm. Father had many loyal to him here, and I couldn't risk one of the courtiers relaying information about me that might anger him. I tossed a wink over my shoulder to the nearest table, and a few of the seated nobles chuckled in response. But a woman with a tall hat meant to mimic our mountain shot me a brief, disapproving scowl.

It wasn't against my father's rules to enjoy the mortals who came through our doors, only to value them. *Mortals are poorly made toys. Enjoy them, but know they will break*, he'd told me.

The woman holding my arm was pressing down so forcefully, attempting to make my arm buckle, that I didn't think she was the type to break easily. Despite her effort straining her muscles, she maintained a dignified posture.

I led her to a table at the center of the cavern. From her seat down on the stone bench before us, Alba looked up, a bright smile breaking across her glittering face. She'd styled her hair with little white mushrooms poking up from the crown of braids that encircled her head.

"Sit," I offered as I slid down onto the bench across from my sister.

"Oh!" Alba said, her eyes flicking between me and the mortal woman. "Oh," she said again, leaning forward, a conspiratorial gleam in her eye.

I resisted the urge to roll my eyes in return. Alba, more than anyone, knew the importance of the mortal games—the importance of my success in continuing my father's wishes while he was away. But the idea of Alba making a wrong assumption about my intention for this woman brought a sour feeling to my stomach.

Zara stared down at the stone bench for a moment, clearly uncomfortable. As I waited for her to sit, I snatched a strawberry, bit off the red part, then tossed the leafy stem toward the cage above our table. A long, furry arm reached down and snatched the tuft of leaves. Zara gasped at the sudden motion.

"This is a mandrill," I explained dully. Mortals saw so little of their world, let alone all the worlds, that there were entire species they'd never heard of.

"It makes a terrible sound," Alba added, "but fortunately, the cage keeps that sound from bothering us."

"Do sit," I said, shooting my sister a glare I hoped warned her not to be too friendly. It was my job to kill this woman, not befriend her.

Finally, Zara stepped down and sat at the table halfway between me and my sister.

"You dance like a flame," Alba gushed, utterly ignoring my silent warning. Her freckled cheeks sparkled with iridescent powder tonight. "Well done. And"—she leaned toward Zara—"my brother never invites mortals to our table. You must have truly impressed him."

I nearly choked on the bite of cheese I'd just popped in my mouth. I swallowed quickly and clarified. "I invited her before I brought her here. I didn't assume she would live long enough to accept the invitation."

Zara's eyes flicked up to meet mine. Her breaths quickened as she stared daggers at me. "Tell me, do you always try to kill us mortals through what we love most?"

The memory of last night's death prickled in my mind as I leaned over my elbow that rested on the table. "It is my duty to ensure my courtiers are entertained, señorita Valencia." I forced a half-hearted smile. "Mortals die with such flare." Last night, the man's drowning gurgles had brought the courtiers to their feet—and the news of it had reached my father almost instantly. My sister's comment about birds nicked at my mind—the fae still valued their songs while we had been taught to place no value on the lives of mortals. "We find it increases the intrigue when you must die doing something you love. It proves all that passion you fleeting creatures claim to have is nothing more than a passing breeze."

"Cas, that's not very nice," my sister said teasingly. But her restrained smile said she was enjoying this.

Zara's brows lifted and a small chuckle sounded in her throat. She leaned back and took a slice of bread from a cutting board strewn with grapes, cheeses, and dried dates.

Needing a distraction from the way her every sound and every glance felt like they were mocking me, I twirled my fingers. The apples began to shift and restack themselves. Zara stared dumbly, bread still in hand.

"Why do you wear white?" she asked. "I thought it was a servant's color."

The apples kept spinning but my attention shot to Zara.

"It is," Alba agreed. "That's why he wears it. It annoys our father to no end."

Zara's eyes went wide.

"Our father dresses in all navy or gray. It's terribly boring," Alba droned on.

"Where is your father?" Zara asked, looking between my sister and me.

"He's—"

"How are your knees?" I snapped, interrupting my sister and flashing Zara a quick smirk.

"Still there," she quipped. "I thwarted your little game, and now you're mad. How old did you say you were?"

Here she was, antagonizing the man with the power to kill her. Prickly little thing.

The apples crashed to the table, then rolled onto the floor. A few faces turned toward us. Zara stiffened, finally showing a hint of fear.

After an uncomfortable silence, Alba whispered loud enough for all of us to hear, "He's a hundred and fifty-seven years old."

Zara's brows lifted almost to her hairline.

"Thank you, Alba," I droned.

"And how old are you?" Zara asked my sister.

Alba's face fell. "I'm only eighty-one. I can't even cast a shadow form yet."

"Alba," I chided. At this rate, she'd be making friends with this mortal.

She shrugged dramatically at me. "He doesn't think it's fun to talk to mortals. We can usually cast a shadow form around one hundred years old, when we reach adulthood. But Cas was able to cast his first one at seventy-two. He's a bit of a prodig—"

"Stop."

Zara jumped at my abrupt word. Alba's lips pinched and she stared down at her plate.

"My sister has not yet learned all the ways of our court." I shot her one more loaded stare, hopefully reminding her what was at stake. She hadn't lived long enough to see it, but she *knew*, as we all did, what would happen when our father returned. If he found anything not to his liking, we would be the ones to pay the price, and I couldn't afford to let Alba pay for my mistakes.

"I love learning about new people and places," Zara said, surprising me with her candor and upbeat tone. How under the heavens above could she be so chipper after what she'd just endured? It annoyed me. "I'd love to learn more about this place," she added quickly, shooting me a quick glance. Underneath her forced smile, I detected a sliver of fear. She had her own motivations buried as deep as my own, and it occurred to me that she might be attempting to uncover secrets about me just as I was about her.

Smart, prickly, little thing.

"See?" Alba said, tilting her head sideways.

I sighed and rolled my eyes at Alba, only to realize Zara was watching me with a slight tilt to her head that suggested she found my interaction with my sister fascinating, almost puzzling.

Zara might be digging for information about me, but I knew mortals well enough to know there were many ways to wound them—and wounded humans often revealed more than composed humans. As I looked again at Zara, my expression hardened. "I do not speak to mortals because there is little point. All mortals are like flowers. They bloom, they get scorched by the sun or trampled by the foot of a passing giant, and then they die." I parroted words I'd heard my father speak countless times.

A scoff rushed from Zara's lips. Alba's face drooped and she looked away.

"You are insulted," I muttered, tasting victory. "But it is only the truth."

Zara spluttered a little before finding her words. "You are...you think you're better just because your lives are longer?"

"And we have magic," I added with a flick of my hand. An apple leaped and spun in the air.

She snorted. "Right. And that. Well, one look at the fae in this cavern, and I can tell you're all miserable. You laugh at death because you hate life, you twist your features because you can't stand your reality, you hide in caves and torture those less powerful than you. I pity you."

I blinked at her, temporarily stupefied. Alba's mouth hung open, a faint smile tugging at her lips.

"Cas," Alba whispered, but I silenced her with a glare sharp enough to cut stone.

"Think what you want about us," I said to Zara, lazily spooning rice with raisins onto my plate. "Insult us if you must, but you do not know what the next game will be, and I do."

She pinned me with a sour frown. "You want me to ask what it is—to ask for your help." A disgusted scoff burst from her lips.

I clicked my tongue. "I think you want my help, yes."

"I do not *want* to be here," she retorted. "I do not *want* to be talking to the prince who told me I'm nothing more than a wilting flower who can die for sport. What I *want*, Your Wickedness, is to get home. So, no, I do not want your help. I simply want to survive long enough to leave this wretched place."

"You will beg for my help one day," I said.

"Never."

She stood from the table and, without waiting for a dismissal, stormed back toward the table for the entertainers.

I watched her go, unable to deny the fact that I wanted nothing more than to make her that angry again.

"Cas," Alba whispered, drawing my eyes away from Zara. "Are you going to let her speak to you like that?"

My lips curled. "Let her taste a little victory. Her guard will lower. You'll see. She might be different from the other mortals who've come through here in my lifetime, but they all have a breaking point."

Alba rested her chin on upraised fists, fighting a smile. "So, you let her go because she'll think you're weaker that way? And that helps us?"

I frowned. "I let her go so she could do exactly what she's doing right now. Watch. She'll go to the mortals. They'll beg to know what we talked about. She's beautiful and bold, and she just spent half the meal talking to us—something none of the other mortals have ever done. They'll hate her."

Alba sucked in a breath. "You're trying to isolate her. I wouldn't have thought of that. I should write down all your ideas."

My attention severed from Zara's retreating form and settled on my sister. "Alba, don't talk like that."

Her eyes avoided mine. "I know. It's just...what if..."

Those two words stung more than iron on my bare skin. Too much rode on those words.

I rested my head in my hands a moment before I met my sister's gaze. "Don't worry. Everything will fall together as planned. I promise. All the humans will die, Alba. Father won't return early."

Alba pinched her lips in a display of emotion most fae would have kept hidden. She was afraid. "And we'll be ready when he does?" she asked.

"We'll be ready."

# 12

## Zara

"May I sit?" I asked as I reappeared at the entertainers' table tucked away in a damp recess of the cavern. As the other humans scooted over to make room for me, my nose twitched at the smell of wet rock. I glanced down to see that the carved space where we rested our feet was slick with water. If this counted as *treating us better* than the servants, I hated to think how they dined. The dragon overhead shifted its weight and huffed, a puff of smoke curling out through the iron bars of the cage.

"I know how you feel," I said to the dragon as I settled my large, ruffled dress around my ankles. The fabric was still damp, and I smirked to think that I'd likely left a small puddle at the prince's table where I'd sat.

Everyone at the table stared at me. The oldest woman, who wore her graying hair up in a neat bun, held her fork halfway to her open mouth, stunned into silence by something I'd done.

The young woman who'd first offered me a seat was looking at me like I'd grown a third arm as she leaned over and whispered, "We don't speak to the dragon."

I made a noncommittal shrug. "Can't see what harm it does. He's as trapped as we are."

The two other women exchanged a wide-eyed glance.

My eyes darted back toward the prince's table briefly, and I saw that he and his sister were engaged in conversation. The fact that he had a sister, and that she clearly annoyed him with her chatter, contrasted so blindingly with his persona of bloodthirsty monster intent on destroying all happiness in the world.

I turned my attention back to my fellow mortals. "I'm Zara, by the way. Zara Valencia Calderon."

"Ivy Quinn," the younger woman replied.

"Eudoria Armond." The older woman spoke next, her voice and posture evidence of wealth.

"Neither of you are from Avencia?" I asked, surprised by their accents.

"We're from Cavaria," Eudoria answered. "Different provinces."

My face brightened then fell. "I was to marry a man from Cavaria. Lord Montrose."

Eudoria did a subtle double take. "*Lord Montrose* was your betrothed?"

I shrugged. "Was. Yes. For about a minute." I explained that my father and I had hoped love, or at the very least, a wedding, might break the bargain. We'd both been wrong.

Silence hung over the table for a moment. The dragon's jerking movements were my only distraction.

"I'm sorry," Ivy said. Eudoria slowly turned her eyes away and didn't look at me again, as if I'd offended her.

"I'm Tomas." The bearded, broad-chested man explained that he was from the island nation of Irdan, but his parents were Avencian, hence his Avencian name. His melodic accent was mesmerizing.

There was Adán from Ruvell, a tiny country beside Cavaria, and his Avencian was less precise. He had gray peppered through his dark hair and the kind of severe expression I'd seen on men who worked out in the sun all day, so perhaps he'd been a farmer before coming here. And a sandy-haired man named Samuel, from Lithera, a country across the sea from Avencia.

I'd never met people from so many countries at once. Excitement bubbled up until I remembered where we were and what we were facing.

As my shoulders sank, Ivy patted my back. "We all feel the same way. It's a terrible place to meet, but I'm...I'm pleased to meet you nonetheless."

I tried to smile, but my stomach had twisted into a tight knot, and my face scrunched into a grimace instead.

After an awkward moment of me staring at the other entertainers, it occurred to me: they all survived their first trial, too. I wondered how many other *mortal games* they'd endured, but if the goal was to kill the humans involved, these people had likely all seen death up close, and I didn't want to dredge up those painful memories for them.

Despite Eudoria's gray hair and prim manners or Ivy's small stature, these women had endured in this nightmarish place. I could learn much from these people.

Nibbling the corner of a chocolate-coated wafer, I considered all the ways I could broach the subject of survival in a polite way. But no matter the words I tested in my head, there wasn't a nice way to discuss the fact that we were all on a collision course with death.

The meal progressed in relative silence, as the others only spoke about the food or the unusual dress of the fae in attendance. Samuel asked what I spoke to the heir about, but after that, we exchanged few words. The other humans trapped here weren't in a talking mood, and I didn't blame them.

Finally, I could hold in my curiosity no longer. "How did you do it?" I blurted, looking quickly at each of them. "How did you stay alive?"

Adán looked confused, and Eudoria looked scandalized by the question. Samuel and Tomas exchanged a weighted look. Ivy alone responded.

"We did what they wanted. We entertained them," she said, not meeting my gaze.

Samuel looked away, clearly avoiding the conversation. Eudoria sniffed. I was suddenly curious what under the stars above that woman had done to entertain the fae.

Tomas leaned forward over his empty plate. "It's not something we're proud of. We don't speak of the trials."

I nodded once in confirmation. But I wasn't satisfied. They were hiding something, and I would uncover their secrets to survival.

After dinner, three servants hustled all the entertainers out of the cavern. The halls of the palace were partly underground, as the massive building was built into the bones of the mountain itself. No one spoke as we walked through the vaulted halls. Magical lights bobbed along the tops of stone walls, casting their cool, bluish glow over the shining stone. Everything here was so well polished that it appeared wet, so I reached my fingers out and traced the stone, half expecting my fingers to come back damp.

"Don't touch anything," the servant behind me snipped. He was tall and thin and had caterpillar brows.

I wondered how my father was faring after my disappearance. Did he know I'd be able to return in a year? Would his broken heart last that long?

I shoved the sadness away and pressed forward into this nightmarish prison, this beautiful, forsaken place. We walked until we reached a long passage with windows on one side that overlooked a sweeping mountain vista lit by bright moonlight on snowy peaks. I rushed to the cold glass panes. A lake covered part of the valley below, and a waterfall burst from the mountainside a level below the windows. I could hear its roar and envied the water's power to leave this place.

Starlight fell across the long, straight hall. Compared to the halls under the mountain, this one seemed bright. On my left were doors. The servant at the head of our small parade stopped.

Ariana was among the servants walking with us, but she'd remained silent. Now she stepped up behind me, a lamp burning in her hand. "Your quarters." She marched to the door at the end of the hall, inserted a key, and opened the room.

As soon as I stepped over the threshold into the cold, dark chamber, I sensed that something was wrong. I felt eyes on me, though the room was so dark I couldn't see. Only the faint outline of what was surely a large four poster bed, barely catching the thin light filtering in from the hall behind me.

Ariana's white tunic glowed in the candlelight as she walked into the room, dispelling the shadows. Polished wood, elegant drapes, and a large armoire greeted me. No one was in the room, but I still had the creeping feeling of someone watching me.

Instinctively, I glanced behind me. A slanted shadow against the far wall moved. I backed into the doorframe with a small clunk.

A man appeared in the dimly lit hall, his features barely discernable, even as the candlelight hit his face. He looked the way Cas had looked when he'd taken me from my home.

"Welcome to Nightsong," said the shadowy fae. He wore a suit jacket but no shirt underneath, exposing his muscled torso.

I looked away with a firm scowl, trying to calm the rising panic in my blood. This man surely had somewhere else to be and would be on his way.

Ariana cleared her throat and stepped toward me, almost protectively. "The fae like to welcome the entertainment who survive their first trial."

My throat closed up and I could barely breathe. The fae was much taller than me, and he leaned one hand against the opposite side of the doorframe, keeping me from easily walking away. But as long as he was there, I was not going to take a single step inside the room.

"I'd love to help you get acquainted with this place," he said with a hungry smile. When he leaned forward, I tilted my head back against the wall, palms starting to sweat. "I can even offer you protection in the next round of games, if you want it." With his last word, his breath ghosted against my cheek and I heard his every intention in the timbre of his voice.

I did the only thing I could think of. I ran.

I darted down the hall, back the way we'd come. This place was fouler than any nightmare I could have dreamed.

I blasted out of the windowed hallway and wheeled around one corner, then two, taking a new hallway, then another. My shoes were making such a racket on the floor that I ripped them off my feet, threw them ahead of me, and kept running.

I would rather have drowned in the lake or been eaten by whatever swam in its depths than be forced to endure the *welcome* that awaited in my room.

What little food I'd eaten threatened to come back up as I ran. I had to escape this place or die trying. Father wouldn't want me to bow my head to these wicked fae.

Another corner, another turn. A corridor, no windows, no doors. Two stairwells, another long hallway. Then a wall. I had reached the end of this escape route. No one chased after me, which only left a sinking feeling in my gut.

A large door braced with crisscrossed metal vines stood at the end of the hall. There was nothing else in this hall save the lights that came on as I ran past them. I still wasn't used to this kind of magic. What must it be like not to have to light a room as you entered it?

I stopped and panted heavily as I stood in the empty hall. I listened, but there were still no sounds of pursuit. I couldn't go back to my room. I didn't want to be here. I didn't want to do anything the fae wanted me to do. I wanted to show them that I couldn't be captured, cowed, and turned into their slave.

But I was so tired. Dancing for my life had taken so much more energy than I'd realized. I leaned against the wall and slid to the floor. My father had always said that *feeling* helpless was what made one truly helpless.

*But Papá, I am trapped here. Thanks to you.*

I fisted my hands and pressed them against my upraised knees. Thoughts of my father brought waves of sudden anger. This was all because of a bargain he'd made—a bargain he'd made for love.

Love had ruined my life, not saved it.

But I couldn't think of him—not now. Fear was poisoning my mind, and I had to be clear-headed to survive the year.

Despite my efforts to avoid thinking of my father, I tilted my head back against the wall and closed my eyes as memories fought their way into my mind's eye. My father had taught me how to wield a knife and told me to always carry one on my body, hidden in my clothes. Though my blades had saved me from more than one greedy hand in the streets at night, they had done little good in the end. Maybe that was why Father had tolerated my dancing, although it wasn't a customary hobby for the upper class. Did he know I would be here performing for my life?

My eyes popped open, and I realized I was not alone in the hall anymore.

A woman slipped out of the massive door, her dark hair wrapped in a braid around her head and decorated with mushrooms.

Alba. The princess of this miserable place.

"Oh, it's you," she said as she spun around, shutting the door quietly behind her. "He thought the mortals wouldn't want to talk to you, but he was wrong." She sounded delighted, and I wasn't certain if it was at the prospect of her brother being wrong about something or at the fact that the other mortals welcomed me. I didn't know how to respond to that, so I said nothing. She nodded slowly, then darted toward me and dropped to her ankles, bracing herself against the wall with one hand. "I'm in need of a dueling partner, and my brother tells me you can fight. Interested?"

So alarmed was I by her question that I shook my head adamantly.

"Think about it." She shrugged and stood. "You know, I hate the way you all have to die, I really do. But for his sake, don't mess this up."

I gawked at her as she walked away on silent feet. Her amber dress draped over the stone floor behind her, rippling like liquid gold as she vanished around the corner.

The subtle sound of a throat clearing behind me startled me, and I jumped up.

The prince walked out of the room. He wore no crown and his hair was disheveled. I tore my gaze away and stared at the shining black wall. What would he do to me now that I was out of my quarters when I was not supposed to be?

"You think you're better than most, don't you?" he asked, voice resonating in the vaulted hall.

I glared at him. "What?"

He cocked his chin up. "You think you can withstand the shadows, don't you? You think that your heart is made of gold? That there isn't darkness in you like there is in everyone else? The hypocrisy of it sickens me."

I lifted my shoulders, straightening my spine. "What makes you think we're all wretched like you?"

"Because you are. You're mortal." He walked in an arc around me. I spun, trying not to let my cheeks flare under his scrutiny. "You survived tonight, so you should celebrate." He clicked his tongue.

"Your version of celebration is repulsive."

His hard expression faltered, but only briefly. "I take it one of my courtiers has invited himself into your room? And you were not pleased?"

I scowled at him. "You are a foul creature."

"I am not responsible for the way my courtiers treat you. They cannot kill you, and they are forbidden from forming attachments, but that is the only restriction on our behavior toward the mortals." He took a step forward. "We may be foul in your eyes, but centuries of studying your kind has shown us what you all desire most. My courtiers want to ensure you are not deprived of anything you might want before your last day."

Without warning, I dry heaved, unable to respond to him for a moment. Finally, I said, "I will celebrate when I'm back home, one year from now."

He paused, tossing me a quick glance over his shoulder as he lifted one hand, his loose sleeve bunching at his elbow. In his upraised hand, an apple appeared. He pulled it toward his mouth and took a bite. The sound made me flinch.

Mouth half full and dripping with apple juice, he added, "Want some?" He held the fruit out to me.

Without thinking, I slapped the apple out of his hand. It clunked against the wall and then rolled back toward us. As he finished chewing his bite, he lifted his brows and tilted his head at me in an appraising way.

"Interesting," he said, his voice dropping to a sinister tone. "How do you think it would serve you to offend me?"

I might have overstepped my bounds just then, but I wasn't backing down now. What difference did it make anyway, if I was set to die in these caverns?

I looked him hard in the eyes. "I'm not going to play your games. I'm not going to bow to your wishes."

"That's nice," he said. He bent down and picked up the apple, inspecting it for any flecks of dust. He found none and took another bite. When he had finished chewing, he spoke again. "There hasn't been one mortal that came through here that didn't crack. All of you are rotten from the inside out. There's nothing good about you—other than that you can be pretty and that you all hate to die so much. My courtiers enjoy watching how hard you fight it."

I wished so desperately right now that I still had my dagger hidden in my clothes.

He flashed me a grin. "You want to hurt me, don't you?" I hated how handsome he was. It was as though he believed he had the right to make every woman tremble before him solely by the way he looked at them.

Talia had accused me of being so pretty that the men forgot themselves around me. Though I had seen many a handsome face in the ballroom, I'd never understood what she meant. But I had never encountered a man as unsettlingly handsome as the one standing before me now. There was something about him, especially the way he looked without his fancy suit on, that made my skin buzz with energy, and I hated it.

He stepped toward me. "I'm glad you want to hurt me, and I hope that one day you try because it will prove that I'm right." His teeth clicked together at the last word.

"You're not as scary as you think you are," I said, stepping deeper and deeper into territory that I should have abandoned long ago. Why hadn't I turned around and walked away?

"Brave little one," he said, twisting the apple in his fingers. "We'll see how brave you are when the next trial arrives."

I swallowed. "When will that be?"

The side of his lips curled up. "The mortals didn't tell you? Pity."

"When will that be?" I repeated, tone lower.

"Does this mean you're asking for my help?"

I rolled my eyes. "No. If the other mortals all know when it will be, it's common knowledge that I could find out from them as easily as you."

The words *other mortals* suddenly reminded me that I hadn't yet asked anyone about Talia.

His dark eyes flashed. "Then go ask one of them." He flicked his wrist as if dismissing a fly.

This time, I held my tongue from all the snide remarks I wanted to say. He must have sensed that I was holding something back, and he quirked his brow at me.

"My friend married a fae. I aim to find out what happened to her."

"Oh?" His eyes brightened with interest. "You said *married*? They gave away their magic and status, then." He tsked. "Shame. Most immortals know better than that." He shoved his hands in his pockets and walked past on silent footsteps. "If you really want that man to leave, just tell him," the prince said over his shoulder before he disappeared around the corner.

He left his bedroom door open. Perhaps he was waiting around the corner to see what I would do. If he wanted me to snoop, then I wouldn't. I turned and marched out of the hall back toward my room, which I desperately hoped was empty now.

It took me a half-hour to find my way back to my room. The black halls all looked the same, save for the chiseled art on the stone walls. I'd been running too fast earlier to take note of the scenes. By the time I found the windowed hall overlooking the mountain range, it was empty.

The magical lights had dimmed, but they blazed to life again as I dragged my feet toward my room—my prison cell.

To my great relief, no one approached me in the hall and no one waited in my room. I was finally alone. My shoulders relaxed, and my arms fell loose at my sides. I realized that my heart was about to break through my ribcage.

When I stepped into the room, the candle glowed brighter as if welcoming my presence. I glanced around the room. It was elegant for a slave's quarters. The sheets had a sheen to them that suggested silk. I ran my hand across them—cool, like spring water. There was a vase of fresh flowers on either side of the bed, along with unlit candles, a silver brush, and several tins that I recognized as containing face powders. A massive armoire stood on the other side of the room.

The room was long and narrow, suggestive of a cell, but full of such nice things that it was easy to think of it as merely a guest room. For twenty years, I'd been on a leash that had been getting shorter every day, a leash leading me here.

My shoulders sank, but I wouldn't let myself dwell on the anger and fear and sadness that prickled in my chest. Shoving those emotions away, I peeked under the bed to check for any monsters hiding there. It seemed like a cruel prank the fae would enjoy. But there wasn't even a speck of dust. I was so disgusted that the fae were trying to lure me into compromising situations solely so they could laugh at me the next day, that I grunted and flopped facedown on the bed, punching the soft sheets over and over again until there were no tears left.

# 13

## Casimiro

Firelight warmed the small reading area of the narrow library to an uncomfortable level, but the mortals who tended the books—looking for mold, worms, or pixies—relished the crackling flames and claimed they helped fight the dreaded moisture of these caves. I'd pushed my sleeves up as high as they would go and unbuttoned the top two buttons of my shirt, hoping to stave off any sweat, but the fire was winning right now. After reading the same sentence three times, I slid down in the wide chair, rested my head against the back, and stared at the glowing orb hovering among stalactites above.

My mind drifted back to the woman I'd brought here this evening. She'd chanced death by sliding into those waters. If I'd thought to enchant the water with a clinging spell, I could have listened in on her conversations with the other mortals. But I hadn't thought she'd do what she did. I'd unleashed our largest water dragon, thinking his presence in the lake would be enough to scare her senseless.

Instead, she'd beaten my game.

A fae entered the long, narrow cavern lined with shelves, their magic brushing against my own like a housecat rubbing against its master's legs. I sat up and tried to find the sentence I'd last read. The approaching fae wore a concealment spell, although not a well-crafted one.

When Alba slipped into the firelit reading room at the back of the library, her features dim beneath a veneer of shadows, I didn't look up from my book.

"I see you," I drawled, reading the same sentence for the fourth time. Daylight hours always made me feel lethargic, and poring over the medicinal properties of various fruit leaves had left me in a state I could almost describe as sleepy.

"King's crown, Cas," she cursed. The shadows fell away from her frame, and she marched into the light coming from the fire and the glowing orb above my head. She had her fists on her hips and a pair of antlers protruding from her head.

I shoved the nearest moveable item into my book—a quill—and snapped it shut to peer up at Alba. "Don't tell me the antlers are permanent."

My sister made a face. "I'm practicing affixing."

Relieved, I nodded and angled my chair outward, studying my sister's expression to see if I could predict her reason for interrupting me.

"What's plaguing you, brother?" she asked before I could so much as inhale.

"Nothing of consequence." Thinking about a mortal was the same as thinking about nothing, so it wasn't a lie.

Alba huffed. "You read that same line at least twice. I saw your hand go back to the beginning. And your magical barrier felt weaker, the way it does when you're distracted or doing magic elsewhere."

"I'm always doing magic in many places."

She crossed her arms and lifted her brows.

"Fine." I leaned forward and propped my elbows on my knees. "The other mortals who survived their first night did so by playing it safe. And each one of them, in turn, welcomed the help of one of our courtiers in return for protection in the next game."

"Yes, and?"

"The woman who arrived last night did neither of those things."

It was a cycle. A predictable, repeatable cycle. Those who played it safe survived, then voraciously accepted the help of a fae in exchange for anything from a single night's company to playing spy for that fae for a matter of months. Eventually, the courtiers withdrew their protection and the mortals died before their year elapsed.

Alba clapped her hands. "She refused help? I like her."

"She chose to entertain, Alba. She has to die."

My sister pouted. "Father is the one who made up the one-year rule for the entertainers. He had to know *some* of them would survive."

The look I sent my sister silenced her objections. Father liked the idea of offering hope but never allowing a mortal to collect on that which was hoped for. Survival for those who chose entertainment was not an option.

"Well," she said, "I still plan to duel with her. Whenever those brutes let her have a day off from the arena."

I lifted a brow. "Be sure to use the wooden training weapons, or you'll kill her without even meaning to. She *is* mortal, you know."

Alba hung her head, as if chastised. I hadn't meant to speak so harshly.

My mind flashed with memories of her standing in my room, head hung low like this, when I'd explained what had happened to our older brothers, Velasquez and Augustín, and so many before them. She'd only been a small child then, perhaps too young to learn of such things. The memory rocked through me, and I sensed my magic faltering in every place it consumed energy. In this room, where I held a thin glamour over my scars, in the halls and stairwells around the library, where I watched for approaching visitors, in my distant Shadow form, where I was currently interrogating a *duende* on the whereabouts of two Moon Court spies who'd been traipsing around the border of our mountain.

I quickly suppressed the memories of the day I'd told Alba of our brothers' murders, reestablishing my spells in the halls first. Far away in the forest, my shadow form faded momentarily, but the little creature I spoke with only stared at me with wider, more terrified eyes. In the library, where my physical form remained, my glamour slipped. The sensation was freeing, until I noted Alba's gaze affixed to my scars.

I reached out to muss her hair between the absurd antlers, but Alba's body vanished from within reach and reappeared several steps away, a few pale strands of hair looped over a prong of one antler. She beamed at me, triumphant.

"Very good," I lauded her. "Not many grown Shadow lords can transport so precisely like that."

Her smile brightened and faded in the span of a breath. "I know you're thinking about them," Alba said, backing out of my embrace. "Your face tightens and you look to the left when you remember them."

My jaw tensed. For a fae without telepathic magic, she could read me better than the books on the shelves. My father had tried for millennia to forge an heir powerful enough and obedient enough to do what he'd always wanted to do: bring the Shadow Court into Rivenmark, making it an official fae court among the other four courts. But when the time came to test the heirs on their ability to lead the court, not one had satisfied the Shadow King.

I pressed my hands down into my pockets so Alba couldn't see the black lines forming on the backs of my hands.

If I hadn't had to watch two brothers murdered by our father, I might never have felt the surge of protectiveness that washed over me the first time I met Alba. I'd seen her face, and I'd known what fate awaited her. Death. As it did for every Shadow heir.

Unless I could stop the cycle.

"Alba," I said, careful to calm my heartrate before the curse in my veins ran out of control. "I won't let you meet the same fate."

She nodded, but her smile had faded. "You said the mortal woman refused protection? Do you think she could spy for you?" A scoff burst from my lips. "She refused help. She won't want mine."

"But the poisonings are starting again. Now that Father is gone, you know as well as I do that another coup will be attempted, whenever they find the right poison." She shrugged. "You need a spy among the mortals. Relying on the journal isn't enough. Eventually, whoever is behind the coup will find a poison that can kill us both."

My heart pinched. "I won't let that happen."

Her expression softened. "I know. But think about it, Cas. She will eventually crack, like all the others. She'll want help. You just need to be the one to offer it before anyone else does. And she seems to have a way of getting even the quiet mortals to talk. She would make a good spy."

"I'd only have to kill her afterward."

Alba bit her lip. "Yes, only that." She sighed. "Well, if you choose not to offer her help, then someone else will, and then she could be spying for the enemy. Think about it. The mortals carry all the secrets around here."

The mortals could lie, so the court employed a network of them to carry secrets and transfer information, enchanting the mortals with spells that prevented them from ever speaking of the secrets they held to unwarranted contacts. Then the fae could then erase from their own minds the information the mortals carried. They were unbreakable lockboxes. The servants had long since been exhausted, and their minds were so filled with secrets and spells that most of them could offer little additional help. But the entertainers cycled through regularly. Their minds were fresh ground to be tilled.

I sat back down and crossed my ankles and threaded my fingers together over my stomach. The woman I'd brought here last night wouldn't crack as easy as the rest of them. She was fighting against my control, and some part of me was enjoying the game. Finally, someone with a little fire in them.

My mouth twitched up at the memory of her small frame pushing violently against my own as we'd danced.

"How can I get her to trust me enough to accept my help?" I asked, glancing at my sister.

Alba rubbed her hands together. "Oh, I like a plan. So, you need to think of something she wants. Not your help, because she's made it clear she doesn't want that. Something she can't refuse."

My brow quirked up. "She mentioned a friend of hers, a woman who married a fae recently."

Alba's face lit up. "You know who that is, don't you?"

Over my crossed arms, I shot my sister a frown. "How would I know who a random mortal is?"

"The news circulated all the courts. A mortal woman from Avencia recently married *Rafael del Sol*."

My lips curled into a satisfied smirk. Yes, I'd heard about *that*. Now that I thought about it, the woman who'd married the Sun prince was said to be from Leor, the same town Zara was from.

"If she wants to know about this woman," Alba said, "you can use that, Cas. Now you've got something she wants: information."

My mind spun with possibilities, ways to ensnare this mortal into spying for me.

"You're welcome," Alba said, wagging her brows at me.

I shook my head, but a small smile played on my lips. "I'd say thank you if we weren't discussing a coup designed to kill us both before Father returns."

Her face paled, and for a moment, she remained speechless. "I'm not worried about the coup. I've got you to protect me. I'm worried about *you*, Cas. How close are you to finding a cure?" Briefly, her eyes darted to my hands.

"Closer than before."

Alba swallowed. "You have plenty of time." Then she bent sideways, drawing my gaze. "How do you keep Father from knowing when you're testing the antidote? Doesn't the curse tell him every time you break his rules?"

I braced one hand against a shelf and drummed my fingers. "The curse only activates on his end if the pain gets strong enough. And I'm very good at ignoring pain."

Alba's frown deepened. "That's a terrible answer."

"And it's the only answer you're getting." I shooed her back the way she'd come, needing to think without her barging in on my thoughts. "Nine more months, Alba. Nine more months to perfect the antidote to an incurable curse and kill all the humans who foolishly chose to entertain our court. And uncover a coup that wants to lop off both our heads. Should be easy enough."

"You'll solve it—all of it. I know it."

To placate her, I nodded, but the pain I'd been denying for the past few minutes was growing, and I longed for a swallow of my tonic to dull the discomfort. I was running low, and Felipe had yet to replenish my supply, which meant I had to keep the last few sips for when the curse in my blood was too painful to ignore.

Until I had a replenished supply, I'd have to stick closer to my father's expectations of me, which meant no speaking to mortals. I only had to hope that Zara Valencia remained as strong for the next few days as she had last night, or someone else might offer her protection before I was able to.

# 14

## Zara

When I woke, my body still lay perpendicular across my bed, face smeared into the sheets as it had been last night. When I lifted my head, my cheek peeled away from the covers. I felt rested but groggy, like I had slept a lot longer than I'd intended.

The only light came from a thin blueish line under the door. The candle had long since burned out, leaving my room full of shadows. I relit the candle with a match and sat quietly in the single chair in my room, staring at the floor for what felt like an hour. There was no timepiece in here, but the line of light below my door grew brighter.

My stomach growled, but I was not going to leave this room—not until they forced me to. Better to be trapped in here than be accosted again by a fae with nefarious intentions.

Boredom overcame my first wave of hunger, and I spent a few minutes stretching, then a few more minutes miming a knife fight with my hands, which morphed into a few quick steps of a dance as the moves came to me. Flamenco dancing was my favorite form of storytelling, and I'd once dreamed of having my own stage at the *Festival de los Cuentos*, dancing the stories that filled my mind as costumed crowds looked on.

My uplifted arms fell limply to my sides as I faced the armoire, a tall, exquisite piece inlaid with bronze stars and capped with a carved, bronze lion that stared down at me mid-roar. When I opened the wardrobe, I gasped. Dresses bursting with color and ruffles sent a spike of joy through my chest. But that feeling was quickly quashed as I realized someone in this court had likely ordered these clothes placed here specifically to create this very response in me. I hated that it had worked—that I'd been *excited* even for a split second.

I didn't want to remain in the dress I'd worn here, and I had no other clothing to choose from, so with a resigned sigh, I reached for the prettiest dress, an emerald gown, sleek and shiny, sewn jewels that might have been real diamonds along the waistline. Every dress in this armoire was fit for a royal ball.

But the dress wouldn't unfasten from its peg, as if it was glued in place. To my horror, a bright fuchsia dress made of shining silk stretched out toward my hand. I screamed and leaped backward. The dress rippled, and I almost thought I heard a rustle of annoyance. I stepped away, my heart beating madly. But the fuchsia dress stretched away from the wardrobe, the bottom ruffles brushing against my legs as I took another step. The dress shook in an angry little fit when I was too far for it to reach. My head turned slowly back and forth in dismay.

I reached into the wardrobe again for the green dress, but the draping sleeve of the fuchsia dress slapped my hand away with more force than I would have expected from a piece of fabric. I snorted, almost amused.

One hand on my hip, I lifted my other toward the fuchsia dress. It enveloped my hand in soft, silky ruffles, and the susurrations of the fabric reminded me of a purr. I rolled my eyes and slipped the fuchsia dress off its hook. I took one look at it and realized I wouldn't be able to get into this dress on my own.

A knock at my bedroom door startled me, and I clutched the dress against me, ducking behind the large bed.

"Don't come in!" I shouted.

"It's me. Ariana. You are required in the training grounds."

"Training grounds?" I repeated aloud, lifting a brow at the fuchsia dress. I laid the ballgown over the bed and walked toward the door. There was no peephole, so I carefully slid the lock out and cracked the door. Behind it stood a white-clad Ariana, her hair back in a tight braid and her eyes downcast. As soon as the door opened, she glanced up at me.

"May I come in?" she asked politely, hands clasped in front of her waist. I scanned the hall. There was no one else nearby. I stepped aside and let her walk into my room. I shut the door behind her, and she spun to face me with an apologetic expression. "Today you'll start your training."

"Training? For what? Aren't they trying to kill me?"

Her expression sank, but only mildly. "They want you to put up a good fight. And if you don't know how to fight, then, well, you can't do much fighting." She had the decency to avert her eyes, and a slight flush colored her cheeks.

I scratched my face, unsure how to respond. "I think that dress wants me to wear it."

She pinned her gaze on the fuchsia dress on the bed. "Oh, yes. The dresses here have mighty strong opinions."

Minutes of silence passed as Ariana helped me into the dress. I desperately wanted to find something to talk about that wasn't death and wasn't this awful place. She'd said she didn't want to be my friend because I was destined to die, but I wasn't resigned to that fate.

"My best friend married a fae last month," I said, trying to make conversation. Ariana spluttered in shock.

That clearly hadn't been the right thing to say.

"She did it to save her family," I added, staring at my feet to avoid Ariana's sharp stare. "I don't think he was from this court. He bred race horses, and I can't really imagine a stable or a race track in this place."

Ariana snorted. "And did you save your family by coming here?"

My mouth hung open a moment before I answered. "My father was the one who made the bargain. Years ago."

Ariana's eyes widened, but she remained silent.

By the time she finished securing the bright dress, I wasn't sure if she was going to add anything else to the conversation, except to give me some marching orders. But when she stepped back to examine me, she tapped a knuckle against her lips, as if contemplating saying something she'd rather not mention.

This dress had a square neckline, soft ruffles that draped over the tops of my arms, and a loose, gauzy skirt so featherlight I worried that my legs were visible through the thin fabric.

Finally, Ariana dropped her hands to her sides and said quickly, "The whole court was talking about a fae horse breeder recently. I believe he was important to one of the other courts."

As I spun in the small room, I locked eyes with her. "Really?"

"I don't know anything else," she snapped.

Excited at the prospect of finding someone here who *did* know more about Talia, I fussed with my dress sleeves and muttered to myself, "I need a mirror."

Ariana rolled her eyes and shuffled toward the door at the same moment an ornate, full-length mirror blinked into existence on the front of the ornate armoire.

"Well, that was easy," I muttered, examining my reflection. Other than the abrasive shade of pink, the dress had its merits. It wasn't nearly as tight as the outfit I'd worn through these halls last night. It didn't follow any of the fashion trends I'd ever seen, but it fit perfectly—a fact I tried not to dwell on—and allowed my legs ample room to run, should the need arise.

I was halfway pleased that this dress had picked itself for my training today, but Ariana's scowl told me she shared none of my happy sentiments.

"Why are you in the Shadow Court?" I asked, my eyes flicking to her wrist cuff despite my efforts not to look at it.

"Follow me," Ariana barked as she disappeared back into the hall.

I wasn't ready to admit it to her, but I desperately needed a friend, someone I could trust not to *die* on me during the next few months. A small weight settled in my already heavy heart, reminding me of the true nature of my predicament.

I hurried after her, wishing I'd had time to deal with my unruly curls. Bright sunlight shone on the mountains beyond the floor-to-ceiling windows outside my door. I stopped, staring at the black and white peaks. The land rose toward the heavens with such grandeur and ferocity. I'd never seen mountains like these. They stretched on endlessly in both directions, though I knew Avencia had no mountain range this large. Besides, our tallest peaks were not rocky or snow-capped. I placed my hands on the window and peered down at a waterfall gushing out of the rock beneath my feet. For a moment, the thunderous sound of the water drowned out the nervous beat of my heart.

The cool air of the stone-vaulted halls pricked against the skin on my neck and arms. Sunlight beat against the opposite mountainside, but it didn't touch the Shadow Court's castle.

"Do you know how to use weapons?" Ariana asked, her voice a mix of nerves and annoyance.

"A blade and a bow."

"Oh, they'll enjoy that."

"And will you?" The words spilled out before I realized that it was a foolish thing to ask.

Her face fell, and she stiffened. "Last night, I had hoped you were here due to some brave bargain you made yourself, like your friend you mentioned. But cursed children are unnatural, born of magic. While I don't enjoy watching anyone die, you were never meant to live." Leaving me with my mouth hanging open, she spun on her heel and marched down the hall.

I stood by the windows for a solid minute, until my breathing slowed. This woman believed I wasn't supposed to be *alive*. I would show her how very alive I intended to stay.

Malik had warned me that the humans here were pitted against each other by the fae. How fitting, considering how much they hated our kind. But I wouldn't let the fae win, not in this battle either. I wouldn't give up on Ariana. Her fate was worse than mine, and she knew it. Enslavement to the fae was worse than death.

A shudder rocked my shoulders, and I rolled my neck, remembering the tune recited to us as children, warning us to stay close to home at night, to never wander into the woods or talk to strangers. *If you think them kind or a good place to hide, you'll die alone in the dark.*

*Maldita* or not, I wouldn't die alone in this dark prison. Ariana's words about finding a solution bit at my composure as I walked through the underground palace. But the possibilities of where to start, what to look for, and how to go about it were so vast that I nearly lost myself to a wave of panic. Chiding myself, I settled on where to start: Talia. I would search out information on my friend first because it felt less daunting than finding ways to survive deadly, unknown tasks crafted by a hateful, conniving fae prince in a court of wicked immortals.

I didn't see anyone in the halls until I reached the cavern where we'd had dinner last night. As I hurried toward the huge doors, I considered all the things I was passionate about. I wondered if Casimiro knew of them, and if he did, how he would try to rip these passions from my chest and smother them. He'd tried with dance. He'd failed.

I adored parties, but I wasn't sure if that counted as something that could kill me. I missed my friends, especially Talia, who'd also been whisked away by the fae. Now that I, too, was in the fae realm, I would determine where she was and how she was faring in her hasty marriage to that horse breeder.

The massive doors to the cavern swung open as I neared. Several stone tables inside were loaded with stacks of baked treats that smelled of cinnamon and sugar. My hunger flared and immediately died as I recalled eating pastries like these with Talia at the *Festival de los Cuentos* only weeks ago.

There had to be a way to gather more news about her. After the training session, I'd find someone who knew about the fae she married.

The cavern was much brighter as white-clad servants bustled around cleaning up from the night before. A few fae lay stretched out across the stone tables, apparently asleep. Others lined the floor in embraces that I didn't want to see. The cages above the tables had vanished entirely.

I saw a servant sweeping up the cavern. "Where's the training session?" The man lifted a finger toward one of the corridors leading from the giant cavern. I raced toward it. I didn't want to know what the fae did to mortals who arrived late to their little torture festivals.

Remnants of last night's food still covered the tables, but almost as much was scattered across the floor. One of the chocolate fountains had been knocked over, and there were puddles of dark liquid shining on the stone floor. *Heathens.*

I scurried down a wide hallway with an uneven rocky ceiling and quickly arrived at a heavy door. It had a small half-circle window filled with bright sunlight reflecting off the opposite peak. This side of the mountain was still in shadow, and the mountain air bit at my skin as I raced down wide stone steps bracketed with ornate balustrades carved to look like flowing water. Below sprawled an open sandy space half-surrounded by curving benches stretching up the mountainside.

Naturally, I was the last to arrive. The same five people I'd met at dinner last night watched me thunder ungracefully down the steps and hustle, skirts in hand, across the sandy space. The other mortals had clearly been given attire to match their *passions* as well. Samuel was dressed as a horse—an actual horse, with a long mask and a strange collar that had a mane attached at the back. Ivy wore a bright red dress as shiny as a strawberry after a late spring rain. The dress had little black dots on it as well, and I wondered if she had a beloved garden somewhere back in the mortal lands. She smiled at me, and I whirled to face the two fae who stood in front of our little class. I coughed, recognizing the long-haired, brown-skinned immortal I'd encountered outside my room the night before. The other fae was unfamiliar.

The man I recognized winked at me and cleared his throat. "For the benefit of our newest arrivals," he flourished his hand first at Tomas, then at me, "I will say that we have mortal games the morning after a full moon, which means our next game arrives in six days."

My throat closed up, and I could hardly breathe.

"Each training session will give you a small taste of what is to come. However, we're not allowed to tell you what the trial will be." He glanced at his friend, who snickered. "But we do want to make sure that you're as prepared as you can be, because we want you to, well, die with flair," he said, giving us a dramatic flick of his wrist. "And, so, we've designed these training sessions in a way that will enhance"—he made a grasping motion with his hand—"our experience of your death."

My shoulders sagged, and I glanced at Ivy. Were they serious? A cool hand gripped my chin and jerked it forward. I hadn't even heard the fae approach. The dark-haired one stared down at me, his eyes as sharp as knives. "You will listen, mortal, or I will visit you again tonight, and I'll bring my friend Viro here." I swallowed, picturing a knife and where I'd stick it.

He dropped my chin and stepped backward.

"Thank you, Erik," the other fae, Viro, said. He had a long blond braid spiked through with what looked like dragon talons, and he took up the speech as though Erik had taken care of some bothersome child.

"It would serve you well in the coming trial if you were, let's say, fast," the blond fae continued. "So today we have designed the training to help you gain as much speed as you can." His voice was strong and harsh, and it reminded me of a pumice stone scratching across my skin.

I glanced at the people beside me, ready for someone to tell me that this was a joke. Who could actually get faster in a week? If anything, if we sprinted every day, we would only be sore and tired and thus slower on the day of the trial—was that their game? But every face staring ahead looked deadly serious. The berry-red Ivy was wringing her hands, and Eudoria shot me an inscrutable look that might have been hatred or desperation. She wore a dress entirely composed of piano keys that clinked together at the smallest movement.

No one protested. No one said anything at all.

"Won't running make us sore and tired come the day of the trial?" I blurted out.

Erik crossed his arms. "Not if you accept our help," he said, lifting a hand to examine his fingernails. "We are nothing but gracious hosts to those who bring us the entertainment we crave. You may have anything at all that you desire, including elixirs to ease sore muscles. You need only ask." He flashed me a wicked smile.

I sneered back at him.

Viro added, "We will leave you here for a little while, and when we return, we hope that you are all a little bit faster than you were when you woke up this morning." His words took on a sinister air. "We'll be watching from up there." He pointed to the stands.

When I glanced up, I noticed several others had gathered to watch us. "You really have nothing better to do than to watch us run around in circles?"

"Oh." His lips curled as he smiled at me. "This is so much more than running around in circles. Enjoy." He and the other fae pranced off toward the stands.

Instantly, everyone around me tensed and tossed nervous glances at the entrances to the arena floor set into the mountainside beneath the stands. I hadn't noticed these gated tunnels until now, and I couldn't shake the memory of the creatures from the cages in the dining cavern. My flamenco shoes were useless in this deep sand, so I kicked them off. Ivy followed suit, but the rest decided to keep their shoes on. This little bowl in the mountainside seemed mostly protected from the frigid breeze that blasted the stone stairs above. A flag emblazoned with a half-moon sigil on a purple background snapped angrily in the wind high above the sand.

Ivy sidled up to me, her small frame taller and thinner than mine. Her shoulders were hunched and her arms clutched across her middle as she walked. She had curly brown hair like mine, but unlike mine, her curls kept their shape and bounced as she shuffled forward in the sand.

"These things only last until the sun hits the arena floor," she said, shaking slightly as she watched the grates covering the tunnels. "Then the fae all burrow back into their mountain to hide from the light."

*They hide from the light*. I tucked that information away beside everything else I'd learned about the Shadow fae.

Then one of the gates slid open with a slow grinding sound and I sucked in a breath.

# 15

## Zara

We all stared at the dark tunnel, and a second before I saw what emerged, Samuel slammed into me as he started to run, his face craned toward the tunnel entrance rather than watching where he was going.

I fell to the ground from the impact as two tigers raced into the arena. I scrambled to my feet as the other mortals scattered like disturbed ants. One tiger arced to the left, chasing down Adán, his dark suit a sharp contrast to the sandy arena. The other tiger shot straight for Eudoria in her black and white dress. The keys played a disturbing melody as she ran. Heart racing, I stood still and considered my options. Everyone was running, save for Ivy and me.

"They're only chasing the ones who run," I said, moving nothing but my eyes and lips as I tracked the movements of the tigers. The tiger took down Adán, who screamed like a girl. I clenched my eyes shut and looked away. The other tiger, distracted by the moving targets, changed direction to chase after Tomas. Ivy lurched forward, but I hissed at her, "Don't move."

Tomas put on speed. He outpaced Samuel, so the tiger took down the slower man instead. But the giant cat didn't destroy Samuel; he sank his claws into him and moved on.

The balding man rolled on the ground, clearly in intense pain. The other tiger had abandoned the broad-shouldered Adán and was now stalking Eudoria. My heart was threatening to seize—it was beating so fast—but so far, the tigers hadn't come for me or Ivy. I remained still, difficult as it was when I felt like prey.

A tomato hit the sand between Ivy and me and splattered. I glanced up at the stands. The fae were booing.

"Come on! You're supposed to run!" They were shouting. "It's no fun if you stand there! Run, little mortals, run!"

The blond-haired fae that had been in the arena with us was pointing and laughing at the man rolling on the ground in pain, blood streaming down his back. I couldn't hate them any more than I hated them in that moment. Our death was their sport. Our pain was their thrill.

I picked up the remains of the flattened tomato and flung the juicy dripping contents back toward the stands. Only the smallest bit of tomato flopped uselessly onto the first bench in the stands. But the point was made. Several of the fae went silent, and the blond man stood, accepting something from Erik beside him. Then he curled his arm backward and launched something toward us. I was only aware that it was a plum right before it hit me in the nose.

I went down, clutching my bleeding nose. I screamed in pain and anger at the purple plum in the sand beside me. The tiger turned his attention toward me. Cupping my bleeding nose with one hand, I stared down the tiger as I hopped to my feet. Sand poured off my dress and stuck to my sweaty skin.

"Run!" the creatures in the stands were shouting. "We want to see you run!"

But I wasn't going to give them what they wanted. The tiger eyed me with curiosity, its shoulders rolling back and forth as it stalked closer and closer. Ivy began to breathe heavily, but she didn't move either. The tiger flicked its attention toward her. On instinct, I kicked sand toward the animal's face. It flinched and turned aside, loping after someone else.

"Thank you," Ivy whispered, clasping her hands over her mouth as she heaved.

One tiger swatted at Eudoria, then flinched and scampered away when its claws met the tinkling piano keys. Internally, I cheered at the stupid fae's outfit. After the tigers chased Tomas and Samuel a little longer, they lazily walked back down the tunnel they had entered. My posture drooped as a relieved breath whooshed from my lungs.

Pressing my palm to my sore nose, I managed to slow the bleeding, but my face ached from the impact of the plum. I might have black eyes tomorrow. I stepped on the plum with my heel and squished it into the sand.

"Thank you," Ivy said, stepping toward me. "I…owe you for that."

"You don't owe me for anything," I said, shaking my head.

"I know you don't want to bow to them," she whispered, leaning closer. "I don't either, not when I might die in a couple of days. What if…would you want to work together? We could help each other in the next trial and buy each other another month?"

It sounded like a reasonable idea, so I offered a faint nod, simultaneously sensing that I'd pay for helping Ivy today. The fae in the stands were angry, their frustration palpable in the air as they jeered at us, hurling insults I'd never heard before.

The tigers had attacked Adán and Samuel and Tomas, leaving each of the men bleeding from scratches of varying severity, but Adán had received the worst injury. He lay in the sand, moaning. Tomas rushed past me.

"Help me get him up," he called to all of us.

Samuel moved to help, but his left arm was bleeding, and he kept his right hand pressed to the wound. I moved toward the man sprawled in the sand. Tomas glanced up at me and nodded, then his attention dropped back to Adán. Together, we lifted him into a sitting position, and Tomas slid his arms under the man's wide chest, helping him stand. With Tomas's help, Adán was able to shuffle toward the stone steps leading from the arena. Samuel followed close behind, blood dripping from between his fingers.

As I watched them mount the steps into the stands, my attention snagged on a familiar face. At some point during the commotion, Casimiro had appeared. He was sitting in a shaded throne carved from the mountain wall in the center of the stone benches, lounged back with his legs angled wide. He lifted a glass when he noticed me staring.

I grunted and turned aside.

"I thought they couldn't kill us except in the trials," I said to Ivy, who was visibly shaking. Out of the corner of my eye, I noticed the heir stand and walk not up, but down the stone steps, into the arena.

Ivy scurried to my side. "They'll heal the injuries. They always do. They want us to love them, remember? It's best to just leave now."

I watched the prince slip into one of the darkened tunnels where the tigers had disappeared.

Ivy tugged my arm. "Never linger here," she warned. "They might get bored and release something else."

I walked toward the stairs, my eyes following the prince's outline as he sank into the shadows of the tunnel leading off the arena floor. Curiosity halted my steps, despite Ivy's rapid protests.

"What's he doing in there?" I asked.

Ivy shook her head and pulled on my arm. "I'm not sure, but he goes in there a lot. Come on, let's go."

My brows shot up. "You aren't curious?" At Ivy's repeated head shake, I said, "Well, I am. The more I know about him, the less power he has over me."

At that, Ivy blinked and let go of my arm, her face pale. "If you're that curious, come back later," Ivy begged, "when he's gone. You could go when the sun slants into the tunnel. It'll be safer."

Her words had a ring of wisdom. I backed up, nodding. "The sun dampens their power, doesn't it?"

She nodded back. "They are not one of the original four fae courts. They created this court by stealing power from both daylight and darkness. They are hated by three of the other four courts, so they hide in this mountain, outside the border of Rivenmark."

"We're not in the fae lands?"

Ivy shook her head. "This mountain is in Avencia."

"I've never seen these mountains on any Avencian maps," I replied.

"That's because this place has always been hidden by their magic. It exists only in shadow."

I pondered this as I collected my shoes, then rejoined Ivy at the foot of the stairs.

"What do you mean they stole power?" I asked, accepting Ivy's arm as she looped it under my own. As we ascended, I used my free hand to dust the sand off my dress, arms, and chest. Grit rubbed uncomfortably in my bosom and clung to my hairline. I longed for a bath.

Ivy kept her voice low as she replied. "According to the fae's own histories, the courts were gifted with power, each from a different source. Sun, moon, stars, and then night. Each draws from a source of light, except for night." She pursed her lips. "But there was an uprising among some powerful nobles in the Sun and Night Courts, and they split off to form this court."

My mind spun, racing in time with my still-thundering heart. A dozen questions rose to the surface, but I was most curious about one thing. "Created?" Each year at Leor's renowned festival, priests or sages from the various religions of Avencia set up booths and attempted to convert listeners to their ways. I'd heard a handful of creation stories; some had made me laugh out loud to the derision of the storyteller, while others had left me feeling empty or worse, unworthy. I'd always assumed there was one true version of history, and that no one really had it right.

My father had never been religious, which made sense now that I thought of the way the bargain had affected him, but it had been a source of contention among the nobles in Leor. Fortunately, my father's wealth turned their prejudices away for the most part, which only further cemented my reasoning that those people couldn't possibly hold all the right answers, if they tossed out their own convictions for the sake of rubbing shoulders with a gentleman of higher standing.

Ivy cleared her throat, a small, high-pitched sound. "Do you know the story?" she asked, concern coating her words.

"I've heard plenty of stories that attempt to explain the creation of the world, but not many that explain the creation of magic or fae or any of this." I waved my arm.

The fierce mountain breeze struck us as soon as we exited the natural bowl in the mountainside that held the arena. My sand-laden curls whipped into my face, and I stopped to rub grit from my eyes.

Ivy clutched her arms around her bare shoulders and hurried up the steps. When we reached the platform where a door led into the mountain, I stopped and looked back at the sunny sky.

In a few moments, it would touch my skin. I hated the cold, but I missed the sun. I wanted to wait and feel its rays on my face. "I'm not ready to go back in yet," I told Ivy.

The side of the mountain dropped off beneath us, and jagged, rocky cliffs stretched between me and any escape route. I walked to the edge of the small balcony and peered over the side. The face of the mountain curved around, creating the small bowl where the arena sat deep in shadow for most of the day.

The cold breeze carried the faint mineral scent of water. To my left, mist rose from one of the crevices in the mountain wall, right below a long row of windows. That must be our hallway. From here, the massive waterfall appeared small as it spilled in a thin veil down the mountainside, disappearing into a ravine.

I smiled over my shoulder at Ivy. "You can see the waterfall from here."

Ivy scurried over but didn't come too close to the edge. "I'm afraid of heights," she said, her olive skin paling.

With a chuckle, I leaned out over the edge of the balcony so far that my feet left the ground.

"Zara!" Ivy grabbed the fabric of my dress and pulled me back.

"I wasn't going to fall," I said. Once again, I tipped forward on my hands, my hips balanced on the balustrade.

"I don't like it. It makes me nervous," Ivy said, chewing on her lip.

"It feels good to hold my life in my own hands," I replied, although that wasn't exactly true. The position was uncomfortable, and I slid my feet back down to the ground and spun to lean against the balcony railing. I lifted my chin and tried to see the top of the mountain, but the sky was so bright behind the peak that it was difficult to look at. Soon, the sun would crest the summit and pour light into this valley.

"My father taught me to never let others control me." A dry chuckle escaped my throat. "Ironic considering his bargain controlled my life. He's a wealthy man, and he's used to people attempting to manipulate him. He knew men would be tempted by my inheritance, so he warned me to watch out for false declarations of love. In reality, I think he believed that true love would end his bargain and set me free. He's a romantic at heart, though he hides it well. I, too, was convinced that falling in love would undo my curse, like it did in so many stories." I shook my head. "I was wrong, but I learned something valuable about myself: the drive to find a solution kept me from sinking into despair over what was to come. But I was terrible at avoiding the bad men," I admitted, my shoulders sinking at the memory of too many mistaken loves.

She averted her eyes and bobbed her chin. "My mother made a bargain for my life," she admitted, "but after I was born. When I was five years old, I fell gravely ill. She'd always believed the stories of the First and Last, the gifter of magic, but when she called on the powers of the fae, she refused the first bargain, which was offered by a man she described as shining like moonlight. He'd offered to save my life in return for making me hideously ugly. Another had apparently offered to switch me out for a healthy fae child she could raise as her own. Yet another fae had offered to take us both into the fae realm, separating us into different cities. When the bargain was offered that I would live twenty years, healthy and well, in the human world with my parents, that was the deal she accepted."

My face fell as she spoke, and when she finished, my eyes closed slowly. "Ivy...I'm—"

"We're both here. Nothing to do about it now."

"Not *nothing*. I refuse to die here. My father raised me to believe I could rule my own life. He taught me I should never bow to anyone, even knowing I would be here, that I would become their slave." I turned around and slapped my hand on the cold stone railing, gripping it so hard that my fingers hurt.

"Maybe he was preparing you for this."

The chill air—or maybe the shock of her words—sent a quiet shiver through my body. She stood close enough to the railing to peer over the edge now, and she wrung her fingers together, clearly nervous.

"We're both going to get out of here," I said. Ivy shot me a skeptical glance. "We're going to make it. We're going to survive this week, next week, and all of the trials they throw at us. And when our year is over, they'll let us go."

Her lips pinched. "Maybe you will."

"Don't say that. We both will. We can entertain them with our lives just as easily as we can entertain them with our deaths. We have one week ahead of us, and we're going to make the most of it." I gripped her forearms, clutching tighter than I intended to. "They may be immortal, but they still have weaknesses, and I intend to find out what they are."

The sun broke over the mountain peak and bright, warm rays poured over my skin. I closed my eyes and lifted my palms at my sides. "Right now, I am more powerful than they are."

When I opened my eyes, Ivy was staring at me with one brow arched.

"I mean it," I said, turning away from her doubtful expression. "They don't want to come outside in the daylight, which means they'll have other weaknesses. I will find them. And with each weakness I find, I'll gain more power to fight them. Two can play this game."

"So you plan to use their weakness to defeat them?" She folded her arms across her thin frame. "Sounds too familiar."

I wheezed as those words hit me like a punch. "They're immortal, Ivy. It's not like I can kill them. But maybe I can learn something that will keep me alive."

"'Maybe I can *learn something* isn't a solid survival plan, Zara."

My lips twitched at her stance and tone. She reminded me so much of Talia, calling out my ludicrous notions. "Fine. You're right. It's a terrible plan. So here's what I'm going to do. I'm going to see for myself what's in those tunnels." I held up a finger to silence Ivy's sputtered protests. "Because they can't *kill me* outside of a trial." Her face lit up. "And if I find where they keep their monsters, maybe I can also discover how to defeat them. I don't know, bring the tigers some meat from my next dinner or something." I shrugged, and Ivy covered a surprised chuckle with her hands.

"You're crazy," she said, matter-of-factly.

"Well, I'm not going to die. I refuse."

Ivy chuckled, but her excitement quickly petered out. "I'll do my best to help you when the trial arrives. Until then, my best advice is to stay as far from the fae as you can."

She turned and slipped through the door.

"The trouble with that," I said once the heavy door had shut behind her, "is that in combat, you need to know where to strike." My weapons instructor had taught me that.

And before I could change my mind, I turned back toward the arena and hurried down the sunlit steps.

# 16

## Zara

At the tunnel entrance, I paused, inhaled deeply, and imagined myself soaking the sunlight into my veins. It was freezing on the exposed mountainside, but in the bowl of the arena, protected from the wind, it was almost warm with sunlight touching the sandy space. If this weren't a place designed to torture me, I could stay here all day.

But if I had any hopes of surviving this year, I needed an advantage. To my dismay, my combat skills likely wouldn't prove as advantageous as I'd hoped, considering they did little good in a race against tigers. To beat these immortals, I needed to know what they craved. Power—I couldn't offer them anything in this department. Escape from their miserable reality—I'd done it in my first performance by surprising them. And I'd do it again.

I stepped into the tunnel, and cold air washed over me. A prickle of fear almost turned my feet back toward the sunny arena floor, but I pressed further into the shadowy space. If they couldn't kill me outside of a trial, I was safe.

My shoes were full of sand, so I slipped them off once again and held them at my side. A shoe could always make a decent weapon in time of need, especially one with a hard sole, like a flamenco shoe. The dress rustled more than I'd like, but otherwise, I moved quietly down the tunnel, deeper into the mountain. Once my eyes adjusted, the sunlight behind me provided plenty of light to see. The tunnel here was rough-cut, unlike the smooth palace halls. The floor transitioned from sand to cold stone.

Less than a minute down the tunnel, the narrow walkway opened up into a small cavern, this one partly natural and partly cut to extend the space outward. Stairs had been carved into the sloping cavern floor. A tiny pinprick of natural light fell from an opening in the ceiling to the stone below, where streaks of pale sand dusted the open space. Along the opposite wall, more tunnels cut into the rock, each capped with a massive iron gate.

The far-left gate stood ajar.

Tiptoeing across the open space, I imagined my heartbeat echoing against the stone, filling the space with thunderous sound, but as I neared the open door, small noises issued from within. I leaned against the wall beside the door and listened.

Snuffling and the friendly snarl of a dog tugging on a toy were accompanied by intermittent laughter.

"Here, boy." The deep voice was much closer than I'd first thought.

Clicking claws on stone raced toward me. I plastered myself against the uneven wall as the happy snarls turned to ferocious, wicked sounds.

A huge black dog with blood-red eyes and a scar across his long snout burst through the door and turned on me, baring its fangs. His shoulders were as tall as my waist, and the hair raised on his hackles made him appear even larger.

A second later, Casimiro stepped through the door, holding something in his hand.

"Diego! Down!" he shouted.

The dog dropped to its belly on the stone, its jaws clamped shut. A low growl still emitted from its throat as it stared up at me.

I flicked one wide-eyed glance at the prince, then pinned my gaze back on the monstrous dog. It was a *dip*, an actual hellhound. As a child, I'd always thought they were make-believe. I could fathom dragons quicker than a blood-sucking dip.

As Casimiro moved into the open space, I saw what he carried: a small piece of rope, frayed at one end and covered with slobber. He tossed the rope at the monster's feet, and the animal's tail actually wagged as it opened its massive jaws to gnaw on its toy.

"Impossible," I said, unsure if the word had slipped out of my mouth or if I'd only muttered it in my head.

Casimiro folded his arms across his chest and stared at me. "Look, I can see why you'd want to follow me—most mortal women do—but coming in here was unwise."

I peeled my back off the rough rock wall and returned his hard stare. "No, it wasn't. I learned your monsters aren't as frightening as all the childhood stories make them out to be. They just need a chew toy."

"He only answers to me. As is the case for most of our pets." He lifted a hand partway in a gesture toward the remaining doors.

"Most?" I repeated. "Not all? How very disappointing that you have something you can't control. I know that must be painful."

Casimiro's jaw muscle twitched. "Diego, hunt."

In a breath, the hound was on its feet, its long fangs bared at me. A single paw took me down, and I was staring up at a foaming, dripping tongue as the vampire dog opened its mouth for my neck. I shoved against its chest, but it did no good.

"Sit," ordered the prince. The dog backed off me and sat.

Trembling uncontrollably, I tried to wipe the slobber from my cheek, but I only succeeded in smearing it. My breaths quickened. I sat up, my rear end and elbow sore from falling on the stone, and pushed myself away from the monstrous dog until my back hit the uneven rock wall. I used the wall to pull myself up, my entire body trembling. I'd never been so scared in my life.

Casimiro clasped his hands behind his back and stared at me with an inscrutable expression.

"H-happy?" I snarled, struggling to speak as the suffocating fear refused to ebb. As long as that dog was looking at me with his red eyes, I couldn't calm down.

Casimiro lifted a hand toward the only open door and snapped his fingers. The nightmarish hound trotted back into its cage and the door swung shut on its own, a satisfying *clink* indicating when it locked.

My back collapsed against the cavern wall again as a relieved moan broke from my lips like water from a cracked dam. Humiliation wasn't enough to silence me, though I hated how ridiculous I must look to him. The fear was so palpable that my stomach hurt.

"There. He's gone."

His words startled me. I was so relieved at the dip's disappearance that I couldn't stop staring at the prince. He could have commanded the dog to chase me out of the cave, gnaw on my ankles, or snarl at me until I cried like a child. Instead, he'd sent it away, locking it back in its cage.

He had done me a favor.

What sort of game was he playing?

He turned to leave, but halfway across the skylit space, he paused. "Fear is the greatest form of control." His footsteps made small clicking sounds as he strode down the tunnel back to the arena.

Anger quickly replaced my fear, and I straightened up, using the wall for support until I was certain I was steady enough to walk. I scoffed as his words echoed in my head. He thought he had full control of me now that he'd made me so afraid, but I would show him—and all these wicked fae—that I couldn't be controlled. Not fully.

I would not let fear win. I would make my father proud.

Eyes fixed on the exit, I stormed forward, but my foot kicked something on the dark floor. The rope.

Staring down at the slobber-covered toy, the prince's words took on a new meaning. I bent down and collected the rope, glancing at the door where the dip had disappeared. Merely looking in that direction sent spears of distress down my arms and legs, but I brought the rope up to my chest and clutched it hard with both hands.

"Diego," I tried, testing the hound's name on my lips. My grip on the rope loosened. "Diego, sit."

The door to the dip's cage remained shut and locked, but the sour knot of fear in my stomach lessened. I inhaled a long, freeing breath.

"Diego, fetch." I hurled the rope at the far wall of the cavern. It slung a few drops of slobber as it sailed end over end and landed with a flop.

A tentative smile spread across my lips. By mentally turning the monster into a pet, I found his memory to be far less paralyzing. I walked forward and retrieved the rope, taking a few cautious steps toward the iron bars of the grate.

"Diego," I called, shaking the rope at the grate as my hand trembled violently.

*Don't let fear win.*

I held the rope against the grate as the massive dog ambled down a narrow tunnel toward me. The iron made me feel safe, but I still jumped when the dog snapped its enormous fangs at the end of the rope, yanking it through the bars.

"G-good boy," I managed as I scrambled backward.

Should I ever see him again, fear would have less control over me.

As I marched back out of the tunnel, the shadows seeming to twist and slink away, I had the distinct feeling someone had been watching me.

# 17

## Zara

I walked back to the massive cavern where I'd nearly died, hoping to find a bit of food, but by the time I arrived, every table was empty and sparkling clean. I saw one servant carrying a platter of fruit out the cavern doors. I followed them up several floors, hungry enough to test the warning about eating fae fruit, until they deposited the food in a small cavern that seemed to be a kitchen of sorts. That room, windowless and dark as all the rest, was filled with piles of fruit, bread, dried meats, and cheeses resting on stone slabs that ran along the walls like counters. There was a massive fireplace hung with pots and a skylight for the smoke. After a baguette and a mountain of dried salami, I felt much better.

A pair of servants came in, took some fruit, and left. Perhaps they were delivering it. Or they had a way to avoid its magical effects?

I left the cavern, wishing I had someone to talk to. By the time I reached the windowed hall outside our bedrooms, the bright midday sun reflected off the mountain peaks with blinding, intoxicating light.

Ivy wasn't in her room.

For several minutes, I stared out at the rushing waterfall pouring from the heart of the mountain. My full stomach churned uneasily at the memory of the dip's fangs so close to my throat. The prince's horrible face filled my mind, and I doubled over, clutching my arms around my middle. To him, I was no different than the rope he tossed to his pet.

I placed my hands on the glass of one of the tall windows, its cold touch pulling my scattered thoughts together. I tried to recall everything I'd ever heard about the fae, anything that might give me an advantage here. These shadow fae hated the sunlight, but they'd found a place to live where the sun barely even touched their windows. But unless I could bottle sunlight, that knowledge would do me little good. My fingers fisted on the glass, the imprint of my hand slowly fading. There had to be something else, some weakness I hadn't yet discovered that could help me beat the fae at their games.

Pushing away from the windows, I strode down the hall, away from the stairwells that descended to the dining cavern and the tunnels that snaked around to the door that led to the arena. The spartan hallways never changed, each opening up with the same smooth walls and lack of adornment, save for intermittent carvings etched in the stone. Memories filled my mind of the artwork hanging in my home in Leor. My father had little taste for art, but he enjoyed having impressive pieces in our home. We had a massive painting of a greyhound, and we didn't even own a greyhound. In the ballroom, the ceiling was painted with scenes of the more popular Avencian myths: the sun god and his wife, a woman who could transform into a red macaw; beings who could wield sunlight in their hands fighting their enemies, dark creatures with black swords; and clouds that parted and led to a place so bright it outshined the sun.

As I peered at the nearest carving on the wall, I chuckled to myself. Art could tell me much about these fae, for art told the truths of a culture.

I ran my hand over the fine lines, expertly cut into the stone. This image depicted stars over water, with what looked like a whirlpool in the center and stars falling from the sky into the massive vortex. I titled my head as I considered what this might represent. The fae had different courts, according to Ivy, and one of them was the Star Court. Perhaps the Shadow Court didn't like the Star Court?

I moved down the hallway, eager now to find another carving, another truth captured in art.

I found an etching of a mountain range with peaks as sharp and majestic as the ones outside my bedroom. Another image showed dragons in flight. And another, dance scenes where the fae in ballgowns and suits held swords and daggers as they twirled. One carving on the ceiling above a stairwell revealed an enormous battle. The ceiling above the top of the flight of steps had pointy-eared fae soldiers with raging faces and pointed swords, and as I descended, I walked beneath depictions of the carnage. Winged bodies sprawled out, lifeless, with others grasping for help, their weapons cast down beside them.

I walked back and forth up and down the stairwell, studying the carving. Without color, the images were difficult to discern, but the white light cast the lines into relief, making them easy to see against the smooth ceiling. Some of the fallen soldiers appeared like two figures emerging from the same set of feet, one standing and the other fallen on the ground. The fae with wings had small swirling lines coming from them. These were the shadow fae. And this was a battle they had lost.

With one hand pressed to the wall, I walked back up the steps and craned my neck to look at who the winning soldiers were. They had no wings. No swirling shadows around them. None of them appeared to have two forms either. They wore armor on their chests marked with a sun symbol.

"Aha," I said, rolling my neck. "So you do have enemies. This must be the Sun Court. And it looks like they beat you. Whenever this was."

I wondered if their hatred of sunlight had anything to do with this battle. Ivy had said the Shadow Court broke off from the other courts. Was this battle a portrayal of that event?

I moved on, feeling like I'd learned something of value, but still feeling like there was so much to learn. One carving looked eerily like it had been defaced with claw marks, and I turned away from that hall, choosing instead the hall branching off the opposite way, which was marked with an etching of two fae locked in a kiss. I frowned and turned away.

But something odd about the image, or maybe my own curiosity, turned me back to it. Swirling lines circled the pair, and upon closer inspection, it looked almost like the pair was bleeding from their entwined hands, their blood mingling in the swirling pattern around them. The strangest part was that a crowd was gathered around them, and flowers decorated every head, almost like this was a fae wedding.

I made a face and forced myself to look away. If that was a fae wedding, I hoped I never had to see one.

After another right turn, the hallway abruptly ended at a solid wall of stone, less polished than the rest of the castle halls. A scene had been carved into the rock to look like an open doorway revealing a world beyond. Within the false doorway, chiseled by skilled hands, was the illusion of overlapping tree branches. In the center of the image was an eye.

My fingers brushed against the stone, feeling the grooves of the design. As my hand passed over the eye, it pulsed a faint blue.

I yanked my hand back and clutched it to my chest.

"I don't think you want to go through that door," someone spoke from behind me.

Felipe strolled toward me, hands clasped behind his back under a cape that billowed lazily at his slow pace. The pale light of the orbs overhead washed his dark skin in a ghostly light.

My heart hammered loudly in my chest. "Where does it lead?" I asked, trying to keep my voice steady. I hadn't broken any rules, but I couldn't suppress the feeling that I was about to be punished. If I screamed, I doubted anyone would hear me—or care.

Felipe stopped a few paces from me. "You needn't worry. I'm not here to punish you." My eyes bulged, but he lifted a hand to silence me. "And no, I cannot read your mind, señorita Valencia. It so happens that we can read mortals like any other language. You speak your thoughts so plainly with your body that we do not have to read your mind."

The fact that he was reading my body sent a shiver of disgust down my back.

"And to answer your question, this door leads to a country called Verindal. It exists on no map you would have studied, as it lies under the protection of the fae. No humans can inhabit those lands."

My gaze flicked to the space beside Felipe, my only escape. "I was only exploring."

He nodded. "Indeed. I expect it of the more...courageous souls we collect."

I couldn't help the way my upper lip curled. "Please excuse me." My heartrate continued to climb the longer I stood backed into this corner.

"May I?" He lifted an elbow. "The evening meal is set to begin soon, and I imagine you are hungry."

Had it been an entire day already? I'd wandered these halls longer than I thought.

The faint gurgling of my stomach was proof that he was right, so I stepped forward and offered a polite curtsey. His features appeared dim and his elbow was slight, wobbling a little under my touch and giving me the impression I walked with a hollow corpse. While Casimiro's arm had been rigid and unyielding, it appeared that wasn't a trait common to all fae.

Felipe strode with graceful, unhurried movements. I yearned to reach the cavern and be set free from holding his arm. My feet clacked on the stone, while his made no sound at all.

"Do you have doors to many lands here?" I asked, hoping to murder the awful silence pressing around us.

"We do. A door to all the lands in which the shadows operate."

"Operate?" I repeated. "Are there some lands without any shadows at all?"

Felipe pinned me with a narrow look. "There are many lands, and in all but one our court has power."

"One?"

"Sunara, of course."

"Oh. Right."

He chuckled. "You've never heard of it, have you?" I pinched my lips, annoyed that I really was that easy to read. "It is a place with no darkness at all, the place in which the First and Last dwells, as the legends go. But as no Shadow Lord or Lady can travel there, we have no knowledge of this place save from rumor and myth."

His tone drew to a sharpened point, and I sensed I was treading on dangerous ground. But I was finally *learning* something. A point of weakness. There was one place where these fae could not go.

"What's in Sunara?" I pressed.

Felipe scoffed. "Besides light without the accompanying power of darkness? I don't know. And considering I hate the light, I've no desire to ever see for myself what lies there. I've no desire to perish from attempting to enter a land I would hate."

My steps faltered slightly, and I gripped Felipe's featherlight arm a little tighter. "But I thought you were eternal."

His dry chuckle surprised me. "We do not die naturally. But we can be killed. Why are you so intrigued by this, young mortal? You seem to be as fascinated with our death as we are with yours."

That stopped me in my tracks, and Felipe whirled to face me, his kind expression replaced with a fiendish one.

"Death is something we cannot have so we crave the experience of watching it," he said. "Death is something you fear so you crave the experience of watching your enemies endure it. You cannot hide it. It's written in your eyes."

Just then, another figure, silent as a shadow, dropped into view from an adjacent staircase, his boot appearing a second before his crinkled white shirt.

"Cas," said Felipe, turning to offer a stiff bow.

The heir's eyes cut to me, then back to his friend. "Having a cup of tea with the mortal?"

Felipe straightened. "Discussing death, Your Highness."

"My favorite topic," he said, flashing me a wolfish smile that twisted my gut. But behind his carefully crafted sneer, I detected the faintest pinch around his eyes. If fae could kill one another, then I wondered how they were that different from humans.

As the heir turned his back to us and sauntered down the hall, I muttered, "In the mortal world, someone like him would have many enemies."

The heir stopped walking but did not turn around. "Oh, and let me guess, you would be one of them?" His profile came into view as he turned his head slightly. "I shake with fear."

My knuckles cracked in my free hand as I fisted it by my side.

"You're afraid of sunlight," I blurted, desperate to shove his weaknesses back at him. "Your court has been defeated before, and I will figure out how."

The heir chuckled and began walking away once more. "The passionate ones always go down in the brightest flames. My court will enjoy watching you burn."

Felipe's hand caught my upper arm a half-second before I lunged for the prince. "I'll let him see me burn, all right," I grumbled against

Felipe's hold, his wraith-like touch suddenly stronger. "And he'll burn with me—I will destroy him."

The fae's grip and the sight of the heir waltzing away as if my threats meant nothing to him tore a crazed grunt from my lips. I jerked my arm out of Felipe's hold, and he did not try to grab me again.

As Casimiro ambled down the long, windowless tunnel, his frame shuddered slightly and his shadow seemed to lurch toward the ceiling, though I couldn't be sure what was real in this dark world. Whatever it took, I would survive, and the most valuable thing I'd learned today was that there were doors here that led to other worlds. Using the art to make a map of this place, I would find the door that led me back home, and then I'd be free of this place.

# 18

## Casimiro

Alba's idea of employing this new mortal as a spy occupied my mind as I scared a pair of dryads away from the base of our mountain, where I'd been reconstructing a weakened part of the magical barrier that hid our mountain from fae and mortal eyes alike. As one of only a few fae in my court with concealment powers and the one with the strongest ability to cast a spell that would last for months untended, this job fell to me when Father was absent. It felt like grunt work, but I was grateful for the fresh air and the moment away from Alba's prying eyes and Felipe's knowing looks. Between the two of them, there was little I could hide, and I didn't want anyone knowing I'd decided to enlist a mortal's help to uncover the traitors in my own court.

There was no sense speaking to Zara until I'd replenished the supply of herbs necessary to mix the antidote, but I'd kept an eye on her. For the remainder of the week, she haunted the paths outside the palace like some demented mountain goat, wrapped in everything from a blanket to a fur cape—an addition I wasn't expecting her wardrobe to supply. Every time I pushed magic through the court to find her, she was scampering around on the narrow, crisscrossing outdoor pathways that were built at the behest of the Sun Sovereign back when this place was nothing more than a prince's home, not the seat of our court. Back when day and night courted each other like lovers. When sunlight wasn't the shackles it had become to my kind.

A different time. My father's predecessor, King Caligo, was born of the marriage between the Sun Queen and a Prince of Night. Caligo took the power of his mother and father and established this court, starting the war that tore our court from the rest of Rivenmark, banishing us to this mountain between worlds. But Caligo's reign was not to last.

My father was the one who killed Caligo, weakened as he was after the war.

And that was the legacy I had to live up to. A three-thousand-year reign of complete, tyrannical supremacy.

From my bedroom balcony, I studied the horizon as two dragons raced each other in the growing twilight. The beasts moved with more grace and speed than any other living creatures, but their fire and their hatred of our magic kept us from admiring them up close. Only the ones we stole as eggs and kept in cages were ours to admire. But even they eventually outgrew our confines and our magic.

They were tolerant enough to let us share their mountain, only because we gifted them with jewels mined as we tunneled deep underground. But our stores of jewels were long depleted, and the dragons would tire of us when the magic of the stones they loved was finally all spent. A dragon could smell magic in the blood, in the air, and quite possibly in someone's intentions, but the only magic they liked was the inherent magic woven into the world at its creation, magic that was mostly gone now.

My fingers rolled a tiny ruby back and forth, back and forth, as my eyes moved from the racing dragons to the curly-haired woman darting along a distant path high above. If she was looking for an escape route up there, she would be sorely disappointed.

One side of my mouth twitched. The woman never stopped moving. Like a tree forced to grow on a windswept hillside, she remained in constant motion. I didn't know what she was searching for, but the ferocity with which she hunted instilled admiration inside me. Most mortals succumbed to despair soon after arriving in these halls. But not her. If anything, she burned even brighter now than she had the night I'd danced with her in her ballroom.

"Burn, little spark." My words were sucked away by the howling wind. I curled my fist around the ruby, angry at the pain shooting up my veins that accompanied my shifting thoughts about this woman.

My father always hated my curiosity about mortals. Curiosity, he'd said, was only useful when it uncovered secrets. I chuckled to myself. At the present moment, the secret I most wanted to uncover was what Zara Valencia was hunting.

Before the trial in two days' time, I would speak with her. Until then, I'd make sure she didn't do anything foolish, like accept anyone else's help.

In my shadow form, beneath a concealment spell, Zara couldn't see me. I slinked silently through the dark passage behind her, indistinguishable from the black stone walls and chilly air that bled through these halls. The trial would take place in two days, and I still hadn't spoken with her. She'd refused Alba's attempts to recruit her as a dueling partner, which only cemented the notion that Zara Valencia wasn't going to say yes to a request from a fae without ample reason to.

My physical body remained in my suite, and when the door to my room burst open and Felipe stomped in, my shadow form flickered briefly at the disturbance in my concentration.

Felipe glanced at a gray-haired mortal woman sprawled on the floor, swept his hair back, and shut the door behind him. He stepped over her body and set a small vial on the desk beside my arm. My veins ran black and thick, raised under my skin like little moles bored through my flesh.

Once again avoiding the mortal like she was nothing other than a piece of furniture to step around, Felipe edged back, his brows lifted. He clasped his hands at his waist and waited for me to speak, to thank him for the replenished supply of ingredients I needed to make my antidote.

In another part of the castle, my shadow form watched as Zara marched obediently toward the arena for her final day of training. If I was to employ her, I must speak with her tonight.

While hearing and seeing in both forms had become easy enough, talking in both forms at the same time was extraordinarily tricky magic. In my physical body, my eyes remained fixed on the vial, its murky contents enough to make my stomach sour, remembering how goosenettle stuck to my throat like drying paint and forced me to endure its lingering taste.

Felipe cleared his throat.

I looked up at him, mind focused elsewhere. The mortal on the floor groaned, and Felipe sidestepped, his lip curling in disgust.

"She's alive," he announced, surprised. "So, it worked."

"Of course she's alive," I said, ripping my awareness away from Zara's bouncing curls two hallways away. My shadow form would have to wait. No one could know I was trailing a mortal or why. I nudged the prostrate woman's shoulder with my bare toes. She jerked a little, and her eyes popped open.

I yanked my foot back. Felipe laughed.

The woman rolled and pushed herself backward toward the door, her face pale as a wrinkled sheet. "What—what did you do to me?"

Pure loathing rolled off of her. I smiled, grateful for her prejudices at the moment.

"You were a test subject. I thank you for your willing compliance." I leaned forward in a mock bow, sweeping an arm across my chest and not taking my eyes off her. Her gaze noted the black veins on my outstretched arm and something in her expression flickered with fear and then glee.

She thought I was cursed, and she was delighted about it.

Good.

She was right about that, but she was wrong about what I'd done to her. If the mortals hated me, all the better. My eyes flickered to the secret compartment that concealed the journal outlining the antidote's ingredients and properties. My great knowledge of herbs and remedies had come from that book, not the countless others I'd studied.

Felipe watched the woman over his massive, crossed arms. She cowered at the sight of him then scrambled to her feet, grasping for the door handle. Her body, weakened from the poison, was pathetic to watch. But when she finally hauled her age-spotted self through the door, I hid my relieved exhale as a chuckle.

Felipe clapped me on the back, which would have sent me tumbling in my own weakened state, had I not seen it coming and grabbed the desk for support.

"You all right?" Felipe asked, noting my hand on the desk.

I nodded. "Just ready for the antidote. Thanks," I added, tapping the vial with a fingernail.

Two halls away, Zara had stopped walking at the door that led outside to the arena. Blinding irreverent sunlight poured in from the small window in the door, and my shadow self recoiled from the light. The tendrils of my magical form, not contained by limbs and veins, curled toward her briefly, then the balcony door slammed shut and I was left floating in the dark.

I dropped my fist on the desk with a hard clunk.

"Something the matter?" Felipe asked. His eyes searched me, and I was thankful his magic did not include empathy. My father's did, and that was more than any living soul should have to endure.

"The brittlenut powder worked well against snake venom," I said, rubbing at a small drool spot on the floor with the ball of my foot. "Worked well, don't you think?"

"Any luck discovering who's behind this?" asked Felipe.

I shrugged. "Alba found her. The woman, of course, didn't remember anything that had happened right before."

"The poisonings are becoming frequent."

"I know. But it will be a while before they find anything I don't have a remedy for."

Felipe rubbed his chin absently as he nodded in agreement. "But as soon as they find a poison that you *can't* cure, they'll strike. Which, judging by all this"—he indicated the shelves of vials—"will be a while. The curse has its benefits, I guess."

My brows shot up. "Oh, yes, blistering pain in my veins has been a childhood dream of mine."

"I only meant that you have so many poison remedies already on hand. You're not only the second-most powerful fae in the court, but you're poison-proof." He let out a dry chuckle. "Hard to usurp a throne from under your rear end."

I wanted to laugh, but all that came out was a raspy huff. "If it weren't for Alba, I might not care. But I can't let her die."

Felipe offered a tight smile. "I know."

My sister had found the latest poison victim in the seldom-used tunnels that led to the dragon's lairs. Those tunnels were used for disposing of things the fae wanted forgotten, and someone had dumped this mortal servant's body for the dragons to find, hoping, perhaps, to cover up the use of a poison known to disarm a fae from his magic for a short time.

A deadly poison, in a roundabout way, and one tightly controlled by the few owners of the particular snake breed whose venom formed its base ingredient. Whoever was testing out the poisons on the mortals had hoped to keep this one hidden from me. Fortunately, Alba had been wandering that way, hunting the glowing lizards that lurked in the quietest corners of our underground palace.

"Ironic that I'm keeping these mortals alive while trying to kill the others," I said.

As I recalled Zara's words about me being the type to have enemies, my stomach tightened. If she had chosen to be a servant, I wouldn't have to kill her before Father returned. But if she had, I would never have spared her a second thought. My eyes lingered on the door where the servant woman had departed, surprised at how oddly tight my muscles had grown when thinking of Zara.

"Not ironic," Felipe corrected. "Ironic would be if you died in your attempts to kill the humans."

"I really don't like your sense of humor," I said to my friend, crossing my arms.

Felipe sighed, finally relaxing a little. "Are you ready for the trial?"

I raked both hands through my hair, pausing with my hands cupped around the back of my head. Ever since Augustín's murder, I had stopped watching the mortal games with rapt excitement, as so many of my kind did. But the others in my court didn't carry a curse that would strip them of life in a short time. For me, death had lost its foreign gleam and now lurked within my very blood—blood that was made to be immortal.

"Ready as ever," I answered.

The deaths of the mortals couldn't matter to me. I saved the ones I could, and it had to be enough. My top priority was protecting Alba from the plot of the usurpers and from the curse that would pass to her, should I die. No entertainer's death could possibly weigh heavier than hers would.

"Don't worry," Felipe said, his chin tilted up in that way soldiers employed when speaking boldly to their captain. "Between your research and my magic, the antidote will keep getting stronger."

The books on the desk mocked me with their proven remedies, time-tested formulas for beating all known poisons and curses. The one inside of me was not among them. And no antidote yet existed that could remove it entirely. The Shadow King had been thorough when he'd crafted the spell.

I nodded firmly, dismissing my friend. An uncomfortable feeling of gratitude had welled up within me. Instantly, pain prickled again in my veins.

Father had never actually left. Not really.

"See you at breakfast," Felipe called as he strode toward the door.

As Felipe closed the door behind him, my physical body dropped into my chair once again. Hallways away, my shadow form peered out a small window onto the balcony at the windswept girl standing in the sunlight like some star-descended saint. My jaw clenched as pain lanced through my veins, warning me that my thoughts were drifting somewhere my father would disapprove of. But I only planned to use this woman as a tool before she died—a shovel to uncover whatever murderous plot was afoot in my court. And *that* was something Father would approve of.

I stood there, watching her from the shadows, temporarily forgetting that she would die in a matter of months. Curse the light. She was a spark, and I was a moth, drawn toward the fire that mocked my existence. But like every other spark that wandered into the darkness, she too would snuff out.

Pity. For what a thing it would be to watch her spark catch fire.

Pain like lightning surged in my veins.

# 19

## Zara

At dinner the night before our first group trial—or rather the first meal of the night, which was equivalent to breakfast for these fae—the servants bustled about with vivid unease, their movements hurried and their shared glances long and meaningful. I'd spent the past several days—after our ridiculous training sessions—roaming the halls again. I found doorways that led to other worlds and doorways that led to libraries, washrooms, and an indoor archery range. To my dismay, the doorways to other worlds hadn't opened for me.

I'd been so tired from switching days for nights that I'd slept through several meals, and no one had woken me. Tonight, however, my empty stomach growled, and I wasn't about to miss another meal. The roasted almonds and Manchego I'd taken from the pantry earlier hadn't been enough to satiate my hunger.

In the cavern, the fae buzzed with magical energy, their skin glittering and their eyes glowing. In the cages above the tables, the animals spun in frenzied little circles.

"What's going on?" I asked Ivy as I settled onto a bench at the otherwise empty table. "And where is everyone?"

Ivy chewed a bite of puff pastry—a delicacy drizzled with honey and positively sparkling with sugar. "Tonight is the new moon. The peak of the Shadow Court's power. When they especially like to go terrorize the mortal world."

"Oh." To think the shadow fae could be *worse* tonight than previously gave me a nasty twist of unease.

She nodded toward the middle of the cavern. "And you asked where the others were."

I squinted, looking around for Eudoria, Tomas, Samuel, and Adán. Ivy lifted her eyes, and I followed her gaze to a cage, hanging above one of the fae tables. Samuel sat inside, his long legs scrunched up to his chest.

"No," I breathed. I caught sight of Eudoria huddled in another cage, her fingers wrapped around the iron bars and her face resting against the back of her hands.

Ivy stared at her pastry with a forlorn expression. "Occasionally, when they get bored, they use us for other types of entertainment. This week was different because two new entertainers showed up, you and the one who didn't make it, giving the rest of us a break for a few days." She offered me a small smile. "It's not always all of us, and there's never any warning. Sometimes it's the cages, sometimes it's the dance floor, sometimes it's"—she coughed and cleared her throat—"standing on the tables dressed in food while the fae pull it off you."

I gaped at her. Her cheeks were so red I knew better than to ask about it.

"How long have you been here?" I asked quietly. I had only been here one week, and it felt like a lifetime. The prospect of surviving here for twelve months sounded almost impossible—*almost* but not quite. One year, and I could return to my father, my life, my house...home, where no one tortured me or humiliated me for fun.

Ivy wore her wavy hair loose tonight rather than a tight bun. "Ninety-six days. The next trial will only be my third. I had to start keeping track of the days by using the kohl they provided. I mark the inside door of my wardrobe. So far, no one has noticed, save the clothes, which always riot a little when I make the marks."

A wry chuckle escaped my lips. "The clothes here do have very strong opinions."

As Ivy nodded in agreement, a disheveled figure stumbled in from a side entrance, his open-collared shirt even more wrinkled than usual. I stared at Casimiro as he crossed the vaulted space to an empty table. The fae puzzled me. In the human world, power was a magnet. Those who had it were like carcasses, and the vultures that buzzed around them never ceased trying to take a bite. Humans flaunted their power, lording it over those beneath them. But here, this fae, who apparently held the highest authority in the king's absence, was a solitary figure. I'd seen him walking the halls mostly alone, save for once with Felipe, and now he chose to sit alone. His sister had eaten with him last night, but she was currently sitting at a different table with two fae women, laughing and smiling beneath Adán as he shook against his cage, his screams silenced by magic. The heir's sloppy appearance suggested he cared very little for his position of authority, but I couldn't figure out why. I was still staring at him when Ivy cleared her throat.

I looked quickly away, staring at the gorgeous fruit they always placed on our table, tempting us or mocking us—or both. As much as the fruit here beckoned to me, I'd been warned not to eat a single bite of it, unless I wanted to risk losing my head to what Tomas had called *el camino loco*, the crazy walk. People who ate the fruit typically woke up hours later without any recollection of what transpired.

My eyes flashed back to Casimiro, who slouched over his book, his goblet pressed against one cheek as if too lazy to sit up and take a sip. The hatred I felt toward him fanned my heartrate to an angry tempo and heat flushed up my neck.

But no matter how much I seethed at the sight of him, the way he'd danced at my party had left an impression I couldn't shake. No man I'd ever danced with had moved with as much passion as he had, and I loathed the fact that I craved another dance with him. Craved the way his hand had directed me with graceful confidence. The way his fingers had gripped mine with ferocity that never hurt. The intoxicating energy that had flamed off of him, leaving me breathless for more.

The heir glanced up from his book, locking eyes with me across the vast space.

I sucked in a breath and stared down at my mostly empty plate until I was certain his attention had returned to his book.

Ivy studied me, a tightness in the skin around her eyes. "They are handsome, but it's only a glamour. They are the enemy, Zara."

I scoffed, unable to meet her gaze. "I know, Ivy. I hate him more than you know."

A voice boomed out over the cavern, startling me so much I let out a small yelp.

"The heir wishes to speak."

When I glanced back at Cas, he was still staring at the uplifted book in his hand hovering over his plate. It didn't look much like he wished to say anything at all, but he set his book down, flipping it over so he wouldn't lose his page, and stepped onto the stone bench and then the table. When he was in the center of the table, he lifted his arms beside him and turned around to address everyone in the cavern.

"Tonight is a special night. Until the sun rises, all rooms are open to you and all doors will open for you. Nothing is off limits. We have everything here that you could possibly want. After all, we want you to enjoy yourselves." The way he lingered on the word "enjoy" made my skin crawl. "Whatever your heart desires, you will find it within these halls tonight. And in the morning, we will see you all at the arena for a little entertainment. I've crafted the next trial with particular enjoyment." He completed his full turn and lowered his arms. Then he leaped down from the table and plopped back down at his seat with his book, his face resting on two upraised fingers.

All eyes in the cavern lingered on him as the fae exchanged excited whispers and the servants shifted uncomfortably where they stood awaiting orders. Ivy and I shared a glance, her crinkled brow and worried eyes reflecting the same unease I felt in my bones.

The next trial awaited us at dawn.

This could very well be the last night for some of us. A violent shudder shook my frame as my imagination painted vivid images of my companions sprawled across the sandy arena floor, never to rise again.

I stood and climbed up from the bench.

"Where are you going?" Ivy asked, voice laced with concern. "I know you wander the halls, but tonight is not a good night to wander."

I pressed my hands against my middle, trying to calm the roiling inside. "Ivy, I can't stay here. Twelve months is an eternity."

Ivy glanced at Casimiro again, clearly reading my intentions. "They won't let you escape."

My hands twisted a wayward curl. She was probably right, but I had to try. After a moment, I said, "Come with me?"

She shook her head.

I nodded once, smoothed out the wrinkles in my dress, and visualized the hallways that led to the door I wanted to try.

As I walked away, Ivy hissed in a loud whisper, "Don't do anything foolish."

My lips quirked. "They're going to try to kill us in the morning, Ivy. I'm not going to sit back and wait until then."

She chewed her lower lip as she nodded once. "Be careful."

I hurried toward the cavern's exits, where several of the fae and mortal servants had already disappeared. I thought I saw a fae in deep green walk away hand-in-hand with one of the servants. Two female fae dressed in tight blue and purple jester suits danced and spun and turned flips as they vanished down the wide stone steps that led to the lower levels. Their magic crackled off their skin and buzzed in the air, snapping in tiny sparks against the stone walls. Maybe that was why these fae lived entirely encased in stone—so that when their magic threw sparks, they wouldn't burn down their castle.

I peeled away from the cavern doors, heading toward the stairs leading up, toward the door carved with a familiar sight.

# 20

## Zara

I hurried up the steps, checking behind me to see if anyone was following. At the top, I turned left, pleased to find the next hall empty as well. At a wide intersection of four halls, a pair of fae in their shadow forms evaporated into the darkness as I approached. They seemed more concerned with avoiding me than following me.

My heartrate jumped as I snaked through the heart of the mountain, hunting the door that I'd found earlier today—a door to Avencia.

The doors to other worlds were all the same, I'd quickly learned this week in my wanderings. Carved directly into the stone walls of the palace, these doors looked like mere artwork, full of perfectly composed etchings of the world beyond. Superimposed over these carvings was always the same eye that would pulse blue at my approach but nothing else. These doors had never opened for me, no matter how hard I pushed or how ardently I screamed at them to open.

But Casimiro had said all the doors would open for us tonight.

It was almost like he was *telling* us to leave. I shook the thought away, not caring why the fae prince might say such a thing, only that if tonight held any chance to escape, I had to take it.

I turned another corner. A pale light pulsed to life above my head, throwing the carved lines into relief at the end of the hall. My heartrate tripled in excitement.

A pointed-arch doorway marked with an eye waited for me. The eye already pulsed a soft blue, as if the magic here was eager, ready to be used. Behind the image of the eye was a vivid cliffside ocean scene, despite the monochrome black of the stone.

I'd seen these cliffs once before.

Up the coast from Leor, the beaches disappeared and tall brown cliffs hugged the sea. Papá traveled often to Risona, a large town perched atop these cliffs, for business, and the summer I was fourteen, he'd rented a small flat in the heart of the seaside town, where I'd spent a month gazing at these very cliffs.

When I'd found the door that had first brought me to Nightsong, the one at the base of the branching stairwells, the image behind the eye no longer showed pine trees like it had the night I'd arrived. Each time I'd seen it, that one door had a different scene etched on it. Which was why, tonight, when I had a chance at escape, I came to this door instead.

I could almost smell the salt and feel the sea breeze on my face as I stepped near the door. Avencia waited beyond this door. *Freedom.* The carved scene in the stone sank deeper and filled with a shining black liquid that rippled along each line and quickly turned to color, filling the entire door like enchanted paint.

A warm breeze tousled my hair.

I gasped.

The cold, underground tunnel whooshed with hot air from another land. A quick glance behind me revealed I was still standing in Nightsong, the home of the shadow fae. Ahead stood my country—my home.

With a yelp of delight mixed with fear, I stepped forward and fell through the opening.

My whoop of victory morphed quickly into a shriek of terror. From my forehead down to my toes, a strange binding sensation cascaded over my muscles, locking me in a rigid stance with my arms pinned to my sides, as I plummeted face-first toward a grassy cliff edge high above the gray sea twinkling with blinding sunlight.

A strong, warm breeze pushed against my body as I fell, angling my trajectory over the calm ocean rather than the grassy clifftop meadow. The sea air, thick with salt and moisture, stung my eyes as I shot toward the gently crashing waves.

Panic blocked the air from my lungs, but my head was about to strike water, and I needed to take a deep breath.

Needed to be able to move.

Needed to back up and decide *not* to jump.

Five seconds ago, this place looked like freedom wrapped in adventure, a welcome friend waiting to take me by the hand. Now, I plunged toward my death, and I couldn't even fight it.

By the time my body shot past the cliff edge, narrowly missing the rocky outcroppings, my skin prickled. A blink before my head pierced the water, my entire body burned like I was falling through flames rather than air.

My only consolation was that I hadn't let the fae laugh at my death. I only wished I'd been able to find real love, the kind my parents had once shared, the kind that never lets go.

Ivy, I'm sorry I abandoned you. Talia, I wish I'd found you.

Father, I wish I could have seen you again. Wish you hadn't let me go...

Sun above, this was going to hur—

*Splash.*

# 21

## Zara

Like an arrow aimed at the sandy sea floor, I shot straight down. Pain lanced through my spine and my awareness dimmed as a massive headache exploded through my skull.

Dark shapes swarmed around me, but they moved too fast, and the light faded too quickly for me to register what these creatures were.

Then something grabbed me.

My entire body lurched as a force yanked me upward, sucking me from my watery grave. The magic binding my muscles vanished, and my limbs floated outward in the water, as did my dress. My hair billowed around my face, obscuring my view as the darting fish swirled and writhed in the waves around me.

Cold hands grabbed my ankle, then my waist, spinning my body until my face pointed up. My eyes stung too badly to register what was in the water with me, but strong arms wrapped around me as we rose.

A second longer and I would've taken water into my lungs. Then cold air washed over my wet body as I was pulled from the waves and toward the clifftop like a bird.

Grasses prickled against my skin as I hit the earth.

My lungs burned as I sucked in air, and my wheezing was accompanied by the groans of my rescuer.

Casimiro stood a few steps away, hands on his knees, heaving air through clenched teeth as black lines pulsed up from his hands toward his elbows. When he spied me watching him, he straightened and slung his hair backward with one hand, tossing a few water droplets into the sunlight.

"I knew you'd try to leave."

Fists formed and loosened at his sides. His white shirt stuck to his skin, and his chin dripped water like a garden fountain. He lifted his face toward the sky, eyes squeezed shut and mouth open in an uncharacteristic grimace.

"Stars, Valencia, you could have died."

The words tumbled from his lips as if by accident, and I found that my inability to stand had nothing to do with the pain in my spine. I stared at him, trying to read the sarcasm that was surely buried somewhere, or the venom that would be hidden in his meaning. I found none.

He leveled his dark eyes at me, his cold veneer quickly returning, then glanced down at the black lines spreading up his arm. "Don't flatter yourself by thinking your life matters to me," he said. "When someone bound to our court escapes, the magic that ties your blood to the one who made the bargain will bind your body until you are retrieved."

Finally, I clambered to my feet in my now heavy dress. "Why not let me die then?" I managed to breathe out.

"Because," he said simply, his tone calm and even once more, "if you die outside of the prescribed trials you've agreed to, my father will suffer. The bargain comes with a price for both parties. And while I'm not opposed to my father suffering, I am opposed to him coming home early."

My brows lifted. Here was a valuable piece of information, almost like he was handing it to me on a platter. But why would he do that? To establish trust? He'd have to do more than drag me from the waters and tell me that he didn't love his father to make me trust him. The warm sea breeze loosened a halo of tiny hairs from my wet curls and tossed them in my face. Casimiro's dark hair whipped backward in the wind, revealing his face in the bright sun in a way that made him look almost boyish—certainly not the grim captor who sulked through his own palace halls.

I glanced at his blackening arms, and though he was trying to hide it, whatever was happening to him was causing him pain. The skin around his eyes was tight and his mouth moved less than usual as he spoke. "And you inherited these bargains from your father?"

His jaw twitched before he answered. "My father left me in charge of ensuring *he* does not suffer."

"Where is your father?"

Casimiro's eyes narrowed. "Away."

"I gathered that. How long will you be *in charge*?" I parroted his words with mock deference.

He stormed forward, and I matched his movements, stepping backward, barefoot, over the dry grass. "Stop running, Zara. I'm only trying to take us—"

But I'd already stopped at the sound of my name, and his chest bumped into my shoulder. In Avencia, men did not use women's first names until they were well acquainted. The only men who'd ever called me Zara were my father and a half-dozen past lovers—or rather, men I'd hoped would be my true love.

But it turned out true love wasn't something I could craft, uncover, or insert within another person, no matter how much I liked them. Love was supposed to be fierce and forever, a force that nothing in the world could stop. Of all the men who'd claimed to adore me, not one had loved me like that. My true love was still out there, searching, as I was, for the match that would finally make this mad world make sense. I would survive my year of torture and find him—one day.

The heir to the Shadow Court wrapped one cold hand around my upper arm, gently but firmly, and in another blink, a doorway opened up in the very air beside us. Another second and he pulled me through after him.

We stood in a black hallway so dim in comparison to the sunlit clifftop that I felt momentarily blind.

My clothes and hair no longer held a drop of ocean water. Casimiro's were dry as well. He turned away from me in the dim hall—no, room—and shoved his sleeves back up to his elbows. His arms were streaked black. As my eyes adjusted, I made out rows of shelves dotted with tiny vials and a fur rug beneath a painted wooden desk stacked with books, loose papers, and an ink pot. A few of the vials glowed faintly, creating the only light in the room. Casimiro again grabbed my arm and turned me so that my gaze was averted away from the desk and wall of shelves and toward a wide archway that led into a small anteroom set with two other arches.

"I didn't bring you to my room so you could stay," he sneered.

"Your room?" My throat closed up a little in fear. My head whipped around and searched for the doorway we'd come through. There was an etching on the wall, the outline of a door with an eye on it, but it was too dim to make out any other designs. "You have a door to Avencia in your *room*?"

He huffed. "It leads wherever I want it to." He noticed the tensing in my muscles and added, "And it only ever opens for me."

He marched me through this small room into a space even darker, with no glowing vials to cast any light. He seemed perfectly capable of seeing in the darkness, and he directed me to another door marked with a small moon-shaped window. Through the tiny window, a thousand stars shone.

Casimiro ripped open the door and starlight revealed the black lines still snaking up his arm. They'd diminished somewhat, now only discoloring his hands and wrists.

"Will that go away?" I asked, staring at his bulging veins. The binding sensation had broken as soon as he'd snatched me from the water, before we'd even returned to these halls. I shivered at the thought that being in his arms counted as being *retrieved* by the shadows.

His eyes held a faint blue glow as he fisted his hands at his sides. "Come. I didn't rescue you just to make you swoon."

He didn't see my shocked grimace as he stormed toward a thin set of steps carved into the mountainside.

"I will never swoon for you," I spat as I followed him out into the icy night. As soon as the cold air bit at my skin, I longed for the ocean breeze and warm sunlight of my world.

"Good, it'll make this easier."

I wrapped my arms around myself and hurried after the heir as he jogged down the stairs.

A veil of ice rested on the banister, so I held my skirts instead. "Make what easier?" The moonless night meant he was at his peak power, and I wanted to get away from him as quickly as possible.

But at the bottom of the stairs, Casimiro turned, trapping me on the narrow stone steps as he braced one arm on the frozen banister. "Your escape tonight was staged. I must say, you played your part seamlessly." He ignored my guffaw and pressed on. "I knew you would try to escape, and everyone here knew I would have to retrieve you or let my father suffer. If I didn't retrieve you, my father would know I was responsible, and—well, let's just say you don't want him returning early any more than I do." He flexed his hand at his side. "But now I need your help."

I blinked at him rapidly. "You need *my* help?"

His jaw tensed, but he showed no other signs of being offended by asking *me*, a mortal, for help. "Unfortunately, yes."

The information washed over me like a bucket of cold water, and for several seconds I was speechless. "I don't want to help you," I finally admitted, crossing my arms, mostly to barricade myself from the bitter wind.

"I didn't imagine that you did. But I design your trials, so it behooves you to do what I say."

"Blackmail. An excellent choice. It befits your station."

He sniffed. "I don't need your approval or your admiration. I merely need your compliance."

"What if I refuse?"

His gaze sharpened. "I will ensure that you never find out about your friend."

My stomach dropped. "You know about Talia?"

He nodded.

"And you won't tell me about her unless I help you?"

Another nod.

"You really are foul, you know that?"

Casimiro sighed. "This will only work if you choose to do it on your own. Any magic I place on you to force your hand would be traceable. This must happen without anyone discovering your true role."

"My true role," I repeated, brows lifting. "If I agree to this, am I your accomplice? Does that mean we're *partners*, Casimiro?"

I threw his given name at him like he'd done to me, and it filled me with a sense of power that shot like lightning through my veins.

His brow quirked at my use of his name. "Think what you like, but I haven't explained yet how this will work." He paused, and the longer the silence stretched on, the more threatened I felt.

"Okay, fine. How will it work?" I needed to get back inside. My muscles were starting to shake.

He smiled, but the expression didn't reach his eyes. "I need you to befriend the servants and find out who is poisoning them."

"Poisoning them?" I barked, my chest rocking forward, putting me dangerously off balance on the icy steps.

Casimiro's arm lifted from the banister as if to steady me, but when I straightened, his hand, now no longer streaked with black, quickly settled again on the icy stone. My eyes stared at his hand a moment too long, and when my attention shifted back to his face, I couldn't reconcile his desire to kill me with his desire to keep me from falling.

"That's what I said," he drawled. "Most of the mortals here have been offered some sort of deal to not speak to any fae of the poisonings by whoever is behind it. But your only hope for finding out about Talia is to do as I say. With a word, I can place a spell on the name of your friend that will silence anyone who wishes to speak of her to you."

"You are despicable, you know that?" It hit me that he would try to kill me again in a few hours.

"People are suffering, and you say I am despicable for wanting it to stop?"

My brows pinched. "What about the trial? Am I supposed to find out all this and report back to you before the trial starts?"

Cold wind tossed his hair across his forehead as he continued. "That would be ideal, yes, but—"

"I see," I said, cutting him off. "You need my help, but you're still going to try to kill me in the morning?" My arms flew out at my sides. "You really should work on your bargaining techniques."

"—but," he repeated between clenched teeth, "since I know you likely won't have time tonight, I will have to make sure you survive the trial tomorrow morning."

My lips parted as breath rushed from my lungs, swirling in the air around the heir's face.

He was going to *save my life* to get this information.

Before words could form on my tongue, my head began to shake in disbelief. "I don't like this. I don't want to be in your debt."

He rolled his eyes. "You won't be. Not after you bring me the information I desire. The mortals who have been poisoned do not know who is behind the attacks. But someone does, and you must find out who."

My head was still shaking, processing. "Why do you care about the mortals? You like to watch us die."

"I don't have to explain myself to you."

"Do you want my help or not?" I shot back.

With a long exhale, he stepped off the bottom stair and took a few steps away before speaking to me over his shoulder. "Whoever is poisoning the mortals is merely using them to test me. My court is well aware of the antidotes and potions I keep, so each poison they concoct is another attempt to see if I have a remedy. They're hoping to find one I do not have a cure for, a poison they can use on—on their target."

"On you," I muttered.

Casimiro did not respond but his silence was answer enough. Someone in this court of nightmares wanted to *kill* the heir. The information shouldn't have been shocking, considering the deplorable nature of these creatures, but it shook me nonetheless to know that this immortal was facing his own deadly trial.

"You want me to help you survive? Don't you think you should have considered that before you tried to kill me?"

He cleared his throat. "I want you to uncover the traitor in my halls. I will not die by his hand."

"Or hers."

He shot me a quizzical look.

"Could be a woman, you know. Especially with as charming as you are."

I glanced up at the stars, unsure how the heavens or whoever lived in them had concocted such a convoluted mess to toss me in. "I don't understand. You said they're poisoning the humans to find out what *you* don't have a cure for. How does that tell them—"

"Because I heal them."

"I'm sorry, what?"

As if moving closer would help me hear him better, I stepped down to the path, blinking rapidly as I tried to assimilate what he'd just said.

"I heal the mortals when they're poisoned," he said plainly.

For several heartbeats, I forgot how cold it was out here. Heat flared in my chest as I stared at Casimiro, his hair and his loose shirt rippling in the harsh wind in a terribly distracting way.

Finally, I found my words. "How can you heal some of us and kill others?"

His hand slid across the back of his neck as he rolled his chin upward. "Do not worry yourself with the ways of the Shadow Court. Find out who is behind the poisoning, and I will tell you what you wish to know about your friend. But ask anyone else of your friend, and my magic will bind their words."

My chin inadvertently turned aside, as if I'd been slapped. "You really are a monster."

But the words felt less true now that I knew he was healing mortals. He could simply let them die and, in so doing, keep his antidotes a secret, but he didn't. He chose to save their lives at the risk of his own, and it bothered me to my core. He was a murderer. A wicked man. And yet he showed mercy.

To some.

Not all.

"But after I help you, you'll watch me die as easily as you'll watch me live." A small scoff escaped my lips.

He clapped his hand so hard on the ice-slick rock wall beside me that I yelped in surprise. "You mistake the reason I am watching you, Valencia." His breaths came fast and hot now, swirling in the cold night air.

For several seconds, I stared at him, unable to respond. My brow worked, trying to make sense of his confession. He *did* want me to die. Didn't he?

"Only so you can use me as a pawn," I finally managed.

He seemed relieved at my words, as his shoulders sank and his breaths slowed. "Here. Take this." He grabbed my hand and slapped something small and pointed into it. "Keep this in your pocket tomorrow during the trial and you'll survive. I'll find you when it's over. We've spent enough time out here."

Casimiro turned, and in an instant, his frame shook as his shadow departed from him, flying off into the starlit night. His body kept walking, vanishing quickly around a corner on the narrow trail cut into the side of the mountain.

I stood there in stunned silence, holding a small ruby in my palm and the memory of his arms around me, pulling me from the water.

# 22

## Zara

As I stepped outside into the frost-coated dawn, an anchor of dread dropped in my stomach. The dress that had insisted on being worn tonight was a luxurious purple ballgown with a daring neckline and heaps of ruched fabric creating a sea of ruffles around my feet. Not exactly the type of gown one would wear for a survival trial that involved running, but the dress did have long sleeves, a fact that I relished as the bitter air stung my cheeks and neck.

The dress also had small pockets hidden among the folds of fabric, almost like the dress knew I needed a small place to store the stone, and inside one of those pockets rested the small ruby Casimiro had given me. The entertainers had been summoned to assemble in the arena below, and I knew I must descend the steep stairs. But I couldn't quite bring my feet to cooperate, to march me toward a deadly trap.

I reached into my pocket and rolled the small stone between my fingers, letting the facets prick at my skin. What lay below was designed to kill me, but the heir had assured me I would survive.

Trusting him felt wrong. I took a step forward. Trusting him could turn out to be a massive joke he and his shadowy friends would laugh about as my body rotted on the sand. Another step. The memory of Casimiro's arms around me as he'd pulled me from the waters of my homeland both chilled and warmed me, and I took three more steps down toward the arena. He *had* saved me. Perhaps he would again.

The way his veins had turned black and his face had pinched with pain pricked my curiosity. He was an immortal, yet he suffered from something he couldn't heal, even with all the potions and spells at his disposal. And he too faced an enemy who wanted him dead.

This felt oddly like it placed him on the same level as the entertainers now assembling in the arena. I burned to know what sort of ailment flowed in his veins, and why he couldn't heal it. His sister seemed overly chatty for a fae princess. Perhaps I could finally accept her invitations to duel and have the chance to talk to her, get her to reveal what plagued Casimiro. But it wasn't Alba I wanted to talk to. A flip of dread mixed with excitement rattled my already frenzied heart as I pictured speaking to Casimiro again. He had the information I wanted about Talia, and I would find out whatever he wished from the mortals in order to hear what had become of my dear friend.

I'd reached the bottom of the long stairway. The arena sands, painted gray with dawn's meager light, waited before me.

My legs felt like lead from the running they'd forced me to do yesterday. We'd been chased by rats that would climb up our legs if we stood still. That was enough to get me sprinting through the sand.

My stomach growled at me, but I ignored it, casting my gaze around the dimly lit arena. The stands were beginning to fill with fae in all states of dress and varying degrees of mental stability. Their night of revelry must have been one for the record books, and I shivered with disgust. Two fae with twisting horns and sparkling dinner suits stumbled down two full levels of stone benches, laughing as they tumbled.

Ivy wrung her hands as she stood on the final stair before the sand. Eudoria had already marched quietly into the arena, her face to the approaching dawn. Tomas, Samuel, and Adán stood near the entrance, their heads close together as they exchanged whispered words. Strategies.

I glanced over at Ivy. "Together," I whispered. She nodded at me, her face pale.

The energy in the growing crowd was reaching a fever pitch as the fae prepared to watch the trial. Goblets of wine clanked in loud toasts, and the volume of the laughter increased as the darkness faded.

My upper lip curled. "Heathens," I breathed, tearing my eyes away from the fae as they tipped forward and back in riotous laughter.

Ivy shot me a warning glance, like I might possibly offend these deplorable fae.

"Hey, over there," Tomas said, pointing behind me.

I swiveled on the last step and spotted two people throwing punches a few rows up. Both were wearing the white servants' tunics. One of the men bent to grab something from a nearby fae. A flash of silver caught the light as he stood and slashed at the other man.

Ivy pressed both hands to the sides of her face. "What are they doing? Somebody stop them!"

Tomas climbed up from the arena into the stands, leaping over the stone benches two at a time.

Samuel crossed his arms and stared at the fight. "The fae probably provoked it. They're itching for blood."

"Be careful," I called to Tomas.

Before Tomas could reach them, the larger of the two men charged his opponent and jammed a knife into the man's stomach. I turned aside, unable to watch. Ivy tugged my arm, and I clung to her.

The wounded man fell to the ground. Cheers rang out from the fae in attendance. My head throbbed, and my chest felt like someone was crushing it.

"Isn't anyone going to help him?" Ivy pleaded, but no one was listening.

Behind us, Samuel chimed in. "The fae love this, don't you see?"

Ivy gripped my arm tighter, and I hurriedly scanned the crowd for Casimiro. He healed mortals. Perhaps he'd heal this man too.

Then I caught myself. Casimiro was the enemy.

"What is it?" Ivy asked, watching my shifting expression.

I gave a small shake of my head. "Nothing."

As I watched helplessly from the huddle of fae and mortals pressed in a ring around the wounded man, Casimiro's words blared loudly in my head. *You mistake the reason I am watching you.*

"Ivy, in the trial, if—"

But before I could tell her she should stay close to me, a fissure opened up in the crowd, allowing Casimiro a pathway to the bloody scene. Felipe flanked him, and Alba trailed behind them, her attention floating across the crowd and up into the sky, as if she barely noted our presence.

The prince's gaze scraped across the arena, pausing briefly on the man holding the knife, then the wounded man, before flitting again to the rest of the people present. His eyes moved quickly until they landed on me, a flash of relief loosening his tight scowl. He then continued his scan of the crowd.

Heat shot up my legs and arms, despite the cold dawn air.

I turned away, angry at the way my mind was in danger of sinking back into its old habit of assuming the best about someone. I'd assumed the best about too many bad men. I had to remember that Casimiro thought of me as nothing more than a tool. Something to use and dispose of. That was my only value to him—that was why he didn't want me to die. I was no more to him than the limp toy I'd seen him throw to his pet hellhound.

The servant holding the knife lifted his shoulders as the prince neared, but he didn't drop the weapon. Casimiro snapped his fingers, and the bloodstained knife jerked free of the man's hand and hovered in the air at his neck, pressed to his flesh with magic.

The man swallowed and lifted his chin away from the blade.

"Cas, let him be," one of the fae beside the prince said. He was shorter than the rest, his skin the purple-gray hue of a fading sunset. His blue eyes were bright against his odd features, like stars in a night sky. "This is the best thing I've seen all week—save that pretty one's dance." His attention flashed to me, and he sneered. Gooseflesh washed over my skin.

Casimiro inhaled slowly. "Fine. But clean up this mess," he ordered the murderer. As he turned to go, he fastened two ebony eyes on me once more.

"Time to go," Erik beckoned, waving his arms and hustling us down onto the sand. He always accompanied us to the arena.

As the six of us shuffled to the center of the arena floor, the fae whistled and catcalled. Magic sparked in the air.

"We've tasted blood now," Erik cooed as he herded us forward. "You all better not disappoint us."

A fae with skin almost as dark as the stone surrounding us snapped his fingers at me from the front row of benches. I'd heard someone call him Manuel. "I wager she'll kill to stay alive."

His words fixed to my mind like shining black leeches, sucking away my confidence and composure. Would I kill to stay alive? The thought had never crossed my mind, and I hated that it did now, along with a flash of heat in my throat that suggested he might not be wrong.

I reached forward and grabbed Ivy's hand, tugging her back to walk beside me. "I won't hurt you," I whispered into her ear. My fingers squeezed.

She squeezed back, her thin fingers stronger than they looked. "I know."

My shoulders lifted.

Ivy cleared her throat and added, "The magic of the arena changes people. Best not to think about it too much after." Her hand slipped from mine, and she smoothed her hair back.

"Magic?" I pressed my hand to the pocket containing the ruby, desperate for it to work and keep me alive.

Ivy flashed me a pinched-brow look. "They can cast enchantments on us while we're in here. Or on the arena. Or on the objects they give us. On all of it. Or none of it. The only rule is that they can't kill us...directly."

The ruby in my pocket called to my fingertips again, but there were too many eyes watching, so I kept my hands at my sides as we turned to face the audience. Our footsteps squeaked in the sand, whereas Erik walked silently, a ghost leading skeletons to their graves.

"I'm not dying today," I snarled, glaring at Erik.

He flashed me a smile that glowed white against the surrounding gray. In his hair, small twisting vines appeared, growing straight out of the air and reaching up into an impressive crown of leaves and stems.

I'd thought the long-sleeved dress would help me stay warm, but this icy morning had claws that raked my cheeks and chest. Curling inward, I wrapped my arms around my body and prayed this torture would be over soon. But I wasn't sure who or what to pray to. Many Avencians prayed to the sun, some to the stars, but now that I was here, in a place the sun had no power, I didn't think it was worth my time. Ivy's words about the First and Last flashed through my mind. She'd said all power gifted to the fae came from this deity I'd never heard of. If he had power over the immortals, he must be truly omnipotent. I worded a quick prayer to this god I didn't know, hoping he cared for little mortals like me, whose lives were but a breath.

The laughter and the chatter of the fae drowned out a fainter sound I couldn't place. A quiet *whoosh-whoosh* that didn't match the silence of the still air.

In the brightening sky above, a dark shape floated across the few remaining stars—a dragon, wings spread wide. It was high above, uninterested in us, it seemed. I watched until its small black outline disappeared behind the cliffs.

"Did you see that?" I whispered to Ivy.

"A dragon," she said with a nod.

"I thought they caged them all."

"Oh, no. The dragons hate the fae. And so the fae capture some of them and train them like horses, just to prove they can."

What I wouldn't give to be free like that creature right now.

My eyes fell and landed on the sole figure standing in the rows of stone benches, arms crossed, feet wide. Casimiro's expression was hidden in shadow, but the faint light of dawn rested on his shoulders and shining hair. When he'd rescued me from the water earlier, he'd worn nothing but an unkempt white shirt, but now he wore a shining black jacket over it, his first button still lazily undone. On his head sat the black crown. He was speaking to Alba, a smile on his face, and I found that I couldn't look away.

"Zara, remember. They can enchant us," Ivy warned from nearby.

The words snapped me back to reality. The trial. Casimiro was about to try to kill everyone standing in the sand but me. I couldn't think of him as *attractive*.

Ivy stuttered a little, then crept closer. "Do you know St. John's wart?"

I lowered my arm and turned to her. "It's a plant. Ariana said it can help ward off enchantments."

The stands continued to fill with other fae prancing in to watch us bleed from whatever perils the heir had cooked up for us. One female fae crept in on all fours, dressed like a white tiger, with actual whiskers and—if I was seeing correctly—a tail.

Ivy nodded. "It can ward off enchantments for a brief period. The mortals here all clamor for it, but it's hard to get. The servants are the only ones with access to it, and they don't give it out freely. Everything here costs something, and these fae value secrets above all else. Pay for St. John's wart if you can, and take it before every trial. If I'd had some left, I'd have given you some, but I haven't gotten hold of any in weeks."

The stands were mostly filled now. Drinks sloshed as glasses clinked. Laughter rolled down over us. Dresses and suits sparkled in the dying starlight, and the sickly-sweet scent of the fae's spiced wine drifted down from the crowd.

I nodded at Ivy. "I will." If I could find that herb, I would feel much better about talking to Casimiro again—and maybe the twisting in my stomach that happened every time he approached would dissipate.

"The games are about to begin!" Felipe shouted. He lifted both arms from his position beside Casimiro and held them aloft until the crowd grew somewhat silent. "Cast your enchantments now."

With a satisfied inhale, Felipe lowered his arms and rubbed his palms together.

Sparks of magic and howling laughter filled the dark arena. Ivy bent down and vomited. I raced to her, but my feet stopped moving mid-stride and anchored to the sand, sending my arms pinwheeling. I pumped my arms, but my feet wouldn't budge. Panic seized my lungs, making it hard to breathe. In my nightmares, I could never run forward.

My eyes cut to the heir. How could he possibly think I'd survive a trial where *running* was required if my feet were cemented to the ground? Hatred tingled in my toes and warmed my blood as the grates leading off the arena slid open.

From the darkness came howls and slavering sounds. Two black hounds raced out into the fading night, fangs bared, hackles raised. Cold, burning fear shot through me.

The first dip chased Tomas. My heart flipped as I watched the dog take him down with ease. I couldn't run, but I could throw. I bent to take my shoe off, but my foot wouldn't lift. The sand scrunched under my foot, and I frantically tore at my shoe until it wiggled free in the soft sand, my foot never moving from the spot. I threw the shoe at the dog as it bit at Tomas's leg. It whirled on me, and I recognized its scarred face. It was Diego, the heir's pet, and it charged toward me.

That was stupid of me.

Ivy screamed. Laughter and cheers poured from the stands.

The hound's red eyes paralyzed me even more than the magic holding me down. For a moment, I considered praying, but I still didn't know who might be listening or why they'd want to hear from me.

In two more breaths, the dog would be on me.

Sheer lunacy drove me to open my mouth and shriek, "Diego! Sit!"

The animal clamped its jaws shut and landed on all fours a handsbreadth in front of my leg. It sniffed my bare foot and my skirt, its nose hovering near the pocket that contained the ruby. Then it sat.

Relief flooded through me. Cas had kept his word.

Red eyes stared at me, as if awaiting my next command. The other hound was snarling and snapping its jaws at someone, but I couldn't tear my attention away from the monster at my feet.

My chest rose and fell so fast I thought I might startle the creature into attacking again, so I lifted a hand and muttered, "Wait."

Then I carefully bent down, slid my other shoe out from under my immovable foot, and held it above the ugly dog's head. Its ridged snout lifted as its eyes tracked the shoe. A snarl issued from its throat.

"Diego, fetch." I hurled the shoe, and to my surprise, the monstrous dog sped away from me.

I bent forward and braced my weight on my knees, whistling with relief. Peals of laughter cut through the awful sounds of the other dip attacking human flesh. I didn't look. Instead, I locked eyes with Ivy, who stared at me with an open mouth.

Then, to my horror, Diego returned with my shoe. He dropped it on the sand at my feet, where it garnered a nice layer of grit on top of the thick slobber already coating it.

The fae were shouting now, some in elation, others in anger, but I focused only on the beast before me. Soon, the second hound left its victim to stalk another. I noted its massive black form trotting across the sand toward Ivy.

"Not tonight," I growled. I grabbed the slobber-coated shoe and chucked it at the second dog, my feet still rooted to the spot. It missed, but the dog glanced my way. I didn't know its name, couldn't command it to sit or fetch. Would the stone cause both hounds to obey me?

The second dip stalked toward me.

Fear rose like bile in my throat. "Dieg—" I moaned, throat tightening. I coughed and pointed at the second creature. "Diego," I tried again. "Hunt."

The dog before me leaped to its feet, whirling to face his opponent. Or so I thought. Instead, the hound lunged for Tomas, who was jogging away from the creatures. I shouted and tried to jump, but my feet were still unable to leave the ground where they were planted.

As the second hound neared, I bent my knees and readied a fist to punch the monster. But as the animal's teeth nipped at my arm, Diego charged back toward me and leaped on my attacker, taking him down with fangs implanted in the other dog's throat. Faster than it took me to straighten my knees, Diego had silenced the second monster.

My hand flew to my chest as I stared down at the struggling black hound. The red light in its eyes faded, and when no light remained, Diego sat back on his haunches and looked up at the stands. A deep, resonant voice called over the din of cacophonous cheers and boos from the crowd.

"Diego! Come."

Casimiro stood in front of the tunnel entrance, his black boots in the sand where the mortals stood. He pointed his finger back toward the darkened cavern where the dog's cage lay.

Diego trotted off into the shadows.

The heir locked eyes on me, and a shiver traced down my exposed skin.

# 23

## Zara

Eudoria and Ivy sank to their knees while Samuel shot a fist into the air. In the stands above us, dark shapes burst from the fae like smoke from flames. The fae didn't seem concerned as they merrily danced their way back into the castle, arms waving and jewelry clinking. Adán didn't rise, and the smell of death hung over the arena, chilling my blood.

Despite my heaving chest, I forced myself to look at the fallen man. Bright light hovered on the horizon as dawn marched on, unconcerned with the life that wouldn't see this new day. The elation in the fae was palpable as they slithered back into their caves. Tomas, who'd fallen as Diego had attacked, labored to his feet, cradling one arm against his middle. He bled from at least two places, but he was alive. He nodded firmly at me and turned to ascend the stone steps, where a fae wearing a glittering golden dress waited for him with one arm extended. She wrapped her arm around his back and led him up the steps.

Puzzled at the sight, I didn't notice Casimiro approaching until his presence at my shoulder made me jump. Without thinking, I ran from him, since the enchantment was finally lifted. But my toes sank into the sand, slowing me down. Ivy was already halfway up the arena steps. She tossed a glance over her shoulder, her eyes wide with relief when she spotted me. She waited, stepping onto a stone bench as Tomas and the fae woman passed.

"Proceed." The heir's voice came from right behind me, startling me for the second time in less than a minute.

Ivy tensed but then gathered her skirts and hurried up the steps.

I whirled on him. "You picked those monsters because you knew I was afraid of them."

The growing light of dawn painted the princeling's sharp features with a soft light. His dark eyes flared with blue magic, the strangeness of it freezing me in place as he rose to stand directly before me on the steps, his face level with mine.

"I picked those monsters because I knew I could control them. I knew I could keep you *safe*, Valencia." His hands slipped behind his back, pulling open the collar of his suit. His neck had a sheen to it that was unnatural—and I couldn't help but swallow as I thought how smooth his skin must be.

I spun and raced up a few more steps.

Without moving around me, Casimiro appeared in front of me, his feet touching down as if he'd flown over my head.

Gasping, I turned to the side and raced down the length of one of the stone benches, turning into the tunnel several of the fae had used. But before I reached the door, Casimiro materialized, his arm propped against the slick stone, blocking my path.

A frustrated scream popped from my lips as I sought another route. Anything to get away from him—from how handsome he looked and how fast my heart was beating at his words. He'd helped me survive, but he was still fae, still the heir of this wretched place, and still going to try to kill me as soon as I helped him. I couldn't stand the sight of him. I hated that I was his pawn and that he held information about Talia over my head.

I hated that he'd saved my life.

Hated that he had a sliver of goodness in him.

That I *wanted* him to have goodness in him.

If he had no goodness in him at all, it would be much easier to forget what he'd just said.

At the far edge of the arena's seats, a path had been cut into the mountainside. I charged down it, trying not to look at the perilous cliff edge on one side. Up ahead, a short stairwell curled up and around to an even higher path. It led, eventually, to a balcony studded with flaming torches, not unlike the balcony adjacent to the heir's quarters. From this part of the path, nearly the entire mountainside was visible, as was the sprawling castle built into the rock. At the very top was a structure similar to the castles I'd seen in Avencia—tall stone walls topped with two towers limned with sunlight, like twin knives pointed at the heavens.

Momentarily awestruck by the sheer size of the castle, I didn't see Casimiro reappear in my path until I ran directly into him. He was black as night and made of whirling darkness—the same strange form he'd taken when he took me from my home.

I shrieked and backed away, nearly stumbling off the edge of the path. Casimiro grabbed my arms and steadied me. For several seconds, my heaving white breaths mingled with the inconsistent outline of his features. Then he solidified and I was again staring at the corporeal Shadow Prince.

I slapped his face.

He caught my offending wrist, but only for a second. By the time I yanked my hand down, he'd already let go. In my hand was a smooth, cold item. I backed away from Casimiro, placing my back to the stone wall on the side of the path farthest from the path's edge.

I lowered my arm and opened my palm, where a small vial, no larger than my little finger, rested. My eyes snapped up to Casimiro's. "What's this?"

"An antidote."

My fingers closed around the tiny vial. "For what?" I tucked that hand behind my back, just in case he tried to snatch it back.

"Enchantments."

My eyes had nowhere else to look but his face, which was too close. Despite the way he made me squirm, I held his stare. "And why would you want to give me this?"

"I need to know that you will not be...tampered with by anyone in my court as you go about your task," he said, the warmth of his breath brushing my chin.

A horrified scoff burst from my mouth. "Your court is foul, you know that?"

"More than you do, I assure you."

That answer silenced me.

He tilted his head, his loose hair falling across his forehead. My attention traveled to his mouth and back to his eyes, but not fast enough. One side of his lips curled up. "You managed just fine back there. Dips have the ability to smell magic, a convenient benefit of using them as spies. Diego took to you so quickly because of the ruby scented with my magic."

Heat flared up my chest, a mix of anger and something I didn't want to admit. "Do you want me to say thank you?"

"You're alive, so, yes, I assumed you would enjoy that outcome."

"*Adán* wasn't protected!"

He averted his eyes, and he raked one hand down his face. "I can't do anything about Adán. He chose to entertain, and his choice ends in death. If I heal him, my father will return. Immediately. And then you will all die."

I straightened my shoulders, putting my face a little closer to his because I couldn't stand the thought of cowering before him. "You are a murderer."

"The bargain and the mortal's subsequent choice are what kill the entertainers. You had the choice to live."

"So you saved me today, but I'll die after I help you. Not exactly excellent negotiation skills."

"Need I remind you that you are still alive because of me." His chest rose and fell faster now.

For a moment, I glared at him. "You snatched me from my comfortable life, made me into a death-defying circus performer for your creepy little court of nightmares, just so you could try to squeeze some fraction of feeling out of your dead heart."

Blue light pulsed in his dark irises, and I recoiled, ready for a spell to hit me, to punish me. But I felt nothing other than the mountain air biting at my skin.

"You humans think your weak hearts are the only ones that feel, but you—"

"No, you listen," I cut him off. "You live forever, and yet you find no joy in life," I pressed, unable to stop myself. "You crave death because you *need* the reminder that some things don't last, and yet it does nothing to push you toward goodness or purpose or happiness. I would be mad, too, if I had to live like this." I lifted my arms at my side. "If I had to live knowing my life could never have as much passion or purpose as a mortal's."

His hand had fallen back to his side. We'd moved away from the rock wall. Freezing wind encircled us, tossing our hair into our eyes and raking icy nails down my exposed back. Casimiro didn't seem affected at all by the cold. He stared down at me with an angry pinch between his dark brows.

"Enough," he growled. His eyes blazed with a different kind of heat, and I let out a small gasp.

I stuffed my hand into my pocket, drawing out the small gem. "Don't you need this back?" I held it out to him, then regretted the movement as the mountain air nipped at my side and a violent shiver shook me.

Casimiro's eyes flickered down my frame. "You're cold."

A laugh burst from my lips. "You live in a frozen wasteland."

"I tend to forget how the cold affects mortals."

I was surprised he had noticed at all. "I was born for hot weather. Coastline, bright sun, happiness." The memory of the waves rolling up onto the pebbled shores outside Leor brought a rush of warmth to my shaking muscles. "Which I fully plan to return to when this wretched year is over."

He tilted his head and narrowed his eyes. Then in a single movement, he removed his sleek suit jacket and, to my horror, swept it behind my head, draping it over my shoulders. The unexpectedness of this strange gesture, and the unfair way my body begged for his warmth still clinging to the coat, left me temporarily mute.

The tiniest flicker of a smile on his lips ripped me from my stupor. I yanked the coat from my shoulders and slung it over the cliff edge. It billowed like dragon wings on the breeze, floating up before it finally twisted and sank out of sight.

Casimiro cleared his throat and took his time rolling up both shirtsleeves before he responded. "You're welcome."

Before I could so much as blink, he fell backward off the path into thin air.

I screamed, but in another second, Casimiro stood on the path again, shadowy wings dissolving into nothing, his suit jacket sliding effortlessly back over his arms. I was so dumbstruck that I didn't resist as he stepped forward, as his arm reached up against the wall once more, one arm over my shoulder, the other slipping quickly into my palm that gripped the vial. His cheek brushed against my hair as he withdrew, twirling the vial in his fingers. He smelled so good—like cinnamon and the inside of a cozy wooden trunk. As he lowered his arm, I breathed in deeply, but the cold air washed over me, and my traitorous mind wanted him to reach back out and block the frigid breeze.

"If you do not want my help, I understand," he seethed, snapping my mind far away from his comforting aroma. "You did say you would never ask for it." He wiggled the vial between two fingers, then hid it behind his back.

"That's not fair!" I pinched my lips and stared where his hands had disappeared behind his waist.

"Fair?" He chuckled. "It wasn't *fair* that I gave you the antidote in the first place and no one else.

Desperate for the antidote and for warmer air, I tucked my hands in at my sides and shuffled my feet underneath me, thinking of a way to change his mind. "Why do you have to be so wretched? What pleasure does it bring you to be cruel to those weaker than you?"

For several seconds, he studied me with eyes I thought might light up with those eerie blue flames any moment. Instead, he withdrew the vial and held it at face level.

"You insufferable monster." I reached for his hand, but he pulled the vial back, out of reach. All that I succeeded in doing was slamming my chest into his and nearly losing my balance. I huffed in embarrassed frustration, trying not to think of how strong he felt.

His brows lifted.

I was about to demand he give me the vial when I recalled that I'd promised never to ask for his help.

Swallowing, I stepped away from him. "Answers. I will talk to the mortals and then I want answers."

"Very well." He took a few backward steps down the frosty path.

A small item flew toward me, and I caught it without thinking. The vial of St. John's wart felt warm against my fingers.

"Keep that."

"But I didn't ask—"

"Mortals don't have to speak to be easy to read."

I let out an exasperated huff, but he was already gone, evaporating into nothingness as I prepared to shout the rebuttal that died on my tongue. Cheeks flaming, I raced back the way I'd come, through the arena, and back into the dark mountain halls, clutching the vial of antidote close against my chest and wondering what under the heavens above Casimiro thought I'd communicated without using words.

# 24

## Casimiro

Two weeks passed uneventfully, with no report from Zara. I was growing impatient. She still roamed the palace, sticking more to the inside halls than the frozen outside ones. I yearned to know whether she sought another escape or simply the information I'd asked her to collect.

In the back of a seldom-used cavern reserved for the royal family's relaxation, I was passing the dreadful daylight hours attempting to read the ancient agreement set down between my father and the dryads who kept the forest at the base of our mountain. They had been lax in their efforts to keep the other lesser fae from wandering too near the border. And while our mountain was invisible to fae and humans alike, the magic of the border was detectable by any high fae if they came into direct contact with it. Fending off an attack from the Sun Court wasn't what I had in mind while Father was away. I had enough to worry about. But the wording of the agreement was so vague that my father could basically charge the dryads with breeching their bargain if and when he pleased. When I'd read the same paragraph three times, I gave up, letting the scroll roll up.

I sensed Felipe's approach before he rounded the little bend that separated the reading space from the rest of the small cavern.

He was in his shadow form, an odd choice considering the hour.

He was also in a hurry.

His billowing shadow form swirled away from his body in little black tendrils, almost like he would blow away if I sneezed.

"You look terrible," I said, standing to greet him. His shadow form was usually much stronger.

"I came this way because I couldn't leave my other location. And I thought you would want to know what I discovered."

"You know how I hate a dramatic buildup."

Felipe laughed, wisps of smoke peeling out of his black mouth. "I found your mortal woman outside the throne room."

A cough threatened to escape my lips, but I masked it by clearing my throat. "*My* mortal? Is that so?"

Felipe's darkened features cracked a smile. "You're the reason she hasn't been chosen as a table decoration yet. Admit it."

I shrugged. "If I am, I have my reasons."

In truth, it was foolish of me, but I couldn't quite shut down the feelings of rage that swept into my blood when I imagined her shoved in a cage. And yet, I was the one who'd brought her here, to this palace, a cage all its own.

"Your father will find out, Cas. And when he does, he won't make a charitable choice."

My expression hardened. "She's hunting for information about the poisonings," I admitted. "If she thinks I'm allowing her that kind of humiliation, she'll change her mind about helping me."

Felipe nodded. "I can see her getting angry about that. She's a fiery one. It's why you can't stop watching her."

The spike of heat flaming through my hands proved he was right. "You're wrong. She angers me."

"You can call it that if you like."

Blue light filled my vision as my magic flared in my veins. "I assumed she could learn something of value from the servants regarding who is planning an attempt on my sister's life."

Felipe finally had the decency to look down. "Of course. And your life. Don't forget yours is in danger, too."

I nodded. "Yes, but killing me early is a waste of poison."

Felipe coughed and pinched his brow. "And did she find anything yet?"

"Not yet." I stood and stepped around Felipe. "But if she's found the throne room, I suppose she needs rescuing again."

Felipe's shadowy features curled into a smirk. "She does. But there's no need for you to stop what you're doing."

Realization struck with a quiet jolt. "Ah. You plan to retrieve her?" A stab of unease shot through my chest. My father liked his throne untouched in his absence, and as such, anyone who touched the throne while he was away would suffer from a withered hand.

"What is she doing?" I asked, careful to keep my tone even and unconcerned.

"For now, only looking around. She hasn't approached the throne."

I scratched my chin. A beard was forming that I needed to remove. *What are you up to, little spark?*

"Want me to bring her back down?" asked Felipe.

"No." The response was too fast. I tried to recover. "I will see that she doesn't touch Father's precious throne."

Felipe nodded, hiding a smile. "Certainly, Your Majesty."

As I moved out of the small cavern, I wasn't sure if I wanted a reason to wrap my arms around her again or not. And the uncertainty of that brought a wave of pain as the curse surged in my blood.

By the time I reached the throne room, Zara was not there.

Her scent lingered on the cool air, and I searched for her with my magic. She was near, in the weapons training room.

*Odd*. She did all of her training outside, with the other entertainers.

As I approached the massive cavern, a smile broke across my face and I paused outside the room. Alba.

My sister's magic resonated against my own from inside the room dedicated to combat training. Had Zara finally agreed to spar with Alba? I hoped Alba hadn't used any coercive magic to push Zara's stubbornness aside.

Part of me wanted to barge in and watch, and part of me wanted to let it unfold. I hesitated outside the cavern. If she befriended my sister, perhaps Zara would not think of us all as monsters.

My hand lifted toward the handle, but I never turned it.

Because I was a monster. I'd never planned to keep Zara alive at the end of my Father's absence. Only Alba. Everything was for her, to keep *my sister* alive.

Everything Zara had said about me was true, and her words cut like knives, exposing me. I would search out the traitor in my court, the one who wanted to poison Alba and me, and I would do it without Zara's help. She didn't need to think of me as good, for I wasn't. Despite all my elixirs and potions, I had no antidote for my father's wrath. And if she was alive at his return, he would end her, without a doubt.

# 25

## Zara

Adán did not recover from his wound. Tomas, however, was back at the table with us by the night following the trial with no visible limp and his arm had only a scar that looked years old. I said nothing and asked no questions, knowing that I was only alive because of a deal I'd struck with the heir himself. If these others had made similar deals, who was I to blame them?

The fae cavorted with an extra measure of glee, but only for a night before their glamoured faces began once more to droop in boredom, fanning the flames of my hatred for them into a raging inferno.

At our table, Adán's empty seat gaped like a missing front tooth.

For days, the rest of us hardly spoke during our meals, which suited me just fine. I couldn't force conversation with these people knowing that I'd survived because of Casimiro's protection. I felt like a traitor every time my eyes paused on the vacant space at our table. The vial of St. John's wart sat untouched in my room, stuffed beneath my mattress, partly from guilt and partly because I knew I now had a powerful bargaining chip that might help me uncover the information the heir sought.

But days slipped by, and I couldn't bring myself to bribe the servants with the antidote. Every time I crawled back in bed I felt angry for not giving it to someone and angry that if I did give it away, it was only because of the Casimiro's grand plan to use me.

The weeks after the trial passed in a strange blur as my body adjusted to waking in the evening and sleeping in the day. At first, I slept in small bursts. Exhaustion would win, and I'd curl into my borrowed bed, fighting off nightmares of dips nipping at my ankles as I ran through a version of my garden back in Avencia, this one choked with brambles and filled with smoke. Then I would wake, march down to the arena for more *training*, which so far had consisted of being chased or fighting with wooden weapons, much the way I had once practiced under my weapons tutor's direction. The absence of Adán pressed like a suffocating blanket over our training sessions, reminding us what was at stake. Even Ivy said no more than a handful of words to me the entire week. I wasn't in the mood for idle chatter, either, except that I needed to uncover *something* useful for Casimiro before he would tell me about Talia.

And I wanted to know why his arms turned black. It hinted at a weakness, and the more I learned about this immortal fae prince, the more it seemed he was weaker than I'd once thought. So, I'd accepted Alba's invitation to duel, hoping to eventually learn more about Casimiro. She'd only come to collect me one time in two weeks, which helped me remember that time passed differently for these immortals. They were never in a hurry about anything. Sparring with a fae had proven every bit as maddeningly unfair as I'd expected, but, in the end, Alba had not hurt me, and I'd actually found myself smiling a few times.

In an effort to hold up my end of the deal with Casimiro, I'd asked Ariana about the poisonings, but she'd given me a stiff look and fastened my dress extra tightly that day, so I'd decided not to ask her again. And every other mortal I'd asked had given a similarly unhelpful response. Casimiro was right—the people here must have been silenced from speaking about this. To get the information, I would have to part with the vial of St. John's wart, but the closer we came to the next trial, the more I wanted to save it for Ivy, to at least keep her safe from enchantments.

One night after a training session, Ivy and I walked mostly in silence through a cavern we'd discovered that housed fascinating glowing mushrooms and equally mesmerizing crystal formations that twinkled in the strange light. This place reminded me of the whimsical illustrated children's books in my father's massive library. I missed the comforting reading space and the welcome feel of the library I'd left behind in Leor. I missed my own bed and the food I was used to eating in my home. I even missed Nina.

"Do you think of your family often?" I asked Ivy.

She nodded but didn't reply.

Speaking of home brought a tightness to my throat, followed inevitably by a sinking feeling that felt like guilt mingled with anger. I huffed as memories of Jorge barged into my mind.

"What is it?" Ivy asked. Her features were painted in a pale blue hue from the glowing fungus that climbed the walls.

"If I hadn't been so bad at reading men, I wouldn't be here right now."

Ivy tilted her head. "You don't know that love would have broken the bargain."

I chewed on that a moment. I'd believed so wholeheartedly that love *would* solve my predicament that I'd never paused to think of the fact that even if I had found true love before my twentieth birthday, I might still have been stolen away.

"Hmm," was all I said in return.

We made another pass through the cavern that was equal parts charming and eerie. Our quiet stroll was interrupted as Ariana hurried into the blueish light, glancing around several times before seeing us.

"There you are," she breathed, walking up to us with quick steps. "You need to come with me. It's time to get ready."

Ivy and I exchanged a glance. "Ready for what?" I asked. "More training?"

"Not training," she said, staring at the cavern's smooth floor. When she straightened up, her eyes locked on me. "You are to bathe and prepare for your first evening as a centerpiece."

My face fell and a shockwave of adrenaline spiked through my blood.

I'd seen the other entertainers endure it. Whatever grace period there might have been protecting me from this humiliation was now over. I couldn't fight the violent sinking sensation in my stomach. I bent forward, hands clasped around my middle.

Ariana cleared her throat. "I brought your chosen outfit to your room already. At least you get to wear a real dress, not just scraps of food. Be grateful."

I stumbled forward and clung to Ivy. "Grateful," I repeated as sweat broke across my forehead.

Ivy squeezed my hand. "They can't kill you tonight," she muttered. "You will survive this."

Ariana nodded firmly. "Come now, to the bath."

The baths were fed from natural hot springs that flowed from the heart of the mountain and housed in an arched cavern dotted with two dozen small pools carved from stone like everything else. The walls in the women's bathing chamber were etched with a pair of massive shadow fae locked in an embrace, their wings arcing from the ceiling and down each wall. Though the baths were more luxurious than any I'd ever seen or used, no amount of lavender oil, salt scrub, or floating roses could distract me from the horrible mental images I conjured as I washed. What would they make me do tonight?

I said nothing to Ariana as she led me back to my room, pulled a brush through my hair and pinned it up, and helped me into a form-fitting white dress entirely covered in glittering beads. Only as I walked toward the armoire to retrieve the small ruby from where I stored it out of sight on the top shelf did I break my silence.

"Ariana," I said as my hand withdrew with the ruby. When I turned around, one of her brows was lifted. The pointed facets of the stone dug into my skin as I rolled it between my fingers, deliberating.

"Yes?" she finally said, setting one hand on her hip.

"I..." I swallowed, briefly picturing what I was about to endure. The ruby in my hand had provided me with a sense of comfort these past two weeks, and I saw now that it was a lie. A pretty little lie cleverly meant to chip away at my resolve to stay strong, to fight back against the fae and their machinations. Casimiro was not my ally. He was a master craftsman wielding a tool he needed for a task. I was nothing to him, and the only reason he didn't want me to die was so he could glean information from me. Then, before I could change my mind, I stuck out my hand. "Here."

"What is it?" Ariana didn't step toward me.

"Take it. Before I change my mind."

She stepped toward the ruby in my outstretched hand, eyes widening.

"It's a gift," I said. "One that will protect you against the poisoner, whoever that may be." I assumed that if the stone had kept me safe, it would do the same for her.

She inhaled sharply. "How did you get that?" She didn't question its effectiveness, as if magical stones were a well-known commodity around here.

"I found it," I said. I had *found* it...in my hand when Casimiro gave it to me.

Her eyes narrowed quickly as she shot me a scrutinizing look. "Then how do you know what it does?" She took a step back.

I shrugged, not prepared to answer this. "I found it before the last trial. It's how I survived." Also true.

Her head tilted. "I see. And why do you want to give it to me now?"

"Because," I sighed, "you need it more than I do. I want to help."

Lips pursed, she took the jewel from my hand and examined it against the candlelight, almost like she'd seen stones like this before. She pocketed the ruby and squared her shoulders. "Thank you. But you really should have kept it."

With that, she turned on her heel and waved me forward.

We walked silently to the dining cavern. It had taken so long to bathe and style my hair that it was close to the midnight meal, the fae court's largest meal.

The massive cavern was mostly empty when we arrived, save for a handful of white-clad servants bustling about, placing food on tables and setting out wine goblets.

"Why are we here so early?" I asked, fighting the trepidation mounting in my jittery fingers.

Ariana bit her lips and pressed her hand against the pocket containing the stone. "You are to be standing there before any of the fae arrive, and sometimes they come early to start drinking."

"Oh. How nice."

Ariana's face pinched slightly, the first expression of compassion I'd seen from her. "I'm sure some will be early tonight, considering the heir is away. They like to revel a little more on nights when he's absent."

"Absent?" My voice cracked a little, but I quickly swallowed, forcing down the knot attempting to shut off my air supply. Giving Ariana the stone had been the right thing to do to, considering humiliation wasn't as bad as getting poisoned, especially now that I knew Casimiro wasn't here to administer an antidote.

"He's collecting another mortal, I believe," she replied.

Another human to torture, whether by lifelong servitude or months of deadly trials. I was no longer sure which was worse. "Where do I stand?" I asked. I was ready to get this over with.

Her head nodded toward a table near the center of the cavern.

The table was covered in heaps of grapes, cheese, roasted nuts, steaming platters of roasted lamb or slivered potatoes, and rice scented with saffron enchanted to never get cold as long as the fae wanted to eat it.

I cleared my throat and nodded, willing the night to pass quickly. Gathering my heavy, beaded dress in my hands, I stepped from the stone bench onto the table, delicately picking my way to the center, which had been left vacant, just for me.

Once in place, I shook out my hands, lifted my chin, and imagined I was awaiting a performance. That's all this was. A terrible, humiliating performance.

My eyes cut to the prince's table. It, too, was spread with food, which meant perhaps that Alba would dine there alone tonight. Even though I'd agreed to spar with her, I doubted that made us friends. My face pinched. No one would get me out of this. As no one had saved Ivy or Eudoria or any of the others.

The air in my lungs whooshed out slowly.

"I'm sorry you have to endure this," Ariana said before quickly striding away.

"Wait," I called after her. That was the nicest thing she'd said to me since my arrival. She turned around, hands wringing at her waist. "After...tonight," I said, scrambling for a reason to talk to her again, to attempt to forge a friendship with her. "I want to know what you were taught about *mal*—about people like me." I offered her a small smile, desperately trying not to cringe at my own words. It was a terrible reason to talk, but maybe if she knew I could respect her views on cursed children, she might be more willing to *change* those views and see me as a friend.

She blinked up at me, her eyes flicking from my face to the food displayed around me. Then she nodded quickly and fled the cavern.

After what felt like half an eternity, fae courtiers began trickling into the cavern. Fresh sweat prickled across my chest and back. Fortunately, the two fae who arrived first did not sit at the table where I stood. They never even looked at me, a relief.

Less than fifteen minutes later, another fae arrived, then another, and soon the cavern was flooding with shadow fae, some in elegant ballgowns and suits, others in attire stranger than any story I'd ever heard. One fae man who sat at my table had feathers all over his body, save for his face and the palms of his hands. A woman came laughing and dancing her way to my table with a dress made of tiny mirrors. As she took her seat, fragmented images of my reflection bombarded me.

Other than laughter and pointing and some rather unpleasant name calling, the table filled without anyone throwing anything at me or touching me in any way. They laughed and talked among themselves, but their sporadic insults were delivered with enough vitriol to make sure I never missed a single one.

The first glass of wine tossed onto my dress came as a complete shock.

The red liquid sloshed from the goblet onto the beaded hem of my white gown. I'd remained mostly stoic, only moving to shift my weight, but I let out a small shout as the fae launched into riotous laughter.

On the far side of the cavern, Ivy's head popped up as she watched me. I couldn't see her expression, but I knew exactly how she felt. I'd been angry when I'd seen her and the other entertainers suffer.

The woman wearing the mirror dress hurled a strawberry so hard that it splattered across my stomach. As they pointed and laughed, heat surged up my throat and burned in my ears and cheeks.

So that was the reason for the white dress. To provide a lovely canvas for the food and wine.

I glanced down at the items near my feet, refusing to meet any of the fae's eyes. There was a gravy boat of some sort and a decanter half full of wine.

Exhaling as loudly as a bull, I fisted my hands and told myself it would be over soon. But when the feathered man stood up and hurled his full glass of wine at my chest, I snapped.

My foot jerked out and kicked the decanter.

Spiced red wine flew all over the feathered fae and the man sitting next to him in a ridiculous yellow suit.

The edges of my lips curled up at their shocked faces.

But the taste of victory quickly soured as the feathered one lifted his hand and cut off my air supply with a silent spell. My hands grasped at my throat, but it was no use. I couldn't draw breath.

Purple dots swam before my eyes and I sank to my knees, knocking over the gravy and a plate of grapes.

When I sank onto my hands, the purple spots turned to gold flecks that blurred the table beneath me. I thought they couldn't kill me, but perhaps these shadow fae didn't bother with the rules while the heir was away.

Just as I was about to collapse onto the table, a loud voice rang out.

"Stop."

Air returned to my lungs.

Head splitting, I looked up to see Casimiro striding between the tables toward me. Without a word, he raked his arm across the table, scattering dishes and goblets onto his surprised courtiers' laps. He propped one foot on the large table and reached two hands under my shoulders. Drawing me forward, he pulled my limp body against his, then lifted me and set my feet on the floor beside him.

The wine on my dress stuck to his white shirt, staining it.

His eyes traveled down my frame, pausing at the strawberry smear and the other stain near my knees. Still lightheaded from lack of air, I gripped Casimiro's shirt in two fists as I heaved ragged breaths.

"Breathe, little spark. It's over now."

I nodded, swallowed, and nodded again. I glanced at the table of silent, shocked fae.

"Look at me, Valencia."

I did.

His dark eyes flared with a magical blue light, and I cowered, still unreasonably clinging to his shirt. He blinked and the light died from his eyes.

"Don't be afraid."

I was. I was afraid of them all. I hated them all.

In a deep and commanding voice, Cas spoke to the fae still staring at us. "You know the rules. You are not allowed to harm them outside of the trials."

Leaving his grumbling courtiers behind, Casimiro led me from the cavern amidst a flurry of whispers. I let him, though my one desire was to flee not just this cavern, but this wretched palace altogether. Perhaps I could find another door to fall through and never again face these vile creatures.

Outside the cavern, I could no longer contain the shudders that started in my chest and worked their way down to my toes. I hated how shaky I was, hated how good it felt to have Cas's arm holding me steady.

He stopped at the bottom of the stair leading up from the wide atrium. "You don't have my stone with you tonight."

"I gave it to Ariana."

Cas quirked a brow at me. "You gave the stone away?"

"She needs it more than I do."

“Do you really think so, after tonight?”

My fingers traced my throat, which still burned on the inside, but I didn’t respond.

"And you didn't take the St. John's wart."

I frowned. "I'm saving it."

“How am I supposed to keep you alive if you give my protection away?” he asked.

I turned so I could look him fully in the face. “I didn’t think you could kill me outside of the trials. I might not have given the stone away had I known you can.”

He flinched at the word *you*. Then his thumb rose and touched my shoulder, where sticky wine clung to my skin. Black lines bulged under his skin, racing up his hands into his wrist. His jaw muscle tightened.

I exhaled loudly at his touch, drawing his eye.

“I wish things were different,” he said as he turned away, eliciting a thousand unspoken questions in my mind.

Finally, I drew up the courage to ask one: “If you’re the heir, can’t you change what you want to?”

A quiet scoff escaped his lips. “Have a good evening, señorita Valencia.” He offered a quick bow and walked back toward the dining cavern, leaving me shaking and confused and unable to dismiss the feeling of his thumb against my shoulder.

# 26

## Zara

After leaving the dining cavern, I'd returned to the bath chamber to wash off the wine and the humiliation, and had sat in the hot water for so long that my fingers turned to wrinkled little raisins and the place where Cas had touched my shoulder had burned from how hard I'd scrubbed it.

But no amount of scrubbing could erase the memory of his touch.

I skipped the final meal of the night, and after an hour of attempting to fall asleep, gave up and got back out of bed. As I took the dress offered by the wardrobe, I reimagined, for the hundredth time, Casimiro's face as he'd walked toward me in the dining cavern. The way my heart had surged at his appearance. The way he'd held me upright until I could stand on my own. None of it made any sense. None of it fit into my plan to hate him endlessly.

The silver dress slipped over my head, and I felt as if I'd stepped into a cool spring. I ran my hands over the fine material, white pearls exquisitely sewn in a pattern across my chest that mimicked the sparkling light on a windswept pool. The immortals did appreciate the finer things in life, at least—anything to push back the relentless boredom of their long lives. Today's dress covered the spot of raw skin on my shoulder, for which I was grateful.

After grabbing the small vial from under my mattress, I glanced at the place I'd stored the ruby as I'd slept. The vacant place on the armoire's lone shelf reminded me I was without his protection now. I'd have to find the information he sought and return his favor of saving me. Then, I'd be free to forget about him. Which was what I needed to do. But as I left my room without his ruby, I felt a small twist of trepidation. The ruby's presence had allowed me to face the halls of Nightsong without fear.

I stole from my room on quiet feet, smiling at the blinding sunlight that glistened on the newly fallen snow outside the floor-to-ceiling windows. One floor below, a waterfall thundered with the sound of constant escape. The water had the privilege of leaving this place, every second of every day. Every time I saw the water fleeing this wretched mountain, it fueled my hope that I, too, might find a way out.

The halls were quiet, as usual during daylight hours, though a few servants shuffled here and there, carrying folded garments, pitchers, or a look of profound purpose. They never so much as glanced at me, but their chins lifted as I passed.

The shock of Adán's death had caused a more pointed silence among the mortals here, but I wouldn't let another day go by without attempting to uncover the secrets of the poisonings.

I nodded at a white-clad servant carrying a small stack of books and heading, I assumed, toward the library, a room I'd discovered during my exploration of the palace. The servant, a tall, thin man with tattoos up both arms, cut his eyes vaguely in my direction, but they never landed on me. He hurried around the corner, and I was left staring at an empty hall.

"Wait," I said, hurrying toward him.

He kept walking.

"Do you know where I can find Malik?" I called after him. I hadn't seen the man I'd met that first night in several days.

The servant paused and glanced back at me. "Malik was sent through a doorway the night of the full moon. Hasn't returned." The man spoke in thickly accented Avencian.

"Sent through a doorway? A magical one? Was he allowed to return home?"

He frowned at me, shifting the stack of books in his arms. "You are the newest one, yes?" The man shook his head. "Second-newest. The heir brought back another one last night."

"He did?"

"Yes. He chose to serve," said the man with an air of pride. "But as to Malik, I suppose you are still new enough to know the fae sometimes bring humans through the doorways with them to help with their nightly raids in the mortal lands."

A disturbed frown tugged at my lips. "Nightly raids?"

Now the man's expression drooped in annoyance. "The fae plague the mortal lands at night. You know this much, yes?"

I nodded.

"They take us with them sometimes, because they need mortal puppets, as they like to call us. And sometimes, we don't return."

"That's awful," I whispered, feeling the loss of the kind servant like a stone dropped in my gut. "This place is a nightmare."

The servant's lips tightened. "You haven't been here for one of their equinox nights."

I shrugged. "No." It was late summer, so the fall equinox wasn't for several weeks.

"They are worse than the new moons. But I suppose you may not live long enough to see one." He turned to continue walking.

"Wait," I said again, not wanting him to leave without a useful piece of information. "I know the servants are being poisoned." The man's steps halted again, but he didn't look back at me. Recalling Cas's words about the mortals being coerced not to speak of the topic, I held out the vial of antidote. "Take this."

The man stared at the item in my hand like I held a large diamond. Then his eyes narrowed. "I cannot speak of it."

I pulled the vial back and clutched at against my stomach. "I only wanted to ask if it's happened to you." Cas had said the ones who'd been poisoned didn't know who was behind it.

The man lurched forward.

"Tell me something," I said, tilting the vial back and forth like some wicked manipulator. At least the contents of this vial would protect him for a short time.

He frowned. "It has not happened to me. And the identities of those involved are concealed from our eyes." He cleared his throat. "I am sorry."

His arm twitched away from the stack of books. I swallowed and placed the vial in his hand. I sighed, dissatisfied with the information as my eyes flicked to the title of the book on top of his stack. *Herbal Remedies of the Southern Plains.*

"Was the heir reading those?" I asked as the man once again turned to walk away.

"Yes."

"Where can I find him?"

"Why would you want to?"

I schooled my expression as best I could. "Maybe I have a poison to test on him."

The servant coughed.

"So you do know something about it," I said.

The man took a few brisk steps, shaking his head as he went. As I hurried to follow, he shot me a puzzled look and said, "He was on his way to the weapons range, I believe."

I stopped pursuing him, resting my hands on my hips. "Thank you."

The door to the weapons range opened to a small tunnel that bored through several feet of rock before opening up into a cavern so smooth it must have been made by magic. No stalactites or dripping cave walls in here. The space was pristine, polished to a shine, and dotted with stone statues laden with weapons of every kind. The statues depicted male and female fae warriors in their shadow forms, wings lifted skyward.

Wide chandeliers—thankfully, not full of monsters—hung down the center of the arched ceiling, casting thin white magical light into every corner and illuminating two lone figures locked in a rapid duel in the far-left quadrant of the vast range.

I paused as I stepped from the tunnel to the wide, arched space, mesmerized by their blurred movements as they fought faster than my eyes could follow. One wore a white shirt and dark pants and had short hair. The other had long hair that paled at the ends and flung wildly around her twisting body.

My lips parted as the two royals jabbed, dodged, parried, flipped, and dove, steel flashing and grunts echoing. I realized then that Alba had gone easy on me in our sparring session the other day—*very* easy. Any human who chose to fight a fae in a real battle had lost before they'd ever begun. The memory of sticking an iron dagger in Casimiro's stomach brought an unexpected chuckle to my lips.

The figure in white paused immediately at the sound, his attention snapping toward the door where I stood.

His sister lunged directly at him with a victorious scream, but he was already gone, a wisp of smoke vanishing near the chandelier over their heads.

I blinked, and Casimiro materialized before me. Sweat matted his hair against his forehead and his chest glistened with droplets that drew my eye. His features appeared *different*, less polished, less glowingly perfect. Then he wiped the sweat with the back of his arm and his features smoothed to their former perfection. He'd had his glamour down.

And before he'd erected it again, I'd seen a pale line running from his throat past the collar of his shirt.

A scar.

This immortal had at least one scar, and I suddenly wondered where else he might carry the reminders of past wounds. Did he have a scar where I'd wounded him? He cleared his throat, and the muscles in my shoulders twitched, as if he'd read on my face that I was envisioning his abdomen.

"Valencia."

My eyes flicked up to his. Why was *I* sweating? I wasn't the one who'd been dueling. I smoothed the front of my flowy dress.

"I...I spoke with a servant but did not learn anything useful."

Casimiro's brow lifted. "You came here to tell me you learned nothing?"

My chin jutted upward. He was so much taller than me that when he stood this close I felt like a petulant child demanding my way. He likely enjoyed staring down his nose at me. "You did not give me any directions or helpful tips." My arms lifted briefly at my sides, but I quieted my unease and clasped my hands at my waist, the way a proper lady should. "You told me only that the servants can't speak of the one topic you ordered me to talk to them about. Seems a bit unfair."

Alba strolled quietly across the vast space, still carrying her sword in her hand. Casimiro's sword lay abandoned on the floor at the back of the room, appearing no larger than a needle from where we stood.

Casimiro leaned forward, his dark eyes narrow. "You'll figure something out."

"Don't you have magic for this sort of thing?" I hissed, feeling Alba's approach like a thief feels the approach of a guard. "Spells you can cast to force the truth out?"

"In certain situations, yes," he replied. "But I don't feel like lecturing you on the difference between a binding spell, a geas, and a curse, all of which can prevent someone from speaking."

I cocked my hands on my hips. "I may not be able to do magic, but I apparently can retrieve information *you* cannot, so I would refrain from the derogatory comments."

His lips quirked as his sister approached from behind, but he didn't break eye contact with me as he stepped aside to include Alba in the conversation.

Alba smiled and lifted her sword so the tip pointed at the ceiling. "Hello! Ready for another sparring session?" Before I answered, she looked at her brother. "You're right, she is good, for a mortal."

I glanced from her to Casimiro. His eyes darted away from me.

"I stabbed him," I blurted, feeling the need to prove that *for a mortal*, I'd been good enough to wound the prince of shadows.

"You *what*?" Alba said, turning to her brother with a gaping mouth.

"And shot him with an arrow," I added.

Alba used her free hand to smack her brother. "You didn't tell me that."

The fact that he'd said anything at all about me to his sister was shocking enough.

Cas turned aside, one hand moving to tousle his sweaty hair. "You wanted a sparring partner. You've got one. Now I can go."

Alba's face fell, then brightened quickly. "But we were having so much fun."

"You said it yourself, I'm too busy to do this with you anymore," Cas said, storming off toward the abandoned sword.

Alba winked at me, then hurried after her brother. She turned back and waved me forward. "Come on!" she whispered.

Cas glanced over his shoulder but only increased his pace. "If you enjoy winning, you'll have much more fun with her."

"She stabbed you," Alba said, catching up with her brother as I walked rather bewilderedly toward them both.

I should have turned around, gone back to my room, and awaited whatever torture was next. But I'd come here to tell Casimiro what the servant had said and to demand he give me some pointers for how to draw out this magic-locked information.

"I wasn't there to fight," Cas retorted.

"Oh, so you *let her* stab you?"

He didn't respond. "Use the wooden weapons." He pointed to one statue. In each hand was a wooden sword and strapped to it in a dozen places were wooden weapons of all shapes and sizes, from a battle axe down to a dagger.

Alba disappeared and reappeared in front of me holding the hilt of a wooden knife toward me. Her sword was gone, replaced by a wooden dagger of her own.

I was too stunned by her fast movement to respond immediately. Finally, I took the proffered dagger, mostly to get it out of my face. Casimiro lifted his sword from the ground with a single move of his foot and caught the blade in the air with his hand. He dissolved into shadow, and I blinked, furiously searching for him.

Alba pinched her lips and nodded toward a statue that now had a sword replaced in its upraised hand. Casimiro had put it there without me ever seeing him move, and he was nowhere in sight. My cheeks flared under her scrutiny. It didn't matter if Cas left without talking to me again. He was the heir of this court of monsters, and he had better things to do than watch us spar.

"You should speak to Ariana, your servant. In the confines of your room, she might divulge some information," Cas said from behind me.

I whirled around, the wooden dagger pointed toward him instinctively. "She hates me."

Cas tilted his head. "Even now that you've given her my ruby?"

"Her religion tells her that I'm not supposed to be alive, that my life doesn't matter."

"Is that so?" He clasped his hands behind his back and tipped his chin at me. "Then you will just have to prove to her that your life does matter."

The way he said it shook me to my bones. This was the same man tasked with ending my life for sport. He'd told me a mortal's life was nothing but a breath, a pointless little blip that could at least be laughed at by those more powerful. He certainly didn't think *my* life held any value.

"But..." I stammered, unsure how to respond or how to keep my heart from racing so much as he looked at me with those two dark eyes.

"Cas, catch," Alba said.

Cas's arm shot up, snatching the wooden dagger Alba had taken from the statue. His eyes never traveled to the weapon. They never even left my face. He twirled the blunt blade in his fingers.

"Shall we even the score?" he asked, eyes still on me.

My stomach flipped over inside me as the heir of the Shadow Court took a ready stance, arms out at his sides, knees bent.

"Are you serious?" I balked.

Alba clapped once. "Better move, Zara, or you'll regret it!"

Casimiro had already vanished. The flat side of the wooden dagger popped the side of my shoulder, alerting me to Cas's liquid presence moving behind me. I spun. Panic sprouted in my veins, and heat surged through every pore as sweat and desperation poured out of me. He was going to kill me. Right here. With a wooden dagger.

All because I'd offended him by stabbing him back in my garden.

Another pop on my other shoulder told me he was playing with me. I was just his toy. His sister cackled nearby, slapping her leg like it was the funniest thing under the stars to see a mortal flounder like this.

There was no beating him. Not if he could move instantly and disappear like rising smoke. But I wouldn't go down without a fight.

I spun away and sliced at the flicker of white fabric blazing past me. My wooden dagger whooshed through nothing but air, but Alba squealed with glee. Tracking Cas as best I could, I turned, dodged, spun, and cut. Again and again and again I hit nothing.

Fury drowned out Alba's excited clapping, and I honed in on my circling adversary. He knew he had me beat, so he was merely prolonging the inevitable. The side of his wooden dagger slapped my upper arm, my ribs, my thigh.

Dead. Dead. Dead.

Or at least I would be if he'd wanted to kill me. I doubted I'd even bruise from the quick taps of the training blade. He was being gentle.

A frustrated growl peeled from my open mouth as Cas knocked the wooden dagger from my hand so fast I barely had time to blink before it clattered to the floor. I whirled on him and stomped my foot, my gossamer dress trailing behind me in the movement and hugging my legs as it finished spinning.

Cas stood still for a single moment, watching me with a slack posture that said he was temporarily stupefied by something. Surely not me.

"It's nice to dance with you again, Valencia," he said with a smirk, his sharpness returning.

I swiped my weapon from the floor and lunged at him, this time purposefully not hitting him with my dagger. I couldn't win by attacking a shadow. Instead, I anticipated his own jab, which I'd handed to him on a platter by exposing my ribcage. A good fighter wouldn't miss that mark, and he did exactly as I'd planned.

His dagger poked at my ribs, and I grabbed his arm, wrapping my hands around him and spinning into his chest until he was at my back. He was much taller than me, so the move was risky, but it was all I had. I yanked forward and kicked up with my hips, hurling his body—which was lighter than I'd imagined, over my shoulder.

My eyes caught the briefest glimpse of Alba staring open-mouthed in sheer delight as Casimiro flipped onto his back on the polished floor.

But I couldn't let go. Casimiro had gripped my arm in turn, and I was sailing forward before I could stop myself. The countermove brought me curling into a roll on the floor to save my neck from cracking.

By the time we stopped crashing across the floor, I lay sprawled beside him, breathing rapidly, fully aware of how close he was. He sat up and propped his elbows on his knees, staring down at me.

"Now we're even," he said through the curtains of his dark hair framing his face.

Alba's peals of laughter and happy clapping countered the thudding of my heart.

He chuckled as he stood up, then held out a hand as if to help me. I stared at his hand like it was tipped with dragon talons.

"Come on, Valencia, haven't I proven that I'm not going to hurt you?"

He had. And it unsettled me because I had no way to know what he would do. A fae who wanted me dead was predictable, was easy to hate. Casimiro was...neither of those. I tentatively placed my hand in his.

He lifted me so fast that my feet left the ground briefly before I found my balance. His grip did not falter as I wobbled, our hands clasped tightly between our chests.

"Steady there, little spark."

I coughed and backed away, unsure if the fae prince had just used a nickname for me or if he'd been attempting to make fun of me in some way. I tried to cram my loose curls behind my ears, but it was little use.

Casimiro bent to collect my wooden dagger from where it had fallen a few steps away, then he handed both instruments out to his sister, who took them with a small smirk and scurried off to replace them on the statue.

"What did you really come here to say?" Cas asked, carefully rolling up his sleeves where they'd come undone.

Words were difficult to form as I studied his forearms, ridged with veins. When he'd finished with one sleeve, he glanced over at me, quirking his brows.

"Oh, I—the servant I spoke with seemed to know something of the poisons." My cheeks had caught fire, and I looked away. "When I asked where you were, he wouldn't tell me until *after* I suggested I had a poison to test on you. Maybe he's working with whoever is poisoning them."

Cas chuckled and looked up at the ceiling. My eyes raked over the point in his throat down to his open shirt collar. Stars above, I couldn't stop staring at him.

"If he knows who is behind the poisoning, then I doubt he assumed you were involved," he said.

"Maybe none of them know," Alba said, materializing beside Cas. I started at her sudden appearance, and Alba giggled at my surprise. "I think whoever is behind this is working without the mortals' help. They isolate a servant, administer the poison, then leave them to die with a spell to erase any memories, should they live." She elbowed her brother. "Which, thanks to Cas, most of them have so far."

The word *most* caught my attention, as did Casimiro's flinch at Alba's words.

Alba cocked her head to the side, her long hair swishing beside her waist. "Cas usually finds them from the trace of magic left on them from the memory spell. But sometimes he's away and...the poison takes them."

"Alba," Cas chided, clearly annoyed at how much information she was revealing. She rolled her eyes. "Speaking to the mortals is still our best bet, for now. I know my court, and I know they employ humans to hide secrets." He stepped toward me. "Speak to Ariana. Giving her the stone might have been the smartest thing to do. She'll feel the need to return the favor."

I nodded and turned away, not waiting to be dismissed. I needed space to think, to breathe. With each step I took, however, the words *little spark* repeated in my head.

"You were wrong about something else," Alba said to her brother as I walked away. "You told me that all humans were weak."

The side of my mouth flicked up despite the strange reminder that fae hated mortals. She thought I wasn't weak. My calves burned from my hurried pace as I approached the small tunnel leading out of the large room. Behind me, their voices dropped to heated whispers, and I could no longer decipher their words.

The door handle cooled against my hand, and I yanked on the door.

A large hand reached over my shoulder and stopped the door from opening.

I didn't turn around, didn't let go of the door handle. I was breathing as hard as I had in the arena after a training round.

Casimiro's forearm brushed against my shoulder as he kept his hand on the door, preventing my escape.

"Don't listen to her," he said, his voice low and closer to my ear than I'd have liked.

"Let go," I said.

"She's never really spoken to mortals, and all she knows of them is what our court has taught her."

"What you taught her."

Cas huffed, his cinnamon scent washing over me. "I too believed all mortals were the First and Last's proof that we were not his worst creation. It is a myth we shadow fae cling to, trying always to prove it."

My hand nearly slipped from the door handle, but I regripped it and kept pulling against Cas's hold. "Believed?" I nearly choked on the word.

"I'm starting to change my mind."

To hide my small gasp, I yanked harder on the door. Cas removed his hand, and I darted back out into the vaulted space bracketed with wide stairwells leading up and down. I wouldn't stop until I was outside in the freezing air, bathed in blazing sunlight. Outside in the sun, I felt strong and safe. The shadow fae wouldn't pursue me there.

My feet raced almost as fast as my heart as I scurried up the wide stone steps, away from the heir and his sister, trying to escape from the strange twist in my chest that his words had caused.

# 27

## Zara

Hours later, I sat on a soft settee beside Ivy in the large room designed to offer us diversions that would weaken our resolve to hate the fae. Sleep had evaded me all day, and my tired eyes drifted as my mind wandered, again and again, over the words and actions of the fae prince since he'd dragged me from that table. In this smaller room—half natural cave, half constructed walls—were bookshelves, a piano, easels and paints, couches for reclining, and even windows that let in the starlight. Of course, we were only allowed to use this room at night, when these fae would accompany us, mixing that which we despised with that which we loved—a brilliant tactic that had likely worked on many a mortal who'd come through these cursed halls.

"Did he hurt you?" Ivy asked, looking up from a sketchbook in her lap. She nodded at my hand. "You keep holding your shoulder."

My hand slipped down into my lap, where a book sat, unread. I shook my head and said nothing, again feeling Cas's thumb as it had peeled from my sticky skin. The book sat ignored in my lap, my mind replaying *him* over and over and over—him leaning against the rock behind my head, him dueling with me, him saving me from that awful humiliation, him whispering that he was changing his mind about mortals.

"Zara," Ivy said, tearing me from my memories. "Look." She nodded at the room's entrance. My eyes traveled toward the door, though my mind remained in a daze. "You said you were waiting to speak to Ariana. There she is."

"Oh." I blinked at the closed book in my lap. "Yes."

I stood and placed the book of poems on the table beside the settee. Ariana noticed me and walked across the cool cave in our direction. Every room here was cold, cooler than my father's estate in the dead of winter. Stalactites hung from the roof's highest point, but as the cavern wall sloped down, the fae had hollowed out more space, and the floor was cut to be perfectly flat save for several wide steps that led from the doorway down into this room.

Ariana approached me and offered a stiff nod, her most polite greeting to date. We were making progress.

"Care to join us?" I asked, indicating the sitting area where Ivy sketched. Eudoria occasionally joined us in here as well to pass the night hours, but she'd fallen in our last training session and twisted her ankle. She'd elected to rest in her room this evening. Samuel and Tomas were playing cards at a table in the far corner of the cavern.

Ariana shook her head. "We are not allowed to enjoy this room."

"Forget what they say," I said.

Her brow tightened. "Unlike you, I am not safe from their tempers. If I break the rules, I'll get punished."

My arms folded as I built a rebuttal that included last night as evidence I was not safe either, but the feeling of Cas pulling me from the table and setting me beside him somewhat nullified my point. I hung my head, wishing I could shake these thoughts of Cas.

"But at least you're safe now," I finally said, hoping to get back in her good graces by reminding her of the gift I'd given her.

Ariana sighed and nodded firmly. "Yes. Thank you. You said you wanted to know what I was taught about *malditos*." At my nod, she continued, "But what I was taught isn't important." I opened my mouth to respond, but she waved my words away. "Last night, I was..." She shivered and started again. "Last night, I was in the hall alone, taking your wine-stained dress to the laundress, and a shadow approached me. It circled me, then moved on." She exhaled slowly. "I think whoever it was thought I would be a good target for poisoning, but the stone protected me."

"Oh, Ariana." I stepped forward, about to wrap my arms around her before remembering she didn't like me. I tucked my hands at my sides. "I'm so glad you're okay."

"Me too." She nodded several times, not meeting my gaze. "I—thank you." She finally looked up at me. "You are meant to be alive, Zara. And without you, I might not be."

Tears stung my eyes, but I blinked them back.

She stepped closer and, to my shock, reached out to embrace me. When her face was beside mine, she whispered, "The fae are stealing from the dragons." Then she pulled back and tucked her hair behind her ears.

I swallowed and realized she'd just shared a secret with me. I couldn't help but glance back at Ivy, realizing too late how suspicious I was acting. I smoothed out my dress, then clamped my hand over my right shoulder again.

Ariana shot a warning glance at Ivy, as if to remind me that someone else was watching us. "Gemstones," she said so quietly I almost missed it. Then she tilted her head, indicating I should follow her. But when I took a step, she gave a tiny shake of her head. "Wait, then follow."

A few minutes later, I could wait no longer, and I excused myself from Ivy, declaring how tired I was, and walked calmly from the cavern, only hurrying once I was alone. Ariana was offering me the first real information I'd gathered since Cas asked me to hunt for answers. How the gemstones were related to poisons, I had no idea, but I rushed down the main hallway back to the stairwell that led to the level of the library.

Ariana's white dress vanished from sight at the bottom of the stairs as she turned onto the lower floor. After a deep breath, I casually descended the stairs, forcing myself to walk slowly. She'd said to wait, then follow—she wanted me to see something without it looking like she was showing me. My blood buzzed with energy as I trailed her at a distance.

I paused at the base of the stairs to let Ariana vanish around the far corner, then I proceeded in her direction, assuming that any dark corner could have eyes watching.

Around the corner was another long, dark hall. The magical lights at this end had faded, but at the opposite end of the hall, a single pale light illuminated Ariana's white dress and red hair. Then, to my surprise, that light faded as well, plunging her into darkness as the one above my head glowed to life.

Ariana hadn't turned from the hall, and to my knowledge the only thing at the end of this hall was another stairway to the left and the library, its ornate entrance complete with double doors and an archway that glowed with ancient fae writing whenever anyone approached. The archway hadn't lit up, which meant Ariana hadn't entered the library, and she hadn't turned left to go up the stairs.

I walked forward, heart pounding. At the end of the hall, the light remained bright above my head. There was no sign of Ariana at the top of the stairs and nowhere else she could have gone. To test the library doors, I walked up to them. The letters emblazoned in the stone pulsed with blue light. So, they were still working. Ariana had simply vanished.

As I spun in the empty hallway, I noticed a small sparkle of light in the scene carved in the wall to my right. Set in one of the deep grooves of the artwork—this scene of a fae fighting a dragon in flight—was the tiny ruby I'd given to Ariana.

With the light above me, I didn't think I could grab the stone without being spotted, even though the hall felt and looked empty. Using the wall for support, I leaned down and pretended to fix my shoe. When I stood up again, in my fingers was the small ruby.

When a knock at my door awoke me the following evening, I was surprised to see a new face.

"I'm Sevienne," said a willowy woman with  and heavily accented Avencian.

"Where is Ariana?" I asked, dread mounting in my stomach.

Sevienne explained that Ariana had fallen ill with a contagious stomach virus. My chest constricted at the news. Ariana no longer had the gem, and she might have been poisoned. This woman quite possibly had been instructed to tell a lie.

Days slipped by without any additional information about Ariana. Sevienne was polite, but her Avencian was choppy and clearly difficult for her. She kept her conversation to a minimum.

I couldn't help but worry each day that Ariana did not return. I half-considered asking Casimiro if she'd been poisoned and if he'd healed her, but I couldn't bring myself to speak to him. His words had rattled me, and I feared the weightless feeling that washed over me every time I thought of him. I couldn't be feeling this way about the prince of shadows. It was wrong. And I'd vowed to never be wrong about a man again.

So, I busied my mind with imaginings about what Ariana had been trying to show me, and where she'd really gone. She'd left the stone for me, that I was certain, and there had been no chatter in the dining cavern about another poisoning. The mortal healer was reserved for the servants alone, as Erik had made clear in training, reminding us that if any of the entertainers were injured and wanted to be healed, our only option was to accept magical healing from the fae. Tomas had accepted this healing more than once, as had Samuel. Eudoria, however, had not, and her twisted ankle still plagued her—while my respect for her increased tenfold.

Since I couldn't find Ariana, all I could do was focus on uncovering where she'd disappeared to that day in the hall.

Between training, which alternately involved physical tasks like running and weapons training, I found reasons to pass by the library and peer at the etching in the wall, looking for gemstones or hidden door handles. But no matter how many times I checked, I never found anything there. The library had two small windows, leaving no room for the mysterious etching on the wall beside the library to lead anywhere but *outside.* So, after having no luck with the carving for several days, I took to once again exploring the network of pathways and balconies lacing the mountainside. This time, I wasn't looking for a way out, but a way *in* that I hadn't seen before.

Two weeks had passed since Ariana's disappearance, and while I wanted to find her, our next trial was upon us. Only as I arrived early for the first meal of the night, putting my back to Casimiro's table so I could avoid the magnetic way my eyes were drawn to him, did it occur to me that at dawn, I'd once again be facing a deadly trial. Neither Alba nor Casimiro had spoken to me since that day in the weapons room—almost like he was allowing me space to think about what he said. I was grateful for the space. But the next trial was upon us, and part of me wondered if he would again corner me to discover if I'd learned anything about the poisonings.

"It's been almost two weeks since I've seen her," I told Ivy as we exited the dining cavern. "And given what's happening in the morning, I can't wait any longer. I'm going to ask him about her."

Ivy glanced at Casimiro and his sister, who strode up the steps ahead of us. I'd refrained from telling Ivy what I'd seen in the hallway outside the library, as it involved the ruby Cas had instructed me to keep secret. Also, if Ariana was attempting to reveal a secret of her own to me, I didn't want to betray her trust by telling anyone, even Ivy.

"If you make them mad, you'll pay for it tomorrow," Ivy warned. She didn't know Cas healed mortals. She still assumed he hated us all.

I swallowed and hurried forward to catch up with Casimiro. As much as I hated to seek him out, he would know if Ariana had been poisoned. And he would also know if she'd survived.

Part of me didn't want to ask, afraid he would tell me she was dead.

I ground my teeth as I scurried up the steps, wishing Alba wasn't with Cas, and wishing my heart wasn't beating so mutinously at the thought of speaking to the heir again. He'd crafted another death trap for me and my friends, proof enough I was a fool to have any feelings for him.

The two royals heard me coming and turned, stepping away from each other in the otherwise empty hall. They said nothing as I approached, their expressions equally confusing. Alba watched me with a bright, close-lipped smile, and Cas stared at me with a flat, shuttered gaze. This place wasn't private enough, but I was out of time.

"Tell me what happened to Ariana," I said without pretense.

Alba blinked and looked at her brother.

"I believe she fell ill."

"Stars above," I breathed. "Don't lie."

"I can't lie."

I bit my lip. "She was poisoned, wasn't she?"

Alba rocked back and forth on her heels, and I tried to ignore her.

"She was not," he replied.

A tiny moan of relief leaped from my lips, but it was quickly replaced with dread. "Then where is she? Sickness doesn't last this long."

Cas shifted his weight forward, just enough to make me uncomfortable. "Do you know she isn't ill?"

I shook my head. "No, I'm not allowed in the infirmary. Entertainer, remember?" I snapped at him, attempting to remind him he'd planned another trial to kill us.

Cas didn't respond, but his stern jaw flexed several times, like he was fighting to remain silent. I peered at the two of them, then Cas turned away, one hand raking through his hair.

"Considering what you will face in the morning, I wouldn't worry about her," he said to me as he walked away. His words stung, but he glanced up at the ceiling, and my gaze followed his. I saw nothing there but shadow, but perhaps he was telling me we were being watched.

Alba sighed heavily and followed her brother, leaving me standing alone under a glowing orb in what appeared to be an empty hallway.

I had to find Ariana. If she'd been trapped behind that door in the passage below, she couldn't have survived for two weeks without water. My stomach dropped as I hurried down the steps, not caring at this point if a shadow was watching. I would open the passage, and I would find her.

The hallway outside the library was empty, or at least, it looked empty. The thick shadows at the far end of the hall couldn't deter me from running my hands over every inch of the artwork carved on the wall. I'd done this countless times already, hunting for a latch or hidden mechanism to no avail.

For what felt like the hundredth time, I pressed my fingers into the small indentation where she'd left the ruby. The cool stone did not respond to my touch.

I dug the stone out of my pocket, tucked it back where she'd placed it, and stepped away, expecting the image to shift or glow or open. Nothing.

A frustrated sigh escaped my lips, and I began tracing the artwork again, faster, my fingers having memorized its sweeping lines.

There.

Along one of the lines in the carved dragon wing was a hole that hadn't been there before. My heart skipped as I traced over it again. Had I not traced it a dozen times without the stone in place, I wouldn't have noticed the difference. But I was certain this was a new indentation. I pressed my finger into the small hole.

The entire image sank into the wall as the glowing light above my head blinked out.

I was plunged into darkness and shivered as the icy cold air washed over me.

Using my hands as a guide, I stepped forward. The stone wall swung open at my touch, and I tensed in shock as the wall gave way to a passage that smelled of snow and howled with distant wind.

On either side, rough rock walls formed a narrow tunnel that glowed with a dim light coming from up ahead. The light was so faint, however, that I could only see a jagged line where the tunnel curved to the right. I carefully hurried forward, bracing my hands on the walls, but before I'd taken two steps, I remembered that Ariana hadn't returned from her last visit to this place.

I backed out of the tunnel and exhaled loudly as my feet met the polished hall floor once again. Pressing one hand to my chest, I tried to calm my breathing as I stared into the darkened tunnel. As my eyes adjusted to the darkness, I noticed a strange shape at the base of the tunnel wall. I assumed it was the uneven rock, but as I squinted at it, I gasped.

The faintest tint of red hair met my eyes.

"Ariana!"

She was jammed up against the base of the tunnel wall, like she'd been shoved aside to let others pass. She wasn't moving, and her arm was limp and cold when I grabbed it.

But not as cold as a corpse would be. A faint pulse tapped against my fingers as I held her wrist. She was alive.

I tugged until she was sitting up in my arms and heaved her out of the tunnel as well as I could. She was taller than me, and her limp weight made it difficult to maneuver her out of the narrow space. As soon as we were in the hallway once again, I laid her gently on the smooth floor and stepped back, hands pressed to my head as I pondered where to go, who to tell, and how best to help her.

Only one face came to mind. I grabbed the small ruby from the carving and tucked it back in my pocket. The door quickly closed and solidified into wall once again. And as it did, the light above me glowed to life.

I told her unconscious body that I would be right back with help and raced up the stairs to find Casimiro.

# 28

## Zara

As soon as my hand touched the cool metal knob of the heir's private quarters, a wave of nerves raced up my arm, lifting every hair and tickling the back of my neck. I was still full of adrenaline from finding Ariana, that was all. I took a deep breath and glanced down at the stone in my hand one more time. He healed mortals. He'd given me the stone. He would help. He *would*. I had to trust that he could heal Ariana.

Before I even knocked, the door cracked open, and Cas peeked out at me. His brows lifted and he propped one elbow up on the doorframe, waiting for me to explain myself.

"I found her. She's not dead, but she's unconscious."

His arm lowered and he pushed the door open wider. "Whoa, slow down, little spark."

"Ariana. She's been trapped in there for two weeks. I don't know how she's not dead, but we can't waste any more time."

Cas tilted his head. "You said trapped."

"Yes, in a secret passage."

"Which one?"

"It's outside the library."

He rubbed his chin, where dark stubble was growing. "The dragon's lair."

"The what?"

He stepped into the hall and closed his door. "You said she's *in* there?"

I nodded. "She disappeared in there two weeks ago—that's when they said she fell ill. It took me that long to figure out how to open it. It's all my fault."

Cas shook his head. "She can't be in the dragon's lair. Nor in the tunnels that lead to it. I've had people in and out of there this week, in preparation for—never mind. Take me to her."

We hurried down the hall, then down three flights of stairs, and finally arrived at the library's entrance. Ariana lay where I'd left her, still and pale as death. Her freckled skin had a blueish hue that made my stomach roil.

Cas dropped to his knees and carefully scooped her into his arms.

I reached forward to support her head as he adjusted her weight. Her neck was so limp.

Cas met my gaze. "She's in a suspended state. It is a poison."

"Do—do you have the antidote?"

"I do."

He moved up the steps as easily as if he carried a stack of papers rather than a limp woman. I was breathing harder than he was by the time we returned to his quarters.

My eyes lingered on Ariana as he set her gently on the floor, though I recalled having come through here after my attempted escape.

Cas stepped over Ariana and sat down at the desk, pulling a book onto his lap and resting his chin in two fingers as he pored over the contents.

I opened my mouth. "Is she...going to die?" That was the only thing that mattered right now.

He tilted his head back and forth as if considering how to answer. "Not if I administer the right antidote," he said.

"Then help her!" I shouted, pointing forcefully at Ariana.

"I need to check the quantity," he replied. "Magical antidotes can kill as easily as poisons if administered incorrectly." He dropped his fist and the book on his desk. "I've personally never seen this poison employed, as it is useless on fae. But the remedy will be in here." He pulled the book back onto his lap.

My brow pinched. "If it's useless on the fae, why did they use it? I thought the poisoner was trying to uncover what *you* couldn't heal."

He shot me a sideways glance then returned to flipping through his book. "Why, indeed. It seems this time, the poison was meant to keep this woman out of the way. Had she spoken to you about anyone involved?"

I shook my head, though Cas wasn't looking at me. "No. She showed me the secret passage, and that was all. Or at least, she showed me where it was, but it took me a while to work out how to open it."

Cas tapped the page before him, then stood and strode to his shelf. "So, whoever did this assumed she was *about* to reveal a secret."

"Why not just kill her then?" I said, staring down at Ariana's lifeless face.

"Good question. Humans who betray fae do usually end up dead." He pulled a vial from the top shelf and calmly moved to kneel once more beside Ariana.

I dropped to my knees on the other side of her. "They wanted me to find her," I said. When Cas flicked his eyes at me, I continued. "They knew she'd led me to the door, they likely knew I was trying to open it, and for some reason, they wanted me to find her like this."

Cas ran his hand down Ariana's front and side.

"What are you doing?"

"I think I know why someone left her like this." His hand paused at Ariana's right hip. He felt through the folds of her skirt at her waist, but before I could shout at him to get his hands off her, he withdrew a small yellow gemstone, cloudy and uncut. He held it up. "Someone is stealing from the dragons. This stone was hidden by a masterful concealment spell, which only a few fae can detect. Even my own magic didn't sense it, but I suspected a stone would be on her somewhere. Whoever left her like this wanted this stone to be found *by a human*, and they wanted Ariana to still be alive when it was discovered."

"Why? Why not just put the stone somewhere easy to find?"

"Because then anyone could find it, and I believe whoever did this wanted *you* to find it." He popped the cork off the vial with his teeth.

I clumsily lifted Ariana's head with one hand and tipped her chin up to open her mouth.

As Cas brought the vial to her mouth, he said, "No one here but you would care enough about this woman to hunt her down after a disappearance, even one so sloppily masked by a feigned illness. Fae can't lie about what happened to her, so by administering this particular poison, she was technically only made ill. And only a few fae know you well enough to know you would do this."

He poured the antidote into her mouth, his hand slipping into her matted hair, as if he'd performed this same motion many times. I pressed her jaw closed with my free hand and held my breath. I wiped a stray drop of elixir from the side of her face.

"She will live," he said, setting the vial on the floor and easing the servant's head back to the rug beneath her.

Only when we made eye contact over her quietly breathing form did I realize Casimiro's fingers were overlapping mine in the tangle of Ariana's hair.

I slid my hand out quickly, looking for somewhere to wipe the amber liquid.

Cas stood and offered me a cloth that I took without question. But as I rubbed away the yellow droplet, I noted the buttons and sleeves on the cloth he'd handed me. It was one of his wrinkled white shirts.

I tossed it back at him. He caught it against his chest, and for a moment neither of us spoke.

My heart was pounding, the only sound in the quiet room. I told myself the presence of the unconscious woman was making my pulse race, not the man staring at me.

"No one steals from the dragons without paying the price," he said, tossing the shirt onto his chair. "They are miserly creatures, and they hold grudges. They can also smell magic, which is why my courtiers employ mortals to steal the stones from the dragon hoard. Whoever employed Ariana to steal this stone wanted you to find her—and the stone—and knew they would be asked directly about Ariana's whereabouts during her absence." He stroked his chin as he set the vial on his messy desk.

"But who would want that? Why keep Ariana silent, and why now, and why would they want me to discover her?" I pressed my hands to my tired eyes. Tomorrow was the next trial, and the reality weighed on my shoulders, my only comfort the small ruby in my pocket.

Cas sighed and propped himself on the edge of his desk. For the first time that I'd ever witnessed, his posture slumped ever so slightly. "Dragons never forget a thief's scent, and in the same way they can smell our magic, they will now smell Ariana on you. I would have said this isn't much of a problem, but..." His words trailed off and he ran a hand through his hair not once but twice. "But your next trial involves dragons." His dark eyes met mine across the room, Ariana's body a silent barrier between us. The reminder that death lurked everywhere here.

"Are you saying someone *framed* me as a dragon thief right before a trial where I have to face dragons?"

Cas stood up. "That's exactly what I'm saying, Zara. Someone who knows how I—someone who wants you dead."

My eyes narrowed. "Don't you all?" He'd left something unsaid, but I didn't dare press him.

"Not all of us," he said, pinning me with his gaze.

My cheeks flamed, and I looked down at Ariana. I needed to remember who he was, and where I was. Staring at the pale woman on the floor cooled the rising heat in my blood. "Can't I just give the dragons their stone back?"

Cas shook his head, tossing a few long strands of hair into his face. "No, that stone has been depleted of its magic. Likely by whoever poisoned your servant." At my confused scowl, he sighed and continued. "All gems have magic in them—natural magic—the kind infused into the worlds when they were first made. It has leeched out of most substances by now, but jewels can hold on to magic much longer than other natural objects. It is for this reason, not their beauty, that dragons hoard them."

"Oh," I said, utterly unschooled on the subject of dragons and their hoards.

"Gemstones are one of only a few items we fae can infuse with our magic, which is what makes them valuable to us, but it is their inherent power that is most valuable, for that is a kind of magic we cannot reproduce. That stone's magic is gone now. The dragons won't want it." The heir shrugged. "You'll have to give them another one."

"I only have this one." I withdrew the small ruby Cas had given me.

His lips turned down. "Not that one. They hate fae magic. They'll only want one with inherent magic, and"—he ran a hand over his mouth—"we've mined all the gems from this mountain. There are none left here." Cas stared at me with unblinking eyes long enough that I felt a burning desire to fidget.

Finally, I could stand his heavy gaze no longer. "What do the dragons do with the magic in the stones?" I asked, trying not to worry about the fact that in a matter of hours I'd be facing the very dragons that thought I'd stolen from them.

He let out a low chuckle. "They don't do anything with it. They just keep the magic from everyone else. Dragons are not sentient in the way we are, but they are some of the smartest creatures that exist. To them, a jewel full of magic is to be protected from those they do not trust. Over the millennia, dragons have learned not to trust any creatures but themselves."

"Have you really never tried to earn their trust?"

Cas laughed again and looked up, giving me ample opportunity to stare at his stubbly jaw. "When they torch anyone who smells of fae magic, it's rather hard to do that."

"Don't some of you *ride* dragons?" I'd seen the fae flying from the mountain on the backs of the beasts.

Cas nodded. "The ones we steal as eggs, we cut the nerve that serves their fire ducts. They can't breathe fire at all."

"Oh," I said, grimacing at the thought.

"My kind likes power," he said with a small shrug. "We don't like knowing they have the ability to kill us."

"Then why live here, in the dragons' mountain?"

Cas stroked his chin as he answered. "My ancestors built the palace on top of this mountain long before this became our permanent home. Back then, all the worlds were still full of magic, and the dragons didn't hoard jewels the way they do now. We shared the space peacefully for centuries. It wasn't until the war between Shadow and Sun, the war that depleted much of the world's inherent magic and forced my ancestors into endless darkness, that we moved inside the mountain and the dragons began stockpiling gems. We needed darkness, which the mountain provided, and the dragons wouldn't abandon their home, stubborn creatures that they are. For a time, the shadow fae stole from the dragons, but if there's one thing that can kill an immortal fae easier than a poison, it is dragon fire when it is infused with the magic of untapped stones." Cas smirked at my look of shock. "When a dragon really wants to inflict harm, it will swallow a stone still full of inherent magic, and you don't want to be around for the fire that results. Flames like that can burn through rock and bone."

I tapped my fingers against my lips. "So you live incredibly close to the one thing most dangerous to you. Sounds a little reckless."

Cas's eyes flashed wide, and for a heartbeat I was afraid I'd offended him. Then he stepped over Ariana toward me. I walked backward until the door was close enough to touch.

"Reckless is what I'm thinking right now." He reached forward, and for a single panicked breath, I thought he might try to kiss me.

I squeezed my eyes shut and for some unearthly reason didn't try to stop him.

Then I peeked one eye open. He was standing right beside my shoulder, his arm extended to the now open door. Black lines stretched up his wrists toward his elbow and pain stood out in his clenched jaw.

"What is that?" I whispered, nearly touching his arm, before I caught myself and clasped my hands behind my back.

"My recklessness," he answered, his tone gruffer than it had been a moment ago. "I need you to leave now." His face was close, and his breath hit my neck in a way that made me almost forget I was supposed to hate this man.

I took a step backward, through the open door. "What am I supposed to do about the dragons?"

He lifted his arm, where the veins stood out like dark ropes against his skin. "This trial was meant to be simple. You'll be given weapons to defend yourselves, and your skill is enough that most dragons wouldn't bother you—they prefer easier game that doesn't fight back. But I chose that before I knew the dragons would be angry. And like I said, they hold grudges." His face tipped forward, and he stared at the ground. "You cannot let yourself get burned. I will find you a stone to repay them. Now leave. We are short on time."

Then he shut the door and left me standing in the dim hallway, the only sound my slow exhale.

# 29

## Zara

"Ivy!" I shouted across the hall as I spilled down the stone steps that emptied into the cramped hallway outside the small kitchen reserved for mortals to use in daylight hours, when fae were scarce. We'd agreed to eat in here before our trial instead of in the main dining cavern, with the bloodthirsty fae. Tins of dates and roasted nuts called to me, as did the smell of hot tea in Ivy's mug, brewed with the eternally hot water emptying from a small hole in the rock into a carved basin.

My friend looked up from her tea and a half-wrapped pastry. "Mm," she muttered, standing up from a small wooden table, her mouth full. "I waited for you," she explained, "but—"

"Dragons," I said, breathless from running through the halls. "We have to face dragons."

A crumb fell from the side of her mouth as she stared with wide eyes.

"And the dragons are angry because someone's been stealing from them." I closed my eyes to try to settle my whirling thoughts. But every time I did so, Casimiro's face flooded my mind's eye. His name echoed in the back of my mind like a drumbeat.

"Zara?"

I opened my eyes.

"How did you find out?" asked Ivy.

My cheeks instantly heated. "I—Casimiro told me. I found Ariana—she was poisoned—and he healed her."

Now Ivy's eyes widened so far that white shone around her dark irises. "But forget that. Do you have anything magical on you?"

"Magical?"

I withdrew the ruby. "Like this. A stone. Or a geas. Or a spell of some sort?"

As she stared at the stone, her expression fell. "So you do have one of those. The others were wondering about it after the last trial. Did he give that to you too?"

"I'm not taking it into the arena tonight. Dragons hate the smell of fae magic. I've already secured servants' attire for all of us for the trial. I'm not going to risk wearing these enchanted clothes."

Ivy's head bobbed as she stared off to the left. "Not long after I arrived, a woman approached me offering me protection if I simply remained silent about the—about—" But Ivy's tongue couldn't seem to form the words. The muscles in her neck strained, and her cheeks reddened, so she quickly gave up, exhaling loudly as her shoulders drooped. "And I guess I can't wash the enchantment off."

"No. I suppose not." We stared at each other for a long moment. "We'll make it through this," I said, grasping her shoulders. "We made it through the last one." *With the fae's protection*. This time, anyone with a fae's magical protection would make us the dragons' target. Casimiro had better return with a stone before the trial began, but even if he did, he was only bringing one stone. And there were five of us.

We were led out into the cold night an hour before dawn would break. The fae clearly didn't think this trial would last long. Samuel had to assist Eudoria up the steep outdoor steps, her ankle still causing her pain. Each of us wore a servant's white tunic, which had initially put a frown on

Erik's glamoured face as he'd assembled us, but then he merely laughed and said it would make us all the more visible to the dragons.

Great.

Even though Ivy and I had raced to the bathing chambers to attempt to dull the smell of magic on our skin—and, hopefully, so that I could wash off any lingering scents of Ariana—I didn't know if scented soaps would do the trick.

The lattice of crisscrossing stairwells, balconies, and narrow paths on the side of the mountain led us upward until we reached a set of stairs so narrow and coated with ice that they appeared forgotten. These impossibly narrow steps lacked a railing, and my fingertips grew numb as I braced my weight against the stone wall to my left. Behind me, Ivy whimpered quietly as she climbed. Eudoria managed to climb on Samuel's back, but I couldn't watch as he carried her up the treacherous path.

Eventually, the stairs became so steep that I had to use my hands to climb, like I did as a child in my father's house. Sadness pricked at my insides as I thought of what my father must be going through, thinking I would never return to him. *I'm coming, Papá. Just a little longer.*

At the top of the stairs, a flat terrace opened before us, banked on two sides by a low rock wall that drew my eye upward. The foundations of an ancient castle were perched atop the highest point on the mountain. This area must have once served as a courtyard. As my eyes scanned the moonlit space, I detected black statues gleaming faintly in the night, some with missing limbs and others toppled onto the wide space like downed soldiers. From this close, I could see that the windows in the castle were empty holes, dark sockets in a once grand façade.

A wave of nausea rocked my body as I looked around—there was nowhere to hide unless we could put our backs against the stone wall and somehow fend off the angry dragons. The rocks glistened from a thin layer of snow.

"Stand over there," Erik commanded us, forcing us past him on the stair. My stomach dropped as I maneuvered around him. "There are weapons waiting for you at the base of the wall. If you can make it that far."

He didn't accompany us onto the platform. As soon as all five of us stood on the exposed flat rock, Erik slipped into shadow and shot straight into the air. I quickly lost sight of his form against the star-studded backdrop, but I noted a wisp of black slither into one of the castle's open windows. Perhaps that was where the fae would watch this trial, safely in the comfort of their stone fortress.

I walked slowly, carefully, cautious of any movements or unusual sounds. After a few steps, the entrance to a massive cave came into view. It had been hidden by the outcropping of rock that formed the castle's foundation. A step later, I heard the sound of wingbeats.

"Ivy," I hissed, drawing her toward me. She was shaking so hard, I feared we might both fall on the slick rock. Samuel, who had already set Eudoria down, quickly took her elderly frame in his arms and attempted to run back toward the stairs that had led us here.

Tomas took a defensive stance beside Ivy and me. My heart soared at the sight.

"Know anything else about these beasts?" Tomas asked over his shoulder as a dragon's massive head came into view over the edge of the cliff.

For a moment, I couldn't respond as I stared at the enormous creature.

The glint of steel beckoned me toward the rock wall, but the sight of the dragon's yellowed eyes anchored my feet to the slick courtyard.

"They think I stole from them," I admitted. I'd already told the entertainers everything else I knew about the dragons, save this one detail.

Tomas shot me a concerned look, and Ivy's nails dug into my skin briefly before she dropped my arm and stepped back.

"Probably best," I said, pushing her behind me so that I stood between her and the dragon. Samuel had paused on the platform, his gaze cast back at the dragon.

The beast hovered in the air, sniffing with loud breaths.

For a moment, all five of us stood paralyzed.

Then Samuel cursed as he took another step and slipped on a slick patch of stone. He and Eudoria went down hard.

The dragon's head cocked to the side and its nostrils flared as it followed the sound and the movement. A strange rattling noise preceded the dragon opening his large jaws. Ivy gasped and dropped to the ground. Tomas and I lunged for the weapons.

Claws clattered on stone, and a strong breeze blasted my long white tunic up around my knees. I grabbed the hilt of a sword, its comforting weight offset by the blinding light of the flames that flared against the rock wall and reflected off the steel.

Instinctively, I lifted my hands to my face. Heat rushed over the terrace and knocked the air from my lungs. Ivy whimpered, and Samuel's deep voice bellowed in agony.

Tomas locked eyes with me.

Then I spun. The dragon perched on an old statue, one taloned foot wrapped around the shoulders of a stately figure, the other gripping its crowned head. Its wings were half-extended over the courtyard, and smoke curled from its snout. Its nose was lowered in the direction of the stairwell, where a few flames still licked a few stray spots of lichen on the rocks.

My chest knotted and I thought vomit might spew from my mouth. I couldn't see Samuel or Eudoria anymore. Samuel's screams told me he'd not moved fast enough.

*Cas, hurry.*

He thought I could survive this. He'd thought wrong.

If he didn't arrive with a stone, and soon, we would all be ashes and teeth.

"Ivy!" I whispered, trying not to draw the creature's attention.

From her crouched position, she pulled her hands from over her head and peeked up at me. She was a body length from the animal's wingtip. I waved her toward the wall, but as soon as she moved, the dragon turned.

A choked scream leaped from my throat.

"Together," Tomas muttered, his deep voice cracking a little.

I nodded.

He jerked his head forward, and we raced toward Ivy.

There were no cheers or taunts this time. The fae didn't want to draw the eye of this mad dragon.

I slipped on the slick stone and crashed to my hip, careful to hold the sword over my head. Tomas reached Ivy first and yanked her to her feet. The dragon stood tall, its wings cupping wind and flinging it back against us as it inhaled as loudly as a rushing river.

"It's going to flame again!" Tomas shouted at me, his eyes clearly panicked about whether to help Ivy or me.

"Go!" I shouted, clambering to my unstable feet. The dragon opened its mouth. Tomas shouted at me to run.

I glanced at the ice, and it gave me an idea.

Taking only a breath to decide, I hurled myself forward in the same move I'd used on my first night in this wretched place. I crashed to my knees, a little less gracefully than I'd hoped, then tipped backward onto my side, letting my momentum carry me across the slick surface.

The jet of flames behind me melted the ice in a single second, and then I was scraping across wet stones. The white tunic bunched, and my leg sliced on a broken paver.

"That did not go the way I planned," I groaned as I rocked onto my elbows. The sword in my hand scraped noisily over the stones as I drew myself to my feet.

Tomas and Ivy had reached the wall, where Tomas was attempting to shove one of the remaining swords into her hands. But she shook her head, her hands still cupped against her mouth.

The scorch marks from the flames darkened the pavement only a step away.

The dragon turned its attention toward me, stepping off the statue and bringing down the carved head with a loud crash.

Licking my chapped lips, I squared my shoulders and lifted the sword in both hands.

"Any time now, Cas."

I nervously began to tap my heel against the pavers. *Clack clack clack.* With this motion came the memorized pattern of a dance, so engrained in me that I didn't even realize I'd made another *click-tap* with my foot until the dragon snorted and I froze.

The dragon's honey-colored face cocked to the side, so much like a dog that I almost laughed.

"You like dancing?" I asked, my voice shaking. I stomped backward, flourishing the sword with a dramatic lift of my arm. At the sound of my heel clacking, the dragon's head tilted to the other side. I grabbed my tunic and tossed it as I spun, creating a flash of white against the endless black. I felt like a lunatic, but I figured I might as well try madness, since there was little else I could do against this beast.

The enormous animal watched me for a moment. Then the sound of wingbeats preceded the scraping of claws raking across stone as another dragon landed on the platform behind me.

A whooshing sound was the last thing I heard before pain lanced against my calf and ankle. I whirled and lunged.

The second dragon's flames had ricocheted off the stone and licked my leg. But the blade in my hands sank into dragon flesh.

The animal leaped into the air, and my blade ripped free. I scrambled backward, toward the wall. Tomas jumped in front of me as my back hit the stones.

With a jab at the larger dragon, he gave me and Ivy a single moment to decide which way to dive to avoid the next round of flames.

I shoved Ivy to the left as I flung myself right, hoping to draw the dragon's flames away from my friend. The creature huffed in annoyance as its targets diverged. I shielded my head with one arm as the dragon breathed flames once more, but this time, the flames didn't even reach my feet. They sputtered in smaller and smaller tongues of fire until the light winked out.

Tomas whooped and backed against the wall. "Must be running out!"

My back slumped against the wall, and I slid down, unable to bear the agonizing pain spreading up my leg. My vision started to fuzz at the edges.

"Cas," I whispered, sinking down onto the paved courtyard. I shook my head, angered that I was helplessly waiting for a fae to save me from a trial *he* designed. There had to be another way to survive. He'd said the trial was meant to be simple. That the dragons would have left me alone if I didn't have Ariana's scent on me. So much for the bath I'd taken, the salts I'd scoured my skin with.

Tomas shot me a worried look as I pushed myself to my feet. I was no warrior. I'd been trained to defend myself from other people but not dragons. The night I'd ridden toward danger with Talia, all to save a racehorse, had been the closest I'd come to needing my weaponry, but that night I hadn't even used a blade.

The pale-yellow dragon snorted and tossed its head, its wings spreading farther out as it balanced on its back legs. The second dragon, this one a dark color indistinguishable in the dim night, was howling as it circled above the platform, eager to repay me for its wound.

Ivy wept. At least she finally clutched a sword to her chest. She'd improved in her weapons training, but she wasn't prepared for this. None of us was.

I stepped forward, sword at the ready, but my injured leg wouldn't cooperate, so I shuffled out from the wall with a step-slide, step-slide. My heel clacked against the stones once more. The pale dragon turned one glassy eye down at me.

"I think it likes the sound," I muttered to Tomas. Three quick times, I lifted and lowered my heel, grunting as my injured leg bore my weight briefly.

The dragon snuffled, then shifted its weight. It almost appeared excited. Or agitated. I was no expert in dragon body language. For two breaths, the one circling in the sky stopped howling.

I tried to clack both heels, but my burned leg buckled beneath me.

To keep from slicing myself, I dropped the sword. It clattered like a trumpet announcing my surrender.

From my hands and knees, I stared up at the beast, determined to keep from gagging on the spit I couldn't swallow. My throat had stopped working.

"Not tonight," I begged through clenched teeth. *I'm going home. I'm leaving this place.*

Casimiro's husky voice as he'd commanded me not to get burned flitted through my mind, and I tried again to swallow. He wasn't here. He hadn't come.

"I didn't steal from you," I shouted at the dragon. My voice came out scratchy and weaker than I'd hoped.

The dragon dropped its snout closer to me and tucked its wings. I reached for my sword, but the animal trapped it with a massive, clawed foot. I clutched my hand back to my chest and attempted to scramble away from the enormous creature.

"What do you want?" I screamed. "I don't have the stone. I don't have anything!"

But the dragon wasn't listening. It was filling its lungs with frigid air. I assumed by the depth of its inhale that its fire had replenished. I was too close. There was nowhere to go.

As it opened its mouth, Tomas hurled his sword, drawing the beast's attention at the last second.

Flames burst from its mouth, and a scream tore from my throat. The fire blasted against the wall and arced over my head. The heat was so intense that I was thrown backward. My ribs ached from slapping the rock, but I tucked my hands over my head and curled my body into a ball where I'd fallen. The fire sputtered out and wingbeats signaled the animal was in flight. The smell of singed hair filled my nostrils, and the backs of my hands burned violently.

My mind slipped. I couldn't stop it. I couldn't hold on.

The world eased out of my grip.

# 30

## Casimiro

"Where is she?" I bellowed as my feet slammed down in front of Alba.

My sister stood among the crowd of mingling fae sipping from wine goblets beside the open windows of the old castle. Magic buzzed in my ears, in the faces of those present, in the wine, in the air. And nowhere in this palace could I sense Zara's presence. My magic couldn't feel her.

Alba looked up from her sparkling goblet but said nothing.

"Tell me what happened."

Her eyes flashed with concern. "Not here."

Leaning into her space, I growled at her ear, "Tell me *now*."

Alba's breathing quickened as all the eyes in the room watched us. I didn't care. Didn't want to waste a heartbeat on what they thought.

"She's alive," Alba whispered a second before she vanished.

I stormed through the crowd into the empty atrium of the castle, where Alba stood against the far wall. She was young, but she had inherited my father's magic, which made her powerful and fast. A barrier surrounded her that only I could sense—a concealment spell.

My gaze snapped to my sister's face. "Where?" In a breath, I crossed the distance, undeterred by the magic that would keep her unseen and unheard by the rest of my court—a perk of also inheriting our father's abilities. "*Where*, Alba?" The fact that I couldn't sense Zara's presence meant only one thing—she'd been burned by dragon fire. A fire of my own kindled in my blood.

"Cas," she hissed. "Look at your arms."

"Tell me where she is!"

The curse tore through my veins, shredding me like a scalpel from the inside. Humans couldn't survive dragon fire, even the smallest burns, if they were left untreated. The magic in the flames would eventually turn their blood toxic. I'd been a fool to leave—to trust I could return when someone here wanted to keep me away.

"Look at yourself! That's why I closed the doorway," Alba exclaimed, pointing at my hands. "Because you don't have enough sense to keep yourself alive."

Shock pulsed through me, dulling the pain for a brief moment. I clamped two quick hands around my sister's shoulders. "You did this."

I had known. I had sensed her betrayal in my room, hours ago, when Zara had stood there asking who would do this. When I'd pieced together that my sister was the only person who knew how I felt about Zara. The only person who would care about me enough to try to stop my feelings. And as I looked into my little sister's face, the face of the one person I cared for more than anyone else in the world, the stab of pain split me in two.

She gripped my forearm, her eyes wide as my balance faltered. "I was trying to help. You know what happens if your curse brings him home before we're ready." Her voice was thick with worry.

"She might die because of what you did."

"And you'll die if you go to her now, Cas. We both will."

Because if Father came home tonight, he'd kill us both. The antidote wasn't ready yet. It wasn't strong enough. We needed more time.

I shook my head. "I won't let that happen, Alba. But I can't let her die either."

Alba's mouth parted in quiet shock. "You really care for her."

A moment of silence passed as I tried to master the pain that would render me useless to Zara if I let it. I had to take control.

My sister tucked her hair nervously behind her ears. Tonight, strands of tree moss hung among the loose curls she'd styled into her hair. "I thought..." She couldn't seem to finish.

"You thought that if she died, I'd stop caring for her, and Father would stay away longer."

Alba nodded faintly, her eyes glistening brighter than before. In my words, she heard what I hadn't said. That even death wouldn't stop the way I felt about Zara. Admitting that shook something deep inside me.

"I've tried to show her that I'm not the monster she met a few weeks ago, but I've failed. All she can see is the danger I've put her in, especially after tonight. She hates me," I said.

"Cas, I'm so sorry. I was only trying to keep you alive. I didn't know it was..."

*Love* hung unsaid between us.

I pinched the bridge of my nose, willing the pain away. "All my life, I've been searching for..." My hand fell away. "I've been searching for her. Now tell me where she is."

# 31

## Zara

From a soft bed, I stared up at star-shaped chandeliers. Voices buzzed around me, but I recognized none of them. Pain danced down my leg and stabbed at the back of my hands. I was in a cave. Cool, moist air and knobby rock formations filled the chamber.

The palace of the Shadow Court. Nightsong. Cas's palace.

Memories tapped against my mind like strangers seeking shelter. I couldn't remember why I was here, or what had hurt me.

I recalled a woman's freckled face and red hair. A white dress. A wide underground lake. Dragons.

My lungs sucked in air, and I tried to sit up.

A cool hand pressed me back down. "There now, she's awake." A man with pointed ears and long blond hair stared down at me. He wore an exquisite suit woven with golden threads, and a beaded headpiece adorned his brow. He was vaguely familiar, but my mind wasn't filling in all the gaps yet.

"Leave me alone," I said in a raspy voice.

He glanced up at another fae, a woman with honey-colored hair and amber skin. She was so beautiful that her skin faintly glowed. No—I reminded myself—that was magic.

Large cushions had been stacked under me, and several fae lounged against other pillows on the cavern floor. A woman played a piano a short distance away, filling the room with a calming sonata.

As I took in my surroundings, foggy memories floated in. Snippets of the trial returned to me. The pale dragon watching me. Dropping my sword. Hiding from the flames. I glanced at my hands. Red blisters bulged across my skin.

"Can you stop the pain?" I asked, desperate for one of Cas's antidotes right about now. These fae had magic. They had the means to heal me, if they chose. I sensed several people watching me and heard a few giggles.

I propped myself on my elbows and took in the cavern and the fae sitting near me. A dark-haired fae still displaying shadowy wings grabbed my hand and pressed it to his lips. The pain in my wounds subsided with a wave. My stomach somersaulted, and my ears heated.

"You want to make the pain go away," he said. "I have just the thing." He reached for a goblet that a woman had extended toward him, and he brought it toward my mouth. "This will make all your pain go away."

Finally, an antidote.

"Where is Cas?" I mumbled as I took the goblet.

The fae exchanged a glance. "The heir is away, tending to court business."

"But he specifically asked that we take good care of you."

"He did?"

One of the fae women pressed her lips together to hide a smile, and I distinctly heard a snort from someone behind me.

A stab of doubt prickled through me, but fae couldn't lie, and I would do anything to stop this pain. If Cas had asked them to take care of me, I was safe. I lifted the goblet in my hands and inhaled deeply. It had a sharp scent, cinnamon and ginger and something stronger. This mulled wine had a lot more than simply grapes. I'd heard of the fae's spiced wine, but I couldn't remember exactly what else I'd heard about it. But if I'd heard of it, it must be famous. And famous must mean good. It smelled good.

The pain was making it hard to think straight. Maybe if the pain disappeared, I'd be able to remember more.

I brought the cup to my lips and took a small sip, afraid I wouldn't like the flavor. But as soon as the liquid touched my tongue, it traveled all the way down to the depths of my body and warmed me. "Oh," I said aloud, embarrassed at my exclamation but unable to contain myself. This was the most delicious thing I'd ever tasted. I took one more sip, a larger one. Several of the fae around me chuckled behind uplifted hands, but the man who had given me the cup smiled with such intensity, such desire that my entire body leaned toward him. I handed him back the goblet and he took it gently, careful to caress my fingers with his own as he passed the cup to the woman behind him.

I stared at my hands. The bulging blisters began to recede, and the skin across the back of my hands began to mend. I let out a small cry of relief, and then my head began to spin. I crashed back into the pillows as dizziness overtook me. The cavern spun as if someone had picked up one end of the floor and was going to flip it over, much like the dance floor I had been forced to perform on my first night here.

Ignoring the laughter all around me, I slammed my fist into the pillow by my head, willing the dizziness to go away.

"That's only the magic of the dragon fire leaving your body," one of the fae women said, suppressing a giggle.

A few people shifted their weight, and the pillows around me moved. Somebody was lying down next to me. My shoulders rocked back and forth.

"The dizziness will go away soon. Don't worry." A hand stroked my back.

And then a sound, different, louder, cut through the dizziness and mental chaos.

"Get your hands off her!" a deep voice boomed across the open space.

The hand that was stroking my back leaped from me like a frightened animal, and the people around me scrambled to get away. I still couldn't open my eyes against the reeling sensation in my head. Even the piano had cased.

I tilted my chin to get a glimpse at whoever was coming, and the entire world began to revolve again. I pressed my mouth into the pillow and groaned. Then, strong hands were turning me over gently, slipping underneath me, pressing firmly under my shoulders and knees. I shook my head, but the movement tortured my dizzy mind.

"Hold on, little spark," a familiar voice said. I knew this voice. I peeked one eye open as my face sagged against a man's chest. Cas's chest.

"You didn't come," I mumbled.

He coughed. "I tried. I was delayed. But close your eyes. I've got you now."

My body bounced and clunked against Cas as he carried me. The gentle swaying of my body kept the dizziness at the forefront of my consciousness. I wasn't aware of where he was taking me. My entire world was still tilting. But when we burst out into the sunlight, my eyes popped open, and I looked around.

Keeping one arm looped underneath my shoulders, he dropped my feet to the ground, where my shoes met tall grasses. I stumbled against him, pressing a hand to his chest as I gained my footing. He gripped my arm with his free hand, steadying me.

"You should sit down," he said, guiding me to the warm grass. We were in the middle of a large field atop a small knoll. Horses grazed in the distance. A breeze tousled his hair and rippled over the ocean of green grass.

"Where...?" I was so dizzy, so confused, so cold, despite the warm air. My head hurt, and my body ached.

Cas sat beside me, squinting in the bright sun. "Rest for now. The sun will help."

When I was settled on the ground, Cas's arm slid off of my back, taking its warmth with him.

"Wait," I mumbled, barely able to form the word properly. "I'm freez..." My loose lips couldn't finish the sentence before I tipped sideways, my face smearing against his warm shoulder. For a second, he didn't move, then he wrapped his arm around me once again. I tucked my face against his chest and breathed deeply into his crinkled white shirt. The comforting scent of cinnamon and cut wood washed over me, soothing me. My tired body melted against his.

With nothing to lean against, Cas rocked backward as my weight sagged against him. When we were lying on the grass, my face pressed against him, he shifted so that I fit in the crook of his arm and propped his other hand under his head.

"Cas," I mumbled, trying to sort through the shuffled thoughts in my head and feeling a strange desire to express them all. "I have to go home. I have to make it back home. Can't you take me home?"

His chest expanded underneath me. "I can't do that, Zara. The bargain still has power over you."

To my shock, he stroked gentle fingers down my back and a sudden, strange thought occurred to me. If I went back home, I'd never get to feel him do that again.

"I'm not what you think," I said, exhaustion weighing heavy on me but still feeling the need to explain myself. The fact that I couldn't see his face made this easier. Or maybe it was the wine. "You wanted me to break, but I'm already broken," I muttered, thinking back over the mistakes I'd made over the years. "I've been broken for years, and I'm afraid that's why I keep messing things up."

His hand paused as it traced lines up my back.

"The sunlight will help," he said again, his voice as firm as the muscles under my smushed cheek.

My body shook with chills and the strange dizziness rattling my mind. He pulled me in tighter, and I tipped against him. As my arm wrapped around his middle, it occurred to me how wonderful this felt, and how I'd never felt safer. Sleep overcame me, and I dropped from consciousness.

When I next opened my eyes, I groaned as my muscles moved from the awkward position of being draped against Cas as we lay on the ground. I glanced briefly around at the sunlit fields and noticed a manor house tucked way in the distance. Cas shifted, looking over at me. The sunlight struck his eyes in a way that made them look lighter.

I struggled to sit up, to pry myself off of him. What in all the worlds had I been *thinking*? He was the shadow heir, not a lounge chair.

And yet, he'd held me.

He sat up, raking a hand through his hair to rid it of the grass that clung to him. His cheekbones created shadowed ridges in his face, and I was struck by how handsome he was. I glanced at the back of my hands. The burn marks had vanished, leaving only a faint pinkish hue where they'd been.

"Sunlight helps the effects of the wine dissipate quicker," he said, his voice rumbling through my bloodstream as panic set in. Ariana had warned me not to drink the wine, but in my confused state, I'd thought they were merely giving me something to ease the pain.

I'd *slept* against him. And he'd *let* me. My mind spun, and a dull headache pressed against my temples. Cas had carried me here. Carried my limp, inebriated body to a place I could sleep off whatever I'd just drank.

"Aren't you weaker in the sunlight?"

His mouth pressed to a hard line. "I am. But it makes you stronger."

I blinked at him, trying to make sense of his words, of why my heart was beating so fast. I couldn't let myself feel this way around *him.* "And the burns?" I asked, examining my leg, which was a deep red, tinged with yellow in places.

Cas rubbed the back of his neck and stared at the ground between us. "The burns have only begun to heal. They won't fully heal for weeks, and that's only if you can get all the poison out of your bloodstream." He glanced up at me. "I healed what I could, but you require magic I don't have. I'm not an expert healer. When we leave here, I will take you to the infirmary, where you will rest until your wounds heal."

Trying to look casual, I lifted my chin. "Where is here?"

He smiled, and for a moment, I forgot that I had been burned by poisonous magical flames. "See that house over there?"

I squinted in the direction he indicated.

A massive stone house sat in the distance. Two barns stood in the wide fields on either side of us.

"That is the home of your friend."

A choked laugh spewed from my mouth. "Talia? She's alive?"

He nodded. "And happy, if one can believe the reports that have arrived from the recent goings on in the Sun Court. I can't take you past the boundaries of the estate, as her husband's magic prevents my court from trespassing, but I thought you might want to see where she lives. She married a very powerful high fae, my equal and my court's ancient enemy."

Covering my mouth as both joy and sadness bombarded me, I tried to stand, accepting Cas's help as he hurried to steady me. When I glanced down at his hands, I gasped.

"Your hands."

Snaking black lines covered his forearms.

"Cas," I whispered, a sinking feeling in my stomach. My eyes flicked toward Talia's house once more, a massive estate of flowers and horses and sunlight—a beautiful place that was better than even the best of my imaginings. But my attention quickly traveled back to Cas, to his arms, his face. The skin around his eyes was tight. His muscles looked taut, and the veins on his arms stood at attention. "You're in pain," I said, feeling rather stupid for my pronouncement. It seemed utterly preposterous that a fae with as much power and influence as he had would sit in the sunlight with a mortal while he was in so much pain. "Shouldn't you go inside?"

For a moment, he didn't answer, but the muscles in his jaw flexed several times. The skin on his face was turning pale. Then a doorway appeared out of nowhere, nothing more than a dim rectangle in the otherwise bright scene. He stumbled toward it, and I moved with him.

"I need..."

His words were cut off, and all of his muscles went limp. As his heavy body teetered, I couldn't move fast enough to extricate myself from him. Together, we crashed sideways through the door.

# 32

## Zara

We hit stone and freezing cold air swallowed my face and shoulders. Cas moaned and rolled to his elbows. I scrambled to my feet, blinking to clear my head and steel myself against the discomfort of my throbbing headache and dully aching leg. "What do you need?"

"In...side."

I grabbed his shoulders and hauled him the rest of the way through the door, my spike of adrenaline the only thing keeping me going. When his feet passed through the strange doorway, it vanished, depositing us on a windy balcony outside of Nightsong. The starry sky was black, with no hints of daylight in the east or west, and I had no idea how long I'd slept in the sunlight on the other side of that magical door.

This time, oddly enough, I was relieved to be returning to the shadow palace once more. Taking hold of his booted feet, I swiveled him around and pulled. He scraped across the balcony's rough stone floor.

"Ow," he moaned, reaching up for his head. "What are you trying to do to me?" His arm was solid black all the way to his elbow.

"I'm trying to help you." I stood and planted my hands on my hips. "But you're too heavy." I was exhausted, but he'd helped me when I'd needed it.

He curled around on himself. His skin was so black now that he looked like he was turning into shadow.

"Help me stand," he said.

I curled my arm under his and heaved upward. It was little use. With a few heavy breaths, I pulled him into a seated position and then shifted my weight so that I was somewhat under his shoulder. From there, I pushed myself up as he shuffled to get his feet underneath him. He was thin but strong and currently so limp it felt like I was lifting an unconscious racehorse. One of his inky black hands steadied himself along the rock wall behind my head.

"Can you take a step?"

He shuffled one foot forward.

"Good. Okay, another one."

A few laborious steps got us to the door, and after another two, we were inside his room.

I peered toward his study through the archway across from us, remembering walking through a magical door in his study the night he'd grabbed me from the waters. But instead of the carved doorway that had been on the wall the last time I was in here, I saw only a burned black scar on the stone wall.

His bedroom was large but not vast, and his massive bed lay in an alcove along the wall to the right. I wondered if he could feel my heart beating against him as I led him toward the bed. That seemed like the most logical place for him in this state, though the thought of him lying in bed in a room that I was also in made my skin tingle.

As I leaned forward to push him onto the bed, I stumbled. My hips crashed into the mattress, and he tipped onto the soft blankets. I backed away quickly, but his hand grabbed mine before I was too far to reach.

"No," he said. He rolled so that he could see me, my hand still gripped in his. "I need you to get something. The antidote."

I could barely hear him over the sound of my own heart beating.

"In the other room. Small bottle. Clear. Top shelf." As I stepped away, he tightened the grip on my hand. "No, wait. It's on my desk." Then he dropped my hand, and I raced toward the archway that led into his study.

I glanced at the place Ariana's unconscious body had lain as I rushed to his messy desk. Half full bottles, some corked, others not, littered the space atop books and loose papers. One book had a vial crammed inside, possibly functioning as a bookmark, and another had only the sleeve of a white shirt draped through it. The rest of the shirt was wadded up at the edge of the desk, and it had clearly been used as an inkblot at some point.

"Stars above," I said, as my hands hovered over each bottle, searching for one that was clear and small. Small must be relative, as the largest bottle was still half the size of a typical bottle of wine. Finally, I settled on grabbing two bottles, both clear, both smaller than the rest on his desk. One was full, the other half-empty.

I ran back to the bedroom. He had pulled himself fully onto the bed and was lying at the edge. I raced toward him and held both bottles up to his face.

"Which one? They're both clear." He glanced between them and grabbed the half-empty one in my right hand. I set the other one onto a small table near the bed, then wiggled the stopper out of the one he'd selected. "Do you need to sit up?" I said, instantly reaching for the back of his head to cradle it. His head was hot, feverish.

I lifted his head a little and brought the vial to his lips, barely tilting it, as I wasn't sure how much to administer. He grabbed my hand and shoved the bottle up, taking one giant gulp. A few drips ran down his chin as he pulled the bottle away.

"Save the rest," he said.

I crammed the stopper back in, but he didn't let go of my hand.

His eyes locked on mine. "I'm going to need one more dose," he muttered, his voice rough. "You're going to have to stay."

I shook my head. I didn't like where this was going.

"Zara. I need you. The pain," he inhaled sharply, wincing. "The pain has never been this intense before."

"What's happening to you?"

"If the lines make it to my heart," he ground out between gritted teeth, "it'll alert my father, and he'll return—and he'll kill us both for what I just did. But I can't take too much antidote at once, or that too will kill me. Wait an hour and then give me more."

His eyes fluttered shut, and his grip on my hand relaxed.

For a moment, I stared down at him, hoping he'd rouse and say something else—anything else. My heart trembled in my chest at his words.

I gently pulled my hand from his and set the vial beside the full one on the table. For several long seconds, I stood there, hands crammed in my messy hair, staring down at the sleeping fae prince, surprised at how badly I didn't want him to die.

Then, I sprang into action and reached for his arm, pushing his sleeve up to examine where the black lines ended. I pushed the sleeve as far as it would go, but the lines disappeared beneath his shirt. His skin was boiling hot.

One hour. I only had to wait one hour before giving him another dose.

I wasn't certain how I could tell when an hour had passed, so I stuck my head back out the balcony door. I marked the first colored hues of dawn and the place where the light grew stronger behind the mountain's jagged peak. I didn't want to administer the antidote too soon or he might die, and it would be all my fault.

But what if I waited too long and the magic—the curse—called his father home? I didn't feel equipped to do this.

Cas had asked me to stay, so I would. He'd waited with me in the sunshine, despite how uncomfortable it must have made him. I cringed at the thought that I might have drooled on him. But hitting my forehead with my palm wasn't going to change what had taken place in that grassy field. I would stay for one hour.

I paced the room, my arms crossed over my chest and my eyes constantly flicking to Cas's form as he quietly breathed. But after four revolutions around the room, a new sound sent a wave of panic down my spine. His body began to twitch on the bed. First his legs moved, and then his arms and chest joined in. Awful gagging sounds issued from his mouth, and I ran toward him. I tried to turn his body onto its side so he wouldn't choke on his saliva, but his jerking movements flopped him back down again. I ran back out to the balcony, but the light had barely changed. It had only been maybe a quarter of an hour.

When I darted back inside, the twitching had stopped. "Cas." I touched his shoulder. "Cas?" I shook him. There was no response. His face had gone slack, his mouth partly open.

Panicked, I grabbed the collar of his shirt and ripped at the first button. I had to know if the black lines were already at his heart. I tore the buttons open and pulled the shirt aside. No black lines touched his chest, so I pulled farther and farther until the fabric of his shirt was all the way off one of his shoulders. There. I could see the black lines. They were at the top of his bicep reaching into the curve of his shoulder, not yet at his heart, but they didn't have far to go.

Relieved, I hung my head and focused on his steady breaths. My hand still rested on his bare chest, and for the briefest moment, I didn't remove it.

What was happening to me?

Memories of the night I'd shot him in my garden played through my head, followed closely by the memory of how well he'd danced.

The fae I'd met in the garden had been nothing but a handsome trickster to me. But now...

The fever had soaked his hairline with sweat. I stroked some of the hair out of his face before moving to pace the room once more. After a few minutes, another fit took him, this time only lasting a few seconds.

The shaking stopped by the time I reached him. I inhaled deeply, trying to calm my own heartbeat.

To feel useful, I whirled around and marched back out to the balcony, marking where the sunlight limned the mountain. I didn't think it had been more than half an hour.

I paced, trying to count the minutes and memorizing every detail of his personal quarters. The rug was mostly purple with silver patterns, not unlike those I'd seen in Avencia, though the pattern was more floral and less geometric than the current style at home. His furniture was an odd style as well, carved all over with swirling lines painted black. Other than books and clothes tossed here and there, and a chair draped with a discarded pair of pants—the sight making me blush—there wasn't much to look at. A single chandelier hung overhead, filling the room with the same cool magical light that lit all the rooms in this palace.

After perhaps another ten minutes, I was going mad with counting. He hadn't seized again, and I reckoned that was a good thing. I strode back over to him and pulled his collar aside once more to check where the black lines were. They were no longer at the top of his shoulder. They disappeared somewhere in the sleeve that was still on his arm. Carefully, I lifted his hand and slid the sleeve off of his left arm.

The lines now ended right above his elbow. I exhaled with relief; the curse was receding. My hands traced gently down his arm, grateful he wasn't awake to see me do this. After placing his arm carefully by his side, I walked back out to the balcony to check the progress of the sun and shadows. I doubted it had been an hour yet, so I counted for what

I assumed was another ten minutes then took another ten laps around his room, just in case I'd counted too fast. At that point, the waiting was killing me. It had been roughly an hour.

I grabbed the vial and slid my hand under the back of his head. "Cas, can you wake up?" At first there was no response. I shook him gently and tapped the cold vial against his chest. "Cas. You need a little bit more of this."

A small groan issued from his parted lips, but his eyes didn't open. I pressed the vial to his mouth and tilted until all the contents were in his mouth. The liquid started to spill out the sides of his lips, and I yelped. I clenched my hand over his mouth trying to shut the antidote in. By then his eyes pried open, and the point in his throat bobbed as he finally swallowed.

With my finger, I traced the corners of his mouth, pushing the last couple of drops of antidote into his mouth. If he needed every drop of it, I wasn't going to let a single bit go to waste. I wiped my fingers on his lips to make sure he got it all. His eyes watched me the entire time, and pretty soon my skin was on fire, though not from a fever. My fingers lingered on his mouth a split second longer than necessary. I jerked them back toward me, but his hand reached up and found mine, and with the smallest of movements, he kissed the ends of my first two fingers before his head lolled to the side and he dropped off to sleep.

# 33

## Zara

My head reeled, but not from dizziness as I stood frozen beside Cas's bed.

Had he just *kissed* me?

At least he wasn't watching me for my reaction. But to be safe, I spun in a circle in case he opened his eyes again. My hands instinctively traveled up to my chest, and I rested my chin on my knuckles, remembering the past few hours as best I could.

Because I'd certainly missed something.

Casimiro, heir of the Shadow Court, couldn't possibly have been in his right mind when he... I fanned out the fingers on my left hand and stared at the place his lips had touched.

When I'd been administering his medicine, I hadn't thought about how my hands were all over him. Or at least, I hadn't thought *he'd* notice. I was merely treating a patient. It's what any nurse would do.

But, stars above, he'd noticed. He'd sensed my hesitation to let go and read it in my eyes. How could I have let him get to me? A fae was definitely on the list of *wrong guys* to fall for, and the prince of shadows—an immortal who despised humans—was at the top of the list.

In my head, I watched that list burn.

I stepped through the doorway that led to his study and back to the halls that would take me to the infirmary where my burns could be treated and I could finally rest again. I'd promised myself that love would solve my problems, not create more, and he was *definitely* more. Perhaps my overzealous heart would calm down after a good sleep.

I glanced back at his quietly breathing form before stepping out of his bedroom. Half of me wanted to run back and check those black lines to see if they'd receded farther. I nearly did. But then I was closing the heavy door to his study behind me and slipping quietly down the cold stone hall.

Samuel was in the infirmary when I got there. Half his body was bandaged, but he was alive. The nurse explained that Samuel had rolled to shield Eudoria from the flames. The elderly woman, Ivy, and Tomas had all survived. Apparently, the dragons had taken flight about the time I'd passed out, leaving us alone and angering the fae.

The mortal nurse, a man named Nadoo with skin as smooth and dark as the palace walls, explained that dragon fire burns could not be healed fully with fae magic. The wounds could be closed up with a spell, but the infection and the remaining burn scars had to be treated the old-fashioned way. With mortal medicine and time.

I'd slept for the majority of the first two days, but after that, time passed slowly. The pain was manageable, but I'd never felt so tired in my life. Staying awake to help Cas had seemed easy at the time—after all, he'd needed me to. But it had taxed me more than I'd realized.

I was not allowed to leave until Nadoo was certain the infection was gone. But three days in the otherwise empty, pristine room set aside for sick and wounded servants felt like six months.

Finally alert when Nadoo came to doctor my wounds, I watched as a second nurse changed the bandages on Samuel's arms. "Why didn't they let him die?" I asked as Nadoo dabbed a thick cream onto my burns.

He shrugged. "The heir commanded that the survivors be treated. The king won't like it. He'll be in a rage when he returns." The man shivered and replaced the lid on the cream. "The heir will go the way of the rest of them."

My heart turned over in my chest. "Go? Is the heir leaving when the king returns?"

The man pursed his lips. "Leaving? No, my dear, he will not survive his father's return. No heir ever does."

"Wha—?" All the breath rushed from my lungs, and I clutched my sheets in tight fists. "What do you mean?"

He clicked his tongue, clearly annoyed at my concern for the prince of this court. "The king kills them all as soon as he returns. Everyone knows it." He leaned forward, oblivious to my quickening breaths. "The coup is this court's best bet for ousting that eternal madman. If they can kill both heirs *and* a handful of the mortals tied to him, breaking several of his bargains at once, they *might* have a chance." He lifted both eyebrows dramatically. "But in three thousand years, no one's ever done it."

I remained in a seated position, staring blankly at the far wall of the infirmary long after Nadoo left and the lights dimmed.

My palms peeled stickily away from my sheets when I finally released them and rose from my bed to relieve myself in the washroom.

I'd learned more in the two minutes I'd spoken to Nadoo than I had the entirety of my stay in this palace. Death awaited Cas, as it had every one of his siblings. My chest ached to think how many brothers and sisters he might have lost in his long life. No wonder he'd lived with such anger—such hate.

He only had Alba now. Their closeness suddenly made more sense.

For hours, I couldn't shake the memory of his chest beneath my face as I'd slept in that sunlit field. He wasn't the man I'd once thought him. And he would die as soon as his father returned.

All I could see as I tried to sleep were the black lines snaking toward Casimiro's chest. *He will not survive. No heir ever has.* The words etched into my mind like the carvings on the stone walls of Nightsong.

As I lay there, tucked into a small ball in my creaky infirmary bed, I whispered his name into the dark.

I said little the following day as Nadoo roused me to tend my wounds and administer my medicine.

Nadoo said nothing of what was happening outside the infirmary, but he narrowed his gaze every time he made eye contact, like he was trying to read my mind. Other than a woman coming in to be bandaged from a fall on the icy steps outside, no other humans came to the infirmary for treatment.

On the fourth day of my stay, Ivy came to visit. She rushed to my side and wrapped me in a violent hug.

"Samuel?" she asked, peering over at him as tears budded in her eyes.

"I think he will recover," I whispered, my stomach tightening with uncertainty.

She nodded firmly and wiped her eyes. "You—the other night. The trial just *ended*. I knew you'd been burned, and then someone yelled that the trial was over. I think it was Felipe. The heir wasn't there, only his sister. None of us knew if you were okay. The fae hustled us all back inside. I didn't even find out about Samuel until he didn't show up at the next meal." She pressed the back of her hand to her mouth and took several deep breaths. "He never said much, but..."

I patted her arm, nodding. "They're treating him."

Her head shook in tiny movements. "It makes no sense. Why try to kill us then try to heal us?"

My throat tightened, and I swallowed. "The trial was supposed to be easy. Then it wasn't."

Ivy touched my arm, her pink cheeks pulling up in a faint smile. "But you survived." She looked down at my hands. "Oh, Zara. I'm so sorry."

I showed her the burn on my leg, and she cringed, then tried to cover it up by saying it didn't look that bad. She told me the court was restless, that many were angry Samuel hadn't been left to die. Others, she explained, were happy with the change. Apparently, not all the fae here hated humans; they were simply less vocal about it until Casimiro had made the first move, commanding Samuel's treatment.

Ivy stood to leave, the bed rising as her weight lifted. "The tension is rising," she admitted. "I'm nervous. I'm afraid we'll...there's talk of another trial. To right the wrong of having a trial where no one died." She wrung her hands.

"Cas won't let that happen," I said confidently.

She quirked her brows and eyed me sideways. "Cas?"

My ears burned, and I looked away. But how could I explain it? And what was there to explain? That he'd shown me Talia's house? That he'd slept in the sunshine with me simply to make me feel better? That he'd kissed my fingers and left an ache inside me that I couldn't shake?

Tilting her head, Ivy said, "To tell you the truth, I haven't seen the heir in a few days. He's probably off collecting more mortals to kill."

To suppress the uneasy feeling rising inside me, I changed the subject. "How is Ariana?"

"She's fine. Feels terrible about what happened, but she's fully recovered. You should probably rest."

"I'm tired of resting."

"At least here they can't make you a centerpiece." Her expression fell. "Have they—?"

She nodded faintly. "All of us." A shudder rocked her shoulders. "But some fae refused to eat at the tables where we…where they made us stand. Others are mad. They're hungry for blood, Zara. Stay here as long as you can."

The following evening, Nadoo checked my wounds and my temperature and declared I was free to go. He seemed nervous, rushing between my bed and Samuel's, cursing as he tried to uncork a medicine bottle.

When I left the washroom a few minutes later, Nadoo looked up at me. Sweat clung to his brow. "It's chaos up there."

I hesitated in the doorway, recalling Ivy's words. Casimiro's actions were throwing the court into a tumult, and if angry dragons were terrifying, angry immortal fae with dark, twisted minds were equally as dangerous.

I wore a fresh white tunic—the only humans who normally received aid from the infirmary were the servants—and barely received a single glance as I made my way up several flights of stairs. Every servant I passed was in a hurry, and by the time I ascended to the more populated levels, my feet moved almost at a jog.

It wasn't until I neared the dining cavern that I sensed how the energy in the Shadow Court had shifted. Shouts sounded from behind the closed doors of the cavern, and several people, white-clad servants and glittering fae alike, hurried across the wide foyer and through the tall double doors. While the entrance was open, I glimpsed the chaos Nadoo had hinted at. Magic sparked in the air, and the low growl of hounds undergirded the courtiers' shouting.

Turning away from the dining cavern, I hurried across the wide space to the grand stair that branched up and down. I needed to hide, to remain scarce until this tension subsided. Two levels down was the library. If I took a moment to grab a book before shutting myself in my room, I wouldn't get as bored.

My moment of hesitation cost me.

The doors to the cavern burst open, and a flood of faces poured out.

"There she is! Grab her!"

I only made it up five steps before a shadowy figure swirled around me, halting my escape. Erik's wide shoulders and square jaw were barely recognizable in this form, but his voice was the same.

"We've got a fun little game prepared for you, mortal. And you won't survive this one."

# 34

## Casimiro

Outside the dining cavern, Zara screamed.

I had my hands out at my sides, my magic bracing two fae from attacking each other as they argued over what some were calling the *failed* trial. But as soon as I heard her, I lunged for the door.

In my moment of distraction, two mortals spun from where they appeared to be pouring wine at nearby tables and attempted to clamp iron shackles around both my hands. Only one succeeded.

But one was all it took.

An immediate weight settled over me as my magic dimmed. My years of building up immunity to iron kept me moving forward, fighting off the attackers as they descended upon me, but I wasn't strong enough to fend off twenty fae as their spells hit me like arrows.

These were the faces of the traitors I'd been hunting, all converging on me at once.

I'd taken to bringing Diego with me to each meal, and the dip defended me earnestly, sinking his fangs into Viro's thigh.

"Alba!" I shouted, hoping she was already gone, already somewhere safe. "Hide!"

The air beside me shimmered right before it split like a cake under a knife. A doorway opened up and I was shoved through.

I stumbled onto a cobblestone courtyard in the center of a sleepy mortal village crisp with cool fall air. No one stirred, save a startled cat. With a grounding inhale, I numbed my mind to the pain of the iron, which for now burned hotter than the pain of my curse, and focused on finding something to break the cuff around my wrist. Whoever planned this had been smart. Iron cuffs were much more damaging than blades, which could be ripped out quickly.

As I raced toward the shabby thatched roof buildings nearby, the traitor's faces flashed before me. None of them were courtiers I considered friends, but among them were some men and women I'd never imagined would be part of a coup. Erik and Viro were not a surprise, but Niv and Reyna and Manuel and—I stopped thinking about them as soon as I spotted an axe leaning against a shabby building with a thatched roof.

I dropped to my knee and placed the cuff on the cobblestones, pressing my arm as far to one side of the iron ring as possible, then slammed the axe blade into the metal.

Sparks flew and the cobblestone beneath my wrist cracked. The broken cuff fell away and my magic surged back through my senses.

The traitors didn't know of my immunity to iron. They assumed I'd be stranded here, dying a painful death as the effects of the iron and my curse consumed me.

But as I attempted to reopen a door in the dining cavern, my magic ricocheted and sparks flew from the air where I'd aimed my spell.

"Clever," I said aloud, fuming as I realized whoever was behind this had at least considered the fact that I might be able to return. Magical doorways had predictable properties, and any door once opened could be *reopened* with the right spell, unless someone sealed it from the other side.

Alba had already sealed the doorway in my study, the one I used most often to return home. I let out an angry yell, not caring who in this mortal town woke from the sound.

My sister and Zara were both in danger now, and I had to get to them. The traitors knew that my father would only be weakened if both heirs were killed within minutes of each other. My body was bound to his with a curse, and severing it would cause him pain. At my death, Alba would become his only living heir, and her life would inherit the curse. To weaken my father, I had to die first, then Alba. And if they really wanted to weaken the Shadow King, the traitors would likely kill every mortal bound to him as well.

If I didn't return soon, it would be a bloodbath at Nightsong.

The traitors couldn't have closed every single magical door in the palace, as some were permanent windows between worlds. Though I sensed I was far from any of these doors, I knew where each of them sat on the various maps of the worlds. Shifting into my shadow form, wings spread at my back and I took to the air.

# 35

## Zara

The moon hadn't yet crested the mountain as Ivy, Tomas, Eudoria, and I paraded out into the freezing night air. Eudoria wasn't allowed help this time, so she hobbled along as best she could. Samuel was still too weak to leave the infirmary, and I hoped he wouldn't have to endure this trial. We peeled out of a tiny, arched door and descended a narrow stairwell that zigzagged down the steep rock face until it spilled out onto a flat, long terrace. On one side was a sharp cliff; on the other, stands had been cut into the mountainside. I'd seen this place weeks ago, at the time being reminded of our back terrace, where Nina hosted tea parties in the spring.

But as the stands filled with fae, I realized that this was no terrace built for parties.

Ivy leaned forward and whispered, "This was where my first trial took place. We were blindfolded and told to follow the person who led us forward." She choked back a sob. "They led us straight over the cliff. Tomas and I only lived because we heard the fae screaming with laughter as...as..."

"Someone fell," I finished.

As I scanned the steps where fae were already assembling, I couldn't see Cas, or his sister. The fae filed onto the steps, laughing loudly as they clinked wine glasses and wobbled into their seats where they would happily watch us die. The air bit at my shoulders and swirled around my feet. Ivy crushed my hand in a death grip as we paraded out onto the terrace.

"The heir isn't here," I observed, trying to sound casual. If he wasn't here, he couldn't save me. I'd have to survive this one on my own.

Tomas turned a deep frown toward us. "The heir didn't order this trial. His father did."

"His father?" I parroted.

Ivy was trembling and staring blankly at the cliff's edge.

Tomas nodded. "The Shadow King is returning. He ordered that no entertainers be alive upon his arrival at midnight."

The blood in my veins pumped hard, barely enough to counter the cold air surging around me. Casimiro would die upon his father's arrival. Even if I somehow survived tonight, he wouldn't.

A hollow sensation filled me, pushing aside the cold, fear, and confusion that clogged my senses. My gaze traveled to the stands, where one seat in the center stood out from the rest of the stone benches. It was clearly the seat of honor. And it was empty.

Empty like the void inside me that expanded as memories of Cas flooded through me.

My stomach knotted and flipped, and I sucked in a desperate breath. If I never saw him again, I'd never know what it felt like to kiss him, and I suddenly wanted very badly to do so.

As we waited on the moonlit terrace for instructions, I tried to take in as many details of our new arena as I could. There was a sheer drop, unguarded by any railings, on my right and stands on my left. At the far end of the platform, a dark tunnel waited ominously. The platform was exposed, a perfect landing site for dragons. But the dragons hadn't killed me, which was why the fae were angry, so I doubted that was what they had in mind tonight.

Erik rose to his feet. "Shadow Lords and Ladies," he shouted, drawing everyone's attention. "Tonight we have some special entertainment certain to delight you." Several cheers rose from the crowd. "As ordered by our sovereign, all five remaining entertainers must die by midnight."

"Five?" Ivy asked, glancing between me and Tomas.

Just then, a burly fae with long black hair walked out onto the terrace, carrying a bandaged Samuel. To my horror, he dropped Samuel without ceremony onto the stone. Samuel barely rocked but his moans pierced my sanity.

I lurched toward him, but Tomas was faster. He reached Samuel and scooped him up. Tomas was shorter than lanky Samuel, but his chest was like a barrel, and he hefted him over to us.

The fae had dressed us all in extravagant white clothing tonight, perhaps angry with our previous choice to avoid wearing enchanted clothes, and we stood like ghosts in the moonlit darkness.

By the time Erik sat down once more, my chest had started to shake from bone-deep cold. The ruffled dress they'd given me pressed against my body in the wind, doing next to nothing to stave off the stinging ache rising in my calves and arms.

I glanced at Ivy, but her face was fixed on the ground near her feet. Her body was trembling. They'd given her a pretty white dress to wear, as well. It was looser than mine, not cut for a flamenco dance, but more the thin, drapey dress that would be worn during a tango. She looked mortified with the slits that went halfway up her thighs.

I heard the hooves before I saw what approached. A thunderous sound echoed through the belly of the mountain. Then, out of a dark archway at the end of the terrace, a bull larger than I'd ever seen barreled forward.

In Leor, I'd seen bullfights. I'd just never once imagined I'd be *in* one.

"Don't run," I yelled over the wind and the hoofbeats. But it was no use.

Ivy darted away, and Tomas staggered with Samuel, clearly at a loss for what to do. Ivy's flashing white dress caught the bull's eye. As it charged, the skin on its neck sloshed from side to side, and its horns reached out and forward, directly toward my friend.

"Turn!" I shouted. Bullfighters never ran away from the bulls. They stood their ground. They even held out capes to attract the bull toward them. Unfortunately, Ivy had nothing but her wispy white dress and the cliff to one side.

As the animal charged toward Ivy, I turned aside.

At the chorus of boos, I yanked my head back around and yelped. Ivy was on the ground, lying on her stomach at the cliff's edge. Her hands were clamped over her head, but I couldn't see any blood.

Still supporting Samuel, Tomas whooped victoriously as the bull arced around for another charge. As he shuffled toward Ivy, I realized what she'd done. And it was *brilliant*. Tomas hurried for the cliff edge with Samuel limping along beside him, but they were too slow. The bull clattered a few more steps as it slowed, then laboriously turned around and grunted, angry that it had missed its target.

It focused on Tomas and Samuel and charged.

"No!"

Tomas couldn't outrun or outmaneuver the bull while helping another man.

He took the horn directly in the back.

It hooked him and Tomas was lifted into the air. Samuel's body lopped off to the side, where he used his uninjured arm to scoot his body toward the cliff edge, where Ivy lay.

I watched in horror as the bull hurled Tomas farther than I'd known was possible. There was so much blood.

Tomas's white outfit darkened, and he didn't get up. I took one step, then pressed both hands to my mouth as silent screams poured out. As long as the bull was on the loose, I couldn't move. Eudoria stood several paces away, slightly bent but unmoving.

A bull wasn't going to charge something that it didn't consider a threat, and my friends, no more than small white heaps lying at the cliff's edge, weren't registering as a threat to this massive animal. It must be torture for Ivy to remain so close to the edge, but she'd been smart to go there, where the animal's instincts would tell it not to go.

The bull's hooves clacked as it spun, searching for the next target. Some of the fae cheered, while others booed. Ivy was right, then. There were fae in this court who didn't want us to die tonight. Despite their protests, they weren't intervening, which meant they weren't as brave as I'd hoped. Cas and Alba were still nowhere in sight. My chest curled forward as sadness and fear warred against my determination to stand completely still.

Something hard hit me on the shoulder, and I spun away in pain. An apple rolled to the stones beside me and in the stands, Erik crossed his arms in a satisfied way.

The bull noticed my movement.

I didn't have time to think. The animal charged toward me so fast that I could take one, maybe two more steps before he was going to maul me. He was so much bigger now that he was running right at me.

Almost on instinct, I stepped back, lifting my arms up and pressing my chest and stomach backward, the way I'd seen matadors arch their bodies. The bull charged through the space that my chest had vacated. The edges of his horns tore through the ruffles in my still moving dress. For a second, I couldn't breathe, startled that I had survived the first pass. People in the stands clapped. Others shouted their disapproval.

I had one aim, and that was to get myself and Eudoria to the cliff edge. I too, could wait out the night beside Ivy, but the windblown ruffles of my white dress, looked too much like the flags the matadors used to draw the bull's attention.

"Get to the edge," I called to Eudoria as I raced toward her. Though we were only a dozen paces apart, there was too much distance between us. The bull would gore me long before I reached her.

Sparks flew as the animal's hooves hit the rocks. The ring in his nose glistened in the moonlight as he charged toward me once again. In the two seconds I had to contemplate how I would avoid him this time, I recalled the way the bullfighters spun away from the bull at the last possible second. But I hadn't trained for this. The complex movement involved arching sideways at the same time you spun. I was a dancer, but I'd never danced with a bull before. Still, I had no choice. He was coming toward me, and I was either going to move or die.

I tried the move again. This time I shoved my hips to the side and tried to spin into the movement, but the bull's horn clipped my stomach and ripped through me, yanking me into a wild spin. I smacked the stone so hard that everything around me went black.

Extreme pain and intense cold were my first sensations when my eyes pried open. My face was pressed against smooth rock, and a frozen wind blasted against my back. I was near the cliff's edge. The stands were still full of fae—screaming, hollering, stomping, laughing. As thunderous hooves clacked against stone, I rotated my face, unable to move my body. Warmth pooled under my stomach, where the pain was sharpest.

Hands started petting the side of my neck and face. "Zara. Zara." It was Ivy's voice. I lifted my head and looked at her. She was still lying on the ground, her arms extended toward me. She must have dragged my body over here to get it out of the bull's trajectory.

My hand moved to my stomach, and I winced. Blood coated my fingers.

"It'll be all right," Ivy was saying. "There's a lot of blood, but it's not as bad as it looks. It's not even deep." Whether or not the cut was deep, it still burned like a branding iron was lying against my skin.

Our white outfits must have caught the bull's attention. He was angry now, and there were no targets left. Eudoria had flattened herself to the stone right where she'd stood—a smart move, considering she couldn't walk quickly, much less spin away from a charging bull. The bull spotted Ivy and me, and he charged, despite our closeness to the cliff's edge. Perhaps he'd been enchanted to come for us or was so mad he no longer cared.

"At the last minute, we roll out of the way," I shouted to Ivy over the hooves. "Ready?" Ivy nodded and tucked her arms against her sides.

It was a stupid idea, dangerous and desperate. But we didn't have time to try anything clsc.

As the bull charged, another sound rose over the clack of his hooves. Drumbeats in the night sky.

Ivy screamed, and I started to roll early, fear and survival instincts banishing reason and logic. I grunted in pain as the wound on my stomach stretched with my movement. The hoofbeats suddenly stopped, and a strong blast of cold air pushed all my hair from my face. I gaped at the sight.

An enormous dragon—the same pale dragon who'd torched me—gripped the bull in her talons and pumped her wings hard to gain height with her heavy load. Every sound on the platform and in the stands was silenced as the dragon flew off into the night.

Ivy pulled me away from the cliff edge and helped me stand. I was lightheaded, and my limbs were going numb. But as we turned to face the fae, I realized that while we might have survived the trial, they were not happy. Several fae leaped from the stands and raced toward us, eyes full of rage.

Others hurried back to the pathways leading into the mountain, while a small number of fae drew swords and attempted to hold back their fellow courtiers from attacking us. Tomas lay unmoving on the cold terrace.

Heaving from the gash in my stomach and the fear clawing at my mind, I clutched Ivy's arm as we hurried to the path that would take us back inside. "Tell me more about this First and Last. Does your god listen to prayers?"

I listened intently as Ivy recited what was clearly a memorized mantra of sorts that described her god. My knees buckled beneath me at her beautiful words, despite the impossible hope in them. As the fae rushed toward us, I fisted my hands and prepared to defend myself and my friend to the end, however quickly that end might come.

A dark shape shot down from the clouds above, wings spread wide.

Cas landed in a crouch on the terrace before us, cracking the stone beneath him. His wings dissipated in the night as he shifted from shadow to flesh. When he stood, authority radiated off of Cas like I'd not seen before. His eyes burned blue and the air around him shimmered with writhing shadows. The skin on his arms was black, and the darkness crept up his neck.

"No one touches her," he said. "No one touches any of them."

# 36

## Zara

I staggered forward, my vision sparkling gold at the edges. "Cas!" But my word was a garbled moan. *You came.*

He knocked a fae back with a single punch, and the rest slowed their approach. A second figure materialized beside Cas, and he whirled as if to attack but quickly stopped. Alba's dark dress and long hair fluttered in the strong wind. Cas shouted something at her, but I couldn't hear her words over the breeze.

A female fae, a blond with ropes of braids, rushed from the stands and hurried to Samuel's side, pressing a kiss to his cheek. I'd seen her walking the halls with him a time or two, and now it made sense. My eyes darted back to Cas. He turned until he met my gaze.

"This way," Ivy said, indicating the stairs. She pressed her lips together and urged me forward. "Let's get you inside. You'll need stitches."

Cas never broke eye contact with me as the fae departed from the terrace, some into the air and others into the mountain. Ivy's words meshed with the breeze and the mutterings of the disappointed fae, and I was left with nothing but my thoughts screaming at me to go to him.

But what if I was wrong? I'd been wrong so many times. I'd misread men. I'd convinced myself that they'd had feelings that were never really there or intentions that were entirely fabricated by my own hopeless longing.

He took a step toward me, and my heart shot into my throat.

Then a shadowy figure holding a sword swooped down in front of him, severing our eye contact. Magic buzzed in the air and I rushed toward the stairs with Ivy.

"The mortal nurse in the infirmary can stitch you up," she said, her words finally cutting through. She was almost shouting at me.

With the hand that wasn't pressing down on my wound, I indicated for her to lead the way on the stairs, heart hammering as I followed. The snap and flash of magic drew my attention back to the terrace, but I couldn't see Cas amid the flying shadows. I placed my shoulder against the rock wall, taking one step at a time.

Each step was agony, even though the cut wasn't deep. The blood just kept coming, oozing between my fingers and soaking into my dress. Each breath stretched the wound a little, and I was so lightheaded by the time I reached the top of the stairs that I had to take a moment to steady myself.

Ivy helped me along the long, black hallways and shuffled me toward the stairs that would lead down to the infirmary. I slowed, not wanting to return there. The carving on the wall beside me caught my attention and I stopped walking. It was the carving of the dragon—the one that led to the secret passage. Ivy tugged on my arm.

"Zara, are you all right? It's not much farther."

"Wait." A voice echoed from the end of the hall.

We turned and saw Alba racing toward us, her black dress covered in white sparkling stones that looked like snow falling.

She stared hard at my wound, then glanced up at Ivy. "Come with me," she demanded.

Neither of us moved.

Her expression sagged a little. "I won't hurt you. Cas told me to make sure you were safe. He's...he'll..." She seemed unable to finish her sentence.

"He'll be okay," I muttered. Her gaze flicked up to meet mine and in it I saw the smallest flash of relief at my words, but it was quickly replaced by a tightness around her eyes that whispered of fear.

Then, to my shock, she clamped both hands over her face and spoke from behind them. "I've never seen him more adamant about anything." Her hands fell away. "He wants me to take you all away from here. Please, come with me?"

Ivy and I exchanged a glance and without a word, Ivy turned to follow Alba.

"But..." I whispered, unable to move. Leaving here would mean never seeing Cas again. As much as I'd wanted to escape this place, now that I had the chance, I couldn't bring myself to go with her.

I leaned against the wall once again, taking a moment to rest. Then my breath caught as Cas whirled around the corner, his white shirt a crinkled mess, parted in the front to reveal dark lines snaking across his chest.

"Cas!" I shouted, the effort punishing my body. I groaned and pressed my back to the wall. In a breath, he was there, a step away, as if he hadn't even moved.

His eyes flicked to my wound then back to my face.

"Take her," he said without looking at his sister. "Take them all. Find a door that leads as far from here as you can and go."

"Cas, I'm not leav—" protested Alba, stealing my own words.

"It'll weaken him," he said to her. "I need you to do this. I'll destroy the door behind you, buy you a little time."

Alba coughed, started to say something, then nodded and pulled Ivy and me down the hallway with her. I jerked out of her grip and turned to Cas.

I wasn't leaving like this.

"You have to go now," he said, his voice deep and strained, as if he was holding back words he wouldn't let himself say.

"I know what happened to all the other heirs," I said, my voice coming out lower and thicker than I'd intended.

Alba rubbed her hands together impatiently, but Cas's eyes remained fixed on me. "Go," he said to his sister. "Find Eudoria and Samuel. I will bring Zara. First, I need to heal her."

I didn't miss Alba's overexaggerated nod before she and Ivy darted down the hall.

Cas took a step toward me and every muscle in my body sensed his nearness. "You're afraid your father will—"

"I'm not afraid of him." He cut through my words.

I blinked. "You're not? But won't he...?"

Cas stepped forward, and my only recourse was to press my back to the wall. "I'm not afraid of him, Zara. I'm afraid that the light I've come to see by will go out, and I will be left alone in the dark."

"What are you talk—"

"You, little spark." He pushed my chin with his thumb until I met his gaze. "You."

My lips parted, and I stared up at him. For two long seconds, he didn't move.

Like I had when I'd jumped through that door, I was falling, falling, and as far as I knew, there were rocks below that would end my fall so I'd never get up again.

I shook my head. "I'm not a spark. I'm not a candle. I'm not some beacon of light."

His mouth went slack as if I had slapped him. "Zara," he said, his voice almost pleading, "you are the stars. Constant, fixed, and ever burning. It is by your light that I see, into your light that I am inescapably drawn. Would that I could call you down from heaven to fall on me and consume me with your light. But I am born of darkness and have no power to command the stars."

I was so startled by his speech that all I could do was blink at him, then his lips pressed into mine, and my body melted back against the wall.

I had a vague awareness of pain in my abdomen, of his hand against mine—moving my fingers away from the wound. But my entire being was lost in his kiss.

Falling didn't describe this. I was soaring.

Warmth spread out from my stomach, blazing up until my cheeks burned and my fingertips tingled.

He removed his hand from my wound, the pain now entirely gone, and slid his fingers behind my back. I touched the place where the wound had been, and my fingers only met smooth skin.

"Thank you," I murmured against his cheek, not ready for him to back away.

He tipped his forehead against the wall beside my head, his hair partially blocking his expression.

I reached up and raked the hair away from his face with my blood-stained fingers.

His mouth curled into a grin. "Is this your way of saying you do not hate me, Valencia?" He playfully caught my hand in his, and I sucked in a breath.

"Your hand!"

It was as black as the stone behind me.

He turned away, tucking one dark hand behind his head and fisting it in his hair. "This is my father's way of ensuring his heirs follow his commands, of seeing who can be worthy to take his place. So far, none have measured up." He whirled back around, eyes blazing. "Not one of my sixty older brothers and sisters."

My eyes slowly closed and opened again. "Sixty?"

"My father has been alive for millennia. In that time, he's fathered many heirs, and each of them have lived short lives for our kind. I only had the pleasure of meeting two of them, not including Alba. The rest died before I was born. I knew it would happen to me, too, and Alba after me, if I didn't change the game."

"I...I'm so sorry."

He waved away my sentiments. "It's why I never cared about my life, and why I was both fascinated and angered by people who *did* care about theirs. I knew I would die if I tried or die if I didn't try, so there was little point. But after Augustín died, he showed me that there was a way—a possibility—that an heir might one day survive. I poured myself into this effort."

"The antidotes?" I asked, wanting to touch him again. My hand moved out to his forearm, which felt hot.

He nodded, staring down at my hand against his cursed skin. "All I wanted before I died was to find something worth dying *for*." He looked up at me now. "We feed ourselves with pleasure, with entertainment, with anything that can shock us from our numb, endless existence. Magic has its charms, but even its thrill dulls over time. You were right—what you said about us, about me. All this time, I've been searching for someone who could wake me up. I was numb, unable to feel the world around me or the life inside me, until I met you." He stepped toward me, but then he bit his lip and angled his face away.

"What is it?" I breathed.

"I am born of darkness. I will not be your condemnation."

My spine straightened. "And I cannot be your salvation." He huffed as if I'd slapped him. "No, listen," I said, poking his chest. "We are all born with darkness inside us. I—I'm not some saint. You have been given power, that alone does not make you condemnable."

He pushed my hair aside with both hands. "Past mistakes don't scare me. I've got a list that will turn your blood cold. But I want to know you,

Zara Valencia. Broken pieces and all. I want—I want more time. But we do not have it."

His words kindled a fire in my chest. "Then all my broken pieces are yours." I pulled his face down and kissed him again.

The edges of his mouth twitched. "How can you have so much life inside that tiny body?" He shifted forward so his hands rested on either side of my head against the wall. "You once said you wanted to watch me burn. So burn me. Light me on fire and take me down because I've never seen light like yours, and I'll be forever blind if you leave. I want to catch fire with you."

This time, I didn't fear the rising flames inside me. I wanted them to consume me.

# 37

## Zara

Before I was ready, Cas pulled away, his hands sliding down my ribcage to rest on my hips.

"My father returns in a little less than one hour. I've planned for this moment since he left, but..." His hands tightened. "My plan no longer supplies what I want."

I swallowed. "Which is what?"

Instead of answering, his hands fell away. He scratched absently at a scar buried beneath the black lines creeping up his neck. If death awaited us both tonight, I could see no reason to hold back. I lifted a hand and traced the scar with one finger.

He leaned into my hand and kissed my wrist. "You can see them. My scars. Where the curse travels, my glamour disappears."

"You don't have to hide them from me." I traced the line of the scar, and he angled his chin away so I could follow the raised skin to where it ended just below his collar. "Who did this?"

"My father."

I pulled my hand back.

Cas let out a dry chuckle. "His dagger was what first showed me I could learn to resist iron. So, in the end, his cruelty saved me tonight, and it saved you." At my raised brows, he added, "I was detained briefly tonight by iron shackles. No one knew I could resist iron."

"I knew that," I said, poking him where I'd stabbed him.

He smirked. "Yes, you did. But, come, I need to get you to a safe place. We're out of time."

Cas took my hand and led me through the palace halls. I'd never felt so high on adrenaline, joy, and fear at the same time. I'd finally found what I'd been looking for my entire life, but I stood to lose it in less than an hour.

We wove our way up a flight of stairs and around two corners, passing servants and fae alike running down the halls, all heading in the opposite direction from us. The servants paid us no mind, but the fae threw us quizzical looks, some nuanced with hate and others with surprise. He paused in front of a carved doorway that depicted an evergreen forest and tall mountains beyond.

"Alba took Ivy and, I assume, the others through this door. I sense that her magic has already passed through here, but I can't tell who was with her when she left." He scratched at the back of his neck. "Now, it's your turn. When you're through, I'll destroy the door so no one can follow you. You'll be far from Avencia, but you'll be safe. With Alba with you, the bargain shouldn't bind you again, at least not until my father realizes Alba isn't coming back. But by then, I hope... well, Alba can help you find your way home when all of this is over." He pulled something from his pants' pocket and grabbed my hand. "Here."

An uncut gemstone rested in my palm.

"I meant to give you this sooner." The stone was yellow and about the size of a robin's egg. It would be worth a fortune in Avencia. "And now if the dragons come for you, you'll also be safe."

He didn't look at me as he spoke, so I reached up and pulled his chin toward me. His dark eyes blazed with apparent restraint.

"Cas," I breathed.

He choked back a laugh. "My carefully laid plan is going up in flames."

"What do you mean?"

He offered me a half smile. "The antidote I've been working on, a magical recipe begun centuries ago by a sister I never met, provides us heirs with an increasing ability to resist Father's curse. Each of us who tweaked and perfected the recipe over the years fully believed that at some point, the antidote would be powerful enough to *break* the curse. But I realized it could never break the curse for someone who already had it. The antidote was never meant to keep *me* alive tonight." His hand, still stained red with my blood, pinched the brow of his nose, then slammed in a fist against the wall. "It was meant to keep Alba alive. I was only taking it to test it."

"You were going to give it to her?"

"I already did," he said as he smeared a hand against his eyes. "As soon as I heard Father was returning, I slipped it into her tea and watched her drink it."

My stomach sank. "So you don't have it anymore."

He shook his head.

A beat of silence passed as we stood and stared at the doorway that now glowed a faint blue.

If I walked through this door, I would never see Cas again. He wouldn't survive tonight. He'd never intended to. It had always been his sister's life he was bargaining for.

My hand slid quietly into his, our fingers lacing.

"You can't stay, Zara."

"I don't have to leave, either."

His fingers tightened around mine. "I need to know you are safe when he arrives."

I leaned into his arm, still so shocked at how easy it was to be this close to him, how right it felt. "Would it help you more if I stayed here and fought by your side?"

He kissed the top of my head. "You are good with a blade, little spark, but against a three-thousand-year-old fae king, a blade would do little good."

"True," I mumbled against his shoulder. Then my head snapped up. "Wait."

Cas eyed me narrowly. "What is it?"

"You gave me an idea." My heart thundered madly, but I couldn't just walk away from him. Not now that he'd held me like this, summoning a fire in my very bones. Before he could retort, I poked him in the chest again. "At least hear me out."

Ariana helped me into my ballgown, the most exquisite one the wardrobe had yet provided. Tonight's dress was a bright red, the preferred shade of flamenco dancers and my favorite color. Under the stacks of ruffles was orange fabric. When I turned a quick spin in front of the mirror, the dress imitated a flickering fire. I nodded at the roaring lion's mouth atop the wardrobe. It was perfect.

Fingers shaking in her haste, Ariana quickly helped me dress and style my hair. The king's welcome ball would begin in minutes. The king apparently preferred for the parties to be in full swing when he arrived, like the noblemen who arrived late to cause a scene.

Tonight, I wanted to simply be me, my wild hair unrestrained. Ariana brushed out my curls until they reached almost as wide as my shoulders. In the wardrobe, we discovered a sparkling hairpin the shape of an orange flame, and she used it to pin my hair off my face.

"You look amazing," she told me, offering me a quick hug. She tucked her hair behind her ears. "And I'm sorry. For thinking—for saying what I did."

I pulled her into another hug. "All is forgiven. Now, we have a ball to attend."

Drawn by the magic of the king that bound them to serve the Shadow Court, the servants all made their way through the halls toward the ball hastily thrown together at the king's command. I wished Ariana and all the others could wait this out in the lower levels of Nightsong, but it could not be so.

At least Ivy was safe. And Samuel and Eudoria and Alba.

We climbed several flights of stairs, my dancing shoes clacking with each step. We had less than a half hour until the arrival of the fae king.

Ariana sighed as we crested yet another flight of stairs, this one narrower than the widely used ones in the lower palace. "Why did the location of the ball change at the last minute?" she mused aloud.

My lips curled at the edges.

Cas had liked my idea.

One of the other servants ascending the stairs behind us said, "At least some of the fae stepped in and moved everything with their magic." He scoffed. "They could do that all the time, but they prefer to watch us run around like rats."

"Perhaps not the ones who helped you tonight," I offered.

The man inclined his head but didn't reply.

"Where are we going?" Ariana asked, her breaths coming slower by the sixth flight.

I hesitated before answering. "The old castle on top of the mountain."

The chilly air in the hallways helped to cool my burning cheeks as we hurried through the palace. Fae in their shadow forms blasted past us, their wings occasionally smacking my arms and shoulders. We finally reached a stairwell that lifted from the heart of the mountain to the sky above. I could smell the outside air, see the bright lights spilling down the stone steps as if they led to a celestial castle rather than the ruins of a once great court.

"Aquí estamos," the man behind us said in perfect Avencian. Then he turned to Ariana. "Here we are." When I turned a close-lipped smile at him, he nodded once and slipped past us.

The final flight of steps rose from the walls cut directly through the mountain into a vaulted atrium so tall I couldn't make out the faces painted onto the ceiling high above. I heard voices and what sounded like a loud party before I reached the top. The air instantly felt fresher, even warmer somehow, as we stepped aboveground.

An archway radiating with golden light spanned the atrium ahead, leading to the ballroom beyond. In the grand room, rows of round tables stretched across a long room buttressed with impressive stone columns on either side. My breath caught at the amount of dripping golden light cascading down from above like glittering rain that stopped before it ever touched our heads. Mounds of night-blooming flowers, moss, and tall white mushrooms were piled on every table, and for the first time, it struck me that these fae might actually have power over *living* nature, the way the stories portrayed them, and not just the dead stone all around us.

Ariana hurried me toward the archway, but as we were about to cross from the atrium into the twinkling ballroom, I glanced behind me, certain I'd seen a shadow flash in the flickering light. My eyes hunted the corners, hoping to see Cas, but there was no one. He said he would meet me here, that he had to destroy the doorway to ensure no one could go after Alba.

As soon as I passed under the golden archway, an awed breath quietly slipped from my mouth. The lights that hung from the ceiling looked like stars against the inky darkness. Candles bobbed in the air above every table, and instead of cages full of angry creatures, this room held a host of magnificent animals. In the nearest cage, an enormous silver cat sat, its paws the size of dinner plates and a tail as long as a dragon's. I'd never seen such a beautiful creature in all my life. There was a white tiger, a pale giraffe with faint spots instead of the usual dark brown, and other animals I couldn't name. All were light in color and exquisite. Several people stood near the cages, peering in. The cages appeared to be made of ice, their frosted bars not entirely reassuring.

In one cage at the far end of the room, a white dragon perched on his hind legs, chest lifted pridefully, wings tucked at his sides. My breath hitched.

In the center of the wide room fae couples already danced, dresses spinning as if made of falling snow or whirling ash. It appeared that the evening's attire was meant to entertain as much as the décor or the animals. One dress appeared to be made of water itself, rippling like a current as the woman spun. I realized my jaw was hanging open when Ariana snorted, trying to cover up a giggle. I clamped my jaw shut.

"It's stunning, isn't it?" she said.

My attention traveled to the windows, which had no glass in them. They stretched almost to the heavens and were wide enough for a full-grown dragon to dart through—wings folded, of course—but no wintry breeze ruffled the sleeves of gowns or the perfectly groomed hair of any of the guests. The room itself was a comfortable temperature, not freezing like I'd come to expect in the halls of Nightsong. And the night outside was brilliant with stars.

Craning my neck to see over the crowd, I scanned the room for Cas. Between the elaborate headpieces some of the fae wore and the tall ice cages, it was impossible to see in every corner. He'd be here. I took a deep breath.

Every dark-haired man with his back to me drew my eye, but after a circuit of the entire room, it became clear that the heir wasn't here.

What if his father had already arrived?

What if our time was over?

I tore my gaze away from the dancing couples, hearing the voice of my father in my head. After I'd first told him I believed love would break the bargain, he'd warned me not to let a man matter so much that I would risk losing everything to keep him. Yet he had risked everything to have me. All my life I'd thought his advice was rubbish, as I'd chased after someone who could *matter* enough to make my father's money and his defense lessons and his snobbery shrink away in comparison. I'd wanted to find a love worth dying for.

Cas and I had been looking for the same thing. For each other.

My heart beat madly against my ribs as I wove through the tables of seated fae. No meals were being eaten here. Piles of small items or stacks of round coins littered the center of each table, and everyone held cards. As we edged around one table, I peeked at a woman's hand, and noticed that the cards were exactly the same as the cards I'd grown up playing. In the center of the table were piles of cut stones. They were gambling.

As I resumed my scan of the crowd, a shining black suit caught my eye as it passed beneath the glittering golden archway leading from the ballroom. I sucked in a breath—it was Cas.

He paused inside the crowded room, his height an advantage as his gaze slowly raked over his courtiers. Tonight, he wore solid black, a striking change that made my heart flutter. His hair was slicked back and his pointed ears twinkled with golden caps. He looked every bit a fae prince tonight.

From amid a small group of fae, Felipe's deep voice announced, "The heir has arrived."

# 38

## Casimiro

The crowd jostled to get a look at me, and I hardened my expression, even though my skin burned with pain under my clothes. As I swept into the party, searching for Zara, I spotted her across the room and froze. Every face in the ballroom followed my gaze, and within seconds, the entire room was looking at her.

The crowd parted as I walked toward her, but I never took my eyes from her face. The mortals bowed, but the fae knew I'd likely not survive the night—they didn't spare me any respectful gestures.

Zara was radiant, and when I flashed her a smile, she lit the room with her own. I walked straight to her, slipped my hand into her curls, and pulled her ear to my lips.

"There you are, little spark," I whispered. Her quiet exhale made the side of my mouth twist into a grin. "Dance with me."

Her hand slipped around my elbow, and I led her onto the dance floor, which vacated as we stepped onto it. The fae melted back into the crowd, not wanting to be seen approving of my choice should the king arrive while we danced. Anyone caught offending my father would die tonight, and beneath the ice-thin veneer of celebration was the buzzing tension of fear.

On the dance floor, I settled my palm on her waist and firmly but gently gripped her lifted hand. Her chest rose and fell in rapid breaths, and her smile, while beautiful, was not fully convincing. She was afraid, and I couldn't very well tell her not to be.

We might not survive tonight. Until an hour ago, I'd not intended to. I'd assumed she would take the chance to leave, to finally have what she'd wanted since I stole her away from her home.

The music began.

But this spark of a woman hadn't left, and now everything hinged on her wild plan.

She followed my lead like we'd been dancing together for years. Her feet knew the moves before I even suggested them, and her timing was flawless. The searing pain of my curse ebbed from my mind as I watched her and held her tiny frame in my hands. This was what it felt like to be alive.

I released her into a spin across the dance floor and her dress mimicked flames as she whirled. Several of my courtiers cheered, and my heart soared. When she landed again in my arms, her back to my chest for a brief moment, I felt like I truly was on fire.

"I love you," I breathed as she spun again to face me. Perhaps she hadn't heard me.

But her eyes were wide and her smile captivating. My body ached to hear her reply, but as she opened her mouth, her words were stolen as a crackle of magic buzzed across the room, silencing all other sounds.

The air beneath the golden arch rippled, and my father stepped into the room.

# 39

## Casimiro

Pain seared in my veins as I reached for Zara's waist, pushing her behind me. Everyone in the room dropped to a knee in a wavelike movement, including Zara, as my father's magic compelled reverence.

His eyes landed on me, the only one still standing. He frowned. Behind him, six guards marched through the arch, followed by two men wearing the liquid black half-cloaks and ghoulish masks of the Wild Hunt.

"Lords and Ladies of the Shadow Court," one of the guards announced, "bow before the King of Shadows, King Rykar Oscuro."

The room hushed, save for the white wolf in the corner emitting a low whine from his cage. Among animals, he might be a prince of night, but he trembled at the king of shadows. Felipe swept toward the golden archway, along with Viro and Erik, pressing the crowd back so all could see and make way for the king. As my righthand man, Felipe was expected to do this, and he was likely only trying to save his own life, but watching him fawn over my father fanned the rage inside me.

My father stepped silently through the crowd toward me.

Zara clutched her fists against my back. She deserved to burn brightly for years to come, but she'd chosen this darkness—my darkness.

I lifted my chin as my father neared, running through the next few minutes in my head. The members of the Wild Hunt sneered at several members of my court. The Hunters belonged to no court but were welcome in all, unlike most solitary fae. They wore their ridiculous black capes like crowns and carried their precious helmets under their left arms, like soldiers.

My father wore a high-collared deep blue jacket with silver buttons and filigree thread stitched across his broad chest. Black, he'd always said, was what he'd worn proudly after the war of Sun and Shadow, but he'd left the color behind a thousand years ago, choosing deep blues and purples and grays instead, the true color of shadows.

I swallowed any indication of the pain in my blood and met my father's gaze. Only when he was chest to chest with me, did he look down at my darkening skin, hungry to see the black lines.

He took a long inhale of breath, making me wait. I cracked the knuckles on my right hand and then my left.

"Father," I finally said, thankful that my height allowed me to look down at him.

"Ah, son. I see that you are looking well."

I translated that as his displeasure to find me still standing. His eyes shone with the same hatred that had been there since I was a boy. As I'd matured, I'd watched my siblings die as they received this same greeting upon his return from an extended absence.

But what he didn't know was that my siblings, his own children, had been quietly rebelling against his magic for centuries, crafting an antidote to his incurable curse that improved as each heir perfected its properties. It allowed us to endure the pain of the curse, although not the end result—our deaths. Survival was only possible if the curse never entered our bodies.

I'd found comfort in the knowledge that Alba would not inherit the curse that had killed every other Shadow Heir. But now, as Zara's small frame stepped boldly around mine, her face firm and fearless, I wanted so badly to stay by her side. To protect her. To *live*.

My father glanced around the room, nodding at the faces silently watching us. "It looks like you have pulled together a rather magnificent celebration tonight, son. And on such short notice." He eyed the pointed dome above us. "An interesting choice, this ruin."

I did not blink. "An homage to the kings of old."

My father cocked me a merciless grin, then lifted his hands and placed them on either side of my head.

I stiffened as he pulled my head down toward his.

I hadn't even kissed Zara goodbye.

"Was it worth it, son?" he snarled, not bothering to keep his voice low.

I jerked my head from his grip, ready for his attack. "Every bit," I shot back, ripping off my suit jacket and plucking at the buttons on my sleeves. I'd watched my father kill two of my siblings and read the accounts of all the others. If there was one commonality in how Rykar killed his heirs, it was that he preferred not to use magic until the very end and always started with a showcase of his incredible skill with a blade. He was a fan of blood.

He sniffed. "The pain wasn't a good motivator, then," he declared, flicking away an invisible piece of fuzz from his jacket sleeve. "It never quite seems to do the trick with any of my children. Pity."

"No, it's you I pity," I said, and before he could say anything else, I turned my back to him. Several murmurs pulsed through the crowd as I grabbed Zara's face and kissed her once more.

"Then I shall have to think of something else," my father growled from behind me. "If my son has found a way to deceive me."

I turned to face him once more. The last dose of my antidote was wearing thin against the fierceness of his anger. "You've taught me nothing but deception. Like any loving father, you should be proud."

My father's fist was on my collar, choking me. Rykar hissed in my ear. "We do not love, son. The shadow heart is black. There is nothing inside of it but power. Love weakens. Power strengthens." With a shove, he let go of my shirt, and I stumbled forward. "The moment that you love is the moment that you become powerless."

He brushed past me, pushing my shoulder hard. At first, I thought he'd attacked, and my hands balled into fists.

But he hadn't been aiming for me.

His hand reached out and clamped around Zara's chin. She stumbled in his grip.

"Let her go!" I shouted. Magic sizzled off my father's frame as he swallowed the two of them in a shield enchantment. No magic could make him let go now. Rykar chuckled, a sound that drew needles into my veins.

Rage blazed through me. I should never have kissed her, never given my father a reason to hurt her. He would use her to prove his point, that love made us weak.

Rykar's fingers squeezed, drawing a small moan from Zara. "This mortal was not supposed to be alive," he growled. "I thought I made myself clear." Zara's cheeks had turned white where his fingers dug in, but she didn't make another sound. "However, it will be more fun to punish her now, so my son can see what his choices have done."

A few goblets rattled against the tables. My father shoved Zara's face away, nearly knocking her to the floor. As I lurched forward, he peered over at me. "And then you will die."

# 40

## Zara

My shoes clacked as I stumbled away from the Shadow King. His fingernails had left indentations on my face that still burned.

"Touch her, and it will be the last thing you do," Cas growled to his father.

In answer, the king drew his sword. The sound of it unsheathing lifted the hairs on my arms.

But then Cas had one too, as the weapon simply materialized in his lifted hand.

My heart stumbled. Time was running out. I glanced at the wide windows, wondering if my plan would work.

The clash of steel broke my hope to shards. My stomach knotted as Cas and his father dueled so fast I couldn't track their movements. But Cas had said Rykar would use steel first. We weren't out of time yet.

Hurrying toward the windows, I hurled a prayer to the First and Last, a god Ivy had said could hear prayers. If this god cared enough about the creatures he'd made to listen to them, he was better than any I'd ever heard of.

"Please let them come," I said. "Please let this work."

At the window, I braced against the casing and leaned out. I gave my hair a shake in the freezing air for good measure. Maybe, despite my dancing and twirling and waving about, there were too many smells in this room for the dragons to smell *me*.

Blades rang out faster than the snap of castanets. The fae were backed against the walls to allow room for the battle between the king and the heir. I'd thought Cas and Alba fought quickly, but this was like trying to watch hummingbirds in flight.

Then I saw blood.

Red dotted the floor and flashed on the hint of blurred gray steel. I couldn't tell whose sword it was. I thought I might be sick, so I turned and held my head over the window ledge.

From this high, the surrounding peaks and the valley between them opened like a spread map before me, illuminated only by the light of the slim moon and host of stars. Above the howling wind, the drumbeat of dragon wings pounded in the air.

A smile broke across my face.

"There you are," I said as the pale peach dragon arced down into view around the corner of the old castle walls. The creature shrieked as it saw me, its large nostrils flaring. "Come to finish what you started?"

I backed into the ballroom, shaking so hard with nerves I thought I might collapse. Ariana wove through the crowd and rushed to my side.

"What are you doing?" She stared at the dragon as it circled outside.

"Inviting the final guest."

Ariana gasped as the dragon pinned its wings to its sides and shot through the open window over our heads.

The entire room broke into chaos.

Servants screamed. Tables flipped as fae launched themselves into the air to flee the one creature they feared. Shadows darted here and there, slipping out the windows like rising smoke. Above the din, I listened for the sound of clashing steel, but I couldn't discern where the fight had moved.

"Down here!" I shoved Ariana forward and dove beneath a table.

A second later, a massive, clawed foot hooked the side of the table and ripped it away. I screamed and collapsed to my knees on the hard stone floor.

The dragon's loud breathing threatened to throw me into a blind panic. But just as my body was giving way to fear, I caught sight of Cas. He stood on a table, sword in hand, shadowy wings outstretched behind him. He had blood splattered across his cheek and chest, but I couldn't tell if it was his. I couldn't see the king.

Cas launched himself into the air and landed with a thud between me and the dragon.

The dragon inhaled, the rattling sound an indication of the impending fire.

I scrambled to my feet, digging through the folds of my dress.

"Here!" I shouted, hurling the uncut stone into the air, away from Cas.

As predicted, the dragon's attention followed the stone. It opened its mouth and caught the jewel with a *snap* of its jaws.

Cas's frame shuddered slightly. "If it swallowed that stone, there is no surviving its flames."

I nodded, but my feet were lifting off the floor as magic drew me toward the Shadow King, who flashed into view at the far end of the room. Then his magic flung me out the window.

"Cas!"

I landed on my back on a hard surface. The air blasted from my lungs, and for several seconds, I couldn't draw a breath. My eyes stared up at the starry sky. Freezing cold air lapped over my body and whistled in my ears. I writhed back and forth, desperate for air to enter my lungs again.

With a jolt, I recognized the courtyard where the dragon trial had taken place.

Quickly, I rolled over and rose to my knees. My lungs finally expanded, and I sucked in a breath. The king had dropped me out here like an offering, clearly assuming the beast would follow me. The king must not have seen me repay the creature. It had no reason to be angry with me anymore.

Suddenly, Cas's limp form slammed down on the stone beside me. A shriek tore from my lungs.

I lunged toward Cas, but wingbeats overhead made me freeze in place. More dragons than I could count circled in the dark night sky. I dropped to my ankles, instinct prevailing, and raised my arms over my head. My dancing shoes clapped loudly against the stone.

The nearest dragon extended its talons toward Cas, but then it flapped its massive wings and rose higher, curling its claws back in. Its narrow face and terrifying eyes watched me intently, as if waiting for something. It was the largest dragon I'd ever seen, its massive blue shape barely discernable in the dark.

"Cas," I sputtered, studying his unmoving frame. The arms splayed before him were entirely black. "Cas!"

I took one step forward, but a growl from the large dragon stopped me.

There was no sign of the Shadow King. Our plan to distract him with the dragon had failed.

I'd led Cas astray, and now he was dead. My heart constricted until I thought it might stop beating.

I jumped as the honey-colored dragon blasted from the windows of the great hall and swooped out into the night, quickly circling back toward the open courtyard.

Remembering the way the pale dragon had taken an interest in my noisy shoes, I curled my fingers over my head into the starting position of a dance. Maybe it would work a second time. The blue dragon's nostrils flared. It beat its wings two more times before settling down onto the stone.

Without knowing what else to do, I stomped my heels in quick succession and launched into the moves of the dance I knew best. It was the dance I'd performed the night Cas had stolen me away. When I thought he was no more than a murderer with no heart at all.

My breaths came faster and faster, but somehow my muscles relaxed as I moved through the steps, stomping and twirling with singular determination to reach Cas where he lay. I added in claps where I usually clicked my castanets. At each stomp of my heel, the dragons settled, one after another, until a dozen of them were perched on the stones around me. Not one of them attacked. I spun, the massive skirt of my red dress flaring out into the night, mimicking flames. With one final spin, I would reach Cas, but I had to move right past the golden dragon that had burned me. I swallowed my fear and pushed toward Cas.

The dragon scooted backward out of my way as I spun across the open space.

My blood pulsed in my veins in time with the stomping of my feet and the clapping of my shaking hands. The fear rushing through my body counteracted the cold air biting at my skin, but after several more turns, I lost myself to a violent shiver. Instantly, the dragons lurched toward me as I broke from the dance. I sucked in a gulp of air and kicked my foot out to enhance the spinning of my dress.

The nearest dragon cocked its head back as if pleased. These dangerous creatures were entirely different than I had imagined. They wanted to be entertained, much like the fae. I wondered how long they would be entertained by my dancing. It seemed that the louder I stomped and the faster I twirled, the calmer they became. But if the king was watching he wouldn't let me go on like this forever.

The end of the dance was drawing near, the final move only a spin away. I could immediately shift into another dance, but what if the dragons disliked my change in tempo? My arms were so cold, and my movements were slowing as my body fought against the frigid night air. I began the final spin, turning and turning, adding two more revolutions. The ruffles of my dress danced over Cas's back and my foot came down right beside him, hands lifted overhead, as I threw myself backward into the final pose.

The dragon nearest me had crept closer as I'd spun across the space, and I flinched, preparing for his fire. But its serpentine head cocked sideways, as if waiting to see if I would keep dancing. Its eyes, those awful orange slits, peered down at me.

I fell to my knees, placing one hand on Cas's chest. It was faintly rising and falling, and I could feel a slow heartbeat underneath his thin black shirt. The dragon's long neck extended, until its head hovered before my chest, nostrils flaring as it sniffed me. I could barely take a breath.

Now that I was still, the cold air sunk into my skin and raced toward my heart. Cas's arms were fully black up to where his sleeves bunched at his elbows.

I assumed I only had another breath or two before I would leave this world. I glanced down at Cas, wishing so badly that his eyes would open. But we were out of time. I bent over and pressed a kiss to his cold face. His mouth didn't respond, and it felt like I was kissing a corpse. A tear dripped from my face onto his, and I smeared it away with my thumb.

The black lines from his curse crept slowly up his neck into his cheeks. I wished I could wipe them away with my fingers as I had my teardrop. As I frantically called to Cas, something scaly bumped my elbow and I screamed, toppling forward.

The dragon had nudged my elbow with its snout. Perhaps it was playing with its food, wanting more of a fight. Unable to control my rapid, ragged breathing, I shuffled over Cas and knelt at his other side, clutching his hand to my chest and staring into the face of the blue dragon. We would die together. Cas's father was right—love would be our end.

I pressed a kiss to Cas's cold, black hand and trembled as the dragon's claws clicked the stone so close I could reach out and touch them. Three more dragons were creeping closer now. I smelled smoke on the wind, as one of them was gathering fire in its belly.

Maybe Cas wouldn't feel a thing when the fire consumed us. I just wished I had been able to tell him how I felt before the end.

Staring up at the enormous blue dragon, I blinked away the tears blurring my vision and lifted my chin. From somewhere in the shadows, I heard the distinct ring of a sword being drawn from a scabbard. The king must be disappointed that we hadn't already been torn apart by the dragons. He was prepared to finish the job.

The dragon heard the sound as well and snapped its long face toward the glint of steel in the darkness. The animal—whether male or female, I couldn't tell—inhaled deeply, a rattle sounding in its massive chest. It released a quick burst of flame in the direction of the shadows, and Rykar's face glowed orange from where he hid. The flames didn't reach him, however, as if the dragon had merely been issuing a warning to say stay back. We were its meal, and it wasn't planning to share. I yelped as the warmth from the flames washed over my body.

The dragon returned its attention to me and Cas.

But the Shadow King was not taking orders from a dragon. He shifted into his dark winged form and stepped across the stones toward us, sword in hand. Several dragons rose on their hind legs, their wings extending and their bellies expanding. The dragon that had been watching us extended one wing over us, its leathery membrane touching the top of my head and arcing down to rest against the stone on the other side of Cas's feet. Was this dragon *protecting* us? Surely it was only protecting its food, the way a wolf might protect its kill from another predator.

I didn't like the thought of becoming a dragon's next meal. I figured being flamed to death would be a quicker way to die than being ripped to pieces by fangs.

The king's guards followed their sovereign out into the night, loosing small arrows toward the dragons. The weapons must have stung as they found their marks, for the dragons attacked. One dragon emitted a stream of flames that stretched across the entire platform. In the light of its blue-white flames, shadowy fae darted away, several screaming in pain. It seemed that dragon fire could even harm a fae in shadow form.

I clutched Cas's arm tighter to my chest, as if his presence could keep me safe from the flames and the battle raging around us. The dragon with its wing over us spun around, its tail knocking into my shoulder. I sailed backward and barely caught myself before my head hit the stone. I flattened myself on the ground next to Cas, pulling his head against my chest.

One shadow landed on the platform beside us. As he walked slowly toward us, I recognized Rykar, with his broad chest and dark sword, the point aimed at the ground.

I clung to Cas, pressing my eyes shut as the sword rose over my head. This was it. My plan had failed.

At the sound of the blade clattering to the ground, my eyes popped open. The blue dragon had snatched the Shadow King from the platform and tossed him in the air, catching him in her open jaws. I covered a gasp with the hand not wrapped around Cas.

Whatever magic the king was performing, the dragon must not have liked the taste, for it spit the king violently onto the stones. For a second, he lay there in a cursing heap. Then, his shadowy form solidified, and the king stood to his feet, fully corporeal once again.

I felt the air shift with a pulse that shook the ground. The king lifted a finger toward the dragon that had protected us, and with a single flick of his wrist, the dragon dropped to the stones and didn't move again, one wing crushed beneath its massive body.

The other dragons grew restless and emitted terrifying shrieks, distressed at the loss of one of their own—one of the largest I'd seen. I knew next to nothing about the lives of dragons, but their rage was clear enough.

In a frenzy, two other dragons descended on the platform, flames engulfing the king.

When the flames died out, the king still stood, unharmed. His magic was so much stronger than I had ever imagined. I shook Cas, praying he would wake up and create a shield around us, but he didn't wake up. I had to do something.

While the king was distracted by the dragons, I stood and hooked my arms under Cas's shoulders. I leaned my weight into tugging him toward one of the gated archways where the fae had watched our trial.

I had only moved him a body length before the king spotted us. As the king turned to face us, the honey-colored dragon hissed and sparks flew from its open mouth. It spun in the air, its hind feet landing just in front of us, tail whipping out so close that I flinched. But its tail never hit me. The creature was blocking the king from us.

"Dragons are protective of their meals. But you will not be safe forever!" Rykar shouted.

The dragon opened its mouth, and a line of white-blue flames shot toward the Shadow King. These flames were brighter and hotter than the rest—it must have swallowed the stone. I dove on top of Cas, shielding his exposed skin as best I could. From the corner of my eye, I watched. The blinding light of the flames illuminated the king as he fell to his knees, arms lifted above him. As his protective spell deteriorated, his screams pierced the night over the sound of the crackling flames and the click of dragon claws.

In a single moment, Rykar lay still. After another moment, his form shriveled into ash, which carried away on the harsh, cold breeze that whipped across the platform.

I pressed a fist to my open mouth, hardly able to believe what I had witnessed. My heart beat madly against Cas's chest as I stared in shock. Then I slid off of him and curled into a sitting position, rocking as I held Cas. Tears dripped down my face as the dragons turned toward us, and I knew that we would be next.

Cas was finally free of his father, but he would never know it.

Except, his arms were a warm color again. The black had drained away the moment his father vanished. Carefully, I laid him back on the stones and stroked the edge of his face. His eyes fluttered open, and one of his hands, now warmer than my own, pressed my palm to his cheek.

"Cas!"

The corners of his lips twitched, but he still seemed mostly unable to move. His eyes flickered around the courtyard. I helped him sit up, and then I kissed him violently.

"I love you," I said through my tears.

His large, warm hand stroked my face and then curled into my hair as he kissed me again. I didn't want to stop kissing him, knowing that I'd rather not see the flames coming, but he pulled my face away and stared at the dragons who were still watching us.

He examined his hands, turning them over, then locked eyes with me. "My father is dead, isn't he?"

I nodded, indicating the space where the king's body had disappeared.

"What did you do to them?" Cas asked, a smile tugging at his lips as he nodded toward the waiting dragons. They hadn't torched us yet.

"I didn't do anything. I only danced to keep them from eating you."

Cas's brows lifted, and he smiled at me. Then he stood, slowly, his eyes on the yellow dragon nearest us. The creature shuffled side to side a little, its wings partially extending then resettling. Cas laughed and offered me his hand. "It seems they liked the show."

His arm wrapped around my waist and tucked me against him. I didn't want to let him go, ever. He pressed a kiss to the top of my head and then looked out at the night.

The dragons faced us expectantly, as if waiting for us to say or do something.

"It looks like we have a new matriarch," Cas said. He bowed politely to the dragon. I followed suit, but Cas shook his head at me. "Not the dragon," he whispered. "You."

The dragon dipped its head, not toward Cas, but toward me.

Cas chuckled as we stood. "To Zara, a tamer of dragons."

With his thumb and forefinger, he turned my jaw toward his and kissed me again. When he pulled away, he stayed close enough that his nose brushed my cheek. "Tell them, Zara. Tell your dragons what you would like them to do."

"*My*...?" The shock of the evening's events was settling into my bones, and I started to shake uncontrollably.

"Dragon clans are ruled by a female, and it appears the blue one over there was the matriarch. Until she died, presumably protecting you. The rest of the dragons see you as their new leader."

Once my head started to shake, I couldn't make it stop. This couldn't be possible.

Cas held me firmly. "In the thousands of years we've lived here, not one of us has ever attempted to *entertain* a dragon. Our ancient foes might be more like us than we realized, hungry for entertainment." He smiled at me. "You've changed the world, little spark. No. I can't call you that anymore." His lips moved down to my ear and warmth poured down my spine. "Wildfire."

My pulse roared in my ears as I looked out at the dragons waiting for a command. "Protect us," I called out. "Protect the new king." I glanced at Cas. His eyes widened.

"I thought you didn't like the Shadow Court?" he said.

"I don't love the cold, but I love you, and you're here. You have a court to rule."

"I can't be the king of darkness," he said, briefly resting his forehead against mine. "Not after loving you and your light."

I stretched my hand up and laced my fingers through his hair. "Yes, you can. *Only* you can. Your power might come from darkness, but that doesn't mean you have to love the darkness the way that your father did."

He crushed me against him, tucking my head underneath his chin. I could feel his heart beating, and I was thankful for each beat as it tapped against my ears. He was alive and he was king.

"Come," he said, "I must greet my court."

# 41

## Zara

Moments later, we were back in the ballroom of the abandoned castle, where flowers and shattered glass littered the floor. Felipe materialized in front of us and knelt amid the debris.

"My king," he said, his eyes down.

"Call the court," Cas commanded as we walked through the littered space, fingers linked.

Felipe stood and called out in a loud voice that reverberated through the stones, "Shadow Court, convene in the throne room."

Shadows soared in from the open windows or materialized on the floor, following us silently as we made our way back through the atrium, down the steps, and through the halls of Nightsong.

We entered the long throne room, partly hewn from a natural crevasse that reached all the way up to the night sky far above. Cas and I walked down the center toward a stone dais boasting a single black throne. Cas's father must never had a queen rule with him. The silent fae streamed in behind us, filling the room and shifting into their solid, colorful forms. Claws clicking on stone announced Diego's arrival as he trotted in among the fae and caught up to Cas. Cas reached out at scratched behind the massive creature's ear. From the opening above, dragons clambered down the uneven rock walls and perched on an outcropping above the throne. Several fae shouted or cursed at the dragons, but at Cas's lifted hand, their protests ceased. He ascended the dais, but I hesitated.

"Sit with me," he said, reaching his hand down.

My heart rate soaring, I took his hand and rose with him. Cas sat down on the throne, settling in with a wide-legged, commanding posture. I stood by his side, my arms clasped nervously at my waist. Diego lay down beside the throne on Cas's other side. Above our heads, the dragons warmed the cold space with gentle flames as they circled. I could get used to them hanging around.

A young red and black dragon, a third the size of the others, seemed unable to find a good place to land. Diego emitted a low growl, but Cas snapped his fingers to silence the dip. The dragon perched on the edge of the dais, his tail draping down the stone steps. I smiled up at the dragon, and its eye that was turned toward me seemed to be asking permission.

I nodded. "Yes, you can stay."

The dragon's nostrils flared, and it kicked its chin up a little bit as if satisfied. The courtiers filling the room collectively took a knee, offering their respect to their new sovereign. Based on what I knew of the Shadow Court, Cas would have a good deal of work ahead of him to truly secure the allegiance of these fae, but at least no one was challenging him tonight.

While they were kneeling, Cas looked up at me and patted his thigh. My chest hitched, but I stepped around in front of him, and then he guided my hips down into his lap. He looped his arms around me and linked his fingers with mine. His chin reached over my shoulder as he looked down at his subjects.

"Now," he said, "we will greet *our* court."

# 42

## Epilogue

The forest blinked with the season's last remaining fireflies, and the wind smelled like a recent rain. On the breeze, I thought I could smell the faintest hint of salt; the winds always rushed in from the sea this time of year. In the distance, I could see the lights of my father's house.

Beside me, Casimiro walked with his hands clasped behind his back, his brow faintly pinched in deep thought. His dark hair was swept back beneath a simple onyx crown carved to look like twining curls of smoke. His black suit shone faintly when the moonlight touched his shoulders.

The fluttering in my chest turned to a full-fledged shake as relief and sadness crashed like opposing waves inside me. As soon as the Shadow King had died, every bargain he'd made dissolved, releasing me and all the other mortals from our confinement to the Shadow Court. Cas had sent a fae messenger to find Alba and let her know it was safe to return, though he wasn't certain how long it would take to find a fae trying to hide. I hoped Ivy and the others were all okay, and that I might see her again one day.

At my request, Casimiro had brought me here. But this place was no longer my home.

In the dim light, I reached for his arm, sliding my hand under his elbow. He sensed my shaking and cleared his throat.

"I can give you as long as you like. If you need a month, a year even, to consider my offer, I will wait."

I bumped his shoulder with mine. "Don't be silly. I've given you my answer."

He'd explained to me when he'd proposed that marrying a fae involved becoming one in more ways than I'd imagined. I would take on a portion of his magic as well as a portion of his extremely long life, and in return, he'd take on some of my mortal weakness and my shorter life span, making us both stronger than a mortal and yet not eternal like the fae.

"But it is customary for a woman's father to give consent before the wedding," I teased, pulling him down the path.

As we approached the golden windows of my childhood home, the gemstone on my finger caught the light. I smiled down at it, imagining how my father would gawk at the ring and its preposterous size when he saw it.

"Thank you," I said, wiggling the finger that held the glittering stone. I spotted Ignacio making his rounds past the garden, past my old balcony. He couldn't see us, thanks to Casimiro's magic pressing the darkness to us like a veil. "My father will appreciate this."

Cas chuckled. "I didn't give it to you for his sake." He jabbed me with his elbow, and I shoved him playfully away. The diamond I wore kept a magical shield around me at all times, Cas had explained. Just in case. "But if a large diamond makes your father happy, he's not that different from a lot of my courtiers."

"We aren't that different from the fae, Cas."

He pulled me in front of him and pressed my chest to his. "I know. You showed me that." He planted a deep kiss on my mouth before releasing me.

Cheeks flushed and heart racing, I walked arm-in-arm with Casimiro toward the grand façade.

"Oh, did I tell you?" he asked as we climbed the front steps. "Your friend Talia's husband—prince of the Sun Court—has agreed to your requested meeting."

I flashed a wide grin and kissed his cheek.

"Apparently, he only agreed to it at the behest of his wife. Sun and Shadow don't normally meet for tea." He raised his brows. "You have only been in the fae realm for a matter of months, and you've already upset our entire world, wildfire. Whatever am I going to do with you?"

"Make me your queen, of course," I said with a dramatic shrug.

On the top step, Cas wrapped his arms around me and lifted me off my feet so that my face was level with his. "Then you'll really set the world ablaze."

And then, after setting me down with a wink, the King of Shadows knocked on my father's front door.

Thank you so much for reading! If you enjoyed this book, please consider leaving a review. It helps more than you know.

If you missed Talia's story, read about her marriage to Rafael del Sol in *The Starlit Prince*.

Scan below to get your copy of The Starlit Prince!

## Also by C. F. E. Black

**Scepter and Crown series:**

Shield of Shadow

Blade of Ash

Crown of Dust

Scepter of Fire

**Secrets of the Fae:**

The Starlit Prince

The Shadow Heir

**Sacrificed Hearts series:**

Labyrinth of Lies and Sacrifice

**Other titles:**

The Veritas Project

Sign up to be a reader VIP at
vip.cfeblack.com/join

# About the Author

C. F. E. Black loves to get swept away in books, both reading and writing them. Fantasy and science fiction have been her bread and butter since childhood, and she can't imagine life without her beloved fictional worlds. She lives in beautiful north Alabama with her superhero husband, sons, and fur-family. Connect with her and explore her books at www.cfeblack.com.

# Acknowledgements

Whew! We did it. This book needed lots of help, and I'm thankful to everyone who poured their time and effort into it to make it shine.

Special thanks to my editor, Sara Lawson, for polishing this story and helping me see the things I'd missed. Also, thanks for loving these two.

To the people who read this story in its incredibly messy early stages, you need an Olympic medal. Special thanks to Myriah for cleaning up the original dictated draft (and for proofing the final product after all its many changes).

Constance, you pulled me out of sticky spots, and your words brought much needed wisdom to this story. Thanks for being there to answer my questions. To Callie and Chelsea, your detailed notes were amazing and invaluable, and it's because of you that Cas and Zara are so much better, from start to finish. To Celeste, you helped me think about this story in a new way and I'll be forever thankful. To Deborah, Tammy, and Kim, your comments helped so much! And to Marisol, your early notes were so valuable—thank you for reading it when it was still so rough.

To my hype squad, you guys are amazing! Thank you for the excitement you showed for this book!

To my early readers, thanks for taking the time to read this book and be the first to establish its place in this bookish world.

To Will, thanks for hanging in there for this one. For the early mornings and late nights and coffee shop trips and deadlines that popped up every other month.

To Mom, for those critical deadline week hours. You saved me much stress.

To my readers, the biggest thanks goes to you. Every note I get from you guys makes my day.

And as always, everything I do, I do for the Lord, to please Him (Col. 3:23). If this story found its way into your hands, He deserves all the credit. Soli Deo gloria.

www.ingramcontent.com/pod-product-compliance
Lightning Source LLC
Chambersburg PA
CBHW020338310726
48979CB00015B/2413/J
* 9 7 8 1 9 6 2 0 6 6 0 7 5 *